COURAGEOUS LOVE

COURAGEOUS LOVE

EASTMONT SERIES
BOOK THREE

BY JAYNE LAWSON

XULON PRESS

Xulon Press
2301 Lucien Way #415
Maitland, FL 32751
407.339.4217
www.xulonpress.com

© 2017 by Jayne Lawson

All rights reserved solely by the author. The author guarantees all contents are original and do not infringe upon the legal rights of any other person or work. No part of this book may be reproduced in any form without the permission of the author. The views expressed in this book are not necessarily those of the publisher.

Unless otherwise indicated, Scripture quotations taken from the King James Version (KJV) – *public domain*.

Printed in the United States of America.

ISBN-13: 9781545616246

DEDICATION

This story is dedicated to my mother, Sawako Tsutsui Guy, who, with great courage, faced many challenges in her life. She grew up in Japan, experiencing firsthand the bombing of Hiroshima and the horror of its aftermath. She eventually met and married my father, then immigrated to the United States where she struggled to learn English and the ways of western culture. Overcoming the racial barriers of being a war bride from an enemy nation, she still embraced America and what it stood for, and eventually she proudly became a naturalized American citizen. Later on in life, after a heartbreaking divorce from my father, she developed an illness called systemic lupus erythematosus, which resulted in chronic renal failure. For fifteen years, she bravely endured both hemo- and peritoneal dialysis. Raised a Shintoist, it wasn't until my mother was 64 years old that she opened her heart to the gospel message and accepted the Lord Jesus Christ as her personal Savior. One year later, my mother went home to be with the Lord. She was without a doubt, one of the most courageous women I have ever known. I can't wait to see her again!

ACKNOWLEDGEMENTS

As always, I thank my Lord and Savior, Jesus Christ, for His precious gift of salvation and for the many blessings He has given me. Some of those blessings are found in some very special people.

To my beloved husband, John. Thank you for always loving me and encouraging me. Having you by my side in this journey has been amazing, and I will forever thank the Lord for bringing you into my life.

To Pastor John Ridings, missionary to Juárez, Mexico. Thank you for sharing your story with me. Your insight and experiences were invaluable in helping me develop Ryan's character. May God continue to bless you and your ministry.

To the special ladies at Old Suwanee Baptist Church that have demonstrated great courage in some very difficult circumstances: Dody Hall, Karen Hamby, Robyn Jackson, and Stephanie Savage. Your faith has been such an encouragement to me. I have watched the way you courageously fought your battles, trusting in Jesus, leaning on His everlasting arms, and reflecting that peace that passes all understanding. You have truly been an inspiration.

Lastly, to my daughter, Samantha, whose endless hours of editing have made this story more interesting and believable. Your honesty has always been one of your strengths. When I watch you live your faith, you truly do demonstrate courage as you stand your ground "...ready always to give an answer to every man that asketh you a reason of the hope that is in you..." Thank you for your continued love and encouragement. You are my biggest fan. This one is for you.

PROLOGUE

"Be of good courage, and he shall strengthen your heart, all ye that hope in the LORD."

Psalm 31:24

The noonday heat was oppressive as the young Mexican woman eased herself down on a wooden bench. She lovingly caressed her swollen belly, feeling for life within her. In moments, she was rewarded by the gentle kick of the developing child, and it delighted her. The sound of her soft laughter floated on the wind and caught the attention of the tall, handsome man across the yard. A broad, boyish grin spread across his tanned face as he blew a kiss to the woman. She raised her hand to wave as a slight breeze teased her long dark hair, and she brushed a few tendrils away from her face.

As she started to rise, she felt a growing tightness in her abdomen. She hesitated a moment, mentally calculating the time remaining for her pregnancy, and then she smiled. Over the past few weeks she had experienced similar intermittent pains as her body began the preparations for true labor. Still a few weeks early, she dismissed the tightness that traveled across her as more of the same. How she wished it would be soon!

The near-end of her pregnancy had dramatically reduced her ability to complete her normal activities, but she still managed to pick a handful of Mexican primrose, her favorite wildflower, for her kitchen table. Fatigue continually plagued her, and she was always grateful when the day ended, and she could lie in a cool bed next to her husband. Tonight, she believed, would be no different.

Sometime past midnight, she was awakened by her discomfort. Rising from her bed, she ambled into the washroom to confirm that her water had broken. Turning the light on, she stared at a small pool of bright red liquid that puddled at her feet. She cried out for her husband.

The nearest hospital was more than two hours away over rugged terrain. Although he drove as fast as possible, the ride was painstakingly slow for the young couple, and despite their prayers for God's help, they both feared the worst.

Upon arrival at the hospital, a nurse ushered the frightened woman into the treatment area, and the man was left alone... standing... staring at the closed doors that separated him from his beloved wife. How long he was there, he did not know for time had stopped for him.

Finally allowed to see his wife, he rushed to her side. The steady drip, drip, drip of the intravenous line and the muted beep, beep, beep of the cardiac monitor assaulted his senses. He resisted the impulse to grab her and run. Instead, he hesitantly wiped away the tears on his wife's face. Her eyes fluttered open; the depth of sadness in them took his breath away. Fear gripped his heart, and he choked back a sob. He had to be strong for her, so he did the only thing he knew to do. He prayed. Holding tightly to his wife's hand, he prayed, and he prayed harder than he had ever prayed before, but the fear within him remained.

"Please don't leave me," she whispered, her hand protectively holding her abdomen as silent tears continued to roll down her cheeks. Her other hand tightened around his fingers. She gazed up at her husband, sorrow on her face.

"I won't. I promise." And he kept his word. When the nurses had asked him to step outside, he refused. When the doctors examined her, the husband stood steadfast by his wife's bedside.

Prologue

And when she drew her final breath, he was there, as he had promised to be.

Cradling her in his arms, he told her he loved her. *"Te amo,"* he whispered as he held her tightly to him. Finally, he relaxed his hold and stared at her now peaceful face. He kissed her one last time, caressed her face, his fingers lingering for just a moment, and then, he cried. Unashamedly.

If only there had been a doctor much closer...

PART ONE – CALIFORNIA

"Be of good courage, and let us behave ourselves valiantly for our people, and for the cities of our God: and let the Lord do that which is good in His sight."

1 Chronicles 19:13

CHAPTER ONE

Surrounded by towering logdepole trees and majestic granite monoliths, the view from the picturesque stone walled church was breathtaking. Nestled beneath the immense rock formations of Yosemite Valley, the rustic house of God was reminiscent of an earlier time when it was not uncommon to see the Ahwahnee Indians walking through lush green meadows while the thundering cascades of mighty waterfalls echoed throughout the valley. This morning, the gentle whispers of the wind through the swaying pines promised another day to remember.

Ryan Devereaux stood quietly near the knee-high rock wall that outlined the churchyard as he gazed out toward the Merced River, full from the melting snows of the Sierra Nevada mountain range. The golden rays of the rising sun danced along the river's sparkling waters as the cry of a lone scrub jay echoed through the nearby pines.

You picked a beautiful day to get married, Maggie.

He smiled as he thought back to when he had first met Maggie Devereaux. A gifted emergency room physician, she had come to Mexico with his brother, Scott, to spend a few weeks working in a small medical clinic that served the tiny rural community of Santa Molina, Mexico. Built on the grounds of the church that Ryan pastored, the clinic still needed improvements to meet the increasing demands of the local population, but it was the only decent medical facility in a one hundred mile radius, so remodeling the clinic was a vital necessity. Staffing was another problem, but Ryan always managed to entice both Mexican and American doctors to donate some of their time in order to keep the clinic operational as often as possible.

Maggie had been a great help to Scott, also a physician, as they worked side by side to improve the healthcare facility while also ministering to the medical needs of the local community. After returning to California, the two had become engaged and soon married. Sadly, a horrible tragedy struck the young couple, and Maggie became a widow less than one month into her marriage. During the time Scott and Maggie had worked together in Mexico, Ryan had fervently prayed for Maggie to accept salvation through Christ and to have a personal relationship with Him, but her broken heart had not been ready to accept God's love.

A few years later, Maggie had met Colin Grant, a very successful gospel singer. Their friendship grew deeper with time, but came close to ending forever until Maggie finally understood the real meaning of selfless love. After a long, soul-searching night, Maggie finally came to understand the meaning of true salvation. Her decision to surrender her life to Christ was the catalyst needed to allow her feelings of love to grow for Colin. Today would begin the next chapter of their romance.

Ryan turned and walked back toward the church. It was empty now, but soon it would be bustling with the arrival of guests eager to witness the long-awaited wedding of Maggie and Colin. Ryan entered through the large oak double doors and paused for a moment in the foyer glancing up at the rough-hewn logs that supported the ceiling. As he strode into the sanctuary, he saw each wooden pew adorned with clusters of white stephanotis and baby's breath on the ends facing the center aisle. A single unlit pillar candle, flanked by two long white tapers, stood on a small oak table at the back of the platform. Pale pink roses in twin crystal vases rested on two other matching tables flanking each side of the platform. Off to the right side of the altar, a fourth table held only a feathered pen in a stand.

Chapter One

Ryan ambled to the front of the church, then sat down on a wooden pew. Bowing his head, he whispered a prayer for the couple.

"Father, thank You so much for this day. It has been such a long time coming. Bless Colin and Maggie as they begin their new life together. Give them more than they could ever imagine or ask. May they serve You faithfully all the days of their lives, and bring You much glory and honor. In the name of Christ, my Savior, I pray. Amen."

As he lifted his head, he turned toward the sound of footsteps near the back of the church. Upon recognizing Valerie Garrett, the matron of honor and sister-in-law of the bride, he stood and walked toward her.

"Valerie, you did a beautiful job with the decorations," complimented Ryan.

A huge smile spread across her face as she brushed a stray lock of dark brown hair from her forehead. "Thank you, Pastor. I wanted to make sure the roses still looked fresh this morning."

Ryan swiveled toward the altar. "They look good to me."

She nodded in agreement. "I'm very glad about that, otherwise—"

"Otherwise, she'd have me out picking wildflowers and replacing those roses," came a deep voice from just outside the doors. Will Garrett, Maggie's brother, walked in carrying a box of corsages and boutonnieres. The tall, dark-haired man set the box on a pew, then turned to shake hands with Ryan. "She's been up since 4:00 am. Does that tell you anything?" He winked at his petite wife.

Valerie playfully stuck her tongue out at Will and walked over to the box. She reached in and pulled out a pale pink rosebud entwined with a white ribbon around its stem. Walking over to Ryan, she said, "Since you're already dressed for the service, I'll pin your boutonniere on you now."

Will chuckled. "Hope you have a Band-Aid handy."

"Just wait 'til it's your turn, dear," said Valerie with a teasing smile. She carefully attached the tiny flower to Ryan's lapel. "There. That didn't hurt now, did it?"

Ryan shook his head. "Not a bit. Thank you." He turned to Will. "How's the groom this morning?"

"More nervous than I thought he'd be, but then we all seem to get that doomed feeling when our carefree lives are nearing an end." He stifled a grin as his wife's narrowed green eyes cast daggers in his direction.

"And Maggie?" asked Ryan, chuckling under his breath.

"Oh, she's cool as a cucumber," boasted Valerie. "As all women are. It's only you men who get the jitters." She laughed as she headed for the door. "C'mon, Will. We've got a lot more to do before the wedding starts."

Will looked at Ryan and shrugged his shoulders. "What can I say? She's the boss today." He turned his head toward Valerie. "Slow down, honey. I can only drag this ball and chain so fast," he called out.

Without turning, she responded, "You just wait, Will Garrett! You're in big trouble now!"

Will grinned broadly as he slapped Ryan on the back. "I always am!" He hurried down the aisle after his wife.

****

As it neared noon, the small chapel began to fill as wedding guests arrived. Many lingered for a few minutes in the parking lot of the church to admire the breathtaking view of Yosemite Falls across the valley floor. Ryan chatted with several of them as they made their way into the sanctuary. As he spoke with Dr. Ben Shepherd, a colleague of Maggie's, Ryan felt a tap on his shoulder. He turned to face Joshua Grant, Colin's oldest brother.

"I'm sorry to intrude, but..." He smiled apologetically at Ben and Ryan, never noticing that his British accent had caught the attention of a few guests. "Colin is asking for you when you've got a moment, Pastor Devereaux."

Chapter One

"Nothing's wrong, I hope."

Joshua smiled as he shook his head. "No, not at all. He just wanted to tell you something before the ceremony."

Ben smiled and nodded knowingly. "It's fine, Ryan. I understand. We'll talk more after the ceremony. Go take care of the groom. He may be getting cold feet."

Ryan shook Ben's hand gratefully. "I doubt that," he said with a chuckle. "He's waited a long time for this day." Turning, he walked with Joshua to the groom's ready room.

****

Clad in a black tuxedo with a small white rosebud on the lapel, Colin Grant paced back and forth in the small room. He stopped abruptly and faced the door as it opened.

"Ryan! Thank you for coming. I wanted—" began Colin as he quickly closed the door behind the pastor.

"Is something wrong?" Ryan's eyes narrowed as he studied Colin's face for a clue to the groom's behavior.

Colin shook his head as he brushed his blonde hair off his forehead. "No. No, nothing. Really. It's just—"

"A case of the jitters?"

Colin looked directly at Ryan and smiled, shaking his head. "No, not at all. I just wanted to make sure I didn't forget to thank you."

"Thank me? I haven't married you yet," teased Ryan as he waited for Colin to explain.

"Not for that. It's just that with Maggie having been married to your brother and all... you've been so supportive of our relationship from the beginning, and I... well, I can't tell you what a blessing it's been to have that support as well as being able to work with you and to get to really know you." He reached into his pocket and pulled out an envelope. "Maggie and I, we wanted you to have this." He held it out to Ryan.

"Colin, this really isn't necessary," stated Ryan, shaking his head as he lifted one hand up, palm forward. Their own relationship had grown over the years, especially since God had led Colin to financially support part of Ryan's ministry in Mexico. Now, they were good friends as well as partners in the work of the Lord.

Colin disagreed. "Yes. Yes, it is. Please take it." He moved it closer to Ryan. "It's from both of us, okay?"

Ryan hesitated a moment, then took the envelope and placed it into the inner pocket of his jacket. "You know I love you both. You're... well, you're family to me. You always will be."

Colin nodded. "I know. And we feel the same." He held his hand out, and Ryan clasped it strongly.

"You ready to do this?" grinned the pastor as his eyebrows lifted.

Colin took a deep breath and smiled. "I'm ready."

****

The glow of candlelight filled the sanctuary as soft instrumental music played in the background. The gathering of family and friends hushed when Ryan and Colin entered through a side door and stood on the platform at the front of the church. As the pianist began to play *O Perfect Love*, the double doors opened, and Valerie Garrett, dressed in a rose-colored dress with a scoop neck and waistline that draped to one side, began her promenade down the aisle. Tiny pink flowers adorned her hair, and she held a bouquet of variegated pink carnations and baby's breath. Slightly behind her, on each side, came Colin's brothers, Joshua and Kurt, clad in black tuxedos identical to the one the groom wore. When they reached the front of the church, the matron of honor moved to the left, while the men positioned themselves next to Colin.

Anticipation hung in the air as the pianist transitioned to *It is Well With My Soul*, and then, almost as a single unit, the congregation stood and eagerly turned toward the rear of the church. The heavy oak doors opened, and Maggie appeared on the threshold with her brother.

Chapter One

Standing still for a few moments, she scanned the familiar faces that filled the church. Her heart warmed, and she smiled. Then, for just a moment, everyone seemed to fade from her view when her eyes moved to the front of the church and fell upon Colin. Her lips parted slightly, and her heart beat a little faster as she stood transfixed, overcome by the moment. The spell was broken when Will whispered, "It's time." Maggie turned toward him and nodded as he reached over and patted her hand. She took a deep breath, and then they began their walk down the aisle.

Maggie's cinnamon brown eyes sparkled, and her smile was radiant as she moved through the sanctuary. Her antique white gown seemed to flow as she headed toward the front of the church. Her upswept chestnut brown hair was adorned with petite pearls and baby's breath flowers, and she held a bouquet of white roses, variegated carnations, and stephanotis. As her gaze swept through the church, her eyes misted over. She blinked several times keeping her tears unshed as she smiled at her family and friends.

When they reached the front of the church, Maggie's hands trembled slightly as she quietly stood while Ryan began the ceremony. When it was time for Will to give the bride away, a single tear of joy trickled down her cheek. As she took her place at Colin's side, he tenderly reached out and wiped away the teardrop.

"Let's all take a moment to reflect on this day and what it means," said Ryan, allowing Maggie time to regain her composure. He waited until her grateful smile signaled her readiness to continue, and then he looked out over the congregation and began.

"Ladies and gentlemen, we are gathered here today to witness the marriage of Maggie Devereaux and Colin Grant. It is a wonderful thing when the Lord brings two people together, and today, we are here to celebrate one such union. Let's pray."

Holding tightly to Colin's hand, Maggie closed her eyes as she listened intently to the words Ryan spoke.

"Father in heaven, we love You dearly, and we thank You for this glorious day You have given us. A day of joy and hope as Maggie and Colin join themselves together in holy matrimony. Lord, we ask Your blessing upon this service and the lives of this couple. May You be honored here this day in this place, and may all that is said and done glorify Your name. For it's in the precious name of our Savior, Jesus Christ, I pray. Amen." Ryan looked up and smiled. "Please be seated."

As the guests sat, Ryan opened his Bible and addressed the couple before him. "Maggie, Colin, it's finally here. The day you've both dreamed about, the day you've planned for, and the day we've all hoped for. The pathway to this day has not been an easy one for either of you, yet you both sought the Lord's will for your lives, and now, here you are, preparing to embark on the next phase of your life's journey. Now you will no longer walk the path alone. You will have a partner. No one knows where life's path will lead or what obstacles you will have to overcome to reach your final destination, so the foundation of your journey must be strong."

He continued his message for the couple, emphasizing three godly principles upon which to build a marriage–trust, faithfulness, and love. As he spoke, Maggie and Colin kept their focus on the pastor until he directed them to face one another.

As they turned, Ryan closed his Bible and addressed the congregation. "At this time, Maggie and Colin have prepared their own vows for one another."

As the bride and groom faced each other, Maggie glanced up at Ryan. His smile and slight nod signaled Maggie to begin. She looked back at Colin and placed both of her hands in his. She stared into the warm blue eyes of the man who had captured her reluctant heart so long ago. She took a deep breath and exhaled slowly. Steadying herself, she quietly recited the vows she had memorized.

"Colin, I love you. I love you more than I ever thought I could. You've opened up my heart to so much, but most importantly, you led me to Christ. You are the godliest man I

Chapter One

know, and I'm so glad that God chose you for me. I promise to walk by your side always, to encourage you when times get hard, and to obey you as God's Word tells me to. I will cherish every moment that the Lord gives us as husband and wife." She paused for a moment, and then added, "I pledge to you this day my trust, my faithfulness, and my love forever and ever." She took another deep breath and then exhaled a relieved sigh as she smiled at her husband-to-be.

Colin forced his eyes off his bride and looked at Ryan. At the pastor's nod, he turned back to Maggie. His calm demeanor was betrayed by the slight tremor in his voice as he began his own vows.

"Maggie, the day I was brought to the emergency room changed my life forever. I think I fell in love with you the moment you stood in that doorway and shooed everyone out. Your feisty spirit, the fire in your beautiful brown eyes... who wouldn't fall in love with that? As time went by, God continued His work in both of us, and soon I knew I didn't want to spend the rest of my life without you. You are the melody in my heart; the song that I sing. I promise I will cherish you as Christ did the Church. I will support you, encourage you, uplift you, and love you for as long as God gives me breath. I, too, pledge my trust, my faithfulness, and my love to you forever."

He raised her left hand to his lips and kissed the top of it, never taking his eyes off of his bride. Despite her resolve, a slight gasp escaped her lips, and she managed a weak smile as, once again, tears began to fall. Colin tenderly wiped them away as he did before. He mouthed, 'I love you,' and she pressed her lips tightly together as she struggled to control her emotions.

Ryan stood quietly, waiting for them to be ready to go on. When Colin looked up with a slight nod of his head, Ryan continued.

"As a token of their love, Maggie and Colin have chosen to exchange rings to signify an eternal love. Colin, please place your ring on Maggie's finger."

As he did so, Colin stated confidently, "Maggie, my love, with this ring I thee wed."

When she received her cue, her hands shook slightly as she gently pushed the gold and platinum band onto Colin's ring finger. "Colin... with this ring... I thee wed." She looked up into his face and an overwhelming joy filled her heart as she continued to hold his hand.

While the pianist played softly, Colin led Maggie to the unity candle, and together, they lit the center pillar candle using the two tapers, signifying their two separate lives becoming one in marriage. Setting the now-extinguished side candles back into the holders, they moved to the second table where they signed their marriage license. Upon returning to the center of the platform, they joined hands once more and faced Ryan for the final part of the ceremony.

"Colin, Maggie, inasmuch as you both have consented together in holy matrimony before God and this group of family and friends, and thereto have given and pledged your love to each other, it gives me great pleasure to pronounce you husband and wife in the name of the Father, and of the Son, and of the Holy Ghost. Amen." He paused for a moment, then grinned. "Colin, you may now kiss your bride."

Colin gently cupped Maggie's face in his hands and kissed her tenderly. He pulled back for a moment, looked into her misted eyes, and kissed her once more before turning with her to face the audience.

Ryan's voice resounded behind them. "Ladies and gentlemen, it is my great honor to introduce to you, Mr. and Mrs. Colin Grant!"

Thunderous applause erupted in the sanctuary as the pianist began to play the recessional. Colin looked over at Maggie, impulsively hugged her, and then led her down the aisle toward the rear of the church.

Ryan clapped along with the rest of the onlookers, and then waited his turn to congratulate the couple in the receiving line.

CHAPTER TWO

The wedding reception was held in the magnificent Ahwahnee Hotel. Massive hewn logs served as beams and supports throughout the building, and huge glass windows provided panoramic views of the valley's granite walls and evergreen trees.

The large conference room had been decorated the night before. Every table had a white linen tablecloth adorned with a trio of white multi-tiered candles, pink rose petals, and loose strands of petite faux pearls. In the background, instrumental music played faintly, and candlelight flickered softly as the wedding guests began to arrive. Shrimp cocktail, Swedish meatballs, and assorted vegetables, cheeses, and crackers were set out around the room. Soon, festive conversation filled the air as family and friends sampled the appetizers and waited for the newlyweds.

As soon as the after-ceremony photos were taken, Maggie and Colin entered the reception room to a fanfare of applause. In moments, the tinkling of silverware against glasses resonated throughout the room.

"I guess some traditions are truly international, love," whispered Colin as he bent Maggie backwards and delivered a dramatic kiss.

Blushing slightly, she draped her hands around his neck. "You are quite the showman, Mr. Grant," she stated as she laughed gaily.

"I aim to please, Mrs. Grant," he replied as he set her back up on her feet.

As they made their way to the head table, they greeted their guests, making sure to spend time at each table and personally thanking each one for coming. They finally seated themselves with the rest of the wedding party as a dinner of prime rib, scallops, and shrimp was served.

One of the last guests to enter the room, Ryan walked in with Ben Shepherd. Although they had just met the previous night, their shared love for the Savior provided a common bond, making it easy for them to engage in conversation.

"Come join us at our table," urged Ben as he gestured toward the far side of the room. They maneuvered around the seated guests, finally stopping at a table where four other individuals already sat.

"That was a beautiful ceremony, Pastor," said Dianne, Ben's wife.

"Thank you," Ryan replied as he nodded at the other three he had met the previous night at the rehearsal dinner. "It's good to see you all again."

Claire Donnelly, one of Eastmont's ER nurses, looked up at Ryan's face through her thick lashes. Her cheeks reddened slightly when she realized she had been staring at him. "I'm sorry," she started, then added, "It's just that you look so much like Scott. You are his brother, aren't you?"

His dark brows lifted slightly in surprise as he turned toward Claire. "Yes. Yes, I am," he answered, placing his napkin in his lap. "Did you know him?"

"I did. He was a really nice guy," said Claire. She turned to Eric Tanner and Jessica Carr, both emergency room physicians, and explained. "Scott was one of the medical school instructors at Eastmont before you two arrived. He was married to Maggie several years ago, but—" She turned quickly to Ryan. "Oh, I'm so sorry. I shouldn't be talking about that... not now."

Ryan's smile set her at ease. "It's fine, Claire." He looked at Jessica and Eric and continued. "Scott was married to Maggie,

Chapter Two

but only for a week or so. He died in an earthquake in Mexico on their honeymoon."

Jessica put a hand to her mouth, and her sapphire blue eyes widened. "Oh, my! That's awful! I am so sorry."

"Thank you. It was a very difficult time, but the Lord brought both Maggie and me through it, and now we're here to celebrate the next part of her journey. So, no sadness today, only joy, okay?" His warm smile relaxed the group, and their conversation easily shifted to other topics.

Eric leaned over to Ryan as he bit into a buttered roll. "You mentioned last night that your church is in Mexico, right? Clearly you're not a national. Missionary?"

Ryan shook his head. "No, not really. I started out helping a missionary when I was in high school, but things happened, and when he could no longer continue his work, the Lord provided a way for me to stay and take over."

"Wow, that had to be quite a challenge," stated Eric.

"It was at times... still is." began Ryan. "Many of the people who live around the church are descendants from the Mayans, so a lot of them hold to very old pagan religions passed down for generations. The concept of a loving God who chose to send His own Son to save them is difficult for most to accept, but each time someone comes to know Christ as his or her Savior, well, I'm reminded and reassured of God's reason for bringing me there."

"You must find that work very rewarding," commented Ben as he finished off his salad.

"I do. There's still much to be done there, but it's very gratifying to see God work in the lives of the people." He paused for a moment as he sipped some water. "I don't suppose I could convince any of you to come and work in Santa Molina? We certainly could use some good doctors there."

"Santa Molina? Where is that exactly?" asked Jessica. "I don't think I've ever heard of it."

"I'm not surprised," stated Ryan as he snapped a breadstick in half. "It's on the eastern side of Mexico near Veracruz, but more inland. It's very rural, but there's a pretty substantial community there. The nearest medical facility is about two and a half hours away on a good day. I've been praying for a more permanent solution for the health needs of the community."

"I can't even imagine what that would be like," admitted Jessica. She moved slightly to allow a waiter to remove her salad plate. "Seems like there's a clinic or hospital on every corner in Los Angeles."

"It's challenging," said Ryan, "but God's been good, and we've had some doctors, like Maggie, that come down and help with our clinic—"

"You've got a clinic?" interrupted Eric.

Ryan nodded. "Yes, but it's not operational full time. Scott helped get it started, and he'd come for a couple of weeks during the year to staff it."

"Staff it for a couple of weeks? You mean the rest of the time, it's empty?" asked Eric.

"Unfortunately, yes. But I'm praying that will change soon."

Claire looked at him through questioning eyes. "Change? What do you mean?"

Ryan set his fork down. "I've been asking God to send us a full-time doctor. Someone with a passion to establish and maintain a year-round clinic. It's a tall order, but..." He grinned at the group. "He's known for doing the impossible."

Ben nodded. "And the Bible does say that 'With God all things are possible,' right?"

"Absolutely," stated Ryan. "I just don't know when He's going to send one."

Eric stabbed his fork into his last grape tomato and popped it into his mouth. He chewed and swallowed quickly, then said, "You never know, when I finish my residency..." He turned to Ryan. "Maybe I'll come down there."

"You would be very welcome, Eric... any time."

Claire shook her head and laughed. "You know there's no McDonald's there, don't you, Eric? How would you survive?"

Chapter Two

The young physician's eyes widened in mock horror. "What? No fast food? I may have to rethink my offer, Pastor."

The entire group laughed as the main course was set before them.

"Ben went on a missions trip one summer when he was in high school, didn't you, honey?" said Dianne.

"Yes, but that was a long time ago, and hardly remote," confessed Ben as he cut through his prime rib. "It was to a sister church in Wyoming, and only for three weeks, but it was an unforgettable experience. I'd recommend some kind of mission trip for everyone."

"Well," began Ryan, "feel free to send anyone who's interested down my way. There's always something to do, medical or otherwise. And it can be short or long term. I've had college students come down for a couple of weeks during their semester breaks, and some others have come for a month or two."

"Really? What do they do? What does Maggie do when she comes?" asked Jessica.

"Many of the college kids are missions majors, so they go out into the surrounding towns, meet the people and share the gospel, invite them to church... that sort of thing. Sometimes, if there's work to be done on the property, they help with that. When Maggie comes, she mostly handles routine medical stuff, like physical exams, vaccinations, and if there's an emergency that comes up, she takes care of that. Oh, she did deliver a baby once. That was pretty amazing. Colin helped her with that one."

"Colin?"

Ryan nodded. "Yeah. She needed a nurse, and he was available." He cut his shrimp in half and dipped it into some melted garlic butter. "It was a very memorable day."

"Man, that sounds awesome!" exclaimed Eric. "Even if there isn't a McDonald's around!"

Ryan laughed. "Well, if you do decide to visit, I promise you won't go hungry. We have an excellent cook on staff. She's the wife of the groundskeeper, and her food is incredible."

Eric cocked his head and grinned. "This is sounding better and better."

Jessica laughed lightly. "I promise if you go, I'll overnight you a Big Mac when you start to have withdrawal symptoms!"

"I guess it's settled then!" Eric winked at her as good-natured laughter filled the air.

****

The next morning, Ryan woke early and caught the shuttle bus toward Bridalveil Falls. It was a short hike from the parking area to the actual falls, and at this hour, few others were on the trail. As he ascended the pathway, the sound of the cascading water falling from the tops of the granite cliffs echoed all around him. Midway to the falls, a three-point buck stepped out of the forest and onto the trail. It stopped, looked at Ryan, and then bounded away through the trees.

As the hart panteth after the water brooks, so panteth my soul after Thee, O God.

Ryan watched the deer until it disappeared into the forest. He inhaled deeply, his lungs filling with the clean, crisp morning air. Continuing his brisk walk, he reached the end of the trail within minutes. He looked up toward the rim of the cliff and marveled at the thin streams of water that fell from the heights. Collectively they created the illusion of a bride's veil against the darkened rock wall. He stood, mesmerized by the majesty of God's creation. He loved the natural beauty of the outdoors, and here in the quiet of the forest, he felt at home.

Before the mountains were brought forth, or ever Thou hadst formed the earth and the world, even from everlasting to everlasting, Thou art God.

Sitting down on a wooden bench, he reached into the back pocket of his khaki slacks and retrieved a small Bible. He opened to Psalm 63, read it silently, then turned his eyes upward and spoke quietly to his God.

Chapter Two

"I do praise Your name, O Lord. You are my God, and my soul does thirst for You. Thank You for Your strength, Your mercy, Your love. I lift my voice in praise to Your holy name. Jesus said if we were to hold our peace, the stones would sing out your praises. I can't imagine what this valley would sound like if every rock here began to praise Your name, Lord!"

He paused for a moment, listening to the sounds of solitude around him. Looking back at his Bible, he silently reread verses seven and eight.

Because Thou hast been my help, therefore in the shadow of Thy wings will I rejoice. My soul followeth hard after Thee; Thy right hand upholdeth me.

He sat for a long time, until finally he glanced at his watch. Looking down the trail, he stood, replaced the Bible in his pocket, and headed back to the shuttle stop.

By the time Ryan returned to the hotel, breakfast had been set up in the conference room for the wedding guests who had stayed the night in Yosemite. Ryan entered and was immediately waved down by Eric Tanner.

"Hey, Pastor, you're up early!"

"It's too beautiful here to stay in the room. I went for a short walk."

"Yeah, it's gorgeous here. God sure did Himself good when He made Yosemite." Eric sat down at a nearby table and gestured for Ryan to join him. "You heading home today?"

Ryan nodded as he pulled out a chair across from Eric. "Kind of. I promised my parents I'd stop by and see them before I flew back home. They're on the way."

"Good morning, gentlemen."

Both men looked up to see Jessica approaching. Her short copper-colored hair was tucked neatly inside a blue knit cap with only a few renegade curls peaking out. She wore a denim skirt that came to mid-calf and a scoop-necked white pullover sweater.

"Good morning." Ryan immediately stood and pulled a chair out for her.

"Thank you," she said as she sat down. "I can't believe how good the air smells here. The pines and the campfires make it so... so... so like Christmas."

"Christmas?" Eric shook his head as he lifted one eyebrow.

Jessica frowned. "Don't spoil my morning, Tanner. If I say it smells like Christmas, then—"

Eric laughed. "I know, I know. Then it smells like Christmas. Okay, okay. Hey, is anyone else up yet?"

"Claire is. She was finishing up with some packing when I left. Said she'd be down shortly," replied Jessica.

"Ben and Dianne?"

Ryan shook his head. "I haven't seen them. Anyone for a cup of coffee?"

"I'd love one," replied Jessica. "Just a little cream with it, if you don't mind."

"Not at all." He turned toward Eric. "You?"

"No, thanks. I'm more of a Coke guy."

By the time Ryan returned, Eric had left in pursuit of a soda and Claire. Ryan set a cup in front of Jessica. "Here you go. Cream, no sugar."

"Thank you." She took a sip. "Perfect. Are you leaving today, too?"

"Yes. I'm going to stop by my parents before I leave the States. They're just north of Los Angeles. My dad's asked me to preach tomorrow morning's service, so I won't fly out until Monday."

"Really?" Jessica's eyebrows rose slightly. "Your dad's a pastor, too?"

"Yeah."

"I guess you were destined to follow in his footsteps?"

"I don't know about that... maybe... but it's kind of a long story."

"I'm not leaving until the afternoon." Jessica smiled sweetly, crossed her arms on the table, and looked expectantly at Ryan.

He looked at her and shook his head with a grin. "Okay, fine. But just remember, you asked." He took a sip of his coffee.

Chapter Two

"I grew up in the church, and I got saved when I was seven, but it wasn't until I was fourteen that I really began to understand that being saved meant more than just going to church. It was at a youth rally where a missionary spoke on the twelfth chapter of Romans that got my attention."

He lowered his eyes and thought for a moment, then quietly quoted verse one of the chapter. 'I beseech you therefore, brethren, by the mercies of God, that ye present your bodies a living sacrifice, holy, acceptable unto God, which is your reasonable service.'"

Looking back at Jessica, he explained. "That verse really hit home. I was supposed to offer myself to God... in service. It wasn't okay to just know I was forgiven of my sins and someday would live in heaven. It was more than that. I had a job to do here... for God.

"That night I really thought about my salvation, what it had cost, and what that meant for me. God had sent His only Son, Jesus, to die on a cross and take the punishment for *my* sin, so that I could have a relationship with Him. And He did it simply because He loved me. I had to ask myself what had I done for Him? Was I really that living sacrifice that Paul wrote about?

"All God wanted of me was *reasonable* service. Not *extraordinary* service, just *reasonable*. I realized I hadn't come close to that. My service had been more obligatory and convenient. I didn't resent working in the church with my parents and brother, but I realized I wasn't serving God out of love, but rather duty, and for me, that wasn't good enough."

Ryan took another sip of his coffee before continuing. "That night, I chose Romans 12:1 as my life verse, and I made a commitment to serve God in whatever capacity He would call me."

"At fourteen? You decided to be a pastor at fourteen?"

Ryan shook his head. "No. I just made the decision to do whatever God would call me to do. In my freshman year of high school, a group of us took a missions trip to Puerto Vallarta, Mexico, and I fell in love with the country, its people, the culture, everything. For the next three summers, I went down there.

In my senior year, I got to help build a parsonage for a church there. I loved that. I thought maybe I'd be involved in a church construction ministry... something like that."

He clasped his hands together on the table. "Then, during Bible college, I had an opportunity to work with a missionary in the eastern part of Mexico. We spent a good deal of time adding on to the facilities as God provided the means. I went there almost every time I had a break from classes. Then after I graduated, I moved there temporarily, or so I thought, to wait for God to show me where He wanted me to go, what He wanted me to do. I figured it would be a great learning opportunity in the meantime.

"When the pastor's health started failing, I'd fill the pulpit for him whenever he needed. When his health forced him to return to the States permanently, the congregation asked me to stay and assume the leadership role of the church. It was pretty overwhelming at the time, and frankly, I fought it. I told God that I was the wrong man for the job. I wasn't a pastor; I was a carpenter. I didn't have many years of experience, especially to take on the role of a senior pastor, and I was..."

He shook his head slightly, and his hands separated. "I was scared. I talked to my dad, gave him every reason I could think of as to why I should tell God that I couldn't do it. Then Dad reminded me that servants of God don't tell Him, 'No.' They do what He asks of them, trusting Him to equip them for whatever He wants them to do. Dad advised me to study the life of Timothy, devote myself to prayer, and be open to God's will.

"When I realized...again... that to be a living sacrifice, I had to yield myself completely to the will of God, which was my 'reasonable service,' I knew what my answer to God had to be. I said 'yes' somewhat reluctantly, but 'yes' nevertheless, and that's how I became a pastor."

Jessica shook her head in amazement. "That's quite a story."

Ryan took another sip of his coffee, then said, "So, tell me about you."

Chapter Two

"Okay, but let's get breakfast, first." She stood, cocked her head, and said, "You are hungry, aren't you?"

He grinned, revealing even, white teeth. "Very. Lead on."

After going through the buffet line, Ryan and Jessica walked back to their table. Jessica's plate held a container of blueberry yogurt, a hard-boiled egg, and a blueberry muffin, while Ryan had a hearty helping of scrambled eggs, hash brown potatoes, and white toast liberally slathered with butter.

"Your arteries must hate you," laughed Jessica as they sat down.

"What?" Ryan feigned innocence.

Jessica smirked. "You forgot the pancakes."

"I'm watching my weight," he chuckled. "So, I believe you were going to share your life history with me."

Jessica cracked the egg with her fork and began to peel it. "Well, I've wanted to be a doctor ever since I could remember. My mom died when I was almost six. My brother had just turned one when we were involved in a horrible car accident. My mother was driving when a drunk driver ran a stoplight and hit us broadside. My brother and I just had minor injuries, thanks to the car seats, but Mom got the full impact of the hit on her side. I was told the paramedics got us to the hospital fairly quickly, but there wasn't a trauma surgeon on staff. By the time one arrived, it was too late for Mom."

Her voice was quiet and low. "When I got older and could understand more of the ramifications of what could have been if there had been a trauma surgeon on site, I decided that was what I wanted to be." She looked up at Ryan. "I guess I didn't want anyone to lose a mother like I did, especially when they could have been saved."

"I'm sorry."

"Thank you." Her smile was genuine. "It's been a long time, and the Lord brought another wonderful woman into our father's life who became our second mother. Anne really showed me what faith is. When my—"

Jessica suddenly felt uncomfortable and fumbled with her napkin. "Are you sure you want to hear all this?"

Ryan nodded his head. "Of course," he reassured her. "You're talking about faith. How could I not want to hear about it? Please, go on."

His genuine interest lessened her discomfort, and when he asked her to continue, any hesitancy she had in sharing her story disappeared. The sincerity reflected in his deep blue eyes put her at ease, and Jessica continued. "My stepmother, Anne, she really helped me when my husband, Nick, was deployed to Afghanistan a year ago. I don't really know what I would have done without her. Dad was great, and so was my brother, but that was a time I really needed a mom."

She hesitated for a moment. "And that was Anne. I don't think a day goes by that I don't thank God for bringing her into our lives."

"Sounds like an amazing woman."

"She's quite remarkable. A real blessing in my life."

"And your husband? He's still overseas?"

Jessica nodded. "Yes. Nick is army through and through. His grandfather was in World War II. He actually was one of those soldiers in the invasion of Normandy on D-Day. Then, Nick's dad was in Desert Storm. He was a helicopter pilot.

"Nick, he's in the special forces, but I don't know exactly what he does. I don't really want to know. I'd like to believe he clerks for a general or something," she sighed. "But I know that's not the case. I try not to worry, but 'casting all my cares upon the Lord' can be very difficult at times for me. I'm hoping Nick will be home for the holidays, but there's no guarantee of that. When we got married, I knew there would be long periods of time when Nick would be gone, but I had no idea how hard it would get sometimes."

"Hopefully, he'll be home in time for Christmas," said Ryan as he scooped a forkful of eggs into his mouth.

"I hope so," said Jessica wistfully. She carefully cut her egg into quarters, then salt and peppered them lightly.

Chapter Two

"So what does a trauma surgeon do that's different from a regular surgeon?"

"Well, we handle patients that need surgery as a result of trauma, like gunshot wounds, motor vehicle accidents, stabbings. That sort of thing. If you came to the ER with an inflamed appendix, you would most likely be referred to a general surgeon, but if you came in with a knife wound to the abdomen, that would come to me. Of course, when there are no trauma cases, I do the other stuff, too."

"Sounds intense."

"It can be, but it's very rewarding, and I work with a great group of people. Ben, Eric, Claire, and of course, Maggie and Valerie. We're a pretty good team. I can't imagine working without them."

CHAPTER THREE

Two days later, Eastmont's emergency room was functioning at a frenzied, but controlled level. A collision between a tanker truck and a hot-rodding Corvette resulted in several major injuries; a drive-by shooting left two dead-on-arrival and one critically injured teen with a gunshot wound to the abdomen, and the recent flu outbreak brought in several families with sick children.

Jessica had been in the operating room off and on for most of her twenty-four hour shift, and now her job was to save the life of the latest victim of yet another senseless shooting. She tilted her head back and brought her shoulder blades in toward each other in an attempt to relieve some of the tension in her neck and back. Within seconds, she returned to the task before her.

"Scalpel."

A masked operating room nurse quickly slapped the requested instrument into the surgeon's waiting hand. As Jessica applied pressure to the stainless steel blade, it easily sliced through layers of skin and subcutaneous fat tissue. Blood began to ooze from the severed capillaries, and suction was applied to prevent the reddish-pink liquid from obstructing Jessica's view. Tiny wisps of smoke dissipated quickly as cauterization put an end to the extra seepage from the tiny blood vessels.

Jessica's focused blue eyes narrowed as she scanned the cavity she had created. Carefully inserting her fingers into the

Chapter Three

wound, she followed the track made by the bullet of the random gunshot just forty-five minutes earlier.

"Vital signs continue to be stable, Dr. Carr."

She nodded, continuing her probing without speaking. Finding no liver or spleen involvement, she turned her attention to the pancreas. Carefully examining the head of the pancreas and the major blood vessels behind it, she felt no abnormalities.

The O.R. team stood poised to respond to any request of the surgeon. Only their eyes, visible above their surgical masks, moved. Roaming from doctor to the overhead cardiac monitor and back to the doctor, the team waited, knowing how critical it was for Jessica to do a thorough inspection of the area.

As Jessica lifted the pancreas to inspect its neck, a small pool of dark red blood began to fill the cavity left behind. Her fingers hurriedly moved around the three major vessels in the vicinity of the hemorrhage.

"Clamp! Suction, please! I can't visualize the vessels!" The urgency in her voice increased the ever-present tension in the operating room, and the team sprang into action without hesitation. Surgical instruments were put into Jessica's hands as fast as she called for them.

"I need more suction now!" Her lips formed a tight line as she found the torn vessel and began the task of repairing its wound. Her hands moved with quick determination to suture the lacerated vein. "Sponge, please." She dabbed at the site as blood continued to ooze.

Come on... hold...

She expertly applied a few more double silk sutures to the site and waited. Her narrowed eyes focused on the now-mended blood vessel until she was satisfied the stitches were doing their job. Relaxing slightly, she continued her probing around the pancreas. Gently maneuvering the pinkish organ to display its back end, she frowned as she examined the exposed section. "Minor laceration present, but no apparent ductal involvement." She paused for a moment, pursing her lips and frowning once more as her fingers continued their blind search.

"Where is that bullet?" she whispered to no one in particular. Under her surgical mask, a frustrating scowl formed.

Where is it? It has to be here somewhere. Is that it?

"Got it!" She gently removed her fingers from the abdominal cavity and held a small metallic object in her fingers. The bullet clanged as she dropped it into a stainless steel metal basin. She quickly returned her attention back to her patient.

Finding no other major injuries, she began the task of repairing the bullet's damage. "I'll need two closed suction drains," she stated as she began to suture the damaged pancreas.

Nearly ninety minutes later, Jessica stepped out of operating room two, dropped her gloves and mask in a biohazard waste bin, and removed her surgical gown. She placed the bloodstained garment in the appropriate receptacle and walked through the O.R. department doors into the nearby waiting room.

"Mr. and Mrs. Pacheco?"

A short, heavy set Hispanic man stood. "*Sí,* yes, I am Luis Pacheco. You have news about my son?" His apprehensive eyes looked up at the surgeon's face. A slender dark-haired woman stood to her feet as she clung to the man's arm. She dabbed her reddened eyes with a crumpled tissue, the fear in them clearly visible.

Jessica quietly explained to the parents about the surgery she had performed on their son, answered their questions, and reassured them that their son's recovery should be without incident if no unforeseen complications arose.

After their brief discussion, she returned to the O.R. department and walked over to the nurses' station.

"Can I see Pacheco's chart, please?" she asked as she leaned on the counter.

"Of course, Dr. Carr. Here you go." Nurse Lorrie Donahue handed the chart to Jessica. "I heard that everything went well with him."

Jessica nodded. "Yes, but keep an eye on his amylase level, just in case. If it rises significantly, I may have to go back in." She scribbled her signature beneath her order for lab work and

Chapter Three

gave the chart back to Lorrie. "This has been one long day," she said as she rubbed the back of her neck.

The nurse chuckled. "And it's only six-thirty; the sun hasn't even set yet!" She turned to the computer on the desk and quickly typed in the lab order. "You off soon?

Jessica shook her head. "No. I'm covering for Ben. He had a conflict with his schedule, so I'm here for quite a while still."

"I hope it slows down, but that's not usually the case for a Friday night."

Jessica tilted her head to one side, shrugged her shoulders and sighed. "True." She glanced at her watch. "I'm going to run and grab a bite to eat while I can. Page me if Pacheco's amylase goes up."

"I will. Enjoy your dinner," called Lorrie as Jessica walked out of the O.R. department and headed to the elevator that would take her to the Eastmont Hospital cafeteria.

****

After finishing a tuna sandwich, Jessica refilled her cup of coffee and headed back to the still-crowded emergency room. Walking over to the nurses' station, she glanced up at the triage board and noticed nothing that might indicate immediate surgical intervention.

"Oh good, you're back."

Jessica turned toward Valerie Garrett, who held out an admission chart. "For me?" she asked, taking the chart from the ER head nurse.

Valerie nodded. "Yes. In two. Lady was washing dishes and broke a glass between thumb and index finger. Looks like a job for a surgeon, don't you think?"

Jessica lifted an eyebrow. "You're kidding, right?"

Valerie's hands went to her hips. "Nope. Everyone else is busy."

"Really?" Jessica smiled skeptically at Valerie.

"Would I lie?" The nurse pointed to the treatment room. "Right in there, Dr. Carr. After all, trauma is your specialty." She batted her eyes and flashed a smile.

Jessica laughed softly as she set her coffee cup on the nurses' desk. "All right, all right, I'm going!"

Half an hour later, Jessica had finished suturing the hand of the dishwashing lady and returned to the nurses' station. She set the completed chart on the clerk's desk and glanced at the triage board again.

Nothing new. That's good.

Taking advantage of the brief lull, she sat down in a swivel chair, put both elbows on the desk, and picked up her coffee cup from earlier. It was no longer hot, but still it enticed Jessica to take a sip. She did, then wrinkled her nose at the coolness of the coffee and set the cup back down. Approaching footsteps to her right captured her attention.

She looked up as Eric Tanner rounded the corner.

"Good evening, Eric."

He smiled broadly at Jessica as he set a chart down on the counter and opened it. He spoke as he began to write. "Evening, Dr. Carr. How'd that GSW do?"

"Okay. Fortunately, the biggest problem he had was a lacerated pancreas. I'm keeping an eye on the amylase because...?" She looked up at the young resident, waiting for his response.

Eric thought for a moment. "Amylase is produced by the pancreas, as is lipase. If these enzymes increase abnormally, it could indicate a more serious pancreatic situation."

Jessica nodded. "Correct. He also had a nick of the splenic artery near the portal vein junction, so he's still critical, but stable now."

"That's good to hear. He was pretty young, wasn't he?"

"Seventeen."

Eric shook his head. "We get far too many gunshot wounds here."

Chapter Three

Jessica nodded her head. "I agree. He was one of the lucky ones tonight though. He should be able to walk out of here and go home before the end of the week."

Eric nodded and said softly, "Thank the Lord for that."

"Dr. Tanner?" called a voice from behind him.

Eric turned around to see a nurse poking her head out of the treatment room from which he had just exited.

"The mother in here has a few more questions about the follow-up care."

"Thanks. I'll be right there." He turned back to Jessica. "I'll see you later."

He walked into the hallway, passing Valerie as she headed to the nurses' station. He nodded and smiled just before disappearing into treatment room three.

Valerie walked up to Jessica and opened her mouth to speak when the ER ambulance bay doors slid open, and a tall, blond man dashed in. He looked around frantically before grabbing a wheelchair and exiting back through the same doors. Neither Jessica nor Valerie had the opportunity to utter a word before the automatic double doors closed silently behind him. The nurse cast a puzzled look at the doctor.

Jessica shrugged her shoulders and shook her head as she stood, watching the now closed doors. "I'm guessing he bypassed the admitting desk?"

Valerie frowned, but curiosity compelled her to head toward the exit. As she neared the doors, they opened once more and the mysterious man reentered the ER frantically pushing a very pregnant woman in the wheelchair. Valerie quickly sidestepped to avoid colliding into the couple.

"Breathe, honey, breathe!" His eyes darted around wildly. "Please, can anybody help us? My wife's about to have a baby!" The desperation in his voice held a touch of fear.

Valerie reached out a hand to stop the couple. She pointed to a treatment room and guided them toward it. "Come right in here. Everything's going to be okay, sir."

Jessica watched them disappear from view, picked up her half empty cup, and headed toward the staff lounge.

That explains it.

She laughed lightly to herself as she entered the lounge. It was empty. She walked over to the sink, rinsed her cup out, and set it on the counter.

"Dr. Carr!" The urgent cry echoed through the hallway. "Dr. Carr!"

Recognizing Valerie's voice, Jessica returned to the corridor and quickened her pace toward treatment room four.

"Thank goodness!" uttered Valerie when she saw the doctor. "I need you!"

Jessica visually assessed the situation. The pregnant woman was breathing heavily and groaning. Valerie had the woman draped for delivery.

Looks like I've just become an obstetrician.

"Ohhh... he's coming! Ohhh...." The woman clenched her husband's hand.

Valerie looked up at Jessica as the doctor approached the bedside. "This baby's not going to wait for an OB! Her contractions are pretty much on top of each other. Fetal heart tones are good." Valerie had positioned the father-to-be at the head of the bed, and now he nervously whispered words of encouragement to his wife as he patted the hand of the soon-to-be mother.

Jessica quickly donned a pair of latex gloves and positioned herself to check the status of the unborn baby. "Val, can you get me a BOA kit?"

Valerie moved to retrieve a "born-out-of-asepsis" kit, the special set-up for babies delivered in a non-sterile environment. She opened it and set up the items that Jessica would need to deliver the baby. She moved the stainless steel table nearer to the doctor who was listening for fetal heart tones.

"Call OB and peds for me, too." Jessica turned her attention to the woman whose moaning was becoming more frequent. "Mrs. Larkin, I'm Dr. Carr. Seems like your little one is ready to be born. I need you to focus and do as I ask, okay?"

Chapter Three

"Yes," replied Mrs. Larkin through clenched teeth. "Oh.... It hurts so much." She tried to stifle a cry, but it partially escaped her lips.

Her husband's face whitened. "She's okay, right Doc?"

Jessica glanced up at Mr. Larkin. "Yes, she's doing fine." She turned toward the nurse. "Val, can you get a stool for Mr. Larkin?" She then looked back at the man. "First baby?"

"Yes..." he stammered.

Valerie moved a chair into position behind Mr. Larkin. "You sit here if you feel lightheaded, okay?"

He cast a thankful look toward Valerie and plopped down.

Jessica completed a quick exam, and then with the next contraction, a gush of amniotic fluid spewed forth. "Spontaneous rupture of membranes. Fully dilated and 100% effacement. It won't be long now."

"Is that bad?" Mr. Larkin asked, his frightened eyes searching Jessica's face.

She looked up and smiled reassuringly. "No. It's perfectly normal. It just means your wife's ready to deliver your baby. Everything is just fine. You doing okay?"

He nodded rapidly, but said nothing as he kept his widened eyes on Jessica.

Valerie quickly replaced the disposable bed pad from under the patient and prepped the warming bed for the newborn. She moved to the telephone and placed a call to the obstetrics and pediatric units informing them of the impending birth in the ER.

"Mrs. Larkin, I want you to push on this next contraction, okay? Hold your breath and bear down when you feel it coming on. Hold it for ten counts. Mr. Larkin, I need you to count to ten out loud for her, okay?"

"I feel the baby coming!" cried Mrs. Larkin. "Ohhh..."

"Bear down and push, Mrs. Larkin," ordered Jessica. She glanced at the petrified father-to-be. "Count!"

In the background, Mr. Larkin's trembling voice began. "Uh... one... two... three..."

"You're doing great, Mrs. Larkin. I can see the top of your baby's head. Do you know if it's a girl or boy?" asked Jessica as she continued her watch on the crowning child.

"A boy," stated Mr. Larkin. "His name is Joel."

"Well, Joel has a nice head of black hair," reported Jessica as she continued to monitor the baby's progress.

Mrs. Larkin's concerned eyes focused on the doctor as the contraction lessened in intensity. "He's okay, isn't he?"

Jessica nodded. "He's doing well so far, and so are you. Mama, get ready to push again with the next contraction."

Mrs. Larkin nodded. "Okay, I... Ohhh... here it comes." She held her breath and pushed.

Jessica quickly felt for the umbilical cord, and when she determined it was not around the baby's neck, encouraged Mrs. Larkin to bear down harder. "Let's get Joel out, Mama!"

Within seconds, Jessica was gripping a vigorously wiggling baby protesting with a loud, lusty cry, its entrance into the world. After quickly suctioning any obstructive mucus from the newborn's nasal passages, Jessica took a warm blanket from Valerie and wrapped the little boy snuggly before laying him on the mother's chest.

"Dad, would you like to cut the cord?" asked Jessica. She looked up at the father's tearstained face.

As he wiped the tears from his eyes, Mr. Larkin nodded and stepped over toward Jessica. His hand shook as he took the offered pair of surgical scissors.

"I... I don't know what to do..." His nervous eyes pleaded for assistance.

Jessica quickly clamped the cord in two places and instructed the new dad to snip between the clamps. "You're doing just fine, Mr. Larkin."

The new father returned the scissors to Jessica, and as his tear-filled eyes met hers, he whispered, "Thank you so much, Doctor."

Chapter Three

She smiled as Mr. Larkin returned his attention to his wife. As Jessica prepared to receive the afterbirth, she spoke to Valerie without looking up. "How's the baby?"

"One minute Apgar is 8," reported the nurse.

Jessica nodded her approval. Checking for respiration, heart rate, skin color, cry, and muscle activity was critical in determining whether or not an infant was ready to meet the world on its own. The higher the Apgar score, the less chance an infant would need medical intervention immediately after its birth. A score between 7 and 10 one minute after birth was good.

After a few minutes of bonding time, Valerie gently took the baby from his parents and transferred him to the warming bed just as the pediatrician entered the room.

"What have we got, Valerie?" she asked as she neared the nurse.

"Hi, Dr. Newton. Healthy little boy. Apgar scores are 8 and 9," stated Valerie as she continued to clean, weigh, and measure the newborn.

"Thanks, Val. How are you doing, Jessica?" Dr. Erica Newton pulled on a pair of latex gloves, and then placed her stethoscope on the chest of the baby, assessing his heart and lungs.

"Fine. Just about done here. Mama's doing great. Baby?"

"This little boy is a strong one." Dr. Newton stood up and faced the new parents. "We'll get him cleaned up and over to you in just a few minutes. Congratulations to you both."

Mr. Larkin beamed. "Thank you! Thank you so much!" He kissed his wife before moving over to the bassinet that held his son. He watched Valerie intently as she gently rewrapped the baby in a clean receiving blanket. As he touched the baby's hand, its tiny fingers closed around his finger. "He's holding my hand, honey! Joel is holding my hand!"

Jessica glanced over at the father just as the obstetrician walked into the room.

"Looks like I'm a bit on the late side," smiled Dr. Rafael Santiago. He quickly pulled on a pair of gloves and changed places with Jessica.

Jessica stood, removed her gloves, and tossed them into a biohazard bin. "No problem at all. I enjoyed this. I love delivering babies. It's always a blessing bringing a new life into the world. I left the easy part for you, Dr. Santiago."

Rafael chuckled softly as he switched places with Jessica. "Noted, Dr. Carr."

Mr. Larkin moved over to Jessica, grabbed her hand, and shook it vigorously. "Thank you, Doctor! Thank you so much!"

"You're very welcome, Mr. Larkin. I wish the very best for you and your new family," Jessica said sincerely. "I'll leave you in good hands now. Take care." Before she walked out into the ER, she looked over her shoulder once more at the little baby now secure in his mother's arms.

CHAPTER FOUR

It was nearly one o'clock in the morning when Jessica finally crossed the threshold to her condominium. She dropped her keys on the small cherry wood table by the front door and walked into the living room. The silence of the house was oppressive, and her discomfort with it compelled her to immediately turn on the stereo system. A soft rendition of traditional hymns began to permeate her home. Closing her eyes for a moment, she allowed the soothing melodies to fill her mind and begin the relaxation process. She began to hum along as she headed to the kitchen.

Opening the refrigerator, she perused the contents, finally reaching for a can of diet soda and a mozzarella stick. She turned around, leaned against the counter, and popped open the can. She took a sip, then set the can on the counter. As she peeled the wrapper from the cheese, she allowed her large blue eyes to focus on a photograph on the refrigerator door. The picture was of Nick standing next to a US army tank. Clad in his desert camouflage uniform, he casually held his weapon as he smiled for the camera. Her eyes misted over as she stared at the picture of the handsome soldier whose ring she wore.

I can't believe it's been so long since we've been together. I miss you so much, Nick.

She bit into the cheese stick as her eyes remained fixed on her husband's picture. Her heart ached with longing, and she was acutely aware of the emptiness that threatened to engulf her. As she reached to touch the photo, the diamonds in her wedding ring glittered in the soft glow of the kitchen's overhead lighting. It caught her eye, and she turned her hand slowly to enhance the sparkle of the gem.

Okay, Lord. You've got to help me. I knew what I was getting into when I married him. Help me focus on... whatsoever things are true, whatsoever things are honest, whatsoever things are just, whatsoever things are pure, whatsoever things are lovely, whatsoever things are of good report...

She closed her eyes as her mind filled with another verse from the same passage of Scripture.

And the peace of God, which passeth all understanding, shall keep your hearts and minds through Christ Jesus.

The sweet assurance that God did understand her feelings, and that He truly cared about her and Nick, began to fill her heart with a much-needed calm. The awareness that she was not alone, despite the solitude she felt, gave her what she needed.

She opened her eyes as God's peace slowly replaced the loneliness she felt in her soul. She looked at Nick's picture one more time. His confident smile reminded her of his deep devotion to his country and his resolve to continue in his father's and grandfather's footsteps as he followed his own dream of becoming a soldier in the United States Army. She took another deep breath, blinked her eyes, and sighed deeply.

I love you, Nick. I always will. Be safe, my love.

She picked up the soda can, then flicked the light switch. Darkness filled the room, but a small light remained in her heart as she made her way up the stairs to her bedroom.

****

Saturday morning greeted Jessica with bright sunshine and a subtle breeze. The sky was streaked with purples, pinks, and yellows without a hint of the light brown haze for which Los Angeles was well known.

Chapter Four

Taking advantage of a rare weekend off, Jessica relaxed on the patio lounge with her feet curled under her as she sipped a cup of peppermint-flavored tea. She cherished this quiet time in the morning. No demands for her attention; no pagers or phones buzzing; no problems with which to deal. She closed her eyes and listened to the silence around her, noticing that it really wasn't silent. The dull drone of the nearby freeway mixed with the muted sounds of a barking dog and its respondent somewhere farther away reminded her that she was in the midst of a thriving metropolitan area.

I wonder what quiet really sounds like.

She rose and walked into the kitchen to make one more cup of tea. As she leaned against the granite kitchen counter, her eyes fell on her Bible resting unopened on the kitchen table. A church bulletin from two weeks ago peeked out from beneath its cover. She picked up the Bible and thumbed through it until she reached the book of Philippians. She turned a few pages, then set the open book down on the counter. She began to read all the verses of chapter four, the same chapter that had been such an encouragement to her the previous night. Her eyes returned to the chapter's first verse.

Therefore, my brethren dearly beloved and longed for, my joy and crown, so stand fast in the Lord, my dearly beloved.

She moved to the whistling copper teapot and filled her cup with the steaming brew. Inhaling its minty aroma, she cupped the mug in both hands, closed her eyes and lost herself in the soothing scent.

"Give me courage, Lord Jesus," whispered Jessica as she opened her eyes. "To trust You. Help me to hold on to my faith. I know You are always by my side." She set her cup on the counter, picked up her Bible, and closed it. As she set it back on her kitchen table, she noticed the church bulletin again. She picked it up and read the verse printed on the front of it.

Casting all your care upon him; for He careth for you.

As she reflected upon the verse, she thought about all the empirical evidence she had experienced in her life that proved God cared for her. She smiled.
How could I ever doubt You?

****

The next day, Jessica arrived at church just in time for Sunday school. She hurried to the ladies' class and found a seat near the back of the crowded room. Sitting quickly, she bowed her head as the teacher began to pray. Her gaze fell on her folded hands and once more, she caught herself staring at the wedding ring encircling her finger.
Nick, I wish you were here with me.
As a veil of darkness encroached upon her, Jessica defiantly sat up straight, raised her head, and smiled at Mrs. Gretchen Draper, the teacher.
I will not let myself be robbed of whatever blessing God has for me today.
She listened intently as Gretchen spoke on godly women and trusting the Lord. She considered the verse that Gretchen read aloud from the ninth chapter of Psalms. "And they that know Thy name will put their trust in Thee: for thou, Lord, hast not forsaken them that seek Thee."
Jessica pondered the verse.
Thank You, Lord, for remembering me in the hard times. I know I haven't always trusted You completely, but You've been so faithful to me. Help me be strong. Help me remember that You are in control of all things, and You always keep Your promises.
Forty-five minutes later, Jessica went upstairs to the main sanctuary for the worship service. Moving toward the center of the church, she glanced around at the gathering congregation and, smiling and nodding to several familiar faces, easily found a place to sit.
A tall, thin man moved to the pulpit and welcomed everyone before proceeding to share some church announcements. When

Chapter Four

he finished, he invited the congregation to join in the opening hymn, *The Old Rugged Cross*.

Reaching for the church hymnal, she flipped through it until she found the song. She joined in, never having to look at the words of the old familiar hymn. At the song's conclusion, the minister walked up to the pulpit.

"Good morning!" he began as he gazed out over the congregation. "It certainly is good to see you all here this morning as we gather together to worship our Lord and Savior, Jesus Christ. Let us go to the throne of grace in prayer." Heads bowed and eyes closed as he began to petition God.

"Heavenly Father, we love You and offer You our praise and worship for who You are. Your mercies are new every morning, and for that, we thank You. Lord, we gather together today to ask for Your blessing upon this morning's service. May it be through Your sweet Holy Spirit's anointing that I am able to share with these people the message You have given me. May Your perfect will be accomplished in this place, and may You receive all the glory and honor for all that is said and done here today. In the name of Your precious Son and our beloved Savior, Jesus Christ, I pray. Amen."

After a few more congregational hymns, the choir began their special selection, a medley of songs that focused on the cross of Christ. Its ending rose to a triumphant crescendo, and several "amens" echoed throughout the sanctuary at the song's finish. As the singers exited the choir loft, the rest of the church stood and greeted one another.

"Jessica! How are you, darling?" An elderly lady wrapped her arms around Jessica and hugged her tightly. "Are you taking care of yourself? Not working too hard? And how's that young man of yours?"

"He's well, Mrs. Jacobson. Thank you for asking. It's very good to be here." She smiled as she moved to shake hands with several others before returning to her seat. Lifting her eyes to the pulpit, she waited expectantly as the pastor moved behind it once more.

"Today's text is the ninety-first chapter of Psalms. Please stand with me to honor the reading of God's Word." He opened his own Bible as the people rose to their feet. "Please follow along as I read aloud."

Jessica opened her Bible and quickly found the chapter to which he had referred. She followed along as he read the sixteen verses, and then sat attentively as he began his message.

"Notice verses one and two. 'He that dwelleth in the secret place of the most High shall abide under the shadow of the Almighty. I will say of the Lord, He is my refuge and my fortress: my God; in Him will I trust.'" He paused for a moment. "What is a shadow? It is the affirmation that something is present. According to the dictionary, the definition of a shadow is a dark area or shape produced by a body coming between rays of light and a surface. A shadow cannot appear independent of anything else. In order for a shadow to be cast, there must be something present.

"In verse one, there cannot be the shadow of the Almighty without the actual presence of God. He may be invisible to us, but God's real presence is there. If He were not, no shadow could be cast. The Bible mentions the shadow of God several times. The first is in Psalm seventeen, verse eight."

He thumbed through the pages of his Bible, stopping when he found the verse. "'Keep me as the apple of the eye, hide me under the shadow of Thy wings.' The Psalmist is asking God to keep him safe and close.

"When we are facing difficult times, we must remember that we can always find refuge in the shadow of the Lord. Psalm fifty-seven, verse one states 'Be merciful unto me, O God, be merciful unto me: for my soul trusteth in Thee: yea, in the shadow of Thy wings will I make my refuge, until these calamities be overpast.'

"We can trust that God is with us even if we don't see Him because we see His shadow, and therein lies our hope."

He continued to expound on several more examples from the Scriptures about the shadow of God. When he began his

Chapter Four

closing remarks, Jessica closed her Bible and leaned forward slightly in her pew.

The pastor stopped for a moment and walked to the side of the pulpit before continuing. "It is often difficult for us to trust God in all things, but when we do, His Word promises that God Himself will keep him in perfect peace, whose mind is stayed on Him. Hidden under the shadow of the Almighty is the best place to be in times of trouble or sorrow as well as times of peace and joy. I encourage you to allow yourself to believe what God's Word tells us, then you, too, will be able to say as the Psalmist did, 'Because Thou hast been my help, therefore in the shadow of Thy wings will I rejoice.' Let's pray."

As soon as the pastor dismissed the congregation, Jessica made her way to the back of the church near the exit doors. She said her goodbyes quickly and weaved her way through the crowded foyer to the parking lot and her waiting BMW. It only took 23 minutes for her to maneuver through the traffic and get to Eastmont Hospital.

CHAPTER FIVE

Valerie Garrett stepped out of the nurses' station and barely missed crashing into Jessica as the doctor rushed toward the staff lounge.

"Sorry, Dr. Carr," she said quickly as she twisted to avoid a collision.

Jessica came to an abrupt stop. "I'm sorry, Val. My fault."

"We just got a call. Multi-car pile-up on PCH."

Jessica frowned and shook her head.

Already? Pacific Coast Highway... this could be a very long day.

"Trauma team's been activated," reported Valerie as she glanced at her watch. "Dr. Shepherd is scheduled to be here within the hour, but I called him, and he's on his way now. Dr. Tanner should be back from lunch any moment."

Jessica nodded as Eric and two nurses rounded the corner.

"Better put on your running shoes, everyone!" exclaimed Valerie as she moved to the triage board and wrote 'Multiple MVAs.' "It's going to get busy!"

Eric's eyes narrowed as he looked up questioningly at the near empty triage board. "Motor vehicle accidents?" He shook his head slightly and frowned. "How many are we expecting?"

Standing with her hands on her hips, Jessica reiterated, "Multiple vehicles and victims. They'll be here soon. ETA is fifteen minutes tops. Initial estimate is seven victims, maybe more."

A muted whistle escaped Eric's lips. "Wow, who've we got?"

Chapter Five

"We're down one nurse," replied Valerie, "but I've got a call in to admin for some extra help. The team's been notified."

"Good. Let's make sure we're ready when they start pulling in."

The ER staff scattered like frenzied ants whose hill had just been disturbed. Within minutes, the trauma team had assembled, and Jessica briefed them with the latest information. The team moved to prepare for the first arrivals. The triage area was well stocked for its incoming patients. Both trauma and treatment rooms were ready to receive the incoming patients. Extra staff were arriving.

Jessica cocked her head as the sound of a distant siren became louder. "Lord, give us wisdom and guide our hands."

Eric glanced over at her. "Amen." He picked up a pen and stuck it in the pocket of his green scrubs.

The emergency vehicle sirens grew louder, then abruptly stopped. Within seconds, the ambulance bay doors swung open. A pair of paramedics rolled a gurney into the corridor, and both Eric and Jessica moved to intercept them as the firefighters pushed the first victim toward the trauma room.

"Seventeen-year-old female MVA victim, unconscious at the scene," came the report as the paramedics neared the nurses' station. "You should see the two cars. Needed the can opener to get her out."

"Put her in trauma one!" called out Valerie as she began to scribble on the triage board.

Jessica followed them toward the treatment area. "I've got this one," she called out to Eric. He nodded and headed toward another patient rolling in behind the first.

"Two others were DOA at the scene," said the paramedic to Jessica as they moved the first motor vehicle accident victim onto the bed. "They were working on another one when we left. I counted at least four others."

Jessica snapped on a pair of latex gloves as Valerie hurried in and began to hook their patient to the overhead monitor.

"What's her name?" Jessica pulled a penlight from her pocket and flashed it into the unconscious girl's eyes.

Unequal and sluggish response. Not good.

Valerie glanced at the field chart started by the paramedics. "Whitney. Whitney Harris."

"Whitney, my name is Dr. Carr. You're at Eastmont Hospital. You've been in an accident. Whitney, I need you to open your eyes for me." She turned toward Valerie. "I need a tox screen in addition to the standard draws," stated Jessica. "Plus a head CT and a chest x-ray."

Removing a pair of scissors from her jacket pocket, Jessica began to cut away part of Whitney's bloodied clothing, exposing large areas of purple blotches across her torso.

At least you had a seat belt on.

She immediately placed her stethoscope on the upper chest of her patient and listened carefully, moving the scope to specific areas that would give her information critical in assessing the young woman's respiratory and cardiac systems.

"Whitney? Whitney? Can you open your eyes for me?" Jessica put two of her fingers into the girl's right palm. "Whitney? Can you feel my fingers? Give them a squeeze for me. Whitney, squeeze my fingers."

The teen remained nonresponsive.

"What's her BP?"

"Ninety-eight over seventy-two and holding." Valerie moved to the phone to order the blood work Jessica had requested. Glancing up at the monitor, she stated, "She's tachycardic. Heart rate's one-thirty-two." Valerie picked up the receiver and dialed.

Jessica glanced up at the cardiac monitor, then placed her fingers on Whitney's abdomen and pressed gently at first, then firmer. As she palpated, she closed her eyes to help her focus on what she was feeling.

What's going on with you, Whitney?

"I need a—" Jessica stopped abruptly as a shrieking voice from the outside corridor interrupted her.

Chapter Five

"Where is she?" a woman's shrill voice screamed. "Whitney! Where is she?"

Jessica could hear Ben's calming voice outside the treatment room as he spoke to the screamer.

"Miss, you have to lay back on the gurney. Whitney's receiving the best care possible. We need to check you over. You're bleeding. Settle down now. Lay back."

"Please, I have to see her," the feminine voice pleaded. "Is she okay? Please! I'm so sorry! Whitney! I just wanted her to see a picture. It was only a second... only a second." The confession changed to loud sobbing, which faded as the gurney moved further down the corridor.

Jessica looked up at Val. "I'm also going to need an abdominal ultrasound." She stood and sighed as she picked up the field chart. Perusing the paramedic's notes, she frowned at the last sentence.

Open containers of alcohol inside the vehicle.

Jessica shook her head as she set the chart on the bedside table.

Later, after x-rays and ultrasound testing had revealed internal bleeding and multiple leg fractures, Jessica stood over Whitney in the operating room.

"Vitals?" she asked.

"No change," came the reply.

"Can I get a little more suction?" Jessica stopped for just a moment while the nurse removed the excess fluid from the surgical site. "That's better."

As she adeptly worked to repair torn blood vessels and a small laceration in the liver, she glanced up when the O.R. door opened. Recognizing the orthopedic surgeon, Jessica nodded as he moved to the other side of Whitney.

"How's it going, Jess?" His deep voice had a hint of a southern drawl.

"Good. I'm almost finished with her. Her x-rays didn't look too good."

"They're not." Dr. Lucas Blackman walked over to the viewing screen to re-examine Whitney's x-rays. "This girl's going to have a lot of rehab in her future, and even with that, I seriously doubt she'll ever dance again."

"That's awful," Jessica said as she finished her last suture. She looked up at the surgical resident. "Can you close this for me?" She stepped back as her assistant took over.

As she headed toward the door, she glanced back. "She's all yours, Luke. Good luck."

He nodded to her as she exited the operating room.

****

It was a little after five o'clock in the evening when the last victim in the traffic accident was brought to Eastmont Hospital. Once more, Jessica fell into step with the paramedics as they wheeled the latest patient into trauma room four.

"Twenty-six year old female. Took a bit to extricate her. Trapped between steering wheel and the seat. C-collar and back board in the field. Slightly tachycardic at 137, respirations in the high 30's with decreased breath sounds bilaterally. BP's low, but holding at 96 over 68. She was responsive when we got there, but she's been out since just before we got her out of the car." The paramedic turned his attention to the other two firefighters who accompanied him. "On my count. One, two, three."

The men moved the still body of the accident victim to the ER bed in one solid movement, and then stepped away so Jessica could easily access the young woman.

"What's her name?" Jessica shined a light into the eyes of the nonresponsive woman. She flicked it back and forth over the clearly reactive pupils.

"Gail. Gail Foreman. Someone said she was a grad student over at UCLA."

Claire had hurried in after the firefighters and was now readjusting the intravenous line started in the field. She attached a pulse oximeter on the woman's left index finger, affixed a blood

Chapter Five

pressure cuff around her arm, and hooked the patient to the cardiac monitor. The overhead console sprang to life with various oscillating lines revealing information vital to the care of the patient.

Jessica glanced up quickly when she heard the first blip, then looked down at her patient. "Gail? Gail, can you hear me? Open your eyes for me, Gail," she coaxed, but her patient remained nonresponsive.

She set her stethoscope on Gail's chest and listened.

Faint heart sounds.

Moving her stethoscope around, she strained to hear the muted cardiac sounds of her patient.

She frowned. "I can barely hear her heart," she murmured to herself. She glanced up at the monitor.

Tachycardic. Her heart is racing.

Reaching down, she felt the arm and lower leg of her patient.

Cold, clammy...

"What's the BP?"

"88 over 58."

Jessica looked carefully at Gail's neck. The jugular veins were somewhat distended. She felt for a radial pulse, but could feel nothing. Her assessment was without error.

Classic cardiac tamponade. Low blood pressure, increased heart rate, faint breath sounds, possible heart trauma from the steering wheel.

"I need a pericardiocentesis set-up now. I need to drain the liquid around her heart," she stated. The declaration of Jessica's diagnosis spurred the ER staff into automatic action.

"Elevating lower extremities."

"Dobutamine ready."

A stainless steel tray was immediately moved to within Jessica's reach with the sterile set-up in place for the procedure. In seconds, she had her latex gloves on and quickly draped Gail's chest with a sterile sheet that had an opening for the targeted region. Hurriedly disinfecting the area, Jessica carefully positioned a syringe and needle over Gail's thorax just below the xiphoid, the lower end of the sternum. Applying steady pressure to the 18-gauge needle, she entered the chest cavity at a thirty-five degree angle, aiming slightly toward the left shoulder.

"Keep an eye on her vitals. Administer the dobutamine," ordered Jessica as she slowly advanced the needle. Her trained fingers felt the resistance to the needle as she pushed it through the muscular wall of the chest cavity. As the needle touched the pericardial sac, the cardiac monitor accelerated its pace.

"Heart rate's increasing, Dr. Carr."

"BP is holding."

Jessica hesitated for a moment, listening to the monitor's rhythmic beeping.

Easy, Jess... take it real slow now...

Skillfully advancing the needle into the fluid-filled sac surrounding the heart, Jessica pulled back on the syringe and began to extract the restrictive fluid. The room seemed to hold its breath in silence; the only sound was the rapid beeping of the overhead monitor. As the liquid inside the pericardial sac was removed, the pace of the cardiac monitor began to drop, and Jessica felt some of the tension in her body dissipate as she glanced up quickly at the readouts. The rhythm and rate were returning to a less life-threatening status, and with the help of intravenous fluids and meds, Gail's blood pressure began to return to normal limits.

"Let's get her stabilized and moved to the ICU," ordered Jessica as she retracted the needle. She removed her gloves and tossed them into a biohazard bin. It had been thirty-eight minutes since Gail Foreman had been brought into the ER.

****

By eight-thirty, the ER had quieted, and only a few noncritical patients were still waiting to be seen. Jessica stood at the nurses' station finalizing a chart. She finished a note, signed her

Chapter Five

name, closed the chart, and placed it in the appropriate tray for the ER clerk. She turned to see Valerie stomping down the hall. The charge nurse was frowning, and she walked with fists clenched. Her lips were drawn in a tight line.

Jessica's eyebrows rose slightly. "Something wrong, Val?"

"Dr. Carr, I know this isn't surgical, but I've got a patient in three who's a little upset... okay, a lot upset, and there's no one I can send in just now. Would you mind assessing her? If I go back in there... well, I don't really know what I'll do." The irritation in Valerie's narrowed hazel eyes spoke volumes.

Jessica smiled understandingly at the nurse. "Sure, Val." She reached for the chart. "Why don't you go get a cup of coffee? I'll take care of..." She glanced at the chart. "Barbara Ortega."

In less than five minutes, Jessica was in treatment room three, listening as the agitated woman rattled on about the incompetencies of the emergency room.

"It's about time someone came in to see me. Where is everyone? On a coffee break? This is no way to run an emergency room!" She scowled at Jessica as her dark eyes moved from the doctor's face, down the lab coat, then back up. "You *are* a doctor, aren't you? And I mean, a real doctor. Not someone who thinks they're one."

Jessica raised one eyebrow as she perused her newest patient. "Yes, Mrs. Ortega. I'm a doctor. What brings you to Eastmont?"

"I know something is wrong, but I don't know what it is. I am just so tired all the time. Even when I sleep nine or ten hours at night, I still wake up feeling exhausted. You need to find out what's wrong," she demanded. "My regular doctor thought it was the flu, but this has been going on for a few weeks. He's incompetent. He said it might be acid reflux, but I've drank enough antacids to drown a rat, and nothing's changed." She frowned at Jessica. "If I thought it would help, I'd drive up to the Bay area. My sister's doctor, now that's a doctor."

Jessica shifted her weight from one foot to the other. "Well, let me do a quick exam. Then, I'll order some lab tests and a chest x-ray. After that, I'll be better able to give you an idea of what's going on."

"I don't want an idea; I want the facts, and I want a diagnosis. Maybe you should call someone else." Barbara folded her arms across her chest.

Jessica said nothing, but pulled out her stethoscope. She held it slightly above Barbara's chest, waiting for the woman to open her arms. "It will be much easier for me to assess your heart if you move your arms off your chest." Jessica's piercing eyes locked on to Barbara's indignant ones.

Barbara hesitated for a moment, then looked away as her arms dropped to her sides.

Jessica remained silent as she positioned her stethoscope several times and listened carefully to each area of her patient's chest.

Lungs are clear. Heart sounds fine. Rate and rhythm are within normal limits...

Jessica carefully scrutinized her patient's fingernails, neck veins, and ankles.

No other obvious respiratory or circulatory symptoms. Hmm... nothing out of the ordinary, still...

"Mrs. Ortega, I'm going to order some tests, and then after I get the results, I'll be back in to discuss them with you."

"I hope so." Barbara rubbed her temples. "Do you think I could get something for this headache? Sitting in that waiting room for a couple of hours has taken its toll. No one should have to wait that long. It's negligence. That's what it is."

Jessica frowned slightly as she took a deep, controlled breath. She forced a smile. "Sure. I'll have the nurse bring something for you." She scribbled some notes on the admittance chart and then headed for the nurses' station.

"Claire, can you get me an EKG stat on Ortega? Also, these lab tests?" She handed the chart to the nurse. "And..."

"Yes?"

"Keep a close eye on her, okay? Something's just not right, but I can't put a finger on it yet."

Chapter Five

"You got it, Dr. Carr." Claire began inputting the lab requests into the computer.

Forty minutes later, Jessica sat down in the nurses' station and began to write a discharge for a young teen with a sprained ankle. As she placed the chart in the clerk's tray, Claire handed her several lab reports.

"Ortega's in there?"

"Yes."

Jessica flipped through the papers until she found the lab slips for Barbara Ortega. She mentally interpreted the results.

Hmm... cardiac enzymes are at the upper limit of normal.

"Did we get the EKG done?"

"I think I just saw the tech go into the room."

"Now? They're just getting to it, *now?*"

Jessica quickly walked into the room of Barbara Ortega and found her patient's skin had developed an ashen hue, and her breathing was shallow and labored.

"I need that EKG *now!*" demanded Jessica, her stethoscope already on the chest of her patient.

The technician quickly placed the electrodes on Barbara's body as Claire entered the room.

"Respiratory rate is escalating as is the heart rate. O-two sat is dropping," reported Claire as she increased the oxygen flow.

Jessica glanced up at the bedside monitor, simultaneously reaching for Mrs. Ortega's wrist.

Oxygen saturation is dropping? That's not good. Heart rate is rapid, and the pulse is thready.

"I can't breathe, Doctor! Do something!" Mrs. Ortega gasped. Her hands moved up toward the oxygen mask over her nose and mouth.

"Leave the mask there, Barbara," Jessica ordered firmly. Maneuvering the stethoscope around Barbara's chest, the doctor's eyes narrowed as she focused intently on the labored breath sounds.

Jessica frowned, then snapped, "Where is the EKG?"

"Almost done."

"What's happening to me?" Mrs. Ortega's anxious voice escalated.

"Let's give her sublingual nitro, and I need a repeat on the cardiac enzymes. And I want that EKG *NOW!*"

"I've got it here, Dr. Carr."

Jessica grabbed the paper and scowled as she studied the EKG. "Elevated ST segments. Well, that's timely." She pressed her lips together tightly and shook her head. "Claire, please get her a bed in the CCU and move her as soon as possible."

"What's happening to me?" Fear was evident in the voice of the once overbearing patient.

Jessica turned to Mrs. Ortega. Her voice softened. "Barbara, you may have had a mild heart attack—"

"A heart attack? Am I going to die?" Mrs. Ortega's voice trembled, and she bolted up in the bed and frantically grasped Jessica's forearm. "Tell me the truth, Doctor! Am I going to die?"

Jessica put her hand atop Barbara's shaking one and squeezed it slightly. "We're going to take good care of you, Mrs. Ortega. I need you to lie back and try to relax. With the right meds and treatment, you should be fine, but you've got to settle down, okay? I'll notify Dr. Markham. He's an outstanding cardiologist."

Jessica's reply did little to alleviate the haze of panic rising in her patient, but Barbara was able to follow the doctor's request and lay back in the bed. Her widened eyes followed Jessica's every movement.

"Please, Doctor. I can't die; I just can't." She began to weep.

"Barbara, listen to me," coaxed Jessica. "You're going to get the best of care. Dr. Markham is the best heart doctor I know. He's going to take very good care of you." Her soothing voice began to penetrate the blanket of fear that enveloped the sick woman.

"I won't die?" she asked anxiously; her frightened eyes focused on Jessica's face.

Chapter Five

Jessica smiled understandingly, this time more genuinely than when she had first met her patient. "We're going to do everything we possibly can to make sure that doesn't happen."

In less than ten minutes, a bed was ready in the coronary care unit, and Barbara Ortega was transported for further care under the watchful eye of Dr. Alex Markham.

Jessica walked over to the nurses' station, her blue eyes flashing angrily. "Claire, explain something to me."

The nurse turned quickly. Her dark brown eyes widened at the harshness in Jessica's voice. "Yes, Dr. Carr?"

"Why did it take nearly forty-five minutes to get a stat EKG on Ortega? Last time I checked, "stat" meant immediately." Her look demanded an answer.

Claire's lips formed a thin line as she shrugged her shoulders. "I wish I could say it was just a fluke, but we both know that's not true."

Jessica shook her head. "We could have had a big problem tonight."

"But we didn't," Claire stated. "You're one of the best physicians I know, Dr. Carr. You trusted your intuition, and your diagnosis was spot on."

Jessica stared at the nurse for a moment and took a deep breath. "Thank you, Claire. I appreciate your vote of confidence, but it would have been nice to have had that EKG about thirty minutes earlier."

"I agree with you."

Jessica sighed. "I'm sorry. I know it wasn't your fault. It just gets so frustrating sometimes."

Claire nodded. "I guess that's just the nature of the beast."

Jessica smiled in resignation. "I guess it is."

CHAPTER SIX

The following day, Jessica emerged from the staff lounge, her stethoscope hanging around her neck, a full cup of coffee in her hand. Walking over to the nurses' station, she spied the charge nurse bent over the printer console.

"Morning, Val."

Valerie placed a stack of paper into the machine, then stood up, closing the printer door. "Good morning, Dr. Carr. How's the coffee?"

Jessica took a sip from her cup as she studied the triage board. "Not too bad." She glanced out toward the waiting room. "Slow morning? That's nice."

"Hey, Jessica..."

Jessica turned, and then smiled at the cardiologist approaching her. "Good morning, Alex."

Standing 6'3" tall, Dr. Alex Markham towered over Jessica's 5'5" frame as he stood next to her. He ran his fingers through his thick blonde shaggy locks and leaned on the counter as he talked with her.

"That was a good call yesterday on Ortega. Those silent heart attacks are easy to miss. Her cardiac enzymes really shot up, which was expected given the EKG results."

The irritation Jessica felt the day before suddenly returned. "Yes, it would've been nice to have had an EKG to work from. She's lucky she didn't get sent home again with just a script for more antacids."

Chapter Six

Alex raised an eyebrow. "What?"

Jessica sighed. "I'm sorry. It just took too long to get an EKG done yesterday, and I seem to be taking it out on everyone. It's a wonder we don't lose more patients around here. By the time we get test results, it could be too late."

Alex reached over and put a hand on her shoulder. He looked her directly in the eyes. "But it wasn't too late, Jessica. You recognized that something was wrong, and you acted on that. It was a good call." He flashed a smile, revealing perfect white teeth. "You know, sometimes the obvious diagnosis is missed no matter what. I'm glad you caught this one. If you ever want to leave the chaos of the ER, we've got a spot for you in cardiology. We usually get our EKGs in a timely manner." He winked at her good-naturedly.

Jessica grinned. "Thanks for the offer, and the encouragement. I'll remember that in case it ever gets too hectic down here."

Valerie cleared her throat as one eyebrow lifted, and she scrutinized Dr. Markham. She pointed a finger at his face and shook it slightly. "I don't know about cardiology, but here in the ER, we don't take too kindly about other departments trying to steal our docs."

Alex held two hands up defensively in front of his chest. "Hold on there, Valerie. I'm not stealing anyone. I'm just saying if she ever wants to jump ship, we'll be there with arms wide open to whisk her away." His grin and the twinkle in his eye made it impossible for Valerie to stifle a giggle.

She picked up a chart and held it out toward Jessica, but kept her gaze on Alex. "You need to mind your manners while you're down here, or I'll put you to work." She looked at Jessica. "As for you, don't even think about it. I tell you what you can do, though. You can see this lady in three. A 44-year-old female with a low-grade fever and coughing. I know it's not surgical, but that's what you get for even considering his offer."

Alex grimaced. "Wow, we treat our surgeons better than that." He lowered his voice just enough so Valerie could still hear him whisper to Jessica. "We really do, and our nurses are not quite so vicious!"

Valerie stuck her tongue out at the doctor, and Alex laughed at the nurse.

Jessica took the chart from Valerie and turned to face the cardiologist. "Thanks a lot, Alex, but being in trouble with the charge nurse is not a position I relish, so I'd best decline your offer." She cast a backwards glance at Valerie as she headed for treatment room three and called out, "We'll talk later, Alex."

"Not if I can help it," countered Valerie with a smirk as Alex disappeared into an elevator, chuckling as the doors closed behind him.

Entering the treatment room, Jessica pulled the curtain behind her to provide a bit of privacy for her and her patient. She observed a woman sitting on the edge of the bed holding a wad of tissues in her hand. The woman looked up hopefully at Jessica through reddened eyes.

"Mrs. Slater? I'm Dr. Carr. What seems to be the problem today?" Jessica stood quietly and waited as Elaine Slater finished a coughing episode.

"I just can't stop this coughing. Sometimes it's so hard, I feel like I'm going to throw up. I get this tickle, and there's nothing I can do to stop it. I've tried some over-the-counter cough medicines, but nothing's worked. My husband told me to go see a doctor, so I–" Another coughing fit ensued, and Jessica handed her a box of tissues.

"Let me listen to your lungs," she said as she put the stethoscope earpieces in place. Moving the bell of the scope to several areas on Elaine's back, Jessica carefully listened to each lobe of the lungs. "Can you take a few more deep breaths?"

After listening again to Mrs. Slater's lungs, Jessica stood up and rehung the stethoscope around her neck. "Mrs. Slater, do you have any history of asthma?"

"No, why?"

"You've got some wheezing in your lungs. Have you been sick lately? Fever?"

Chapter Six

"No, not that I remember."

"I'd like to get some blood work, a chest x-ray, and then a breathing treatment. After that, I'll come back and see how you're doing."

Forty-five minutes later, Jessica was writing two prescriptions for Elaine Slater. One was an antibiotic and the other a steroid to help decrease the inflammation in her patient's breathing tubes.

Valerie walked up beside Jessica. "For Slater?"

"Yes. Can you see that she gets these, and remind her to follow up with her regular physician in a day or so?" asked Jessica as she handed the prescriptions to Valerie.

"Sure, if you can see the man in one. Said he felt nauseated and weak." She held out another chart.

Jessica grimaced. "Another medical? Where's all the surgical consults?"

"You'll be the first one I call when we get one," promised Valerie as she headed toward room three. "I'd hate for you to get bored and transfer to another department." Her mockery was impossible to miss.

"Cardiology is starting to look very appealing!" Jessica called out as she watched Valerie walk off. The doctor laughed lightly, shook her head, and headed for treatment room one.

****

It was nearing two in the afternoon when the ambulance bay doors slid open once more. A team of paramedics pushed a gurney into the ER. Claire met them in the corridor. She listened to the report as they walked side by side.

"Several knife wounds to the abdomen. Patient is nonresponsive. Pressure dressings were applied. Vitals fluctuating. IV started with Ringers."

Claire motioned them into trauma room two and assisted in the transfer of patient from gurney to bed. She connected the cardiac monitor to the patient's chest and readjusted the IV as Jessica entered the room.

Pulling on latex gloves, Jessica quickly moved to assess the patient.

Claire read from her chart. "23-year-old male. Name is Jonathan Dresden. Multiple stab wounds to abdomen. IV started in the field. No meds given. Nonresponsive, but vitals are holding." She began to cut away his clothing.

"Jonathan? Jonathan, open your eyes." The man did nothing.

Jessica put a stethoscope to his chest and expertly assessed his cardiopulmonary status. She quickly moved to his abdomen. As she removed a dressing, blood began to ooze over his belly.

"Better type and cross-match for 2 units. I need an ultrasound of the abdomen stat and have an O.R. room on standby," ordered Jessica.

Claire nodded and made the necessary phone calls. Within twenty minutes of ultrasound confirmation, Jonathan Dresden was prepped and ready for surgery.

Jessica entered the operating room, holding her hands up in front of her. A nurse assisted her with sterile gloves and gown. She nodded her thanks and moved to the side of the operating table.

"Is he ready?" She made eye contact with the anesthesiologist.

"As ready as ever, Dr. Carr."

Jessica looked up at Eric, who was to assist her in the surgery. "Dr. Tanner, you take the lead, okay? I'll assist you when necessary."

Eric nodded and held his hand out toward the O.R. nurse.

"Scalpel, please," he said. The stainless steel blade was quickly set into his waiting palm. Placing it over Jonathan's abdomen, Eric applied firm pressure to extend the major knife wound and separate the upper layers of skin tissue. As quickly as capillary bleeding appeared, Jessica mopped it up with sterile dressings. Making a deeper midline incision, Eric squinted to visualize the internal abdomen. He began to carefully examine the damage inflicted upon Jonathan's liver. Several small

Chapter Six

wounds had already stopped bleeding, so he ignored them as he spied two larger cuts. He skillfully cleaned up the jagged edges and then applied overlapping sutures to close the wounds.

After carefully checking for any more injury to the liver, Eric thoroughly examined the abdomen for any other wounds that may have been overlooked. Finding none, he raised his head and looked at Jessica.

"I'm ready to close, Dr. Carr."

Jessica nodded and continued to observe as Eric brought together the edges of the incised abdominal wound. He carefully stapled them together, spacing the metal sutures evenly from one end to the other.

"Lorrie, will you dress this before he goes to recovery?"

The O.R. nurse nodded her head as Eric glanced up once more at his supervising surgeon, who nodded her silent approval. As Jessica and Eric walked out of the operating room, she tossed her gloves, mask, and gown into the appropriate receptacles.

"You did a good job in there, Eric," stated Jessica.

He dropped his used gown into a laundry bin. "We make a good team, Dr. Carr."

Jessica agreed. "We do, don't we? You know your stuff, and I can depend on you."

"Thank you. I really appreciate that." Eric hit the button that would open the double doors to the recovery room and waited for Jessica to walk through before he followed.

After checking on their patient, Jessica studied the resident as he wrote a few more orders on the chart.

"So, what's this I hear about you maybe leaving us for Papua New Guinea?"

Eric whipped his head around to face Jessica. "What?"

"I said, what's this about you going to Papua New Guinea?"

Eric shifted uncomfortably. "Where'd you hear that?"

"Is it true?"

"I've been considering my options after my residency is completed," he admitted.

"I thought you liked it here at Eastmont."

"I do, but I believe God's calling me to something more."

"Really? And that 'something more' is being a missionary? What about your medical career?"

"Oh, I'd still be a doctor, just working in a different venue."

Jessica cocked her head slightly and looked intently at Eric. "A little more remote?"

"A lot more, but I'm still in the planning stage. I want to be sure God's really the One calling me for missions work." He looked up and away from Jessica, as if he saw a different place. "Remember Maggie's wedding? Well, I talked a little more with Pastor Devereaux about the work that Dr. Devereaux, I mean Dr. Grant, the work she did in Mexico. It just seemed so... so... right." He returned his gaze to Jessica. "I know that's hard to understand."

Jessica shook her head. "No. No, Eric, not at all. It sounds, well, it sounds like someone who God is working on." She poked him in the chest and smiled. "If anyone can do it, you can. I have faith in you."

Eric looked at her, his eyes widened in surprise, then he grinned. "Thank you, Dr. Carr. That is so encouraging. I really appreciate it."

"You're welcome. Just promise to keep me posted, okay?"

****

"Really?" Valerie shrugged her shoulders. "I had no idea Eric was thinking about that, at least not seriously. He mentioned something about it a while back." She brushed her hair away from her face. "I really haven't talked to him about it since then. I've always wondered how people know, I mean really know when they're *called* to do something by God. He doesn't actually speak to you, so how do you know it's really Him and not something you've just imagined?" Valerie looked at Jessica expectantly.

Jessica shook her head. "I'm not really sure. God's never actually called me to do something."

Chapter Six

"I just don't get it," continued Valerie. "Why Papua New Guinea? What's wrong with Eastmont? Can't he work for God here? He's a good doctor. He's almost finished with his residency, and he's had some pretty good job offers from what I hear. Now, he's going to throw it all away?"

"I wouldn't call it throwing everything away. He's just going to be working in a different place, that's all." Jessica narrowed her eyes as she looked up and studied the triage board.

"For our sakes, I hope he changes his mind," lamented Valerie. "I suppose that's being selfish, but doesn't it seem a bit strange to you that he would want to go into the mission field? I mean, I'm all for serving God, but—"

"But only if it's where *you* want to go?" Jessica's eyebrows lifted as she turned toward the nurse. "I don't think that's how it works."

Valerie hesitated for a moment. "No. No, I didn't mean that. I don't really know. It just seems kind of scary to think God might send me somewhere away from my friends and family. I wouldn't even know where to begin."

"I think if God's going to send you some place, He'll prepare your heart for it."

"Yes, I suppose so." Valerie thought for a moment. "So, you really think God wants Eric to go to Papua New Guinea?"

Jessica shrugged her shoulders as she shook her head. "I don't think it matters what I think. If Eric believes God is calling him there, then he's right to go."

Valerie sighed. "I guess so, but it seems so sudden for Eric. He was just talking about how great it would be to be finished with his residency. I guess I just assumed he would be staying here." She turned toward Jessica. "Would you go, Dr. Carr?"

Jessica hesitated. "If God called me?" She shook her head. "I can't imagine Him doing that, but if He did, I'm sure He'd prepare my heart for it. I guess I would... I mean if I knew for sure He was leading me there...but He'd never call me to do that. I'm destined to be here forever."

CHAPTER SEVEN

"Dad! Come eat!" Jessica called out as she lit two orange tapered candles on her dining room table. Between them sat a golden brown turkey nestled on a bed of onions, crabapples, carrots, and a few sprigs of rosemary. The aroma of the roasted bird wafted through the entire house. From the living room, the soft music of an inspirational CD could be heard.

Anne Merrick walked in holding a large glass bowl heaped with mashed potatoes. "Everything looks lovely, Jessica!" She set the dish at one end of the table next to a green bean casserole and a very full gravy boat.

"Thanks, Mom." Jessica smiled as she blew out a match. "Dad?"

At that moment, Paul Merrick walked into the dining room. "You called, dear?" He grinned at Jessica as he pulled out a chair for his wife.

As Anne sat down, Paul moved to pull out a chair for Jessica. "It looks like you two have prepared quite a feast!"

"I hope you're hungry, Dad," smiled Jessica as she sat in the chair her father offered.

"We even made you a key lime pie," stated Anne as she smiled up at her husband.

"Key lime? My favorite!"

Jessica rolled her eyes and scrunched her face in mock disgust. "Who eats key lime at Thanksgiving? It's supposed to be pumpkin pie, Dad!"

Chapter Seven

He chuckled as he bowed his head, and then held his hands out to the ladies. When he had each one's hand in his own, he began to pray. "Father God, how we love You. We thank You for Your mercy and Your love especially this Thanksgiving day. We thank You for this feast You've provided for us, and ask that You bless both the food and those who had a hand in its preparation. Be with those we love from whom we are separated today. Keep them safe in Your hands." He paused for a brief moment before continuing. "Please help us to be ever mindful of all that You've given us. We thank You mostly, O God, for our salvation through Your precious Son, Jesus Christ in whose name we pray. Amen."

Jessica whispered, "Amen," then placed her napkin in her lap.

"I can't believe your brother isn't here," lamented Paul.

"Why would he be when his fiancée's family invited him to their home for Thanksgiving?" Jessica defended her brother's choice.

"You mean you would've gone home instead of spend the holidays with me, dear?" Anne asked Paul with a twinkle in her eye.

As he lifted his head, his eyes met those of his wife's. He hesitated, smiled, then picked up a carving knife. "Okay, who wants a leg?"

****

"Are we ready?" Jessica's eyes sparkled with excitement as she sat in front of her computer screen. A small dessert plate with a half-eaten piece of key lime pie was on the desk next to her as well as half a cup of coffee. Her parents flanked her on each side.

"We're ready!" they chorused.

Jessica clicked several times, and within seconds, she was staring at the face of her beloved husband. The young lieutenant's smile was radiant, and the family's joy was overflowing as the overseas contact was established.

"Nick!" Jessica's elation manifested itself in a cascade of tears when she heard his deep voice. She hastily swept them away with her fingertips.

"Hello, sweetheart. Wow, it's so good to see you! Hey, Mom, Dad! Happy Thanksgiving!"

"Happy Thanksgiving to you," they echoed.

"Nick, you look so good," declared Anne. "Are you eating okay?"

He laughed. "As well as anyone else here, I suppose. We had something that resembled turkey and mashed potatoes last night, but who knows?"

"You're staying safe, right?"

"I'm doing my best, Mom."

After a few minutes of conversation, Paul and Anne thoughtfully left the room, leaving Jessica alone with her husband.

"I miss you so much, Nick," admitted Jessica. Her voice trembled with emotions that threatened to spill forth.

"I miss you too, Jess. You look... you look so beautiful." His voice was strong and resonated with love. "I wish I was there with you. I wish I could hold you in my arms."

Her smile wavered, and her voice softened. "I wish you were here too, Nick. Are you... are you really safe?"

Nick's brown eyes were solemn. "I am very careful, Jessica. We are in a volatile area, but we are very, very careful. I'm as safe as I could possibly be, given the circumstances."

Jessica swallowed hard, forced a smile, and nodded. "Please come home to me soon."

His grin broadened. "As soon as I can, sweetheart. I love you."

"I love you too, Nick. See you soon."

"I hope so, darling."

After a few more minutes of conversation, she took a deep breath, blew him a kiss, and logged off the program. Closing

Chapter Seven

the laptop, she sat for a few minutes before rising to head into the living room.

Anne looked up as Jessica walked in from the den. "Everything okay, honey?" she asked quietly.

Jessica sat beside her mother. "Yes. I am so grateful for technology, but saying goodbye each time is so hard."

Anne nodded her head. Reaching out to squeeze Jessica's hand, she said, "I understand, honey. I wish it could be easier for you. Will he be coming home on schedule?"

"I hope so, but you never really know. We're still praying he can make it for Christmas. I miss him so much."

****

Two days later, a steady drizzle of rain kept Jessica inside the house, and her dismay at not being able to go Christmas shopping was somewhat alleviated by her decision to cuddle under a blanket on the sofa and watch a marathon of Christmas movies. She pushed the 'play' button and relaxed with a cup of hot tea in hand as George Bailey appeared on the screen.

"This movie never gets old," stated Jessica to no one as she glanced out the window. The outdoor Christmas lights that her father had helped her put up the day after Thanksgiving twinkled brightly in the rain.

Jessica sighed wistfully. "It will be a wonderful life when you're back home with me, Nick." Her thoughts turned heavenward. "Lord, please keep him safe. Put a hedge of protection around him. Give him courage to face the enemy and strength to do what he has to do. What time he is afraid, help Nick to trust in Thee."

Her personalization of verses was something Anne had taught her to do when she was a little girl. One of the first times was when Anne had led Jessica to Christ. As Anne had instructed, Jessica had inserted her own name into John 3:16. "For God so loved *Jessica* that He gave His only begotten Son, that *when Jessica* believeth in Him, *Jessica* should not perish, but have everlasting life."

When Anne had gently explained to the small child how much God loved her and wanted to forgive her sins so that one day she could live in heaven with Him, Jessica had eagerly responded. Accepting Christ's forgiveness of sins not only provided eternal life for Jessica, but it gave Anne great insight on the tremendous guilt her beloved stepdaughter carried regarding the death of Paul's first wife. That night, Jessica poured out her heart to God, begging for forgiveness for an accident that never could have been her responsibility, but somehow in her young mind, she had believed was hers. Through her tears, Jessica had opened her little girl's heart to God and allowed His love to flow in.

When she had finished praying, she looked up at Anne with hopeful eyes and asked, "Will I be with Mama some day?"

Anne had embraced Jessica and held her tightly. "Yes, my darling. You will be, and your Mama will be waiting for you with open arms." Anne's tears of joy fell freely as she silently praised God for His saving grace.

Jessica's faith had grown through the years, nurtured by a woman who loved her as her own. As Jessica's spiritual role model, Anne helped her understand the importance of church attendance, Bible study, and prayer. Now, Jessica often inserted the names of family and friends into verses as she brought them before the Lord.

As she tucked her feet under her blanket and sipped her cup of hot tea, her attention turned to the bay window. She saw an unfamiliar car slow down and then stop in front of her house. She stared at the military markings on the side of the vehicle. The rain made it difficult to see clearly, and Jessica strained to make out the two figures that emerged from the car and begin their walk to her door. She raised a hand to her mouth. Time seemed to stand still.

No, dear God, please... no!

Before she could rise, the doorbell rang twice.

Chapter Seven

Fearing the worst, she stood slowly, her body trembling. She took a deep breath and walked apprehensively toward the door. *Please give me courage, Lord.*

On the third ring, she opened the door and stood face to face with an Army captain. She saw nothing but the dark brown eyes of the officer as he stood at her threshold. Everything else faded away, even the other soldier, who stood somewhat behind the tall captain. Her knees weakened as she closed her eyes tightly, and she willed herself to stay standing. Bracing herself against the doorjamb, she took a deep breath and slowly opened her eyes, waiting for the words no military wife wanted to hear.

"Mrs. Carr?"

Jessica stared at the officer, slowly raising her hands to cover her mouth. Her eyes brimmed with tears, and she swallowed hard.

No! No! What? What did you say?

"Mrs. Carr, I said I have a special delivery for you." As he stepped slightly to his left, revealing the man behind him, he smiled and exclaimed, "An early Merry Christmas from Uncle Sam!"

Jessica's eyes widened in astonishment as her worst fears vanished in a moment's recognition. "Nick!" She flung herself into the open arms of her waiting husband. "I thought... Oh, Nick!" She wept uncontrollably, both from relief and joy.

Nick's arms tightened around Jessica, and he held her long after the captain had discreetly departed. Loosening his embrace, Nick looked into Jessica's tear-filled eyes. "I'm sorry. I didn't mean to scare you. I guess I never thought—"

She pulled his face down and kissed him, wrapping her arms tightly around his neck. "You're home! That's all that matters," she whispered. "You're home!"

"I have missed you so much, Jess." His husky voice choked with emotion as he inhaled the fragrance of her perfume.

When she pulled herself away, she stared into the loving brown eyes of her husband. She reached up to caress his cheek. "I can't believe you're here!" She kissed him once more before admitting, "I saw the car... I thought... but Nick, you're home!" She held him tightly.

"Yes, I am, sweetheart. I'm home." This time, tears flowed down Nick's cheeks as he held his wife closely and whispered tenderly, "I love you so much, Jessica."

****

"A little rain never hurt anyone, Jess, and I can't think of anything else I'd rather do right now than go out and get our Christmas tree." Nick grinned at his wife.

Jessica put her hands on her hips and feigned disapproval. "A little rain?" She indicated the steady downpour outside.

"Barely drizzling." Nick raised one eyebrow. "Besides after living in a desert for so long, I welcome a walk in the rain!" He cocked his head and stuck his lower lip out. "C'mon, Babe. What's Christmas without a tree?"

"That's supposed to win me over?" Jessica laughed. "If only your men could see you now! Okay, but I insist on jackets and umbrellas."

"It's a deal!" He swept her off her feet and spun her around, then kissed her soundly on the lips.

Jessica playfully chastised him. "Enough of that young man! I believe we have to go get a Christmas tree!"

Within minutes, they were driving down to the local Christmas tree lot. Together, they happily searched the lot for the perfect tree, getting thoroughly soaked in the process. Upon deciding which one would best fit their home, Nick secured the fir tree to the top of their car and headed back to their house.

Later that night, after the tree had been decorated, Nick reclined on the sofa with Jessica nestled in his arms. Together, they watched the twinkling lights dancing among the hanging ornaments as a CD of Christmas carols softly played in the background.

"I wish I could stay here forever, but I'll have to go back right after Christmas."

Chapter Seven

Jessica sighed. "I know. I wish you could stay too, but I'm happy with any time I can get with you."

"I talked to my C.O. about a stateside transfer, and after this deployment, I think it'll work out."

"Really?" Jessica's eyes lit up as she turned to look at her husband. "That would be wonderful!"

"I thought you might like that," he grinned. "I know I sure would." He paused to give her a small kiss. "I love serving my country, Jess, but sometimes being away from you is about the hardest thing I face."

Jessica smiled knowingly. "I understand completely, but we both knew it would be like this."

"Yeah, but knowing and going through it are two different things. I am so grateful for technology. Being able to talk with you and see you, well, I can't tell you how much I cherish those times."

Neither wanted the night to end, so they sat together long after the carols had stopped playing and the flickering candles ceased to glow. It was well after midnight when they fell asleep in each other's arms on the sofa.

****

The day after Christmas, Nick left for Afghanistan, and three days after that, another military car was parked in front of Jessica's home. She gestured for the two army officers to come into her house. This time, Nick was not one of them.

"Please..." Her voice caught in her throat. She indicated the kitchen, following them to the dinette table. The captain pulled out a chair for her. Jessica sat down. She felt her heart pounding in her chest as he sat down opposite her. The other soldier, a chaplain, took the chair next to Jessica. He reached a hand out to hers.

"Mrs. Carr, we regret to inform you..."

When they left, she stumbled into the living room and dropped down onto the couch. As she struggled to comprehend

Courageous Love

the loss of her husband, she collapsed into the large throw pillows and sobbed.

"God, what am I going to do without him?" Overwhelming grief turned to anger, and she struck out at her heavenly Father. "How could You let this happen?" She pounded her fists into the cushions as she cried out, "No, he can't be gone! He just can't!" She wept throughout the night until she had nothing left within her.

The following morning, she stood in front of her bathroom mirror, her reddened eyes staring back at her. She washed her face, brushed her teeth, and combed her hair.

What am I going to do?

She staggered out to the kitchen table and sat down. Her downcast eyes fell upon her Bible. She slowly reached out and pulled it toward her.

What time I am afraid, I will trust in Thee. Oh, God, help me trust You.

She opened the Bible randomly, not caring where the pages fell. She began to read, desperate for any words that would ease the oppressive sorrow that threatened to engulf her.

Oh, Nick...

Later in the day, after her parents had come and gone, Jessica sat alone on the sofa. Her feet were tucked beneath her, and she hugged a throw pillow to her chest. She could still smell the scent of Nick's aftershave in the fabric. Again, her tears fell freely, and she did nothing to stop them. Her numbed mind failed to make sense of what was happening to her life, and her heart seemed to beat furiously. Her breathing came in short gasps as her anxiety rose.

She forced herself to take slow, deep breaths. She closed her eyes tightly. "I know nothing happens that You aren't aware of, Lord," she began. Her voice shook in desperation as she whispered, "I know You're with me. Even though I feel alone, I know I'm not. You're here. I know You're here."

You know you're really alone, Jessica. No matter what you say, you are alone.

Chapter Seven

Her eyes snapped open, and she shook her head determinedly. "No!" The pillow fell to the floor as she abruptly sat up. "No!" She wiped the tears from her face and looked upward. "Please, Lord, help me!" As she sat expectantly, God's sweet Holy Spirit brought to her mind a verse she had memorized years before.

Fear thou not; for I am with thee: be not dismayed; for I am thy God: I will strengthen thee; yea, I will help thee; yea, I will uphold thee with the right hand of my righteousness.

Retrieving the small pillow she had dropped to the floor, she pressed her face into it and found solace in the musky scent. She curled up once more on the sofa as exhaustion finally caught up with her. A tiny candle flickered on the coffee table, burning itself out long after Jessica had fallen asleep.

****

The next few days were a blur for Jessica. She functioned on automatic for the most part. The U.S. Army had been incredibly supportive, helping her with funeral arrangements and the official return of Nick's body from overseas. Anne often stayed over at her daughter's house while Jessica struggled through the first few sleepless nights of tears and emptiness.

When it was time for the funeral, Jessica had graciously accepted everyone's condolences and managed to smile at the appropriate times, breaking down only when she was handed the folded American flag. Despite knowing it was to happen, she jumped with each round of gunfire from the twenty-one gun salute. She held tightly to Anne's hand, drawing strength from her stepmother's presence and support. Jessica had no idea how her life would change from this horrendous event, but she knew it would, and she prayed God would give her the strength to endure and the courage to face whatever the future held.

Although it was against the advice of her family and close friends, Jessica made the decision to return to work after only two weeks had passed. She had yearned for her life to have some semblance of normalcy once more, and she believed it was unhealthy for her to continue to stay at home and grieve. However, even after returning home from her exhausting shifts at Eastmont, Jessica often woke in the middle of the night, her cheeks damp with tears. She repeatedly turned to the only source of strength she knew could sustain her.

Oh, Lord, please help me go on without Nick. It's so hard. I miss him so much it hurts inside. Please help me...

CHAPTER EIGHT

After another sleep-tossed night, Jessica arrived at the ER and was assaulted by the cacophony of chaos all around her. Nurses and technicians were scurrying through the halls. The triage board was full as was the waiting room. Jessica noticed one nurse in the paramedic relay station jotting down notes.

Valerie rushed out of a trauma room and saw Jessica. "Dr. Carr, am I glad to see you! Can you help Dr. Grant in one? She was asking for a surgical consult, but I can't find anyone. Car accident victim. No air bag. Paramedics said he was trapped between the seat and the steering wheel."

Jessica nodded and hurried over to trauma one. Upon entering, she saw Claire adjusting the IV, while Maggie Grant was attempting to insert a laryngoscope in her patient.

"What can I do, Maggie?"

"Almost completely crushed larynx, and his oxygen levels are dropping. If I can't get this in, I'll have no choice but to trach him, but I'm not sure that'll do the trick."

Jessica put her stethoscope against the patient's chest and listened while Maggie tried to maneuver the tube into place one more time.

"I can't get in, Jess. Will you give it a try?"

Jessica changed places with Maggie and peered through the instrument. "You weren't kidding about the larynx. I can't visualize the cords... wait, I think... yes, there they are." She painstakingly threaded the flexible tubing through the scope and down the patient's throat. "Am I in?" She remained poised to retry if needed.

Placing her stethoscope on the chest of her patient, Maggie listened intently to the patient's lungs as Claire compressed the artificial respirator bag twice. Maggie nodded her head. "Yes! Bilateral breath sounds. You're in," she announced, then whispered, "Thank you, Lord."

The respiratory technician took over, forcing air into the patient's lungs via manual compressions of the airbag.

"BP's dropping. Heart rate is tachycardic," reported Claire as she finished securing the endotracheal tube in place.

Jessica and Maggie simultaneously glanced up at the cardiac monitor. The numbers confirmed the report.

"We need two units of O-neg blood stat," ordered Maggie.

Jessica frowned. "Look at that belly. He's got to be bleeding internally."

Maggie noted the rigidity of the lower abdomen and agreed.

"We've got to get him up to the O.R.," Jessica stated, "or he's going to bleed out."

Maggie nodded in agreement. "Let's move him."

In less than ten minutes, their patient was being prepped in the O.R. while Jessica scrubbed for the surgery. She walked into the operating room and pushed her arms through a sterile gown that an O.R. tech held out for her. She turned to get it tied into place as a nurse slipped a pair of latex gloves over Jessica's hands.

"Let's get to work."

Jessica made a precision cut into the mid-abdominal region. As soon as the blade penetrated the abdominal cavity, blood began to spew forth from the incision.

"I need suction! Get me some lap pads now! Clamp!"

Instruments were repeatedly slapped into Jessica's hand as fast as she called for them. As soon as one bleeder was clamped or cauterized, another one shot out a stream of blood. The assisting surgeon worked furiously across from Jessica, and together, they fought to control the profuse bleeding.

Chapter Eight

"I need a new pair of goggles!"

The nurse quickly removed the blood splattered eye protectors off of Jessica's face. Another pair immediately found its way over her eyes.

"BP's dropping. Ninety over fifty. Heart rate is one-sixty five."

"Get that blood hanging!"

"Lab's out of O-neg. They're calling local hospitals now."

"Hang plasma then. We don't have time to wait for a delivery. He'll bleed out before we get it. Get that fluid into him. Open up the IV! Clamp!"

This frenzied pace continued for over two hours before Jessica and her team had the bleeding under control and the patient stabilized. Jessica stood back as they wheeled the thirty-three year old man out of the O.R. and to the recovery room.

Nick was thirty-three...

****

Forty minutes later, Jessica sat down in the ER physician's lounge for a moment's respite. Ben Shepherd followed her in and poured himself a cup of coffee.

"Would you like a cup?"

Jessica shook her head. "No thanks. I'm good."

Ben sat opposite her in a well-worn brown easy chair. He sipped his coffee. "Ah, nice and strong. This'll keep me going for another few hours. How are you doing?"

Jessica sat quietly, looking at her hands.

Ben studied her for a moment before repeating himself. "How are you doing, Jessica?"

She jerked her head up to see his dark brown eyes looking compassionately at her. Uncomfortable with his concern, she looked away from Ben momentarily, but then answered as she turned back. "I'm sorry, Ben. I'm fine." The corners of her lips dipped downward, and she sighed. "Well, maybe not fine, but I'm okay. It's been hard, really hard. I find myself praying a lot more, asking God to get me through each day. I was hoping

Courageous Love

being at work would help, but every day still seems to be a struggle. Sitting at home, remembering our last time together, and asking myself 'Why?' isn't very productive."

Ben nodded. "I can only imagine how hard it must be for you. You know Dianne and I are praying for you."

"Thank you. I really appreciate it." Her saddened eyes betrayed the hint of a smile that appeared on her face.

Leaning forward, Ben reached for her hand and gave it a squeeze. "If there is anything we can do, don't hesitate to ask."

"Thank you. I won't." She sighed, then looked up at him. "For the first time in my life, I feel so lost."

"You're not lost, Jessica. You're grieving. It's normal."

Jessica nodded solemnly, then confessed, "I guess so. I just never thought he wouldn't come home." Her voice was almost a whisper. "Even now, I keep thinking it's all a bad dream, and I'm going to wake up, and everything will be fine."

"I am so sorry, Jess."

She looked over at her colleague and forced another weak smile as Ben handed her a tissue.

"Thank you so much, Ben–"

"Code Blue – ICU. Code Blue – ICU." The hospital announcement filled the room.

Jessica rose quickly. "I'll go." She hurried out the door just as her pager began to vibrate. In less than three minutes, she entered the room of the young man on whom she had just operated. Frenzied activity centered around the still figure on the bed.

"What happened?" she asked as she moved nearer her patient. Manual CPR was being performed. Anti-arrhythmic medications were being administered via the intravenous line in hopes to calm the unpredictable and irregular ventricular contractions.

"Started throwing PVCs, then his blood pressure began to drop, and his heart rate skyrocketed. No response to meds or IV fluids. Within minutes, he arrested. We got him back briefly, but he went back into v-tach."

Chapter Eight

Premature ventricular contractions... ventricular tachycardia... what's going on with you?
Jessica's mind quickly reviewed everything she knew about her patient, but nothing gave her a clue as to what was responsible for this post-surgical cardiac event.
EKG was normal. No evidence of cardiac trauma. What happened?
Despite her best efforts, her patient was dying, and there was nothing she could do about it. The medications were ineffective. The advanced cardiac life support measures were fruitless. She glanced up at the cardiac monitor. The previously erratic line now only showed the movement of each artificial compression performed by the ICU nurse.

It had been twenty-two minutes since the code had begun. Jessica looked up at the cardiologist. As he shook his head, Jessica sighed deeply and pressed her lips tightly together.

Her blue eyes sparked with anger, but she spoke without emotion. "I'm calling it. Any objections?" No one spoke. She looked up at the clock. "Time of death: fourteen fifty-five."

Jessica yanked off her gloves and flung them into the biohazard bin as she exited the room to notify the family.

****

Rounding the corner into the ER, Jessica almost collided into Maggie.

"Hey, slow down!" Maggie's brow furrowed as she viewed her colleague's irritated face. "What's wrong?"

"It's just not right, Maggie. He was so young." The anger in Jessica's voice matched the fire in her eyes. She set her lips in a hard line and looked away from her friend, but allowed Maggie to escort her into the staff lounge.

"That was my patient that coded in ICU."

"I take it he didn't make it?"

Jessica lowered her head. "No," she said curtly, dropping down on the sofa.

Maggie took a deep breath. "Unfortunately, we can't save everyone. You know that." She sat down beside Jessica.

A deep sigh escaped the surgeon's lips. "I know, but it's so unfair. He was so young... and married. Had two kids and one on the way." She stood up and paced the room. "Then I had to tell the wife, Maggie. I had to stand in front of her and tell her that despite all our efforts, her husband died. And what does she do? She thanks me for trying to save him."

"Every—"

Jessica held up her hand, palm facing her colleague. "I know, Maggie. Everything happens for a reason." Her look hardened as she crossed her arms in front of her.

Maggie's eyes narrowed as she studied Jessica's face. She sat back and clasped her hands together in her lap. "I was going to say that every time I lose a patient, no matter what the reason, it's hard to take. So, I understand how you feel."

Jessica took another deep breath, instantly regretting her earlier sarcasm. "I'm sorry. I just have a hard time accepting it sometimes, that's all. He had his whole future ahead of him, then some person runs a stoplight, slams into his car, and this is the result. Now his wife is left to face the world on her own. Was that really God's plan for them?" Jessica dropped her head in her shaking hands as she plopped back down on the couch.

Maggie sat quietly, then softly asked, "Are we still talking about your patient?"

Jessica lifted her head slowly and stared at Maggie. "I guess it just hit too close to home today."

Maggie nodded. "I understand, Jessica. This has got to be a difficult time for you."

"Difficult? That's an understatement. It's been really hard. My faith, well, it just doesn't seem enough right now. I feel so alone, and I seem to be always questioning God. I keep praying for strength, Maggie, but it doesn't seem like He's answering me. Maybe He's not even listening anymore..." Her voice drifted off.

Chapter Eight

Maggie offered a silent prayer for wisdom before she spoke. "Maybe it's not strength you need, Jessica."

"Meaning...?" She reached into her pocket for a tissue.

Maggie looked compassionately at her friend. "When Scott died, a part of me died with him. I was so angry with God. I didn't admit it. I just needed someone to focus my anger on, and sadly, God took the brunt of it. Scott's brother, Ryan, spent a lot of time helping me come to terms with Scott's death, but each day was still so hard for me. Going home to an empty house. Coming to Eastmont to work and knowing I wouldn't see him here. Everywhere Scott should have been, he wasn't. I needed more than strength to carry on; I needed, well, I needed courage to face the future without him."

Frowning, Jessica shook her head slightly. "I'm not really following you."

Maggie continued. "I needed to allow myself time to grieve and know that I wasn't going to lose it. I needed to give myself permission to be brokenhearted. Permission to cry until I could cry no more. I needed to mourn the loss of my husband."

Giving Jessica time to absorb her words, Maggie waited a moment before speaking once more. "The Bible says, 'Wait on the LORD: be of good courage, and He shall strengthen thine heart: wait, I say, on the LORD.' Sometimes we have to wait. You know, for God. Our strength isn't *from* Him, it's *in* Him."

Jessica's shoulders slumped, and she looked away from Maggie as she whispered, "I thought I was so strong. You know, I could handle anything, but I'm not."

"Jess, sometimes, we Christians set ourselves up to a higher standard than everyone else. We figure we have to be strong because 'all things work to the good,' right? If we feel lost and alone, we think we must be losing our faith, but that's not true. We're human beings. God created us to have feelings, just like He does. He grieved over mankind just before the Flood; His heart broke over the death of His Son, and we're created in His image."

Courageous Love

Jessica blinked her eyes to hold back her tears as she turned to focus on Maggie's face.

"Maybe," Maggie continued. "Maybe you just need to allow yourself time to be held in the arms of God. Let yourself be the one to depend on *His* strength, not your own." Maggie's voice softened as she remembered. "I still miss Scott. I don't think anything will ever fill the emptiness I feel when I think of all that could have been, but in those times when I still hurt, I try and let God cradle me in His arms, and then I cry on His shoulders."

Jessica swallowed hard and nodded. "Oh Maggie," she whispered. "I miss Nick so much, and sometimes it hurts so badly inside. I can't even begin to imagine a life without him. Sometimes I don't think I have the courage to live without him, and that scares me."

Maggie smiled understandingly at Jessica. "I know, Jess. I really do. But God still has a plan for your life. You just need to have the courage to believe it. He's not going to let you fail. And remember, Nick's passing did not take God by surprise."

Jessica wiped her eyes with a tissue. "I know, but no matter what I do… read my Bible, pray…it seems like all I really do at home is cry."

"It's okay to cry, Jess. It hurts for a long, long time. I think crying is part of the healing process. You're still walking through the valley of the shadow of death, but you have to remember that God promised He'd be with you. Nick's gone, but the awful shadow of his passing remains. Lean on God as you go through these dark times, Jessica. I know it's difficult to see it now, but one day, I promise you, you will be able to look back and see how God got you through it all."

Jessica took a deep breath and exhaled slowly. She squeezed Maggie's hand. "Thank you, Maggie. Thank you so much. You don't know how much I needed this."

"I'm here for you, Jess, but more importantly, so is God. Don't ever forget that."

Chapter Eight

At that moment, a nurse poked her head into the lounge. "Sorry to interrupt, but we need one of you in treatment four." Maggie stood. "I'll take it." She moved to the door and as she pulled it shut, she turned to her friend. "You're going to be okay, Jessica. You just need a little more time."

PART TWO – SANTA MOLINA

"And David said to Solomon his son, Be strong and of good courage, and do it; fear not, nor be dismayed: for the Lord God, even my God, will be with thee; he will not fail thee, nor forsake thee, until thou has finished all the work for the service of the house of the Lord."

1 Chronicles 28:20

CHAPTER NINE

The bright yellow tropical sun was nearly overhead as Ryan Devereaux stood quietly in the rural Mexican church courtyard watching a small group of young men and women huddle in prayer together. In a few moments, the group broke up and scattered, each with a specific task to complete.

Less than two weeks earlier, Ryan and the people of Santa Molina had faced one of the frequent tropical storms that often raged through the area. Although its winds were fierce, the storm missed being categorized as a hurricane by a wind speed only five miles per hour below the minimum rate. Still, rivers had overflown their banks bringing streams of mud and debris through the church grounds, and tree limbs had come crashing down on several courtyard structures including the tiny medical clinic he was trying to maintain. Thankfully, the sanctuary and parsonage had suffered minimal damage.

A few phone calls and emails to his father, a pastor and professor at a southern California Bible college, resulted in a small group of dedicated and determined college students arriving in Mexico to help Ryan clean up and rebuild as needed.

Ryan wiped his brow and accepted the glass of *agua fresca* held out to him.

"Thank you, Akna." He took the offered glass of fresh fruit juice from the dark-skinned Mayan woman and quickly downed half of it.

The humid weather never seemed to fluctuate in Santa Molina. Spring, summer, fall or winter, the temperature usually remained in the mid 80's, and the humidity was rarely below 85%. Today was no exception, and drinking water or other liquids was a necessity to keep the body hydrated.

Pressing the blade of his shovel into the dampened soil and angling its long handle against him, Ryan finished the refreshing blend of cold papaya juice and water. He scanned the activity all around the courtyard and admired the volunteer workers from America who tirelessly labored to clean up the grounds and repair the small medical clinic.

Thank You, Lord, for bringing such an energetic group of young people here to help us rebuild. They are such a blessing.

As if reading his thoughts, Akna Canul, the wife of the church's groundskeeper and self-appointed mother to Ryan, smiled at the young pastor. "They are hard workers, Pastor Ryan. The Lord has truly blessed us."

"That He has, Akna. I can't believe how much work has been accomplished in just a few days. If they keep this pace up, we'll be near completion sooner than we thought."

Akna smiled. "That is good. It needs to be completed by the time He sends our doctor to us." She took his drained glass and walked toward the church fellowship hall leaving him to contemplate her departing statement.

Ryan shook his head and grinned as he watched her disappear into the building, then turned back toward the workers. His deep blue eyes squinted as he scanned the activity around him.

Lord, it would be great to have a doctor here. You've provided everything we've needed to get this clinic built, now if You could just provide a physician...

It had only been a few days since this group of enthusiastic Christian young people had arrived to offer their assistance in clean up and repairs. Ryan had welcomed them, shared his plans, and the group immediately went to work.

Now as he scanned the young volunteers, his attention was drawn to one of them. Standing over a wheelbarrow, a tall lanky

Chapter Nine

teen with tousled brown hair, a shirt half tucked in his pants, and determination on his face, struggled to stir a batch of concrete. Sweat beaded on his forehead as he strained to move the resistant cement. He stopped for a moment, pushed his sunglasses up on his nose, then put all his effort into moving the large wooden paddle. Ryan walked toward him.

"Need some help?" he asked as he reached for the wooden stirrer.

The young man smiled sheepishly and nodded. "I didn't know concrete was this hard *before* it dried." He gratefully handed Ryan the paddle, then inspected a blister forming on his palm. "I spend way too much time in the library. I can't even remember the last time I did manual labor."

"Owen, right?"

He nodded. "Yes, sir. Owen Hamlin."

Ryan pushed against the stiffness of the cement as he began to move the paddle. "I really appreciate all the work you and your group are doing. Your help is really going to get this clinic back up and running much sooner than I had hoped."

Owen nodded. "I'm glad we could help. To tell you the truth, Pastor, I was kind of afraid to come."

"Really? Why?"

"Well, you can clearly see I'm not the 'hands-on' labor kind of guy. I figured I'd just be in the way, but these guys, well, they kept encouraging me to come, so now, here I am. Don't get me wrong, I'm glad I'm here. I mean, I'm ready to work if God can use me, but I'm not a Marty. Now he's a real go-getter. If you have a job to be done, he's your man. He's blessed with brawn *and* brains."

Ryan stopped stirring and turned to Owen. "Hmm... I guess you aren't familiar with the story of David."

Owen looked questioningly at Ryan. "David? You mean the one who fought Goliath?"

"Yeah, that's the one. He was a shepherd and from what I understand, a bit scrawny in stature. He hadn't been trained as a soldier, and he couldn't even wield the weapons that were provided for him, yet he was the one God chose to defeat the giant. The Bible even calls David 'a man after God's own heart.' Guess you never know who God will call for a job."

Owen looked at the pastor thoughtfully, then smiled and nodded his head. "I get it. Here, let me have that." He reached for the wooden paddle, eyeing the cement. He painstakingly moved the stubborn board through the unyielding concrete. "I think it's ready... at least I hope it is." He gripped the wheelbarrow handles and glanced at Ryan. "And... I think I can manage this."

Ryan nodded, but walked by Owen's side. "What are you planning to do when you're not building clinics in remote villages in Mexico?"

"I'm majoring in music, so I'm hoping for a position in a Christian school or a church after I graduate."

"When's that—"

"Hey, Owen!" A voice called from the roof of the existing clinic.

Owen set the wheelbarrow down and looked upward as he shielded his eyes from the noon sun. Ryan squinted and scanned the roof.

"Where are you? I can't see you?" Owen called.

"Sorry!" A head poked over the roof's ridge. "I thought I heard you down there. Oh, hi there, Pastor Devereaux. Do either of you know what time we eat lunch?"

Owen chuckled. "That's Marty. He's always hungry."

Ryan nodded and called out, "I'm guessing in about an hour or two, Marty."

"That long? I'm starved! I hope I make it 'til then! Oh well, thanks, Pastor." He disappeared once more to the far side of the roof.

Owen maneuvered the wheelbarrow next to the footing that had been dug earlier. He hesitated for a moment, then held out his hand. "Thanks, Pastor."

Chapter Nine

Ryan's grip was strong as he shook the young man's hand. "My pleasure, Owen. I really appreciate all you're doing here. Keep up the good work."

Owen grinned and nodded, then turned back to the wheelbarrow and the cement.

****

As promised, lunch was a feast. Akna prepared fish tacos, skewers of spicy beef and vegetables, rice seasoned with cilantro, and sweetened plantains. Glasses of *licuados* – various fruits blended with either orange juice or milk – were at each place setting. As soon as everyone took his or her place at the large table, Ryan offered a prayer for the meal.

"Lord, thank You for this food that You have provided for us. Please bless it to the health and nourishment of our bodies that we may better serve You. Thank You for those who prepared this meal for us, and bless them as well. May You be honored and glorified around this table. In Jesus' precious name, I pray. Amen."

As soon as the soft echoes of 'amen' dissipated from around the table, platters heaping with food were passed around.

Marty was the first to speak after taking a huge bite of a taco. "Wow, this is good stuff! If I'd known what a great cook Mrs. Canul was, I'd have come here much sooner!" He took another big bite and added, "I may never go home!"

The other students concurred as they eagerly sampled everything set before them. Ryan noticed Akna standing near the kitchen entrance with a satisfied look on her face. Her dark eyes moved from one young person to the next, her smile spreading across her face as she disappeared into the cooking area.

"Hey, would someone pass the rice?"

"Toss me one of those skewers, would you?"

"What kind of fish is this? It's amazing!"

"Does Mrs. Canul give cooking lessons, 'cuz Bethany could sure use some!"

Bethany elbowed the man who made the cooking comment as she laughed. "I won't be cooking for you when we're married, Caleb. You'll be taking me out to dinner every night!"

Grinning, Caleb held his hands up as if surrendering. "Help me out here, Pastor Ryan. Isn't she supposed to obey me?"

Ryan chuckled. "This is a luncheon, not a marriage counseling session, Caleb. I think I'll just enjoy my fish taco if you don't mind."

Bethany playfully punched Caleb in the arm. "You know, there is something I can make very well in a kitchen."

"What's that, my dear?" asked Caleb as he reached for a warm tortilla.

Bethany paused for dramatic effect, looked at Caleb squarely in the eyes, and then announced, "A dinner reservation!"

Caleb rolled his eyes. "I'm doomed!"

Good-natured laughter filled the dining room as everyone continued to eat and chat. Soon the plates were empty, and everyone's hunger had been satisfied.

"I'm stuffed!" stated Marty. "Is it time for a *siesta*?"

"Sounds like a good idea to me. Beth, want to go for a walk?" Caleb asked as he stood.

"I'd like that," she responded as she rose. The two joined hands as they exited the dining hall.

"Have they set a date yet?" Ryan asked as he watched the couple leave.

"They're both finishing their graduate programs in May, so Bethany is planning on a summer wedding this year," answered Olivia, Bethany's roommate. "Caleb would marry her tomorrow, but they both thought it would be better to graduate first. They've both got a heart for missions, so they're anxious to see where God directs them."

Ryan nodded. "That's smart of them."

Owen took a big bite from a plantain. "Yeah, Caleb is one lucky guy. Bethany is one of the sweetest girls I know. Well-grounded in the Word, loves the Lord–"

"And Caleb!" added Marty with a big grin.

Chapter Nine

Owen laughed. "Yeah, that too."

A brief respite from work had already been planned for after lunch, so within minutes of the plates being cleared from the table, the rest of the young people wandered off to their own choosing for the customary afternoon siesta. Ryan walked toward his office, pausing to look at the clinic. He stopped, put his hands in his pockets, and surveyed the morning's work on the building.

Thank You, Lord, for sending such a sweet spirited group.

****

Four days later, in the late afternoon, Marty and Caleb worked side by side on the roof of the clinic. Repairs to the roof had gone slowly due to the frequent rain showers, but now they were nearing completion.

"Can you hand me that bag of nails?" Caleb reached an empty hand in Marty's direction.

"Sure." Marty picked up a small bag of roofing nails and leaned over toward Caleb. "Here you go." He relinquished his hold on the bag a split second before Caleb had a grasp on it, causing Caleb to try to catch the nails before they fell to the ground, twelve feet below.

Thrown off balance by his attempt to snatch the bag, Caleb's left knee slid slightly, and before he could regain his stability, he began to slide.

"Caleb!" Marty's cry echoed through the courtyard, and the workers near the dining hall looked up just in time to see Caleb fall to the ground with a thickening thud.

Marty scrambled down a ladder and reached his friend before anyone else. "Caleb! Caleb! Are you all right? Hey, Caleb! C'mon man, talk to me!" Marty looked around frantically. "I need some help here!"

Within moments, Caleb was surrounded by Bethany, his friends, Ryan, and the Canuls. He slowly opened his eyes.

Ryan knelt by the young man. "Caleb?"

"What happened?" His eyes fluttered open as he asked a slow, but understandable question.

"You fell off the roof. Does it hurt anywhere?" Ryan waited for an answer.

Caleb looked at the pastor, his frightened eyes widening. "I... I can't feel my legs."

Ryan took a deep breath and looked at Akna and her husband, Joaquin. "Get the truck. We need to get him to the hospital."

Bethany knelt beside Caleb, whispering words of encouragement to her fiancé. "Don't try to move, Caleb. We'll get you to a doctor. Everything will be okay." She held tightly to his hand, closed her eyes, and silently prayed.

Still kneeling beside Caleb, Ryan scanned the work area. "Marty, get me that piece of scrap plywood over there. We'll use it as a stretcher. We've got to get Caleb on it without twisting his back or neck. I need a towel, too. We'll roll it up and use it to brace his neck."

Working together, the men moved Caleb on to the makeshift backboard, secured him in the bed of the truck, and headed to Veracruz. Marty and Owen sat with Caleb in the back, stabilizing him against the bumps and jostles during the ride. Ryan and Bethany rode in the cab with Joaquin driving as fast as he dared go.

The road was slow going as the first section was unpaved and recent rains had left it muddy and rutted. As they came out of the denser rain forest region, the road conditions improved somewhat, but it was still nearly three hours until Caleb was being seen in the emergency room of Veracruz's main trauma hospital.

As the group sat in the ER waiting area, hoping for encouraging news on Caleb's status, they prayed. Again and again, they prayed, both collectively and individually.

"Do you think he'll be paralyzed?" Marty's guilt-ridden face betrayed the seeming calmness in his whispered voice.

Chapter Nine

"I don't know, Marty," Ryan admitted. He sat with his elbows on his knees, and his hands clasped in front of him. "I don't know."

"Man, I'm so sorry," Marty's voice choked up as he dropped his head into his hands. "If only I'd—"

"It wasn't your fault, Marty." Bethany reached out, placing her hand on Marty's shoulder. "No one is blaming you. Things happen. We just need to pray for Caleb, and be there for him no matter what the outcome."

Marty looked up at the young woman. Tears filled his eyes. "I'm so sorry, Bethany..."

She looked at the distraught man and repeated, "It's not your fault, Marty. Please don't blame yourself. I don't blame you, and I know Caleb won't blame you. Whatever happens, we'll face it together. God's here. We need to remember that He's here, and He's totally in control. We just have to trust Him."

The entire group lifted their eyes and focused on Bethany and Marty.

Ryan watched the grief on Marty's face lighten.

Trust in the Lord with all thine heart, and lean not unto thine own understanding. Help us to trust in You, Lord.

****

Two hours and many tests later, Ryan stood by the bedside of Caleb's bed. The cardiac monitor was beeping a steady rhythm, and an intravenous solution was flowing into Caleb's right hand.

Ryan looked into the fearful eyes of the young man.

Caleb's voice shook slightly as he spoke. "So far, they don't really know anything conclusive. The neurologist said that it could be permanent or temporary; it just depends. He said sometimes the spinal nerves get compressed, and that can cause paralysis, but it's not permanent. He won't know until the swelling goes down around the spinal cord, and he's still waiting for an MRI test."

Ryan nodded. "I think I should notify your parents."

Caleb reluctantly agreed. "I guess they should know," then added, "Bethany?"

"She's here. She wants to see you, Caleb."

Caleb didn't answer. He looked away from Ryan before speaking. His voice was shaking. "What if I am paralyzed permanently? What if I never walk again? What if she…?"

Ryan chose his words carefully. "She loves you, Caleb. She wants to be with you. Give her a chance."

The young man swallowed hard and whispered, "I do want to see her, Pastor. It's just that…"

Ryan put his hand on Caleb's shoulder. "I know it's hard, but it's in times like these that we need to trust God. I can only imagine how frightening this must be for you, Caleb, but you're not alone."

Caleb swallowed hard as his anguished eyes looked at the pastor. "I know," he stammered. "Would you pray with me, Pastor?" He bowed his head, and before Ryan could begin, Caleb began to weep.

As Ryan prayed, Caleb quieted, and when Ryan had finished, the young man looked up at the pastor through misty eyes.

"What if I never walk again, Pastor?" His head dropped, and his shoulders shook.

Ryan stood watching Caleb, unsure of what to say at that moment. Instinctively, he knew that Caleb wasn't really seeking an answer, but was simply voicing the fear in his heart. Quietly, he reassured the young man. "Caleb, whatever happens, God will be with you. You won't be facing this alone. No matter what lies ahead, I promise you, God will be with you."

Caleb lifted his head and nodded. "If you would ask Bethany to come in, I… I would really appreciate it."

****

Chapter Nine

Five and a half hours later, Ryan and everyone except Bethany and Caleb were back in Santa Molina. Caleb's family had been notified, and now everyone was just waiting.

Exhausted, Ryan sat in his office. He had tried to soothe the worried students, but he really had no solid hope he could offer regarding the recovery of their friend. He sat down at his desk, clasped his hands together, and bowed his head.

Lord, please take care of Caleb. Whatever lies ahead, take care of him. I know You are in complete control. Nothing happens without Your allowance of it, but Father sometimes it is so hard to accept. Help us... help me... to trust You. I pray we did the right thing in moving Caleb, but I'm not a doctor, Lord. You know how badly we need one... a full time doctor. Someone who can meet the needs of this community... someone who can help these people, Lord. Please don't let this clinic stay empty. Please bring us a doctor before... before... someone else gets hurt... or dies...

He prayed long into the night, finally falling asleep at his desk.

CHAPTER TEN

It was nearly eight in the morning when Ryan walked into the near empty waiting room in the Veracruz hospital intensive care unit. Bethany sat in a corner chair, her legs tucked under her, her head resting on her folded arms on the thin, wooden armrest. Her eyes were closed, and her breathing was rhythmic and slow. Ryan quietly turned and headed down the corridor to Caleb's room.

The door was partially open, and Ryan poked his head around the privacy curtain. Caleb was talking on a cell phone. Ryan started to leave, but Caleb motioned for him to come in as he finished his conversation.

"Really, Mom, I'm doing okay right now. Don't worry. Tell her there's no rush. Believe me, I'm not going anywhere." He paused for a moment. "No, I'm not alone. Bethany is here, and..." He looked up at Ryan and managed a weak smile. "And so is Pastor Ryan." Another pause. "Yes, Mom. I promise. I'll have her call as soon as she gets here." He nodded his head. "I love you, too." He set the phone down, looked at Ryan, and shrugged his shoulders. "My mom."

"How's she doing?"

"Okay. Worried, but that's what moms do, right?" He tried to sound nonchalant.

Ryan pulled a chair over by the bedside. "Yeah. Mine's like that, too. I guess it's a maternal thing." He sat back and crossed his legs. "How are you doing this morning?"

Chapter Ten

Caleb pressed the bed control button and rose to a more upright position. "About the same, I guess. Still no feeling, but the doctor says it could take a long time for the sensations to return... *if* they return. My mom asked my sister to fly down, so she ought to be here tonight or tomorrow."

"Your sister?"

"Yeah, she's the best. We've always been close, me and her." Caleb looked up at Ryan. "She's a few years older than me, but as long as I can remember, she's always been there for me. If anything happened to me when we were kids, she'd always be there to back me up. And she..." He stopped for a moment, unable to speak, and glanced away from Ryan for a moment.

Caleb swallowed hard, turned back to the pastor, and continued. "She lost her husband a couple of months ago. It hasn't been easy for her. I know because for the first time, I got to be there for her. My shoulder got waterlogged sometimes from all the tears, but the Lord really gave her an extra dose of grace, and, well, she's getting through it. And now, she's dropped everything, and she's coming here." His voice broke, and he said nothing for a few minutes.

Finally, he looked up at Ryan. "That's how she is." His voice trembled when he added softly, "I'll be glad when she's here. My stomach's all tied up in knots. I have this sick, scary feeling deep inside. I can't even begin to imagine my life without the use of my legs. I've got so many questions, and no one's giving me any answers. My sister, she's a—"

"Caleb, this would be difficult for anyone." Ryan leaned over, putting a hand on the young man's shoulder. "There are too many unknowns right now. I think we've got to wait until we get some results back from the tests."

Caleb nodded. "You're right. I know that, but it's so hard to not know anything. I stayed up most of the night just thinking. The 'what-ifs' can drive you nuts."

"I can imagine."

"Beth and I... we talked for a long time yesterday. She says nothing's changed, but if I can't... if I don't regain the use of my legs, everything changes." His tortured face turned away from Ryan.

"Isn't it a bit too early to make any decisions? You did say the doctor said this could just be temporary, right?"

Caleb nodded, then finally turned back to Ryan. "Yeah, but I kind of wanted to look at all my options."

"Do you even know what your options are?"

Caleb sighed deeply. "No, I guess I don't. I just know I don't want Bethany to be obligated to spend the rest of her life with me if I can't—"

They both turned their heads as the privacy curtain whipped open. Bethany stepped into the room; her eyes filled with unshed tears.

"Caleb?" She hesitantly walked toward his bed, shaking her head. Her anguished eyes remained fixed on her fiancé. She swallowed hard and took a deep breath, sorrow in her voice. "I'm sorry, but I couldn't help but hear what you were saying. Please, I thought we talked about this last night." She begged softly as she reached a hand out to take his, "Don't give up on us... please." She stared at his face, and the tears finally spilled over. "I love you, no matter what happens." She looked over at Ryan. "Make him understand, Pastor... please..."

Ryan opened his mouth to speak, but Caleb interjected before any words came.

"It's not that easy, Bethany!" Caleb protested. "I might never walk again."

"But you might. And even if you don't, that won't change how I feel about you. It's you I love, not your legs." She hesitated for a moment, then asked bluntly, "Will it change how you feel about me?"

Caleb looked at Bethany, then Ryan, his questioning eyes seeking help.

Ryan raised one eyebrow, shook his head slightly, then nodded toward Bethany.

Caleb sighed deeply in resignation. "Bethany, please come sit by me." His voice was subdued, but clear. "No, Beth. It

Chapter Ten

will not change my love for you. I just... I just don't want to burden—"

"Stop, Caleb." Bethany put a finger to his lips. She lifted her tear-stained face, and her features softened as her loving eyes met Caleb's. "No matter what happens, God will see us through. He didn't bring us this far together just to abandon us here." As Caleb drew Bethany to him, Ryan quietly left the room and went to find a strong cup of coffee.

****

Later that morning, per Caleb's request, Ryan sat with the couple as the neurologist, Dr. Alejandro Romero, discussed the treatment options and prognosis.

"I would definitely not advise traveling at this time," the doctor began. "This injury is too recent, and we don't have enough information to guarantee that travel will not adversely affect your situation." Dr. Romero paused for a moment. "The MRI shows a small fracture in the lower back region. Part of the vertebra has chipped off. It needs to be removed to prevent further damage to the spinal cord. If it should shift, it could injure the lower spinal column possibly leading to a more permanent paralysis of the body from that point down.

"Until the surgery, I cannot be absolute in my diagnosis. Even with surgery, I may not be able to tell you whether or not there is irreparable damage to your nervous system. Once I can visualize the affected areas, I will be able to give you a more definitive prognosis." He sat back in his chair.

"I don't understand. You won't be able to tell him anything after the surgery?" asked Bethany, her brow furrowing.

"Hopefully, I will have some answers, but I may not have *all* the answers at that point. Spinal injuries take time to heal, and because of that, definitive prognoses are difficult to make early on," explained the doctor.

Bethany frowned. "And why can't he have the surgery in the United States?"

Ryan leaned forward in his chair, his elbows on his knees, and his hands clasped. "The travel is basically too bumpy. Without the surgery, his back is unstable and any jarring movement could potentially make things worse."

Dr. Romero turned to Caleb. "I assure you, you are in good hands here. We have an outstanding team of doctors and nurses; many have been trained from all over the world."

"What happens if I don't have the surgery?" Caleb asked.

The doctor took a deep breath. "That's difficult to say for certain. You could recover on your own with the passage of time, but if that bone fragment isn't removed, it could shift, producing more damage to the spinal cord. The surgery is not without risks, of course. There is a chance that even with surgery, the paralysis will remain. I wish I could be more exact, but unfortunately, I can't be at this stage."

Bethany looked at Caleb. "What do you think?"

"I don't want to lie in this bed indefinitely waiting for who knows what." He glanced at Ryan, then back to Bethany. "I think I should have the surgery."

She reached for his hand. "Maybe we should get a second opinion?" she said softly.

Caleb smiled tenderly at the young woman. "Beth, Dr. Romero has been here since I came in. He hasn't pulled any punches with me. I trust him, and if he thinks that surgery is my best option, then I think I should do it."

Bethany nodded her head and feigned a weak smile.

Dr. Romero stood up. "I will let you speak privately to discuss this before you give me your final decision, and Señorita Porter..." He smiled at Bethany and placed a hand on her shoulder. "I can arrange for Dr. Escalante to see Caleb and give us a second opinion. It is no problem at all. Will that help?"

Bethany's cheeks reddened. "I'm sorry–"

"No apology needed. I would want the same if it were my fiancé." Dr. Romero turned and looked again at Caleb. "I will ask him to see you this afternoon. If you decide to have the operation, it would be best to do it as soon as possible. Do

Chapter Ten

you have any other questions for me right now?" He waited patiently for their answers.

"No. Not now, but I'd like to wait until my sister gets here." replied Caleb. "She should be here by tomorrow."

Dr. Romero nodded. "Of course. I understand completely."

Caleb held tightly to Bethany's hand as the doctor left the room, then turned to Ryan. "What do you think, Pastor?"

Ryan sat back in his chair and crossed his arms. "I know that the doctors here in Veracruz are very well trained. Through the years, I've had several times when I've been here with someone from Santa Molina, and they've always been treated well. I think the second opinion will help ease everyone's minds, but I do respect these physicians, and I'm confident in the care you will receive here."

"Thanks, Pastor," said Caleb as he continued to hold tightly to Bethany's hand.

"You really think it'll be okay to have the surgery here, Pastor?" Bethany's soft voice quivered.

"I do, Bethany."

She pressed her lips together and nodded her head. She turned to Caleb. "Whatever you decide, I will support you," she whispered. "Whether it's here or the U.S., God is still in control, right?"

Caleb nodded. "Yes, He is. We've got to remember that. It'll be okay, Beth. Whatever happens, it'll be okay." He tried to sound confident, but his voice shook as he clung to Bethany's hand.

****

A deceptive aura of peacefulness filled the hospital corridors in the early morning hours. Somewhere in the distance, muted, unsynchronized beeps fought their way through the silence announcing to the new day that the business of saving lives still continued.

The dim lighting of the ICU waiting room did little to promote a good night's rest, but Ryan had managed a few hours of uninterrupted sleep in the now empty place reserved for family and friends of the critically ill patients. Somewhere off in the distance, the sound of rhythmic clicking became louder in the semi-consciousness of Ryan's mind, and despite his subliminal desire to remain asleep, his eyes opened slightly as the sound intensified. He sat up just as the light flickered on to its full brightness. He blinked his eyes and sat upright coming face to face with a young woman.

"Oh! I am so sorry. I didn't see you. I thought—" Her mouth dropped open. "Ryan?"

"Jessica? What are you doing here?" His widened eyes focused on her face.

"I just got here from Los Angeles. My brother had an accident, but they won't let me in to see him just yet. Change of shift and all. They asked me to wait for a few minutes while they finished their rounds."

Ryan cocked his head slightly. "Are *you* Caleb's sister?"

She stared at him, then replied, "Yes. Yes, how did you...? Are *you* the pastor he was working with?"

"Yes. His accident... it was at my church." He indicated the sofa. "Please sit down."

Jessica gratefully accepted the offer and eased herself down on to the stiff cushion. She crossed her legs, then smoothed the fabric of her light gray skirt over her knees. "Please, tell me what happened. My mother was quite upset, and her rendition of the accident left me with many questions."

"Of course." He sat down opposite her in a hard-backed faux leather chair and recounted the accident up to the last doctor's report from the previous night.

Jessica listened stoically; her intense blue eyes focused on Ryan's face as he shared the details of Caleb's injuries and prognosis. The sudden misting of those blue eyes betrayed her calm demeanor, and she bit her lower lip as Ryan finished

Chapter Ten

describing the recommended plan of treatment proposed by the neurologist.

She blinked several times before speaking. "How's *he* doing?" Her voice resonated with concern as she clasped her hands together in her lap and leaned forward.

"He's doing okay for now. I think he's struggling to hold on to any kind of hope the doctors can give him. I suppose any of us would be doing the same. I know he was greatly relieved to hear you were on the way."

Jessica forced a smile. "Not the best of circumstances to be seeing my little brother."

"No, it's not," Ryan agreed as an ICU nurse entered the room. "Dr. Carr?"

Jessica stood, and Ryan rose to his feet beside her.

"You can come see your brother now."

"Thank you." She turned toward Ryan and raised her eyebrows questioningly.

Ryan shook his head. "No, no. You go on in. I need a cup of coffee right now. I'll come in after you've had some time alone with him."

Jessica smiled gratefully, and as her somber gaze met his, she turned toward the door.

He watched her exit, then sat back down. He reflected back on his conversation with Caleb about Jessica.

What was that he said? Her husband died? And now this?

He bowed his head and quietly prayed to the Lord on behalf of Caleb and Jessica.

****

"Caleb?" Her voice was barely audible as Jessica entered her brother's room. She glanced at his sleeping form, then automatically looked up at the bedside monitor.

Heart rate and rhythm within normal range. BP is fine. Well, that's good.

She looked back at Caleb. His eyes were closed, and his breathing steady. She quietly pulled a chair near the head of the bed and sat, putting her hand through the bedrails and placing her fingers gently around his hand. She studied Caleb's sleeping face as her eyes filled with tears. She dropped her head down slightly.

Please, Lord, don't let him be paralyzed... please...

"Jess? Is it really you? You're here?" The whispered voice interrupted her silent prayer.

She jerked her head up and met the sleepy brown eyes of her brother. She smiled at him and squeezed his hand. "Yes, it's me. I'm here. How are you doing?"

He reached for the bed control and raised the head of the bed up slightly. "I'm doing okay. It could be worse, I guess." He stared at her face. "It's good to see you. Really good. Are Mom and Dad okay?"

"As well as could be expected considering everything that's happened lately. They're both worried, of course, and send their prayers. If Dad hadn't just had his surgery, they'd both be here with me. I am expected to report in on a daily basis, which I will do, of course."

Caleb grinned. "Of course. Dad's doing okay?"

"Yes," she nodded. "If he hadn't slid into second base so hard, he'd have saved that ankle, but now he's bionic. Three pins later, he claims he's as good as new, but the orthopedist wants him in the hospital for a few more days just to keep him off of it. You know Dad. He's ready for a marathon!"

Caleb nodded. "Yep. It'll take more than a broken ankle to keep him off his feet." He easily pulled himself up in the bed; his arms tanned and muscular from athletics and outdoor work.

"So tell me what you know." Jessica sat back and waited.

Caleb took a deep breath and shook his head. "I'm not sure what I know. I fell off a roof, and when I came to, I couldn't feel my legs. They brought me here, and I've had a ton of tests. I still don't have any feeling there, but the neurologist said something about a bone fragment and swelling. He said right

Chapter Ten

now he can't know whether it's going to be temporary or not, and he... he recommends surgery."

"Surgery? Here? In Mexico?"

"Yeah. He said it would be too risky to travel back home for it. Said something about stabilization of the spine and possible nerve damage. Will you talk with him?"

"Absolutely. How far up does the paralysis go?"

"About here for sure." He indicated his hip region. "I got some kind of shot here. I felt that." He pointed to his upper right hip. "But it's a weird kind of numb to the waist, I guess. I'm not sure if I really feel stuff this high or not."

Jessica's eyebrows rose. "I presume you've had several MRIs?"

"I don't think there's a test I haven't had since I've been here. I've been poked, prodded, scanned, rescanned, and then some."

"Your doctor... he speaks English?"

"Yeah. Quite well, actually. He said something about studying in the States. He's been very informative, and he seems quite knowledgeable, but I don't know if I'm a good judge of his competency."

At that moment, as if on cue, Dr. Alejandro Romero entered the room.

"Good morning, Mr. Merrick." The doctor moved to the far side of the bed and faced Caleb. "Your sister, I presume?" When Caleb nodded, Dr. Romero turned toward Jessica. "You are the sister I've heard so much about. I'm Alejandro Romero." He leaned over the bed and extended his hand.

Jessica rose and shook it. "Jessica Carr. *Encantado*."

"Ah!" the doctor smiled. "And I am pleased to meet you as well. You are a physician also, no?"

"Yes. Emergency medicine."

Dr. Romero turned once again to Caleb. "Mr. Merrick, do I have your permission to discuss your case with your sister?"

Caleb nodded. "Anything and everything you can tell me, you can tell her."

Jessica's eyes moved from Dr. Romero to her brother as she sat back down. She smiled at Caleb, then focused her attention on the neurologist.

Dr. Romero pulled a chair over beside Jessica. He sat down facing her and Caleb. "It's one of those situations that cannot be determined until the offending bone fragment is removed, and time for healing has occurred. Caleb has a small vertebral fracture in the lumbar region that resulted in a chip of bone breaking off near the spinal column.

"There is a considerable amount of edema in the surrounding tissues which may be causing the loss of sensation in the lower extremities, but it is hard to say at this point whether or not the damage is permanent."

The doctor's eyes narrowed as he continued. "My recommendation is surgery to remove the bone fragment, and then we will be better able to evaluate Mr. Merrick's paralytic status."

Jessica cocked her head and crossed her arms in front of her chest. "Would it be possible for me to see Caleb's MRI films?"

Dr. Romero nodded. "I thought you might want to do that. I will get them for you, and the results of the nerve studies as well. If there is anything more, I will be happy to provide you with whatever you need."

"I appreciate your spirit of cooperation. It's not always easy to allow someone else to... to..."

"Scrutinize your work?" He chuckled as his facial features softened. "Consider it professional courtesy, Dr. Carr. I would hope if the situation was reversed, you would do the same for me," explained Dr. Romero.

"Of course," replied Jessica. "Would you be the one performing the surgery?"

"Yes, with my colleague, Andres Escalante. He is an excellent neurosurgeon. He received his medical degree from a school in the States. Perhaps you've heard of it? Johns Hopkins?" He winked at Caleb.

Chapter Ten

Jessica's mouth opened slightly as her surprised eyes darted from the doctor to her brother again. She smiled, "Yes, I've definitely heard of it."

Dr. Romero chuckled, then continued. "As for me, I trained here in Mexico, but did additional work afterwards at the University of Miami medical school. I completed my residency there as well, but eventually returned home to Veracruz to work with the people of my country." He paused for a moment.

"I know there is the misconception that our medical services are somewhat substandard here, but I can assure you, Dr. Carr, nothing could be further from the truth. In fact, here in the city, we have very high standards for medical care. It is only in the very rural areas that the health care of our people suffers. Unfortunately, that is where the outbreaks tend to occur, and that is what the media tends to report."

Jessica's nod was barely perceptible. "I understand, and I apologize if I gave you the impression—"

"No apology necessary, Dr. Carr." Dr. Romero held up his hand, his palm facing Jessica, and gently waved it back and forth. "You said nothing to offend me, nor did you imply it. I simply wanted to take advantage of the opportunity to brag about my country's health services." He smiled once more as he stood. "I will give you some time alone with your brother now, but I will return later with his medical information. If you have any concerns that should arise before I return, please inform our nurses here. They will be happy to help you." He shook her hand once more, then turned to Caleb, nodded, and left the room.

"Well, what do you think, Jess?" He turned his head to look at her more directly.

"I like him," admitted Jessica. "It seems God is already answering prayers about your medical care."

Caleb raised an eyebrow. "How so?"

"I've been praying for a doctor who would be somewhat sympathetic to our cause. You know, willing to share information with me and not be difficult to work with. Plus, speaking

English works so much better for me. My Spanish is more conversational than medical, so I am very grateful he is fluent in English."

"Yeah, that was really a blessing for me, too. I think I'd have been terrified if I had no idea about what was going on. He's been real good about explaining everything to me. Good or bad."

Caleb hesitated for a moment, averting his eyes from Jessica. He continued speaking, but the tone of his voice became solemn, almost apologetic. "It's been really hard to... uh... hold on to my faith, you know? I didn't want to tell Mom or Dad, but it's been kind of..." He stared at his hands, not moving until one of Jessica's hands moved into his range of vision. It settled on top of his own.

"I can't imagine what you're going through, Caleb, but whatever happens, we'll get through it together. You know Mom and Dad are praying for you, and so are lots of other people, but right here, right now, it's just me and you." Jessica spoke with confidence. "There's nothing we can't handle together, right? We've always been a great team. You just make sure you do your part, and don't give up, okay?"

Caleb turned his head and looked at his sister. He managed a faint smile. "I won't. I promise, but if it gets too hard, give me a little help once in a while, okay?"

"I'm not expecting you to be perfect. No one is, Caleb. You shouldn't either. Remember when Moses had to hold his hands up for the Israelites to have victory? When it got too hard to hold them up, he had help from those closest to him. That's what I'm here for. I've got your back; you've got mine, always and forever," stated Jessica.

Her brother smiled and reclined back on his pillow. "I can't tell you how much better I feel just having you here. Was anyone else here when you got here?"

Jessica shook her head; her coppery curls bouncing around her face. "Just the pastor. I spoke with him for a few minutes, but then they let me come back here. He said he'd come back later today."

Chapter Ten

"He's been great, Jess. Really great. He's been here every day, and it's a good two-hour trip one-way from Santa Molina. He's prayed with me, listened to me, and… I don't know where I'd be right now without him." Caleb's voice broke as he struggled to maintain composure. "He's really helped me hold on."

"I'm so sorry this happened to you," whispered Jessica. She looked at Caleb through her thick black lashes, now moist with tears, her hand tightly holding his.

Caleb smiled weakly at his sister and became the comforter. "It's okay, Jess. Everything will be okay. Isn't that what God promised? All things work to the good… not just some things?"

Jessica nodded. "Yes," she said softly. "He did."

CHAPTER ELEVEN

The Veracruz hospital cafeteria was not unlike that of Eastmont, and Jessica felt a strange familiarity in sitting at a window table while she ate. She stared out the window watching people walk by, some in lab coats, others in scrubs, but the majority dressed in everyday clothing, hurrying off to somewhere. She held a white plastic fork in her hand and absentmindedly stirred the lettuce around on the plate that held her small salad and a cup of soup.

"May I join you?"

Jessica looked up and saw a pair of warm blue eyes. "Pastor Devereaux! What a pleasant surprise. Yes, please sit down."

He sat down opposite her. "It's Ryan, remember?"

Jessica smiled. "Yes, I do. Not eating?"

"Just finished. I was actually going to go see Caleb when I saw you sit down. Anything new?"

"Actually, yes. I had a long talk with both Dr. Romero and Dr. Escalante last night. They'd like to operate tomorrow morning."

Ryan studied her worried face. "Are you good with that?"

Jessica pursed her lips, then sighed. "Yes... and no. I suppose there's a part of me that wants him to have his surgery in the States. I guess I'd feel better if he were under the care of one of my colleagues, but in reality, I know it's not safe for him to travel in his condition, and Dr. Romero seems very competent." She shrugged her shoulders and shook her head. "It's not really up to me though. It's Caleb's decision."

Chapter Eleven

"True, but I'm guessing you've got a lot of influence in that decision. He trusts you."

"I know." Jessica looked up at Ryan. Her lips formed a thin line, and she crossed her arms in front of her. "I know what the right answer is. Of course he should have the surgery."

"You don't sound convinced."

"It's just that I... I guess I'm afraid of the outcome."

Ryan nodded in understanding. "The longer the surgery is postponed, the longer the diagnosis of permanent paralysis remains unconfirmed."

Jessica looked away from Ryan and whispered reluctantly, "Yes." She returned her gaze to the pastor. "I really think—"

A soft whirring sound emanated from Jessica's pocket. She reached in and pulled out her cell phone. "I'm sorry, it's my mother..." She accepted the call and began to chat with Anne.

Ryan sat back in his chair and listened as Jessica talked with her mother.

"He's doing as well as can be expected, Mom. They're thinking about doing the surgery tomorrow. No, no, I can't. I don't have a license to practice medicine here, plus it's never a good idea to treat family members. We tend to lose our objectivity."

Jessica's eyes met Ryan's, and she shrugged her shoulders and sheepishly grinned as she listened to the voice on the other end.

"Yes, I think it's the right thing to do. If he's transferred without the surgery, and the bone fragment moves, it could sever some of the spinal nerves, and he could be paralyzed permanently."

As Jessica lifted her hand to brush a small lock of reddish-gold hair from her forehead, Ryan considered the young woman seated in front of him.

This has to be very hard for her, Lord. Please give her strength to get through this and the wisdom to help Caleb make the right decisions.

As she replaced the phone in her jacket pocket, Jessica spoke, interrupting Ryan's silent prayer. "Mom wants to fly down. I told her to stay with my Dad. He just had surgery for a broken ankle." She frowned as she looked at Ryan. "I hope that was the right thing to say."

"Why wouldn't it be?"

Jessica thought carefully before answering. "Truthfully?"

Ryan nodded and waited.

Jessica's lips parted slightly. She turned away, and then said softly, "If the surgery's not as successful as we hope it will be, I don't want Mom to be here to hear that, especially not without Dad. I guess I... I want to soften the blow if it's not the best news." She looked up remorsefully at Ryan. "Not much faith, is it?"

Ryan smiled sympathetically and took a deep breath. "Sometimes, I have found that the depth of our faith is not seen in the waiting, but in the accepting of the reality that is set before us. Sometimes it takes more faith to accept what God gives you than in anticipating what the future holds."

Jessica's brow furrowed as she stared at Ryan. "I'm sorry. I didn't quite get that."

"What I meant was don't be so hard on yourself. You're doing just fine in the faith department. You're here because your brother needs you; your folks need you here, and God needs you here. You'll find the strength you need, when you need it. He'll get you through the waiting, and then He'll get you through the outcome if you let Him."

Jessica nodded and smiled. "Wise words from a wise pastor."

Ryan grinned. "I try."

****

The following morning Jessica sat in an empty waiting room. She had arrived nearly an hour earlier to be with Caleb before he had been taken to the operating room. They had talked about the possible outcomes, and Jessica had promised

Chapter Eleven

she would not return to the United States until he could go with her. She also had agreed to oversee his care and rehabilitative therapies, and take care of any other needs he would have. They had finished praying together just as the orderlies had arrived to wheel Caleb to his surgery.

Now she sat alone, and the possibility that Caleb may never walk again was overwhelming. She held her head in her hands and for the first time in a long time, allowed herself to cry.

I'm so sorry, Lord. I've tried to be strong for Caleb, but I'm so afraid. I'm afraid he'll never walk again, and he's got so much life to live. Please don't let him be paralyzed.

"Jessica?"

She quickly wiped her eyes and raised her head, coming face to face with Ryan. He sat down beside her.

"Are you okay?"

Self-conscious, she rummaged through her purse. "Yes... yes, I'm fine."

"Here." He handed her a tissue.

She looked up and sighed as she took it and dabbed at the corner of her eyes, careful to keep her make-up from smearing. "Thank you."

"Caleb's in surgery?"

"Yes. They took him about a half an hour ago." The tremor in her voice was minute, but not unnoticeable. "It's not easy being on this end."

"I imagine it's not."

Jessica lifted her eyes and looked at Ryan through her long black lashes. "Could we pray together?"

"Of course." He watched her close her eyes, then bowed his head over his interlaced fingers. "Father in heaven, we love You so much. You are our strength, our joy, and our hope. You have told us to come boldly before Your throne for any and everything on our hearts. This morning we come on behalf of Caleb. We ask for Your healing touch on this young man. Even as we speak, knit the bones and nerves together correctly so there is no paralysis. Give wisdom and guidance to the surgical team as they work."

He paused for a moment. "Lord, we ask for Your peace... the peace that truly passes all understanding. Help us to trust You in this situation. Comfort Jessica and her parents as they await the outcome of the surgery. Give Jessica wisdom as she helps her brother through the recovery period. Help her know Your presence in every moment of every situation surrounding Caleb's health.

"Help us to trust in You, leaning not on our own understanding, but acknowledging You in all things, and allowing You to lead and guide us in Your perfect will. Lord, we are frail creatures. Give us the courage to stand against the fears that may arise. Keep our faith strong. In Jesus' name, amen."

"Amen."

"Amen," came a third voice.

Neither of them had heard the young woman enter the waiting room. Clad in a pale green sundress, the young, dark-haired woman looked at Ryan apologetically.

"I'm sorry. I was going to wait outside, but then I saw it was you praying, and I didn't think you'd mind."

Ryan immediately stood up. "Bethany, of course not. Please come in. Sit here." He gestured next to Jessica.

"He's in surgery?" Her fearful eyes remained fixed on his face.

"Yes. A little while ago."

Jessica noticed a faint floral fragrance as the young woman sat down next to her. Recognition dawned.

Bethany? This is the girl Caleb wants to marry!

"Bethany," began Ryan. "This is Jessica Carr, Caleb's sister."

Bethany nervously straightened her dress and brushed her long, dark hair from off her shoulder. "Dr. Carr, I'm a friend of Caleb's. Well, kind of more than a friend." She smiled uneasily, cast a quick look at Ryan, then looked back at Jessica.

"So you're Bethany," smiled Jessica warmly. "I've heard so much about you. It's nice to finally meet you."

Chapter Eleven

"I wish the circumstances were different, Dr. Carr."

"Me, too," she began, "and please call me Jessica. After all, from what I understand, we're going to be sisters one day."

Bethany lowered her eyes. "Maybe... I hope so."

"Maybe?" Jessica's brow furrowed. "What do you mean?"

Bethany spoke without looking up. "I don't think Caleb wants to get married anymore. He thinks if he's unable to walk that we don't have a future together, but..." She lifted her head and looked directly at Jessica through her tears. "We do, Dr. Carr... Jessica... I want to marry Caleb. It doesn't matter if he's in a wheelchair or not. I love him."

Jessica nodded. "Be patient with him, Bethany. He has a lot to think about... a lot of uncertainty in his immediate future. Not with you, but with himself. He's going to need you now more than ever to help him through this. But I believe when it's over, you two will be together, stronger than ever." She smiled reassuringly. "Trust in the Lord, Bethany. If God has brought you two together, this won't tear you apart."

Jessica glanced at Ryan and saw him watching her intently. A small smile formed on his face, and Jessica found herself returning one of her own.

Bethany nodded. "I'll try, but sometimes it's so hard. At first, I was so worried that he wasn't going to walk again, but now all I worry about is that he won't want us to be together. I love him so much, Dr. Carr. I can't even imagine my life without him in it."

Jessica moved closer to Caleb's fiancée and opened her arms slightly. Bethany looked up through hurting eyes and fell into Jessica's embrace.

"I love him so much," she whispered as she hugged Jessica. "I really do."

Jessica blinked several times and then spoke softly. "It'll be okay, Bethany. Don't worry. God's will will prevail. He hasn't abandoned any of us. He's here in this room with us, and He's with Caleb right now in that operating room. No matter what happens, God is with us. He'll get us through this."

Bethany hugged Jessica again and whispered, "No wonder Caleb loves you so much. You don't know how much I needed to hear that." Releasing her hold on Jessica, Bethany reached into her purse to retrieve a tissue. She dabbed at her eyes as she spoke. "Did they say how long it would be? The surgery?"

Jessica shook her head. "No. It's hard to say. I would think at least five or six hours, if not more. It just depends on what they find when they open him up."

Bethany grimaced.

"I'm sorry," apologized Jessica. "What I meant was... when they examine the affected area and see the position of the bone fragments, they will determine exactly what they need to do. It takes time."

Ryan stood up. "I could use a cup of coffee. Would either of you ladies care for some?"

Jessica smiled gratefully. "I would love a cup with—"

"Cream, no sugar. I remember," said Ryan.

"That would be so nice, Pastor," said Bethany as she tossed her tissue into the trash receptacle. "I guess it's going to be a long wait, huh?" She reached out and squeezed Jessica's hand. "I'm so glad you're here."

"Me, too," Jessica agreed. "Me, too."

****

Nearly seven hours had passed since the surgery had begun, and Caleb's friends had now gathered in the waiting room. They dealt with their rising anxieties by laughing together, crying together, and most importantly, praying together.

Needing some quiet time, Jessica excused herself and paced in the corridor just outside the waiting room. Every few minutes, she glanced at her watch. Every step she heard caused her to pause and look for the source, hoping to see Dr. Romero or Dr. Escalante approaching.

Chapter Eleven

I've got to make sure I send someone to the waiting room more frequently when I'm in surgery. This is killing me. What's happening? Why is it taking so long?

She leaned back against a wall, closed her eyes, and rubbed her temples.

"Are you okay?"

Before she opened her eyes, she knew it was Ryan. His deep voice resonated with compassion, and she forced a smile as she opened her eyes. "I'm fine."

He looked at her skeptically. "Did you just lie to me?"

Her smile broadened, and she laughed lightly. "Yes, I believe I did."

"Shame on you."

Jessica looked into his concerned blue eyes, and for a moment, she couldn't look away. He repeated, "Are you really okay?" and the spell was broken. Feeling the warmth rise in her cheeks, she looked quickly down the hall. "I'm sorry. What did you say?"

"I was wondering how you were doing."

She glanced at her watch once more, then sighed. "I want to be in there." She turned her head toward the closed doors of the operating rooms.

"Someone once told me that no news was good news. Isn't that the way it is with the medical profession, too?"

Jessica shrugged her shoulders as they began to walk the hallway. "It all depends. Sometimes no news can mean things are progressing well in the O.R., and you don't want to stop; you want to finish before talking with the family, but other times, it can mean you've run into something you didn't expect, and you've got to focus every bit of energy into saving that person's life. There's no time to send someone out to update the family."

"Hmm... so let me ask you again, how are you?" He walked next to her, his hands in his pants pockets.

"Honestly, I don't know," admitted Jessica. "Part of me... the doctor side... knows that surgeries are not black and white.

No two seem to be alike, and they never seem to follow the prescribed route from start to finish. The other part of me... the sister part... well, it's struggling to hold on, but I have to. For Caleb, for Mom and Dad."

"That's a pretty big burden, Doc."

"I know."

"I guess you know who you ought to share that burden with?"

Jessica smiled as she eyed Ryan. "Spoken like a true pastor."

"Really? Well, then let me offer you this. I have found that in times like these, I cling to one or two verses of Scripture that can offer me the greatest support for the moment, and I repeat them to myself. You see, Satan is more than happy to attack you at your weakest point. Sometimes we don't even know what that point is, but he is there waiting. You know, the roaring lion waiting to devour?"

"Are you calling me lion fodder?" Jessica teased.

Ryan grinned. "In a sense, I guess I am. But you don't have to be." The tone of his voice became serious. He stopped and turned to face her. "It's one thing to say that God is in control, and you don't need to worry, but it's another altogether to quote a verse that supports that. For example, instead of fighting my fears on my own, I can meditate on Isaiah 26, verses three and four. 'Thou wilt keep him in perfect peace, whose mind is stayed on Thee: because he trusteth in Thee. Trust ye in the Lord for ever: for in the Lord Jehovah is everlasting strength.' The more I say it or repeat it in my head, the more peace prevails in my soul.

"It's the power of God's Word that causes Satan to flee and brings you to the place you need to be to get through whatever you're going through. Christ was our example for this. When He faced Satan in the wilderness, He used Scripture to cause the devil to flee."

They stopped at the end of the corridor where the sunlight was streaming in through a partially draped window.

Jessica parted the curtain and looked out over the hospital grounds. "How do you know which verses to use?"

Chapter Eleven

"Well, that would be the job of the Holy Spirit. You know all those verses you memorized as a child? He'll bring the right one to mind," stated Ryan confidently. "You need to be open to Him though. That's one unique thing about our God. He's not a demanding forceful God. He doesn't intrude; He only comes when He's asked to come." He pointed out the window. "See that car there? The one waiting at the gate?"

Jessica shaded her eyes with her hand. "The red one? Yes."

"Well, that car won't come into the parking lot until the attendant raises the guard rail. That's kind of like God. He won't barge into your mind unless you invite him in," explained Ryan.

They both watched as the black and white striped bar pivoted skyward, and the tiny red car drove into the lot.

Jessica turned toward Ryan. "So right now, when I'm feeling those doubts and fears inside me, I need not only to pray for God's help, but find a verse to help me stay focused?"

"Yes. That's like lifting the gate and allowing God in. It'll make the battle easier for you. That car could've gone in without the bar being raised, but we both know it wouldn't do that. It'll just wait until the attendant allows it in by raising the barricade. That's how God works. He'll come in when we invite Him."

"So for me, right now, the verse that comes to mind is 'What time I am afraid, I will trust in Thee.' Is that what you mean?"

"Exactly," smiled Ryan. "You know, that's from Psalm 56. The next verse says 'In God I will praise His Word, in God I have put my trust; I will not fear what flesh can do unto me.' Kind of applicable to us right now. No matter what happens to Caleb's body, we can trust God for our deliverance and for Caleb's."

Jessica nodded, then repeated, "What time I am afraid, I will trust in Thee." She looked up at Ryan and smiled. "Thank you."

"My pleasure."

Together they walked back to the waiting room. As soon as they entered, a hush descended, and four heads turned toward them expectantly.

Ryan shook his head. "Sorry, no news." He waited for Jessica to take a seat before sitting down.

"You know, Pastor," began Marty. "We were all talking, and if it's okay with you, we thought maybe we'd extend our stay. You know, we could keep on with the project while Caleb's on the mend, and be here in case he needs us."

"Yeah," said Owen, "you know, all for one and one for all. We all came together; we'll leave together."

Olivia giggled. "Spoken like a true Musketeer, Owen."

"Yeah, I know," he stated. "We never leave a man behind."

Marty smirked at Owen. "That's not the Musketeers, D'Artagnan; that's the Navy Seals."

"Whatever! You get the general idea, right?" Owen feigned insult.

Marty rolled his eyes.

"So would it be okay, Pastor Ryan? I really want to stay," pleaded Bethany.

Ryan scanned the room, pausing to look at each student's hopeful face. "Of course, it's fine with me, but you need to get permission from the school and your parents."

"All right!" Marty and Owen high-fived each other. "We can call as soon as—"

Conversation abruptly stopped when Dr. Romero stepped into the waiting room. "Dr. Carr, may we speak?"

Jessica stood immediately. "Of course." She cast a furtive glance at Ryan, then smoothed her skirt and followed Dr. Romero into the hallway. Five pairs of eyes watched them exit the waiting room.

Dr. Romero stopped near the nurses' station and turned toward Jessica. "First, I need you to know that the surgery went well, and Caleb is doing fine. The bone fragment was imbedded in a rather precarious position, but we were able to extract it. Obviously, it took longer than I anticipated, but I believe we had the best possible outcome. There is some swelling at the site, but when that has subsided, we will be able to determine more about the extent of any permanent paralysis."

Chapter Eleven

"How did it look? The cord?"

"We didn't see any obvious damage, but you know that can be deceptive."

Jessica nodded. "Yes, yes, I understand. I'm sorry. I was just—"

"Dr. Carr," he smiled at her. "I think the outcome will be very good."

Jessica stood staring at the physician her mouth slightly open, and her eyes widening as hope replaced fear. Suddenly, she grabbed his hand and shook it vigorously. "Thank you, Dr. Romero. Thank you so much. When can I see him?"

"He's in recovery right now. It may be another thirty minutes or so before you can go back, but as soon as possible, I will have one of the nurses come get you. We're going to keep him sedated for a while. I don't want him moving around right now."

Jessica nodded her head rapidly. "Of course. I understand. I just would really like to see him as soon as I can."

"Of course, Dr. Carr. I will send someone out as soon as he's settled in. Again, if you have any more questions, please feel free to ask me or my colleague. We are at your service," reminded Dr. Romero before he walked back toward the surgical unit.

She shook his hand once more and headed back to the waiting room. She took several steps, and then stopped and glanced upward.

Thank You, Lord. Thank You so much.

****

Later that evening, Jessica sat quietly beside Caleb's bed while he slept. She kept a watchful eye on the cardiac monitor while she pondered his latest scans and her recent phone call to Dr. Edward Sorenson, a well-known neurologist at Eastmont.

Ed says there is the possibility it's spinal shock, especially since Dr. Romero didn't see any observable cord damage. Even though the healing process would be long, he could recover from that. He's going to look at Caleb's medical records as soon as I get them to him. I hope his findings agree with Dr. Romero's. I wonder how long before Caleb can fly home—

"Jess?" Caleb's groggy voice disturbed her thoughts. "What time is it?" He reached for the railing.

Jessica stood quickly. "Don't try to move Caleb. It's about six in the evening."

"Really?" He closed his eyes. "I am so tired."

"That's the medicine. They're trying to keep you quiet."

He chuckled softly. "Did you tell them that's impossible?"

Jessica smiled as she sat back down, relieved that her brother's sense of humor remained intact. "I should have, but I cut you some slack. Are you in any pain?"

"No, not really. A little dull ache, but otherwise I'm okay. So what's the verdict?" he asked sluggishly.

"Dr. Romero is cautiously optimistic."

Caleb lazily chuckled again. "That's pretty noncommittal. Guess I won't sign up for any 5 K's for a while." His eyes closed, but a smile remained on his face. "Why are you still here? Go get some rest."

"I will, but I wanted to be here when you woke up."

"Did you see Bethany?"

"Yes. Yes, I did. She's a lovely girl, Caleb."

"She is. She really is..." His voice drifted off as his smile faded.

"Caleb?" Jessica whispered. Receiving no response, she simply bowed her head and quietly prayed. "Father, thank You so much for my brother. Thank You for Dr. Romero and his team, and the excellent care they've given Caleb. Thank You for the good report so far. Please let it be only a temporary paralysis. Please help his nerves heal and start working again. Please help our faith to remain strong. Help us not to be afraid." She stopped and allowed her mind to focus on spiritual things. "'What time *Jessica* is afraid, *she* will trust in Thee.' I'm trying, Lord. I'm really trying."

Chapter Eleven

She raised her head and stood up, reached over the rail and squeezed her brother's hand. "I love you, Caleb. I'll see you tomorrow," she whispered. She cast a final glance at the cardiac monitor before turning to exit the surgical ICU.

CHAPTER TWELVE

Jessica walked slowly through the quiet corridor leading to the intensive care waiting room. Her vision blurred as her watery eyes tried to focus on her watch.

Hard to believe we're miles apart, yet only an hour difference. Mom's probably still at the hospital slipping Dad an In-and-Out burger or something else not allowed on his diet.

She smiled as she reached into her purse for her cell phone. As her fingers wrapped around it, she leaned against the wall, looked to her left and right before hitting the speed dial for Anne. She took a deep breath and suppressed her emotions as she heard the ringing begin.

Anne's worried voice answered after the second ring. "Hello? Jessica? How's Caleb?"

"Hi, Mom. Caleb's doing okay."

"Oh, Jessica. I'm so glad you called. We've been so worried. How did the surgery go?" There was an edge of controlled concern in her question.

Jessica carefully related her brother's situation, taking time to answer each question Anne asked about Caleb's condition. "We don't know anything really about the paralysis yet, but there's no evidence one way or the other that it will be permanent. It's just too soon to know, but Dr. Romero says it looks good." She paused, waiting for Anne to ask another question. When none came, Jessica quickly asked, "How's Dad?"

Chapter Twelve

"He's doing well, Jessica. Of course, he wants to be there with Caleb. We both do. How are you doing, sweetheart?" Her voice had lost its edge.

"I'm doing well, Mom. Caleb's college friends are here, so that helps, and then there's Ryan."

"Ryan?"

"Yes. Ryan Devereaux. He's the pastor of the church where Caleb was working. He is the nicest man, Mom. You and Dad would love him. He's been here with Caleb every day since the accident," Jessica's eyes misted over once again as she confessed in a hesitant whisper, "He's been such an amazing encouragement to all of us."

"Oh, Jessica, praise the Lord! I am so glad you're not alone there."

"I'm not, Mom, and I promised Caleb I'd stay until he could fly back home with me."

"Can you do that, Jessica?"

Sadness accompanied Jessica's response to her mother. "I have plenty of vacation time, Mom. I was saving it for when... for when Nick came home, but now I can stay with Caleb a little longer." She swallowed hard, willing her voice to remain normal. "I promise as soon as I know anything more, I'll call. Give Dad my love, okay?"

"You know you're covered with our prayers, Jessica. We love you and your brother so much."

"I love you too, Mom." She ended the call, stepped away from the wall, and brushed a tear from her face.

"Hey, are you all right?"

Jessica hastily wiped away another tear before looking up into Ryan's questioning face. She nodded as she looked down, then took a deep breath.

"I was just talking with my Mom."

When she looked back up, he was holding a tissue out to her. She smiled gratefully as she took it from him. "Thank you."

"How about joining me for dinner? There's actually a great Mexican restaurant nearby that also serves pretty good

American food if you're not game to try the local cuisine. It's just a short walk from here." He cocked his head slightly as he waited for her reply.

She sighed deeply, preparing to decline his offer, but when her gaze fell upon his warm eyes, she heard herself say, "That sounds wonderful. Thank you."

****

Ryan guided Jessica across the street, and they walked a few blocks to a sidewalk café with outdoor seating. They sat at one of the small rod iron tables in the restaurant's patio. Burning torches illuminated the perimeter of the outside eating area. From their seats, they had a panoramic view of the setting sun over the western edge of the city. In the center of the table, a glass vase was filled with freshly picked pink and lavender flowers.

Jessica touched a petal with her finger. "I love these! These are Mexican primrose, right? They're my favorite flower!"

Ryan lifted his eyes from the menu and stared at Jessica.

She continued admiring the flowers. "I have these in my backyard at home. I just think they're so lovely." She looked up, and for a moment, her sapphire eyes shimmered in the waning sunlight.

Ryan shook his head slightly. "I'm sorry. You were saying?" He set the menu on the table.

"I just said that these flowers are my favorite. It's funny. They're so delicate, yet they're a pretty hardy wildflower."

He watched her pick up the glass vase and inspect the small bundle of flowers. "Yes. Yes, they are."

She set the vase back in the center of the table and looked up at Ryan. "Thank you so much for all you've done for Caleb. I can't tell you how comforting it is to have someone with us that speaks the language so well and knows the system."

"No problem. I'm happy to help." He looked up at the young boy who set their drinks on the table along with a basket of

Chapter Twelve

tortilla chips and a dish of salsa. *"Gracias."* Ryan picked up his soda and took a sip. Leaning back in his chair, he crossed his legs. "I used to wonder why we had to take Spanish in high school. Now I'm grateful I did, but I sure wish I'd paid more attention."

Jessica laughed lightly. "You know what they say about hindsight."

"True."

As the waiter returned for their order, Jessica hastily picked up the menu and scanned it. She glanced over at Ryan with raised eyebrows and a questioning look.

He shrugged his shoulders slightly, turned an apologetic palm up in front of him, and shook his head slightly. "I always order the Mexican. I thought I'd have *filete a la plancha*."

"Okay. Well, then..." She started hesitantly, eyes moving rapidly from Ryan to the waiter, "I guess I'll have what he's having."

"Si, Senorita," smiled the waiter as he scribbled the order on his pad. *"Eso es una buena opción.* A good choice." He picked up their menus and left them alone to resume their conversation.

Jessica turned to Ryan. "So what did I order?"

He chuckled. "Grilled fish in a spicy green sauce. It comes with rice and vegetables usually."

"Ooh! I did make a good choice!"

Their conversation was light, avoiding the deep concerns within both of them, and in less than ten minutes, their dinner was set before them.

"This looks delicious!" exclaimed Jessica as she bent over slightly and inhaled the aroma of the food.

Ryan quickly offered a prayer of thanks for their meal, and they continued their conversation as they ate. He swallowed a bite of fish and wiped his mouth with a napkin. Reaching for his drink, he asked, "So, do you like it?"

Jessica swallowed a bite of fish and answered truthfully, "It's a bit spicy, but it's good."

By the time the sun had set, they had finished their meal and were ready to return to the hospital. They walked back across the street and followed the sidewalk leading to the main entrance of the medical facility.

"Caleb told me about your husband. I'm very sorry, Jessica."

She looked up at Ryan and managed a weak, but sincere smile. "Thank you. I just never thought Nick wouldn't come home..." Her voice trailed off. "He was a good man. A wonderful husband." She stopped and turned toward Ryan. "Listen to me. I'm rambling on. I'm sorry."

"It's okay, Jessica. Sometimes it's good just to share your thoughts with someone else. Let's sit here for a minute." He motioned to a bench near the entry of the medical center.

They sat in silence for a few moments. A gentle breeze caressed the early evening air as the far-off cry of a macaw could be heard.

"I really miss him." Her voice was barely audible, and she stared out at the city street. "And now this happens to Caleb. Why is God letting this happen?"

Ryan shook his head. "I don't think I have an answer for that."

Jessica's sad eyes misted over as the earlier brightness in them faded. "How do you keep your faith when things like this happen?"

Ryan took a deep breath and thought carefully. "Right now, your heart is broken; your outlook on life is shrouded in sorrow, and your faith is being tested to its limits, or so it seems. It's an awful lot to expect someone to go through on his or her own. You have to hold on to the truth of God's Word, and then you reach out to those you know are there for you, those who are standing strong in their faith and can carry you when you can't carry yourself. Right now, the one thing you probably most want to do is crawl under a rock and be left alone with your grief, but you can't. You have responsibilities, family, work, friends. So you automatically go through the days. No one really knows what you're going through inside if you don't let

Chapter Twelve

them see how difficult the journey is. But, it's not enough to just survive, Jessica. You need to find a way to live again.

"You must hold on to that which you know is true, no matter how you feel. The truth is..." He looked into her teary eyes and spoke with confidence. "The truth is God does love you. He's not punishing you for something you did or didn't do. He's not trying to break you for some ethereal purpose. But Satan is. He'll fill your head with doubt, confusion, fear. Trust God, Jessica. Allow the Holy Spirit to bring to the forefront of your mind all those Scriptures you've read and memorized. He alone is your refuge and strength, and your help in time of trouble. When you feel like you're drowning, hold tighter to God's hand. He won't let you go."

She stared at him in amazement. "Seems like you understand exactly how I feel."

Ryan's dark blue eyes clouded for only a second and then he softly answered her. "Well, I've been there."

It took a moment for Ryan's words to register in her mind. *I've been there?*

"What do you mean 'you've been there'?" she whispered somewhat apprehensively.

Silence hung between them until Ryan cleared his throat and quietly admitted, "I was married once."

Jessica stared at him, her mouth slightly open, and her eyes glued to his face. Hesitantly, she asked, "What happened?"

"She was expecting our first child. Her labor was complicated. The only doctor was hours away in Veracruz. By the time I got her there, there wasn't anything they could do. Placentia abruptio, they said. I lost her and our daughter that night. They both died in my arms."

"Oh, Ryan, I'm so sorry," murmured Jessica. She struggled to keep her tears from falling.

"I was numb for quite a while. Ready to quit the ministry. Hide under that rock so to speak. I couldn't imagine a life without Gabriela. And I was angry. Angry with God. Angry with myself. Angry at everybody. And then Scott came. My brother. He had come for the funeral, but he stayed with me until I could move past just surviving."

"Your brother? The one that was Maggie's first husband?" Her eyes rose questioningly.

Ryan nodded. He leaned forward, resting his arms on his knees. Looking forward, he continued. "Yes. He let me talk, and when I talked, he listened. And then he talked, and I listened. He showed me through God's Word that God was still on my side. In fact, he made me understand that God wasn't responsible for Gabriela's death, but sin was. Not sin in her life, but sin in this world. He kept talking to me until I was able to understand that we live in a sinful world, and sometimes, bad things happen. And sometimes, they happen to God's people."

He spoke from his heart, and his vulnerability touched Jessica. She sat perfectly still, quietly listening to him bare his soul to her. She studied his face as he talked. There was no anger there, no sadness, no despair. All she saw was a man who loved and trusted his God. A man who had walked through the valley of the shadow of death and had emerged victorious at the other side. Her respect for Ryan grew as she continued listening to him.

"Jessica, I can't tell you why God allowed Nick to die, any more than I can explain why He allowed Gabriela or Scott to die, but I can tell you that no matter what happens in my life, good or bad, God will continue to be my God. I put my trust in Christ a long time ago, and that's not going to change. My faith is based on His Word, and it tells me to 'Trust in the Lord with all thine heart; and lean not unto thine own understanding. In all thy ways acknowledge Him, and He shall direct thy paths.' So, that's what I choose to do. It's not always easy, but it's my 'reasonable service.' He's brought me this far, and I know He'll see me through anything that comes my way."

"So it gets better?"

"Better? I don't know if that's exactly the word I'd use. For me, I can say it doesn't hurt as much as it did before. I can talk

Chapter Twelve

about it without as much pain. And God has given me a secondary purpose for being here."

Jessica straightened up as realization dawned upon her. "The clinic! That's why you decided to build the clinic!"

Ryan smiled as he turned to face her. "Yes. I didn't know how I'd accomplish it, but by the time Scott left, we had a pretty good plan. I figured if it was God's will, it would eventually come to fruition in His time. It's been a slow process, but we're getting there." The sadness had left his face, and he was able to smile at Jessica again.

"Your brother, he helped you reach that understanding?"

"Yes."

"He sounds like a wonderful man. I wish I could have known him." Jessica squeezed Ryan's hand. "Thank you for sharing that with me."

"You're welcome." He stood up. "You ready to go see Caleb?"

She rose to her feet. "I am."

Together, they walked into the hospital.

****

"Caleb?" Jessica spoke softly. "Caleb?"

The rhythmic beeping of the cardiac monitor at the side of his bed was the only sound in the room.

Jessica looked at Caleb, who remained asleep, despite her intense desire to talk with him. She mentally interpreted the numbers on the monitor, and satisfied with the information they conveyed, left the room.

She walked to the ICU waiting room and found Ryan sitting in a dimly lit corner reading his Bible. She glanced around, but other than him, the room was empty. He looked up when she approached him.

"Is he okay?"

"Sleeping. I thought it best to let him rest until tomorrow." She sat down next to him. "You really should go home and get some rest." She tapped her watch. "It's almost 9:00."

Ryan closed his Bible. "I wanted to wait until I knew how Caleb was, and how you were doing."

"We're both fine. I think I'll go to the hotel and maybe, just maybe get some sleep myself. I'm exhausted."

Ryan stood up. "Walk you out?"

"Yes. I'd appreciate that."

The moon was nearing its full phase, so their walk to Jessica's hotel was well lit. She kept up with Ryan's long strides, but found herself slightly short of breath by the time they reached the hotel lobby.

"Thank you, Ryan," she began. "For everything today."

"You're very welcome. Promise me you'll try and get some rest, okay?"

"I promise. I'll probably be out the minute my head hits the pillow."

He left her standing in the lobby, and she watched him exit the hotel and cross the parking lot.

She walked over to the elevator and pushed the button. While she waited, she thought about the things Ryan had said to her.

Can life be good again, Lord? Without Nick? With Caleb never walking again? Please give me the courage to face tomorrow, Lord.

CHAPTER THIRTEEN

Jessica woke to the sunlight streaming across her bed. Her eyes darted around the room, finally coming to rest upon her still unpacked suitcase opened on the luggage stand.

She stifled a yawn, glanced at the clock on the nightstand, then bolted to a sitting position.

Ten o'clock! I've got to get to the hospital!

Jumping out of bed, she rushed into the bathroom. She frowned at the image in the mirror. Grabbing her makeup, she attempted to cover the dark circles under her eyes. They refused to hide.

Ugh! I look like...well, like I just woke up!

She ran a brush through her hair, but the uncooperative copper curls simply did their own thing, and Jessica gave up in frustration. Finishing her morning tasks, she scurried back into the main room and hastily donned a navy blue skirt and pale blue blouse. Hopping toward the room door on alternate feet, she pulled on a pair of low-heeled black sandals and headed toward the elevators. In less than fifteen minutes, she was rushing out the lobby doors to the hospital across the street.

As she hurriedly walked past the large glass windows at the hospital entrance, she viewed her reflection. Half of her shirt was hanging loose. She quickly tucked it into her skirt, taking a few moments to catch her breath.

I really need to exercise more.

As she walked through the main lobby of the hospital, her stomach protested its empty state. She wrestled with the decision of whether to forego breakfast or to head to the cafeteria for something light to eat. Her desire to see Caleb overrode the need for a morning meal.

I can eat later. Besides, that fish didn't seem to agree with me last night.

As she rounded the hallway leading to the entrance of the intensive care unit, Jessica neared the waiting room. She slowed down and peaked in.

Empty. I wonder where Ryan is. Maybe he's with Caleb. Maybe he's not here yet.

She continued to the nurses' station, and upon receiving permission, walked quietly to Caleb's room. Entering slowly, she saw her brother lying on his side with his eyes closed.

"Caleb?"

His eyes opened slowly. "Hey, Jess. How are you?"

Jessica sat down to be at eye level with her brother. "I'm good. How are you feeling?"

"Okay, I guess. The nurse gave me something for pain, I think. I'm not too sure. Gotta stay on my side for awhile." He closed his eyes again before speaking. "What day is today?" His speech was slow, but clear.

"Wednesday, and it's almost eleven o'clock in the morning."

"I am really thirsty. Do you think I could have some water?"

Jessica quickly scanned the room for anything that would indicate Caleb was designated as NPO status. If so, he would not be allowed anything to eat or drink, including water. Seeing no precautionary label, she poured some ice water into a cup and held its straw to his lips.

"Here you go, Caleb. Just a sip or two. Swish it around in your mouth before you swallow."

He followed her instructions, and as he whispered "Thanks," he closed his eyes once more and drifted off to sleep.

Chapter Thirteen

Jessica didn't know how long she had been sitting in the chair when a familiar voice seemed to beckon her from somewhere. It began quietly, then seemed to escalate in volume.

"Jessica?"

She felt a hand on her shoulder as she opened her heavy eyes. Ryan's face slowly came into focus.

"Good afternoon. How long have you been sitting here?" he asked in hushed tones.

Jessica looked around, then at her watch. It was 12:15 pm. "Oh my!" She sat up quickly. "I've been here for about an hour and a half. I guess I fell asleep." She looked at her brother's bed. It was empty.

"Caleb?" Her voice held an edge of fear.

"I just passed him in the hall as they were taking him for some kind of test. He said you were in here sleeping, and he told the staff to let you rest. C'mon, let's go wait where it's more comfortable. It'll be a while before he's back." He led her to the waiting room.

Jessica shook her head disbelievingly. "I can't believe I fell asleep in there."

"Go easy on yourself. You've been under a lot of stress," reminded Ryan as he sat beside her on the black faux leather sofa. "You want a cup of coffee?"

"Do you think—" She unsuccessfully tried to stifle a yawn. "I'm sorry. Do you think I need one?" She smiled at him.

"I know I do." He stood and moved to the door. "I'll be right back. Take a nap if you feel like it. It should take me, oh, I don't know, five minutes or so." He grinned and walked out of the waiting room.

Jessica took a deep breath and exhaled slowly, coughing slightly as she did.

Just great. Now I'm getting a cold? That's all I need.

After a few minutes, she stood up and stretched, taking time to look out the window. Branches of palm trees danced in the gentle breeze, and cotton candy clouds dotted the afternoon sky. "And so life goes on," she stated somewhat introspectively. "No matter what happens to each one of us individually, corporately, we all move forward."

"Are you a philosopher now?"

Jessica turned around abruptly, coming face to face with Ryan. She felt her cheeks warm as she smiled meekly. "Just reflecting."

"Only cream." He held out a steaming cup of vending machine coffee.

She nodded and took the cup from him, murmuring a subdued 'thank you.'

"So what was that you were saying? Something about life moving forward?" He sat on the arm of the sofa and sipped his coffee.

Still embarrassed, she tried to explain. "Everything out there looks the same as it did yesterday and the day before. It will probably be the same tomorrow. The same trees are blown by the wind. The same white clouds will float by. Even the same people will pass this way. But in here, people are sick. Some die. Lives are being changed forever, and it doesn't matter how bad it gets, life out there just keeps on going. The world doesn't care that Caleb may never walk again or that your wife and brother and my husband all died."

Ryan studied the sadness reflected in the thoughtful blue eyes that looked at him. "You're right. The world doesn't care." He took another drink from his cup. "But God does, and that's what matters. God cares about each one of us personally."

"Do you think He really cares about whether or not Caleb will walk again?" Her words craved hope.

"Absolutely. I think God cares about each one of us. And He wants what's best for us." Ryan chose his words carefully. "That may not be what we think is best."

"You really believe that?"

"I do."

"Do you really believe that Gabriela dying was best for *you*?" challenged Jessica. She crossed her arms in front of her.

Chapter Thirteen

He sighed, then answered truthfully, "Jessica, I have never known as much hopelessness as I did when I lost Gabriela and our daughter. I had never been in such a dark place before, a place where all I felt was pain and emptiness and abandonment. But in the midst of my despair..." His voice was confident, and he took another deep breath. "I read Isaiah 41:10 over and over and over. 'Fear thou not; for I am with thee: be not dismayed; for I am thy God: I will strengthen thee; yea, I will help thee; yea, I will uphold thee with the right hand of my righteousness.' And I called on God again and again to give me the strength to go on."

He ran his fingers through his thick dark hair. "And then God reminded me that there was nothing I was going through that Christ hadn't already gone through for me. No sorrow, no loneliness, no abandonment that He hadn't already experienced. He knew what I was going through, and He was with me every moment that I was going through it, and as I continue to go through it.

"I had to believe that no matter what was going on, God would sustain me. I chose to believe His Word because I had to. It was all I had left, but it was more than enough to get me through undeniably the most difficult time in my life.

"So, to answer your question, I may not understand why things happen, but I do believe God allows things in our lives that will help us know Him, love Him, and serve Him better, and that is always best for us."

"Will I ever get to that place?" Her voice was less antagonistic as she wiped her weepy eyes with a tissue.

Ryan smiled in understanding. "If you let God help you, you will."

****

The golden sun had nearly disappeared below the horizon by the time Jessica and Ryan left the hospital for dinner. Elongated shadows stretched across their path, and only a faint glow could be seen through the buildings of the city.

Jessica had started coughing more as dusk approached, and now she was concerned about visiting Caleb again.

"I can't believe this," she lamented. "This is not the time to get sick."

Ryan put an arm out to stop her as she started to step off the curb. A white and green taxi sped by tapping its horn as it passed them. Jessica jumped and stepped backward.

"Oh! Thank you so much. I'm sorry. I should be paying attention, shouldn't I?"

"Only if you want to see another day," chided Ryan playfully. He gestured for her to cross the street.

Jessica kept pace with Ryan as they moved to the opposite sidewalk. "If I don't feel any better than I do today, I'm not too sure I want to."

"Are you feeling that bad? Maybe you should see a doctor tomorrow. There's an urgent care facility a few miles from here. I'd be happy to take you. At least you'd know if it was something contagious. Maybe it's just an allergy," suggested Ryan.

"That's not such a bad idea. It could be allergies, couldn't it?"

"Maybe. You are in a strange place, and if it is allergies, you won't need to worry about your visits with Caleb."

They entered a small seafood restaurant and were seated immediately at a table on the outside patio. A votive candle flickered as it sat deep inside a red beveled glass holder.

"This looks good," commented Jessica as she glanced at the menu.

"I don't get here very often, but it is one of my favorite seafood restaurants in Veracruz."

Her eyes peeked over the top of the menu. "Any suggestions for tonight?"

"If you like shrimp, I'd recommend the *camarones y pollo*. Grilled shrimp with a mild red sauce served over rice. However, if you prefer—"

Chapter Thirteen

Jessica grabbed a napkin, covered her mouth, and coughed. "Ugh! That's it. I'm going to see someone tomorrow."

He set his menu on the table. "Are you feeling up to dinner? Because if you're not, I can grab something quick for you to eat in your room."

She shook her head. "No, I'm fine really. It's just irritating me more than anything else."

"If you're sure."

"I'm sure." She took a sip of soda as a large basket of hot tortilla chips and two bowls of salsa, one red and one green, were set between them.

Ryan dipped a chip into the green one and popped it into his mouth. Jessica did the same, but as soon as she bit down on the chip, her eyes widened and watered, and she reached for her glass of diet soda.

"Sorry! I should have warned you. It's hot," apologized Ryan. His deep blue eyes reflected remorse as she hastily gulped her soda.

The heat of the salsa caused her to cough uncontrollably for a few seconds. Finally it subsided, and she was able to talk again.

"Hot? You call that hot? That's more like a ten-alarm fire!" exclaimed Jessica with a slight wheeze in her voice. She dabbed at the corners of her eyes with her napkin. "That was crazy!"

"Hey, be careful with that. You don't want to get any of the salsa near your eyes. They'll start burning, too." He raised his hand to cover his mouth.

Jessica glared at him suspiciously as she set the napkin back in her lap. "Are you *laughing* at me?"

"I'm really sorry," he stammered apologetically, trying to sound sincere. "You already had it in your mouth before I could say anything."

Jessica pursed her lips and drew in a breath to cool the salsa's heat. "You *are* laughing at me!"

Ryan shrugged his shoulders and stifled a chuckle. "You should've seen your face. It was priceless."

Jessica's eyes narrowed, and she shook her finger at him. "You just better hope I never have to remove your appendix. We'll see who's laughing then!" She smiled slightly, her lips tight together. "Okay, I suppose it was comical. I just thought green would be a milder salsa. Clearly, that wasn't correct."

"No," Ryan said under his breath. "It wasn't."

****

It wasn't long before their dinner was set before them. Laden with ten plump Gulf shrimp nestled in a bed of wild rice, Jessica's dish beckoned to her to take a bite. A red chili sauce, drizzled over the large prawns, caused Jessica to hesitate after she speared one. She glanced up at Ryan. "Is it safe?" she said as she sat poised with her fork in mid-air.

Ryan nodded, a hint of laughter in his voice as he answered. "This sauce is fine. It's got a mild spicy flavor, but it won't burn your tongue." He pulled the tail off one of his shrimp, cut it into two pieces, and ate it. "I think you'll like it."

Jessica gingerly bit into one of her shrimp, ready to wash it down with soda if the need arose. Pleasantly surprised, she swallowed and reported, "This is delicious!" She pulled the tail off a second one and munched on it a bit slower, savoring the flavor. "These are amazing!"

"I'm glad you like them."

They spent the rest of the meal trading more of their life stories, and as Jessica finished her *flan*, a light Mexican custard dessert, weariness began to take its toll. She stifled another yawn as she put her spoon down.

"I'm sorry. It's not even eight o'clock, and I can barely keep my eyes open. Even the caffeine isn't working," Jessica admitted as she finished the last of her after-dinner coffee.

"No apologies necessary. Let's get you to the hotel, and then I'll pick you up tomorrow around ten. We'll go to the clinic, and by the time you're finished there, Caleb should be awake,

Chapter Thirteen

and we can go see him. How does that sound?" Ryan pulled Jessica's chair back as she stood.

"That sounds perfect. I really appreciate you taking me tomorrow. Will you be my translator if no one speaks English?"

"Absolutely."

They walked down the street and turned the corner toward Jessica's hotel. Many of the shops were still open, and the avenue was still bustling with people going to and fro.

Ryan walked Jessica into the hotel lobby, said goodbye, and watched her enter the elevator. He stood there for a few moments, his hands in his pants pockets before exiting the hotel.

He walked out into the night air, and as he neared his truck, his cell phone vibrated. Pulling it out of his pocket, along with his keys, he looked up at the hospital building. Its seven stories were dotted with illuminations from patient rooms and hallways. He glanced at the text, put his keys back in his pocket, and walked toward the hospital entrance.

A couple of minutes later, he knocked lightly on the door to Caleb's room.

"Come in," came the reply. Caleb's eyes brightened when he saw Ryan.

"I got your text. What's up?" asked Ryan as he pulled up a chair.

"I've been doing some thinking, but I need some advice. Is Jessica with you?"

"No." Ryan shook his head. "She was pretty worn out, so she went to her hotel." He eased himself into the chair, crossed his legs, and relaxed back into it.

"Good. I kind of wanted just to talk with you," admitted Caleb as he maneuvered himself to better see Ryan.

"Okay. What's going on?"

Caleb cleared his throat. "I hate to sound like a pessimist, but remember when I said I liked to consider my options? Well, I'd like to get your thoughts on something." He swallowed hard, then continued. "If I can't ever walk again, how will I be able to serve God? I went to school to be a missionary. I majored in missions. I wanted to take the gospel to people that had never heard about Jesus, tell them about how much God loved them and wanted to save them. How can I do that if... if nothing changes?"

Ryan looked at the young man lying in the metal-framed bed and leaned forward in his chair. "Caleb, you understand that your accident didn't catch God by surprise, don't you?"

"What do you mean?"

"I mean, God had a plan for your life before this happened, and He has that same plan now. This accident, regardless of the outcome, didn't change those plans. He knew this was going to happen. In a sense, it was always part of that plan." Ryan waited for his words to sink in.

"You mean God wanted this to happen to me?"

"No. I didn't say that. I said it didn't take God by surprise. He didn't look down at you and wonder what He was going to do with you now that you were injured. His plan for you will continue despite this accident. Despite whether or not you walk again. If you surrender your life to God, He'll accomplish His will through it."

Caleb thought for a moment. "So, you're saying if God wants me to be a missionary, I should still plan on that? Even if it means being a missionary in a wheelchair?"

"Exactly. Where were you thinking of serving?"

"I don't know. Wherever God wanted."

"Really?"

Caleb cocked his head, and his brow furrowed as he pondered Ryan's question. "Well, yeah. Of course. I want to serve God, no matter where, but Bethany and I, well, we have talked about some places overseas."

"What if God's not calling you to some place overseas? What if His will for you involves some inner city gymnasium with kids that are disabled? Would you go there?" Ryan sat calmly with his hands in his lap while Caleb fidgeted in the bed.

"I... I never thought about that. I guess I always had a picture of some far off exotic land."

Chapter Thirteen

"There's nothing wrong with that, but there are other places that aren't quite as exotic that have people who need to hear the gospel, too. Downtown Los Angeles is just as needy as the jungles of Africa.

"Those kids in that gym, well, they need Christ, too. And who do you think they'd pay more attention to? Some guy like me, who walks in with a handful of tracts to pass out, or someone like you? Someone who understands exactly what they're going through. Someone who can tell them how Jesus helped him and made life meaningful when everything seemed hopeless. Who do you think God would choose to send to those kids?"

Caleb swallowed hard, his voice almost apologetic. "I... I get what you're saying."

"I'm not saying that's God's plan for you. I don't know what His plan is, but I do know He has one for you," stated Ryan confidently.

"What about Bethany?" asked Caleb.

"What about her?" Ryan tilted his head as he waited for the answer.

"Does His plan include her?"

"I can't answer that."

Caleb shook his head slightly. "I don't know anymore. If I never walk again, then she'll be stuck with... " He turned away from Ryan, then added, "...half a man."

Ryan waited for a moment, allowing time for God's Holy Spirit to lead him before he spoke. Then he said, "Caleb, your inability to walk doesn't make you any less a man than I am. Who a man is depends upon his relationship with Christ. It's that relationship that defines your character, your integrity, your heart. We're all flawed in one way or another. Some of those flaws may be more visible than others, but that's not how a man is measured.

"A man is measured by his words and his actions, and if that man lives for Christ, he stands tall with or without legs. There are many people who live full, happy, productive lives with disabilities. A disability can be mental, physical, or emotional, but regardless, your life is not invalidated because you have one. It continues to be precious in the sight of God, and if you let Him, He will use you to do great things for Him.

"Don't count yourself out because you've hit a stumbling block. The Bible tells us we can do all things through Christ. Not some things, but *all* things. God never said it would be easy, but it would definitely be doable. If you don't want to marry Bethany, you need a better reason than this accident, and if you want to be a missionary, go for it, but let God take the lead."

When Caleb turned back toward Ryan, his cheeks were wet. "I'm afraid, Pastor."

Ryan's lips came together in a thin line, and he nodded. "That's understandable, Caleb, but you need to remember that you're not in this alone. Jesus is with you, and He'll never leave your side. The Bible says 'Trust in the Lord with all thine heart; and lean not upon thine own understanding. In all thy ways, acknowledge Him, and He shall direct your paths.'"

"Easier said than done."

Ryan shifted in his chair. "Let me tell you about a time when I was scared."

****

By the time Ryan arrived home, it was well after midnight. He knew he would need to be on the road by seven-thirty the next morning, but he needed some time to unwind from the day. He strode over to the sanctuary, walked up to the front pew and sat down.

His mind replayed his conversation with Caleb, and he sighed. "Lord, please help Jessica and Caleb. I know You've got a plan for them, but they're struggling. Give them the strength they need to get through this. If there's anything I can do to help them, please show me."

How long he prayed, he didn't know, but when he had finally shared all that was on his heart with his Savior, he rose

Chapter Thirteen

and walked to his home, fell into his bed, and slept until his alarm woke him five hours later.

By the time he arrived in Veracruz to take Jessica to the urgent care facility, she was already dressed and waiting in the hotel lobby. She waved to him when he walked in through the revolving doors and walked over.

"Good morning!" he said. "You're looking much more awake than last night."

She smiled warmly as she strolled beside him into the morning sun. "I'm actually feeling much better. Maybe a good night's sleep was what I needed."

Ryan looked at her questioningly. "Are we still going to the clinic?"

Jessica nodded. "Yes, just in case this reprieve is only temporary." She lifted her face toward the sky. "This sun feels so good!"

He led her to his truck, parked in the passenger loading zone, and helped her to her seat. Sliding in behind the steering wheel, he put the truck in gear and moved out into the traffic.

"You might want to put on the seat belt," he cautioned.

"Are you that bad of a driver?" she asked, fastening the safety restraint.

"Not me," he explained, "but sometimes people or cars appear in front of you when least expected. I'd hate to have to explain how you broke your nose against my dash if I had to hit the brakes hard."

Jessica laughed. "That would be awful." She gave the belt an extra tug. "I am securely strapped in."

The drive was short, and within minutes, Ryan and Jessica were standing by the registration window of the urgent care clinic. A young girl with a head of black curls smiled up at them.

"*Buenas dias! ¿Puedo ayudarlo?*"

Ryan leaned over the counter closer to the woman. "*¿Habla usted Inglés?*"

"*Sí.* Yes, I do. How may I help you?"

Ryan turned to Jessica. "How's that for service?" He turned back to the girl and explained that Jessica needed to be seen for a continuing cough. The receptionist handed him a set of registration papers attached to a clipboard, directed him to complete them and return them when he was finished.

He gestured to two chairs. "Let's sit there." He handed Jessica the clipboard.

She lifted the pen to begin, then sighed.

Ryan glanced at her. "You okay?"

"Yes, but I'll need your help with this."

He took the clipboard from her and noticed the writing was only in Spanish. As he wrote her name on the top of the first paper, he said, "I promise I won't ask your weight or age, okay?"

"Deal."

He asked the questions and wrote her answers in the indicated lines. When finished, he gave the clipboard to the receptionist and returned to Jessica. "Do you want—"

"Señora Jessica Carr?"

Ryan and Jessica looked at a nurse who stood by a now opened door next to the receptionist's window. Jessica stood, but Ryan remained seated.

"Please come this way." The nurse moved to the side of the door as she smiled and gestured toward the corridor behind her.

Jessica turned to Ryan. "You're coming, right?"

"I thought since—" Suddenly aware of the uncertainty on Jessica's face, he rose. "Are you sure? Everyone seems to speak English."

"Yes, we all do," affirmed the nurse. "We treat many Americans. Dr. Santana speaks English very well."

"You okay with that?" Ryan asked.

Jessica thought for a moment. "You'll wait, right? And I can come get you if I need you?"

"Of course."

Jessica pressed her lips together and nodded. She followed the nurse to the treatment room, sat in a chair next to

Chapter Thirteen

the exam table, and scanned the room. The nurse closed the door behind her.

"My name is Lydia. I am Dr. Santana's nurse. You have a cough?"

Jessica nodded. "Yes, for a few days. No more than four or five, I think. I didn't really pay much attention to it until I started to feel rundown. It's not productive though."

Lydia looked over Jessica's paperwork, then began to pepper her with additional questions. As Jessica answered, Lydia entered the information into a computer.

"You are not from here?"

"No. I'm from California. I'm here visiting my brother. He's at the hospital."

"The hospital? He's sick?"

"No, he had an accident."

"He is doing okay?"

"Yes. He's getting better. I don't want to expose him to something that might make him sick."

"I understand. You are wise to see the doctor." She stood, placed a thermometer in Jessica's mouth, and then wrapped a blood pressure cuff around her left arm.

Jessica sat very still as the pressure in the cuff increased. She watched the sphygmomanometer dial as the air was released; the red indicator pulsated as the pressure dropped. Lydia finally removed the cuff and wrote the numbers on a piece of paper, and then removed the thermometer.

"Your blood pressure is very good, Señora." She popped the thermometer cover into the waste bin. "And you have no fever. Dr. Santana should be in shortly. Is there anything I can get for you to make you more comfortable while you wait?"

"No, thank you. I'm fine." As Lydia exited the room, Jessica pulled the sleeve on her blouse back down on her arm.

Within minutes, a short balding man in a lab coat entered. His bushy black moustache covered his entire upper lip, and he wore a pair of gold-rimmed glasses. The name "Miguel Santana, MD" was embroidered over the pocket of his coat.

"*Señora Carr. Encantada de conocerte.* I am Dr. Santana. It's a pleasure to meet you." He sat down on a rolling stool and flipped through the registration papers. "So you are not feeling too well?"

"It's just this cough, and I've been really tired. I'm hoping it's allergies plus jet lag. I don't really know. I'm here visiting my brother at the hospital, and I just need to be sure I'm not going to give him something I caught."

"I see." He perused her paperwork once more. "I just have a few more questions for you, if you don't mind." He smiled at her and as he did, his moustache curled up at the ends.

After Jessica answered several more questions for the doctor, he began the physical exam. Jessica obediently breathed in and out as the doctor moved the stethoscope over her lungs. She watched his face for clues to his findings, but the doctor merely moved the stethoscope and listened intently to another part of her lungs without any facial expression. Jessica took another deep breath, which triggered her cough reflex. She covered her mouth and coughed, while the doctor kept the bell of the stethoscope in place. He moved it to the other side and listened once more. Finally, he placed it over her heart while simultaneously reaching for her wrist. As he closed his eyes, he palpated her radial artery.

Hanging his stethoscope around his neck, Dr. Santana stood upright. "Señora, I would like to do some standard blood tests, urinalysis, and an x-ray of the lungs. *Un momento, por favor.*" He opened the door, then paused. "I'll be back in just a moment. I will tell your husband that he can come in to sit with you now."

Jessica's eyes widened. "He's not—" Before she could finish her sentence, Dr. Santana had closed the door. Jessica frowned.

Mental note: Always take time to listen to the patient before leaving the room.

In a few seconds, Ryan knocked and entered the room.

"Hey, everything okay?"

"Yes. He wants to do some labs and an x-ray. I hope I don't have pneumonia. That would certainly explain the fatigue and

Chapter Thirteen

cough." She sat quietly, looking at her hands now clasped in her lap. "This is definitely not a good time for this."

"I don't think it's ever a good time for pneumonia." He sat down across from her, leaning forward; his forearms resting on his knees.

"True." She shrugged her shoulders slightly. "Well, if it is, better to know now than later."

"You really think it could be pneumonia?"

"I don't know. Maybe, but I don't have a fever, so I'm still hoping it's allergies, but who knows?" She shrugged her shoulders again.

"Well, hopefully, it will be nothing major. Maybe you'll just need some antibiotics, a little cough medicine, and you'll be good as new."

"Always the optimist?"

"No point in being anything else."

"That's why it's so good being around you. You are so encouraging."

Ryan grinned. "I try. You know 'A merry heart doeth good like a medicine.'"

She laughed lightly. "Spoken like a true man of the cloth!"

He chuckled under his breath.

Jessica drummed her fingers on the cot upon which she sat. "I just don't have time to be sick. I want to get over to see Caleb."

Ryan nodded understandingly. "Hopefully, it won't take too much longer." He glanced at his watch.

Within minutes, Lydia came back in to draw the blood needed for the lab. She smiled. "Just a little stick, *Señora*."

Jessica smiled. "It's fine." She pushed up her sleeve, held out her left arm, and watched Lydia apply a tourniquet. She turned her attention back to Ryan. "How's the building coming along?"

"Great. The kids are doing well. They're pretty hard workers. Of course, Akna keeps them well fed, so they're happy. I've kept them updated on Caleb, and they've been praying for him regularly. Bethany spends more time here with Caleb than in Santa Molina, but that's to be expected. She's been a real encouragement to him."

"I've noticed."

Lydia released the tourniquet and put a small dressing and bandage on the site of the blood draw. She handed Jessica a small cup. "Come with me, and I will show you the bathroom."

Jessica pulled her sleeve back down on her arm and stood up. "This just wasn't in my plans."

Ryan nodded. "Sometimes His plans aren't the same as ours."

Jessica smiled teasingly. "Did you just put on your 'pastor' hat again?"

"I never took it off."

Jessica smiled as she followed Lydia. "I'll be right back."

****

"How long has it been?" asked Jessica.

Ryan checked his watch. "About forty minutes."

"I really want to see Caleb."

"I'll go see what's taking so long. I'll be right back."

He left Jessica sitting in the room and rounded a corner nearly bumping into the doctor. "Dr. Santana, I was wondering about how long before the x-rays are taken?"

"Ah, I was just coming to talk with you both. Based on the lab tests, no x-rays at this time." He grinned and extended his hand. "Congratulations!"

Ryan hesitantly shook the man's hand. "For what?"

"You are going to be a father!"

Ryan stood speechless, his mouth slightly agape. He shook his head slightly, then stammered, "I… I'm sorry. What did you say?"

"The test is positive. The *señora*… she is going to have a baby. I do not want to do an x-ray because of this, and also I do believe the cough is most likely related to allergies. Her lungs sound clear and the white blood cell count is normal, so no indication of any serious lung problem or any other infection, but I

Chapter Thirteen

saw signs of allergies in her nasal and throat passages. I would recommend fluids, but no medications unless approved by her obstetrician." He paused, waiting for a reaction, but Ryan said nothing. "*Señor?*"

Ryan snapped out of his fog. "I'm sorry. Yes, of course. I need to tell Jessica."

"Of course, *Señor*. I will give you two a moment alone. I will be right here if you need me."

Ryan took a deep breath and regained his composure before entering the room. He forced a smile as he walked in, closing the door behind him.

"Did you find him? Does he have the results?"

"Yes. I… uh, I just spoke with the doctor. He said your white blood cell test was normal, and he didn't believe there was any pneumonia—"

"No pneumonia? Great! So can I have an antibiotic and maybe some kind of steroid for the cough?"

"No. No medications." Ryan swallowed hard.

Jessica studied Ryan's face.

Something's definitely wrong.

Her stomach tightened, and her breathing began to increase as her anxiety rose. She took a deep slow breath and waited. "So what is it you're not telling me?"

He thought for a moment, sat down beside her, and reached for her hands. "Jessica, there's really no easy way to tell you this. The blood tests had some unexpected results."

Jessica's apprehensive eyes focused on his face. "What's wrong? Tell me, please."

"He says," Ryan hesitated, then stated. "He says you're pregnant."

CHAPTER FOURTEEN

They sat together on a bench in the hospital courtyard. The sun was now high in the sky, but the cool sea breeze caused Jessica to shiver. Ryan didn't ask for permission; he just put his jacket over her shoulders. She sat unmoving, not saying anything as Ryan silently prayed for words to ease her mind.

Finally, he spoke. "He said he ran the test because you complained about fatigue, and that he ran it only to rule out a pregnancy. He didn't expect the results to be positive, since your history didn't really support it," explained Ryan, even though Jessica hadn't asked.

"I can't believe it." Her voice was monotone and barely above a whisper. "It never crossed my mind that I could be pregnant. I just can't believe it."

Tentatively, Ryan shared his concern. "Jessica, maybe you shouldn't be alone right now. Maybe you should come back with me to Santa Molina and stay there for a day or so? We've got plenty of room. You can have your own cabin. You won't have to socialize if you don't want to, but I'll be there if you need anything. Plus, Akna's there; she's a good one to talk to if you need someone to listen, and I promise I'll bring you in to see Caleb any time you want." He waited for her to answer.

Finally, she turned to him, and with troubled eyes, she nodded. "Thank you. Maybe that would be good for now." Her trembling voice was just above a whisper, but the absence of joy was deafening. "Promise me…"

Chapter Fourteen

"Anything."

"Promise me you won't say anything to Caleb or anyone else, okay? Not yet."

"I promise."

And then, she started to cry. She buried her face in his shoulder and sobbed.

Ryan hesitated for only a moment, then put one arm around her and held her gently as she wept. The wind continued to blow, the sun kept shining, and the world passed them by, unconcerned with the heartbreak of one individual.

****

Half an hour later, Jessica felt ready to go see her brother. They entered the hospital and walked quietly through the main corridor.

"How do I look?" Jessica stopped by a glass window and studied her reflection. "Do my eyes look like I've been crying?"

"A little, but maybe it's only because I know you have been," answered Ryan honestly as he stood behind her scrutinizing the same reflected image.

She took a deep breath, then turned to him and smiled. "Think he'll notice?"

"I doubt it. Guys tend to miss those kinds of things. At least I always did," admitted Ryan.

She took a deep breath just outside Caleb's door. "Here goes," stated Jessica as they entered his ICU room.

Caleb was sitting up in bed chatting with Bethany, who sat in a chair while holding his hand. He smiled when Jessica and Ryan entered the room. "Hey, Jess! How are you feeling? Did you get enough rest?"

"Yes, I think so. Hi, Bethany. Anything new?" asked Jessica as she sat down, ignoring the look of concern from Caleb's fiancée. Ryan moved to stand behind Jessica, his hands resting on the back of her chair.

Bethany cocked her head slightly as she studied Jessica's face. "Not really. Yesterday, they did another nerve study. No results yet, but Dr. Romero seemed optimistic. And the physical therapist started some exercises."

"It's good to not be stuck in this bed all the time. I just wish this IV could come out. It's aggravating," grumbled Caleb with a lopsided grin.

"You must be feeling better if you're complaining about something," noted Jessica.

"After Pastor Ryan and I talked last night, I am better."

Jessica turned her head and cast a quizzical look upward at Ryan. "Last night?"

Ryan explained. "You turned in early, remember? I dropped by for a short visit before I headed home."

Caleb nodded. "I'm sure glad you did. I shared some of what you said with Bethany."

"I'm glad it was an encouragement to you," said Ryan.

"Yes, thank you, Pastor," echoed Bethany. "I haven't seen Caleb this content since the accident." She paused for a moment, her cheeks reddening. "We've been able to move forward, too." She looked lovingly into Caleb's eyes.

Jessica looked apprehensively at her brother.

He grinned. "Don't look so alarmed. This shouldn't be such a surprise. You knew I was thinking of getting married after grad school, well, we just decided to keep our plans on track… no matter what happens." He looked over at Bethany and squeezed her hand. "I won't let her set a date though until I get her a ring."

"Must have been a powerful talk you two had last night," teased Jessica with a slight smile. "Congratulations to you both!" She leaned over the bed and kissed Caleb on his cheek. Walking over to Bethany, she wrapped her arms around her and said lovingly, "I'm finally going to get a sister!"

Bethany smiled shyly. "Thank you, Jessica," she said softly. "I want you to know that no matter what happens, whether he

Chapter Fourteen

walks again or not, I will love Caleb with all my heart for the rest of my life."

"He is very, very blessed to have you in his life," affirmed Jessica as she hugged her once more. "Welcome to our family!"

****

"So you talked to my brother last night?" asked Jessica as she sat down in a corner table in the hospital cafeteria. She poked her fork into a large mixed green salad, playing with the vegetables.

Ryan answered without looking up from the roast beef sandwich he was cutting in half. "Yes."

"What did you two talk about?"

"He had some questions about his future."

"Is he going to be okay?"

"I think so. He has a good support group." Ryan took a bite out of his sandwich, then wiped his mouth with a napkin. "You really should eat something."

Jessica continued to move the lettuce around on her plate. She nodded as she put a forkful of greens into her mouth. "I feel so disconnected. Like everything that's happening is not really happening to me. The accident, a baby, and now, Caleb's getting married." She set the fork down and stared at Ryan.

"It's an awful lot to take in, Jessica."

She nodded, somewhat automatically. "How can I help Caleb now, while I'm carrying a child?"

"What do you mean?"

"I want to be there for him, but now, I have to be there for this little one." The solemn look on her face concerned Ryan.

"Why can't you do both?"

Jessica shrugged. "I don't know. When I think about what Caleb might have to go through, I want to be there for him. You know, help in whatever way I can. What if I can't do it all?"

"Then someone else will," Ryan said matter-of-factly.

"Who?"

Ryan sat back in his chair. "Jessica, you're not the only one in the world who can help Caleb recover."

Jessica eyes narrowed as she looked up at him through her long, black lashes. She opened her mouth to speak, then shut it quickly before saying anything. She looked down at her plate.

Ryan leaned forward on the table. "You do understand that God does have a plan, don't you? And it's a plan that nothing can thwart."

The frustration in her eyes betrayed her artificial smile. "I guess so. Maybe."

Ryan put down his sandwich. "No. There is no 'maybe'." He pushed his plate away from him. "None of this, Caleb's accident, your pregnancy, took God by surprise. It's all been allowed by God to fulfill His plan in Caleb's life and in yours."

"What if I don't like the plan?" she asked bluntly as she stabbed a small grape tomato.

Her response caught Ryan a little off guard, and he sighed deeply before responding. "Well, I suppose you'll have to take that up with God." He sat back and took a sip of soda as he watched her play with her food.

Finally, he spoke. "Jessica, I know it's overwhelming right now, but this is the time you need to trust God the most."

She looked up at him and frowned. "Right."

He ignored her glare and continued. "You know, the Bible is full of stories about people whose plans changed for various reasons, and they had to trust Him for the outcome."

Jessica set her fork down and glanced away from him. "It would be a lot easier if I knew how the story ended."

"We're not often privy to that. We're told to live by faith, not sight, and frankly, that's not an easy thing to do, especially when the unexpected happens in our lives."

She turned back to him. "So you really believe that Caleb's accident is part of God's plan for his life?"

"I didn't say that," said Ryan firmly. "I do believe if we're living for the Lord that His plan for each of us cannot be thwarted by what happens to us in this sinful world. So, in

Chapter Fourteen

regards to Caleb, I definitely believe God's plan for his life is still intact, paralysis or not. Whatever God wants Caleb to do will not be hindered by this accident unless—"

Jessica looked at Ryan. "Unless what?"

"Unless Caleb allows it to." Jessica's mouth curved downward as she pursed her lips and shook her head.

What is that supposed to mean? Sometimes Ryan, you can be so frustrating.

Ryan took a sip of water, then set the cup down as he explained. "God's will for Caleb will be accomplished if Caleb allows God to lead him."

A pair of skeptical blue eyes accompanied her confrontational query. "So whatever God has planned for my life will still happen regardless of Nick's death or this baby's birth?"

Ryan's eyes never wavered from her face, nor did their compassion fade. "Yes, if you submit to His will. You see, God's plan moves us from point A to point B. Along the way however, there are detours, and the road winds around them. Some of those detours are illnesses, problems with family or friends, accidents, financial woes, personal choices. There are a myriad of things that try to throw us off course. Many of them are simply a result of living in this sinful world. Others are attempts by Satan to draw us away from God, to plant seeds of doubt. Sometimes, unpleasant things happen in our lives, and God allows them for different reasons, but all to help us get to where He wants us to be."

"So the road is never direct?" She crossed her arms in front her and sat back in her chair.

"Rarely. It's those bumps in the road that help our faith grow. Those detours help us learn to trust God more. Think of it like a long road trip. You know where you're going, and you're driving along, when all of a sudden, there's a sign directing you to an alternate route that promises something more interesting. You know you should stay on the main road, but you decide to take that little side trip, not realizing that it may lead you to a place that's far from your original destination, and you have to backtrack to return to the main road to get on the right path again.

"At other times, those detours are just an inconvenience. We are forced to go another way due to circumstances beyond our control. That detour may take you where you didn't really want to go. Most of us grumble and complain, but we follow the signs and eventually end up back on the right path.

"Some refuse to heed the warning signs and plow on straight ahead. Whatever looms further on usually leads to disaster. Maybe a bridge has washed out, or part of the road is missing.

"Well, we have the same kind of thing in life. Our journey through life leads us toward our heavenly home with Christ, but there are a lot of twists and turns as we travel. As I said, some of those detours are directly from Satan himself, while others are just a natural part of life, and some are from God. But no matter where those detours originate, the Bible says that God causes *all* things to work together for good to them that love God. If we trust in the Lord to guide us through, our faith will emerge stronger for it."

Jessica thought for a moment, then questioned him once more, her voice less antagonistic. "So *everything* will work out?"

"If you trust God and allow Him to lead you, everything will definitely work out. It has to. God promised it, and He always keeps His word," stated Ryan with certainty.

She rearranged the lettuce on her plate, then looked up and pointedly asked, "Has everything worked out for you?"

Ryan studied Jessica's face before responding. The sincerity in her eyes removed any doubt he harbored in sharing his innermost feelings with her. "Everything is working out for me, but it's a work in progress, and it's not exactly how I thought my life would be. I don't think I'll ever know exactly why the Lord took Gabriela when He did until I get to heaven, but I do know my life didn't end that night, even though I thought it would. I don't know what tomorrow holds for me, but I know

Chapter Fourteen

that God has a purpose for me here. If He didn't, He'd have taken me home, too."

Jessica's eyebrows rose slightly, and a long pause in their conversation passed between them. Ryan sat quietly, allowing Jessica time to process his words.

Finally, she took a deep breath. "I never thought about it like that." She tilted her head slightly as she spoke. "That makes sense to me. If God was finished with me here, I guess He would take me to heaven because my work for Him would be done. So, He really does still have a plan for me, and Caleb, and this baby?"

"I believe He does."

For the first time in a long time, Jessica felt a glimmer of hope inside her heart.

****

The next morning, Jessica awakened to the not-too-distant crowing of a rooster. She opened her eyes, and as the fog of sleep lifted, she glanced around her sparsely decorated room, remembering she was in Santa Molina. Another loud call from the unseen fowl reluctantly stirred Jessica into action. Stretching her arms above her head, she swung her legs over the side of the bed and moved over to the window. Peering out, she saw her morning alarm clock strutting around outside her cabin.

"Aha! There you are, you scoundrel. Not everyone gets up with the dawn, Mr. *El Pollo Loco*," scolded Jessica. The rooster flapped his wings defiantly, stood ramrod straight on his legs, and emitted another loud squawk.

Jessica laughed. "Okay, okay, you crazy chicken! You win, I'm up."

She stood, and with her feet clad only in socks, she padded her way to the door. Partially opening it, she peeked outside and saw several other small buildings nearby, a house in the distance, and what appeared to be a church.

Courageous Love

I don't even remember the ride here. I must've really been tired.

She walked into the bathroom, stood by the sink, splashed water on her face, then vigorously brushed her teeth. Looking into the mirror, she tried to fluff her unruly curls.

I look horrible. Ugh! Please let there be a scarf in my bag.

She scowled at her reflection, then turned away and walked back to the bed. Pulling out a denim skirt and a white eyelet peasant blouse from her overnight bag, she dressed quickly. She dug into the bag once more and found a white scarf, which she knotted into a makeshift head covering, tying it securely at the nape of her neck.

"Shoes. Shoes. Where are you?" She lifted the bedspread and spied her white sneakers under the bed. She put them on, straightened her skirt, then went into the courtyard. Noticing Ryan's parked truck, she headed in its direction.

He's got to be here somewhere.

As she walked through the courtyard, she felt something in her shoe. Spying a small wooden bench beneath the thick foliage of a ceiba tree, she ambled over and sat down. As she pulled off her shoe, a small pebble fell to the ground. From somewhere in the canopy of the trees came the screech of an animal that was yet to be seen. Nervously, she slipped her foot back into the sneaker and quickly tied the laces.

What was that?

Jessica scanned the perimeter of the courtyard. The flutter of wings could be heard, and when she turned toward the sound, she saw a flash of red disappear into the nearby jungle.

"Hey there!"

Jessica jumped, then turned toward Ryan's voice.

"I'm sorry. I didn't mean to startle you." He sat down beside her. "You're up early." He wore a pair of worn jeans and a gray shirt with the sleeves rolled up.

"Yes, I am. Thanks to Mr. Rooster, I am wide awake." She looked toward the abundant vegetation at the courtyard's edge. "What was that sound I heard earlier? Was it a bird?"

Chapter Fourteen

Ryan followed her gaze toward the rainforest. "Probably a monkey or a macaw. Nothing to worry about."

Jessica smiled in relief. "That's good to know. Besides, it wasn't nearly as loud as that rooster!"

"I'm sorry. Paco's been here a long time, ruling with an iron beak, so to speak. He was a gift to us from one of the villagers. The intent was for us to have a hearty meal, but Gabriela refused to let me kill it. Now, we all suffer for it," he explained with a crooked grin.

"Well, he's very efficient at his job."

As if on cue, the multicolored rooster pranced across the courtyard, then flapped his wings and crowed once more.

"Does he have a hen to keep him company?"

"No. He's a bachelor. Way too ornery for a hen to put up with him, I suspect."

Jessica watched the proud bird scratch in the dirt, then said, "I probably didn't thank you last night for your concern and your generosity in allowing me to stay here."

"You're welcome. As you can see, we've got plenty of room here." He gestured toward the group of guest cabins from the area she had stayed the night. He then pointed to the house across the courtyard. "That's the parsonage. I live there. And that..." He indicated a wood-sided building. "That's the dining hall and a couple of offices. Over there, see that smaller building? The one with the planks against the wall? That's the clinic. And of course," he pointed to a large stone and wood building. "That's the church."

"Wow, this place is a lot bigger than I thought. You did all this?"

Ryan shook his head. "No, not me. I got the clinic going, but the rest has been here for several years. My brother and I helped build the parsonage when we were in high school. The church itself has been here for a little more than fifty years, but it's only been the last fifteen years or so that this whole courtyard was completed. It's been used for church camps during the summer, visiting missionaries, and I hope one day, we'll have a Christian school here, Lord willing."

"Sounds like you've got a lot of work to do."

"It does keep me busy. Are you up for breakfast? Akna, she's the groundskeeper's wife, she's the best cook I know, and breakfast is probably ready. She and her family live on the grounds over there." He indicated another building slightly beyond the dining hall.

Together, they walked into the hall, and Akna met them with a big smile. *"Buenas dias!* I am Akna. Welcome! Sit here." She hurried off into the kitchen and returned with two cups of coffee. "Pastor, he tells me you are the sister of Caleb? He is well now? Milk? Sugar?"

Jessica looked at Akna, then Ryan, then back to Akna. "Yes, I am his sister. Just milk, please."

Ryan quietly sipped the hot brew.

"I will bring you both something delicious for breakfast. You stay right here," ordered Akna as she disappeared into the kitchen once more.

"She's beautiful," whispered Jessica. "I don't think I've ever seen hair that black."

"She's of Mayan heritage. Combine that with the Mexican blood and you get that. She's a really kind lady, and she loves the Lord," informed Ryan, taking another sip of his coffee.

"Where are the others? I thought Caleb's friends were here," said Jessica as she looked around.

"They headed into Veracruz to see Caleb early this morning. I told them we'd be there a little later." He sat down across from Jessica. "Yesterday was a rough day, but you made it through."

She looked up at him and smiled gratefully. "Barely."

"Maybe, but you made it." He took another sip of coffee as Akna came out with two plates of scrambled eggs, fresh flour tortillas, pork sausage and salsa.

"If you need something else, you just call me, okay? I will be in the kitchen." She headed off, leaving Jessica and Ryan to enjoy their breakfast.

Chapter Fourteen

Jessica stared at her plate. "Goodness! Do you think she gave us enough food? I don't think I can eat all this."

"Just eat what you want. She has a tendency to pile on the food," explained Ryan as he poured some of the salsa on his eggs. "You'll never be able to say you left Akna's kitchen hungry."

Jessica took a small bite of the eggs, then set her fork down. "I can't believe this is all happening, Ryan. First, Nick, then Caleb, and now this. I can't even think straight." She moved the eggs around on her plate. "Having a baby, that's supposed to be a joyous thing, but I'm not feeling too joyous. I guess that makes me a pretty terrible person."

Ryan set his fork down. "You're not a terrible person, Jessica. You've been given an awful lot to absorb. It would be overwhelming for anyone. My advice for you is to just take everything one day at a time. Maybe even one step at a time."

"You make it sound so easy."

"Do I? I don't mean to trivialize it because it's not easy. Struggles are always a part of life, and they're rarely easy to navigate through."

"Maybe I just don't have the faith I should have. After all, lots of people go through hard times, some of them worse than what I'm going through, and they do just fine." She sat back in her chair and looked directly at him, her eyes searching his face. "How do they do it?"

Ryan swallowed his bite of sausage, then answered. "A couple of reasons, I think. One, they weren't alone. They had family or friends to help them. When I thought I couldn't go on, I had my brother. Deep in my heart, I knew he loved me unconditionally. I could share anything with him. My fears, my frustrations, whatever was inside of me. I knew he'd always be there for me. Secondly, and most importantly, they turned to the only One who could provide real comfort and peace… God. Something from His Word, or maybe just that still, small voice of His Spirit speaking to a needy heart."

"And it's different for each of us, right?"

"Probably, and probably for each situation as well. It's not easy to trust God when things are bad, but we need to try because in trusting God, we find peace."

"So much easier said than done," she sighed.

"Yes, it is. That's why we are so encouraged to build relationships with other Christians. To help us in our struggles. To bear one another's burdens. To pray for each other. Sometimes we have to allow other Christians to help us through the hard times."

Jessica nodded with a frown. "I wish I knew how to do that. We doctors tend to like to be in control of everything. And admitting when we're not, well, that's not easy for us. It tends to spill over into our personal lives, I think."

Ryan nodded in understanding as he took a bite of buttered tortilla. "I imagine it could be difficult."

Jessica's smile was half-hearted. "You have no idea." She bit into a piece of sausage. "I like to have a well thought-out plan, and I definitely don't have one now."

He chuckled. "No, you don't. But God does."

She sighed. "Yes, He does. My head tells me it will get better, but right now, my heart doesn't think that's possible. It's pretty overwhelming, and sometimes I feel like I'm alone."

Ryan studied her face. "Jessica, there's no way to predict the future, but I can promise you that from what I've seen, you're not going to face things alone. You've got a great family, good friends, and most importantly, you've got God."

"You're right. I do." She took a deep breath, then exhaled slowly. "And I have you."

He looked up quickly, his eyebrows slightly raised, then smiled. "Yes. Yes, you do."

She took another bite of eggs, followed by a sip of coffee. "Oh! I shouldn't be drinking this!" Setting the cup back on the table, she frowned as she shook her head. Her reddish curls danced around her face. "I've got to rethink so much. No coffee, no soda, no artificial sweeteners, ugh!"

Chapter Fourteen

Ryan brought his hand up to cover the erupting smile on his face. He quickly looked down at his plate.

"What are you laughing at?"

He responded without looking up. "Who? Me?"

"Yes, you. What's so funny?" Her narrowed eyes bore into Ryan's lowered head. "Well?"

He stood, picked up the plates, and moved toward the kitchen. "I probably should help Akna clean up."

Jessica watched him as he walked away and smiled to herself.

Thank You, Lord, for Ryan. I can't imagine what I'd do without him right now.

****

Jessica strolled into her cabin after leaving Ryan to his studying. She sat down on the edge of her bed and her hands moved to her abdomen. She gently moved them across her belly, knowing it was too soon to feel anything. As she sat and pondered her situation, doubts began to rise within her. A fearful frown appeared on her face.

"Why did You let this happen, Lord? It wasn't supposed to be like this. Not without Nick. It wasn't supposed to be me with a baby *alone*. And what about Caleb? I have to help my brother! How can I help him when I've got a baby to think about?"

Out of the corner of her eye, she saw her Bible on the nightstand. Reaching her hand out, she picked it up, and a piece of colored paper fell to the floor. She stooped down to retrieve it, opening it up to see her notes from a previous sermon written on the back of a church bulletin. She had scribbled, 'If God is your co-pilot, you ought to change seats.' It was circled in red. She sat back on the bed and stared at the quote.

"I'm not trying to fly the plane!" she argued.

Her thoughts began to challenge her. *More like wrestling for the controls.*

She scowled. "No, I'm not! It's just that this is more than I can handle."

With God all things are possible.

"If You think I can endure this, You've made a mistake," she countered.

God never makes mistakes.

"I don't even know which way to go. If You really knew me, You'd know I need a plan, but I've got nothing!" she maintained, sorrow threatening to engulf her.

"What am I supposed to do? How am I supposed to help Caleb when I can't even help myself? I can't raise a child alone. I'm a doctor. I work crazy hours. How am I supposed to do this?"

She dropped her face into her hands and sobbed, "Why don't You tell me what I'm supposed to do!"

Trust in the Lord with all thine heart and lean not unto thine own understanding. In all thy ways, acknowledge Him, and He shall direct thy paths.

"Oh really? Like that's supposed to be an easy thing to do?" She sat very still and moved only her eyes around the room. She looked up and down, then side to side. The guilt from her rampage with God stifled her voice, and meekness overcame her. "I'm so sorry, God," she whispered as she cried. "But I don't understand why You won't answer me. Please, I need to know what to do."

Ryan.

Jessica grimaced. "Ryan? I've already talked to Ryan." She got up and paced the floor, stopping at the door the third time she passed it.

Go talk to Ryan.

"He's studying. Besides, he's just going to tell me to trust You." She resisted the urge to go, but the conviction of her thoughts grew too strong for her to combat. Finally, after exhausting every other mental argument for not talking with him, Jessica hesitantly opened the door and stepped out into the courtyard.

Chapter Fourteen

"Okay, Lord. If that's really You, here goes my step of faith." Her skepticism was mingled with a touch of fear knowing her anger had been misdirected. She warily walked toward the dining hall. Reaching its door, she turned the knob and peered in.

"Ryan?" It was empty. She turned and went back out into the courtyard. Glancing over at his truck, still parked in the same place, she sighed, somewhat disappointed that it was still there.

Well, he's still here. But where? If I can't find him, I guess I won't have to talk to him.

She ambled over to the parsonage and knocked on the door. "Ryan? Ryan, are you in there?"

Where are you?

She turned around, put a hand to her forehead, and scanned the courtyard until her eyes rested on the church.

Of course.

As she entered the sanctuary, she saw him kneeling at the altar.

He's praying. I shouldn't stay.

She hesitated.

If I leave now, how will I know for sure that God's in this?

Despite feeling like an intruder, she resisted the impulse to flee. Instead, she sat down quietly, never taking her eyes off Ryan. In the stillness of the church, she could easily hear him, and tears began to fill her eyes.

His voice was strong and clear as he knelt in prayer. "Father, I can't tell you how much my heart hurts for Jessica. I cannot imagine what must be going through her mind right now. She has so much on her platter, and she is overwhelmed. Please envelope her in Your love. Place a hedge of protection around her. Strengthen her faith, and help her stand strong in it. Give her the courage she needs to face whatever lies ahead.

"Protect her child, Lord. It will be such a blessing to her. A reminder of the love she shared with her husband. Give her body the touch it needs to endure this time of pregnancy, especially these first few months. Bring people into her life to encourage and support her. Give her the energy she needs to do the things she needs to do, and work all things to good in her life."

After a few quiet moments, he finished his prayer and sat back on the front pew. He kept his head bowed and his hands clasped together, resting his arms on his legs.

Jessica hesitantly rose and walked softly toward the front of the church. As she neared him, she cautiously spoke his name. "Ryan?"

He came to his feet instantly and turned. "Jessica! Are you all right?"

"Yes. Yes, I'm fine. Ryan, I'm sorry I eavesdropped on you." She averted her eyes from his caring gaze. "It's just that when I heard you, I, well, I didn't want to interrupt and then..."

"No apologies necessary." He looked into her guilty eyes. "Really. It's okay. Did you need something?"

Jessica inhaled deeply. "Yes. I need your help."

"My help? For what?"

"I need you to help me stop flying the plane."

"What plane?" He looked at her quizzically. "What are you talking about?"

"Can we sit over there?" She moved into an adjacent pew.

Ryan sat down beside her and waited for her to speak.

"I guess I feel like I've totally lost control, and frankly, that terrifies me. I am helpless over everything that's happening to me, and God said I should talk to you."

Ryan lifted an eyebrow, and his mouth opened slightly. He shook his head as if trying to get rid of a pesky insect. "He told you *what*?"

"I don't mean He *spoke* to me, but you know, sometimes He puts ideas in your head. I mean, you get thoughts, and you just know it wasn't anything you thought of yourself, so then you decide it has to be God? Those kind of thoughts. Well, that's what I mean." She sat expectantly, looking up at Ryan.

Chapter Fourteen

Ryan's eyes narrowed as he studied Jessica's hopeful face. "Okay. I understand. What is it you're supposed to talk to me about?"

She took a deep breath and simply stated, "How to let God fly the plane."

"Fly the plane?" He looked at her bewildered, and cleared his throat. "Well, first of all, can you give me a hint as to where all this has come from?"

Jessica nodded. "After I left you, I went to my cabin and..." Her cheeks reddened as she admitted her tirade with God. "I yelled at Him."

His amused eyes widened slightly. "How'd that go for you?"

She smiled sheepishly. "I didn't get zapped with lightning, so I think it went pretty well, all things considered. I started thinking about everything that's been happening, and how to fix it all. After I was done ranting and raving, I saw my Bible, and I thought maybe if I picked it up and dropped it open, it would miraculously flip open to the verse that would give me the answers I needed, but instead, this note fell out. It said 'If God is your co-pilot, you should switch seats.'

"Maybe that was what I needed to read the most. I don't know, but it made me realize something was very wrong with my attitude. I don't think I've let God be in total control of my life, and I'm not sure if I really know how to do that, and I'm kind of afraid to let Him."

"I see."

"Wow, I was hoping to get more than that." A hint of a smile appeared on her face.

"Well, let's see if I can do better." He thought for a moment as he rubbed his chin. "Jessica, when you asked Christ to forgive your sins and become your Savior, you established a very special relationship with God. You became part of His family, a child of the King as Christians are often called. He's your heavenly Father. However, your obligation to God doesn't end when you get saved. As Christians, we are called to serve Him.

And as servants, we follow His lead. Not the other way around. Jesus said we were to pick up our cross and *follow* Him.

"Now, think about the relationship between a servant and the master. The master's responsibility is to take care of the servant's needs, and the servant's responsibility is to do what the master requests. The servant never goes out on his own, never tries to usurp the master's authority, but instead, in whatever he is asked to do, he does to the best of his ability. That's his reasonable service."

Jessica nodded in remembrance. "You mentioned that before. The 'reasonable service' thing." She leaned against the back of the bench. "How did you get to that point? How did you give up everything?"

"I haven't given up anything, really. Well, nothing that hasn't been worth giving up. When I made the decision to follow the first verse in Romans twelve, I made a conscious decision to trust God in that He would be a fair and just Master. I believed there would be nothing He would require of me that I wouldn't be willing to do or give up."

"Including your family?"

A brief glimmer of pain crossed Ryan's eyes, but he continued. "He didn't ask me to give up my family. They died as a result of living in a sinful world. Their deaths were not God's fault, just like Nick's death wasn't God's fault. The Bible tells me that God causes 'all things to work together for good to them that love God, to them who are the called according to His purpose.' I don't know yet what the 'good' is in their passing, but I choose to believe He'll show me one day." Ryan leaned forward, his forearms resting on his knees. He lowered his head and sat silently for a few moments.

"I'm sorry," she whispered. "I didn't mean to cause you pain."

"Jessica," he said, turning to look at her. "I don't know why God has allowed all of this to happen to you, but I am one hundred percent certain that He will eventually use it all for good if you let Him. Surrendering your entire life to God and giving Him complete control of the plane, so to speak, is a

Chapter Fourteen

choice that only you can make. I honestly believe if a person loves the Lord with all their heart, soul and mind, as Jesus said, that person becomes a living sacrifice and a devoted servant. When that happens, listening to and trusting God in every part of life becomes 'reasonable service.' In other words, you then let Him fly the plane."

"What do I do if He asks me to do something that's really hard?"

"What would a servant do?"

"I guess he would just do it."

"Yes."

"That's kind of frightening."

"It takes courage to accept the role of a servant. The servant must surrender his or her life completely to the Master. That's where the trust part comes in. You need to remember that God's your heavenly Father. He's not out to hurt you or cause you great heartache. He loves you. If He asks you to do something that's hard, it's only in your best interest, and He'll see you through it. Not only that, but He'll help you through it. Trust Him; He'll never lead you astray."

Her fearful blue eyes looked deep into Ryan's reassuring ones. "What if I *can't* do it?" Her voice was barely audible.

"Maybe *you* can't, but God can. He'll help you, and remember, God will never require something of you that He will not equip you to do."

She lowered her head and quietly recited Philippians 4:13. "'I can do all things through Christ which strengtheneth me.'" She looked up at him and hesitantly asked, "Will you keep praying for me?"

"I will."

Jessica stood as a timid smile spread across her face. "Thank you. Thank you so much. I wish I could tell you how much I appreciate you."

Ryan rose to his feet, and together they walked toward the back of the church. "Could I interest you in a ride to Veracruz?"

"I'd love that," she answered. "By the way…"

"Yes?"

"You told me that once you thought you wouldn't be a good pastor? You were wrong." She smiled sweetly, then headed toward her cabin.

CHAPTER FIFTEEN

Ryan and Jessica bumped along the road leading to Santa Molina and then to the larger highway that would ultimately end in Veracruz. Jessica held on tightly as they swerved around a large mud-filled hole in the middle of the road. Wide-eyed, she grasped the dash to keep herself in the seat.

Ryan glanced over at her and let his foot off the accelerator. "Sorry. I'll slow down a bit."

Jessica smiled gratefully. "I'd hate to see this road after a good rain."

"There's a lot more sliding around. It's kind of fun, if you like that sort of thing." He looked over at her, then added, "I guess you'd prefer a smoother ride?"

"Oh, why would you think that?" She laughed lightly as her curls bounced around her face.

"At least we don't have to dodge any livestock."

"Livestock?"

"Yeah, sometimes there's a donkey or a goat wandering down the road."

"Really?"

"Really. Sometimes I—" Ryan slammed on the brakes, and the truck groaned to a stop. He shifted into reverse and backed up a few yards. "Look!" He pointed up toward a large branch in one of the trees bordering the road.

Jessica squinted her eyes and scanned the area to which he was pointing.

"It's a howler monkey. See there? In the crook of that branch. That black— there he is! He's moving!"

Jessica's eyes widened when she saw the animal. "Oh my! It's staring at us!"

"Yep, he sees us."

At that moment, the monkey opened his mouth and began to grunt. Resonating through the tropical foliage, its low, guttural call rose in volume as the creature continued staring at Ryan and Jessica.

"He's telling us that this is his territory, and we need to stay clear."

"Is he dangerous?"

"Well, as dangerous as any wild animal, I guess. Usually, they're not aggressive unless they feel threatened. I've never had one attack me."

Ryan slowly maneuvered the truck forward, giving Jessica a better view of the animal. She steadily watched the monkey, her gaze fixed upon it, until it moved out of her visual range.

"That was amazing!" Her eyes sparkled as she turned to Ryan. "I've never seen anything like that! I can't believe I saw a real monkey!"

"They're all around us. You can hear their howls for two to three miles. Mostly in the early morning and evening."

"So that's what I've been hearing!"

Ryan scanned the vegetation on the sides of the road as they continued along, pointing out various tropical plants and one iguana, but they saw no more monkeys as they made their way to the city.

The narrow dirt road widened enough to allow two cars to pass as they approached the actual town of Santa Molina. As he drove through the rural village, he slowed down, watching for stray animals or children playing in the street.

While Ryan chatted about the people he obviously loved dearly, Jessica looked back and forth at the scenery. Small wooden homes at the edge of Santa Molina were randomly spaced in areas cleared of tropical vegetation, but as they

Chapter Fifteen

neared the center of the community, the homes were clustered closer together. Small stores dotted the main street, and Ryan always waved to everyone he saw.

He slowed down a bit as a skinny dog lumbered down the middle of the road, sniffing along the ground. He gave the horn a slight tap, and the pup looked up abruptly, then scampered off. As they continued through the village, they drove past a man pulling a donkey hitched to a cart laden with melons. The man waved at them, his smile broad and friendly.

"*Buenos tardes!*" Ryan called out as they drove by.

When he finally neared the far end of Santa Molina, he turned toward the major thoroughfare that would take them to Veracruz, Merging easily into the traffic, Ryan rested one arm on the door while steering with the other.

"I've been thinking," began Jessica as she relaxed back into the seat.

"Yes?"

"I think I need a flight plan."

"A flight plan?"

"Yes. Not one set in stone, though. After all, I'm just the co-pilot. But every pilot and co-pilot have to file a flight plan, right? Anyway, I thought maybe I'd run it by you. Get your thoughts on it?"

"Okay. Shoot."

"First of all, there's really nothing to do about the baby right now. I'll see an OB when I return to California. So, while I'm here, I'm going to focus all my efforts on getting Caleb well enough to travel, so he can finish his recuperation at home, if that's what he wants, which I hope he does. When I get home, I'll schedule an appointment with my OB, and after that, I'll decide more of what to do. So what do you think?"

"Sounds like you've come up with a pretty good flight plan."

"I do need to be proactive, right? I can't just sit around and make God do all the work, can I?"

"Proactive is good, as long as you remember who's in control, and you seek God's wisdom and will," reminded Ryan.

Jessica's eyes brightened. "That's exactly what I was thinking about! 'Be careful for nothing; but in every thing...'"

Ryan joined in with her as they finished quoting Philippians 4:6 and 7. "'by prayer and supplication with thanksgiving let your requests be made known unto God. And the peace of God, which passeth all understanding, shall keep your hearts and minds through Christ Jesus.'"

Jessica laughed lightly, then became somber. "Maybe, just maybe, there'll be a way they can find to safely transport Caleb back home for rehab treatments." Her voice waivered in its confidence, and she turned quickly to look out the window. "But I don't need to be worrying about that, right? Because if he has to have rehab here, well, God's got that covered, doesn't He?"

"Yes, He does." Ryan glanced over at her and saw her wipe her eye. "I will definitely be praying for that."

"You really do believe God cares about every little thing, don't you? I mean, He could fix all this, couldn't He?"

"Yes, He could," replied Ryan.

Jessica looked at him. "You really think so?"

"I know He's still in the miracle business, so I'm not ready to count Him out on this one," admitted Ryan. "Look, Jessica. I know it's hard to trust God right now. The obstacles Caleb is facing are tremendous, but you've got to hold on to your faith, and help support him when his faith wanes. Don't let the unexpected things shadow what you know to be true. God loves both you and Caleb, more than you or I can imagine, and He's at work in each of your lives right now.

"I don't have all the answers, and I'm sorry I don't, but someway, somehow, God will see you through all this. I promise you, I will pray for you every day until God gives you victory over this. I will pray for a hedge of spiritual protection around you; I will pray for your health and the health of your child, and I will pray for your heart, that it will be strong, yet surrendered wholly to the Lord. I promise."

"Thank you, Ryan. I can't tell you how much you mean to me." She sniffed as he handed her a tissue. "I don't know what

Chapter Fifteen

I'd do without you." She blew her nose, and then managed a weak smile in his direction.

****

Jessica sat quietly in her brother's room as Dr. Romero detailed the results of the latest tests that had been done on Caleb. "It is difficult to be optimistic with these results. You may want to get a second opinion when you return to the States," stated the doctor honestly.

Caleb pulled himself up in the bed and extended his right hand to the physician. "Thank you, Dr. Romero, for all you've done. I can't tell you how much easier you've made a very difficult time for me."

Dr. Romero shook his hand. "I wish I had better news for you, Mr. Merrick."

Caleb nodded. "Well, God's got something in mind for me. I guess He'll let me know what that is when the time comes. Thanks again."

As Dr. Romero turned to leave, he stopped and faced Caleb. "Young man, you are most remarkable in your faith. We must discuss it before you leave us."

Caleb glanced at Jessica, then back to the doctor. "I'd like that, Dr. Romero. I'd like that very much."

As the doctor moved toward the door, Jessica shook hands with him. "Thank you, Dr. Romero. You've been a real answer to prayer. May God bless you always." Her eyes followed him as he left the room, then she slowly turned her head back toward her brother.

"Jess? You okay?"

Jessica finally raised her head, her eyes filled with tears. "I'm so sorry, Caleb. It's just that, I was hoping for better news."

Caleb nodded. "I know. Me, too, but it could be worse." He looked at her compassionately.

"Worse?"

"Sure. I could've injured my neck; Bethany could've walked out; the doctors could've been inept. There's a ton of worse things."

Jessica stared incredulously at her brother. "You almost sound happy."

Caleb looked at her and grinned. "I am happy. Did you hear him? He wants to talk with me about my faith! I'm going to be able to share the gospel with my doctor. How cool is that? You've got to promise me you'll be praying for him."

"Of course I will, Caleb, but I meant—"

"I know what you meant, Jess. I can't explain it, but whatever happens, it'll be okay."

"How?"

"I've had a lot of time to lay here and think. First, I was really angry about everything. I kept thinking, 'why me?' How could God have let this happen? What did I do to deserve this? Then Pastor Ryan and I talked, and afterwards, the 'why me?' became a 'why not me?' There's really no special reason why I should be spared from hard times any more than anyone else. After all, God's only Son wasn't spared from pain and suffering in His life. I'm certainly not better than He."

He brushed his fingers through his hair, then continued. "I guess the most important thing Pastor Ryan told me was that this accident didn't take God by surprise. God didn't plan it, but He allowed it for whatever reason. My life is still in God's hands. Whatever He's got planned is still in effect, and since He knew this was going to happen to me, and He still called me to serve Him, this whole thing must fit into His plan somehow."

Jessica tilted her head and stared at Caleb. "So if you never walk again, you're okay with it?"

"Okay with it? I don't know about that. Sure, I'd rather be able to walk out of this hospital on my own, but if not..." He shrugged his shoulders. "It's up to God to find a place for me to serve Him from a wheelchair if that's what He still wants. I know it's what I want."

Jessica smiled halfheartedly. "You really believe that?"

Chapter Fifteen

Caleb looked at his sister tenderly. "I know it'll all work out. We can't see the big picture, but God can. We just gotta trust Him. It'll be okay. It's just a change in plan. Our plans, but not His. I know it's going to be hard sometimes. I'm pretty sure there'll be times I'll want to quit, but I've got Bethany and you, and Mom and Dad to help me through those times. And God, of course."

"Yes, we do have God, don't we?" She impulsively stood up and hugged her brother. "I am so proud of you, Caleb."

His grin broadened. "Thanks, Jess. You've still got my back, right?"

She laughed softly. "Of course. That'll never change. How about some coffee?"

"That'd be great, and if Bethany's here, would you ask her to come in? I need to talk with her."

"Of course."

Jessica left his room and stood outside watching the activity in the intensive care unit. It was still early, but the ICU never slept. Nurses were busy going in and out of rooms; technicians were already drawing blood; doctors had begun their rounds. She leaned against the wall and sighed.

What did Caleb say? God wasn't surprised by his accident? His plans for Caleb are still on track? Is that the same for me? Do You really have a plan for me, Lord?

She stood quietly, expectantly.

One day at a time. Trust God. He's in control.

She scanned the ICU one more time, then went into the waiting room before heading to the cafeteria for the coffee.

Ryan was sitting in a corner, reading His Bible. He looked up when she entered. "Everything okay?"

She walked over to him, leaned down, and embraced him.

His arms automatically went around her, but he didn't pull her close. When she stood, she wiped silent tears from her cheeks before she spoke.

"You are incredible." It was a simple statement, spoken softly, but her voice broke as soon as the words came out.

"What did I do?" He closed his Bible as Jessica sat in the sofa next to his chair.

"I don't know exactly what you said to Caleb that night, but he's facing a lifetime in a wheelchair, and your words have given him hope," explained Jessica. She continued to dab at her eyes with a crumpled tissue. "The doctor came in and said there wasn't much of a chance he would ever be able to walk again, and Caleb took it all in stride. Much better than me, in fact."

Ryan handed her another tissue.

"Thank you." She blew her nose. "Then Caleb thanked the doctor, and that was that. He wasn't upset or angry, simply accepting. I know it's because of your talk with him."

"Not me, Jessica. God's working in his life in ways neither you nor I can see. He loves Caleb, more than anyone else does, and He has plans for him, just like He does for you and me. It's just up to us to determine whether or not we're going to let Him love us and accomplish His will through us."

She nodded. "I'm beginning to understand that."

Ryan smiled. "It's one of those journeys that lasts a lifetime. As we travel along, we learn more and more about the Lord, and how much He loves us. It's that undeniable love that connects us to Him in such a profound way that we're almost compelled to serve Him. How can you not want to do everything for the One who sent His own Son to die on the cross just so we could have our sins forgiven and have restored fellowship with Him?"

Her hand rested on her abdomen, and she looked down at it. "I wonder what His plan is for this little one."

****

The next week passed quickly, and now, Jessica stood in front of Ryan at the Veracruz airport.

"You know, I never got the chance to hear you preach to your congregation," she stated. "I hope I do one day."

He smiled at her. "If you ever get down this way again, you know you're welcome. Akna would love to see you again."

Chapter Fifteen

She glanced over at her brother, seated comfortably in a wheelchair and talking with Bethany. "I think they're going to be just fine, don't you?"

Ryan looked over at them. "Yes, I do. It'll be interesting to see what God has for the two of them. Whatever it is, they're going to be used in a special way."

Jessica looked into the warmth of Ryan's deep blue eyes. Tiny flecks of azure seemed to dance in the blue richness of his gaze. She impulsively raised herself up on tiptoes and kissed him on the cheek. "I'm going to miss you, Ryan." She then quickly turned and walked toward her brother as the sea breeze tossed the curls in her hair like a wind fanning the flames of a fire.

"I'll miss you too," he said to himself as he stood with his hands in his pockets watching her leave.

Jessica walked beside Caleb's wheelchair as Bethany maneuvered him through the doors of the terminal. As the doors began to close, Jessica stopped for a moment and turned. She smiled and waved at Ryan, then disappeared into the crowd of travelers.

PART THREE – LOS ANGELES

"Wait on the LORD: be of good courage, and He shall strengthen thine heart: wait, I say, on the LORD."

Psalm 27:14

CHAPTER SIXTEEN

It had been hard saying goodbye to Ryan, but Jessica knew returning to Los Angeles would provide the best opportunities for Caleb to have a positive outcome in his diagnosis. Now back at Eastmont, as she slipped into her lab coat, the brightness and background noises of the hospital almost seemed overpowering to her senses.

I wonder what that crazy rooster is doing right now.

She walked out into the corridor of the emergency room and quickly stepped aside as a gurney was hurriedly pushed past her.

"Sorry, Dr. Carr," came the apologetic voice as it passed her.

Jessica watched as the gurney disappeared into the elevator and then walked over to the nurses' station. She gazed up at the triage board. It was nearly full.

Valerie Garrett looked up from the desk. "Dr. Carr! Welcome back! How did everything go in Mexico?"

Jessica smiled at the charge nurse. "Good, Valerie. It was good. How's it been here?"

"Same old, same old," replied Valerie. She finished writing a note in a chart, then swiveled to look at the board. "I just put a guy in four if you'd like to evaluate him. Chief complaint is epigastric pain. I put in a call for someone upstairs, but now that you're here…"

Jessica smiled. "No problem. I'll handle it."

"Hey, good to see you back, Jessica! All is well, I hope?"

Jessica turned to face Ben Shepherd. "Hi, Ben. All is well, for now, anyway. We'll catch up later?"

"Sounds good." They headed off in opposite directions as Valerie wrote another name on the triage board.

Jessica entered treatment room four and picked up the admission chart. She read the notes quickly, then looked up at the patient.

"I'm Dr. Carr. What seems to be the problem, Mr. Kennedy?" She glanced up at the cardiac monitor then returned her gaze to the older man on the bed.

"I think it's my heart."

Jessica visually assessed him as he continued.

No tachypnea; breathing is normal. Skin color is good.

She glanced up at the cardiac monitor once more.

Heart rate and rhythm are within normal limits; BP is okay.

"I probably need some nitro or something. You know, something to open up my clogged arteries."

"What makes you think you have clogged arteries?" She pulled out her stethoscope, but waited for him to answer before placing it on his chest.

"Just about everyone does, Doc. You know, we Americans eat high fat diets." He pointed to the center of his chest. "Been getting chest pain too. Off and on now for a few weeks. I figured I'd better get it checked."

"A few weeks? What made you come in today?"

"I had some time before my golf game. I will be out of here before noon, right?"

"I'll see what I can do." She placed her stethoscope on his chest and listened carefully for any indication of a cardiac abnormality, then proceeded to check his lungs. "Breathe in for me a few times, please. Slow and deep."

Jessica stood straight and picked up his chart. She wrote as she spoke, "Mr. Kennedy, I'm going to order some tests that should give us more information about your heart. After I get the results, we'll talk okay?"

Chapter Sixteen

"Sounds good, Doc, but don't forget, I need to get out of here by noon."

Jessica pursed her lips and forced a smile. "I'll keep that in mind." She walked out of the room and toward the nurses' station.

Valerie walked up behind her. "How's the guy in four?"

Jessica turned around and handed her the chart. "Standard lab tests, plus add cardiac enzymes just in case, but sounds more like acid reflux." She looked up at the triage board just as an older, gray-haired man approached her. His steel blue eyes darted back and forth from Jessica to Valerie, and his facial features were tense.

"Excuse me, ma'am, but could someone help me? My wife is having trouble breathing. I'm sorry, but I don't know where to sign her in," apologized the man.

Jessica reached out a hand to the man's shoulder. "Show me where she is, sir."

He led her into a crowded waiting room, and they meandered their way through coughing children, tired parents, and two or three lone adults quietly waiting for their names to be called. In the corner sat an older woman whose frightened eyes and ashen skin tones indicated a potentially serious medical problem.

"This is my wife, Evelyn Cauldwell. She's having trouble breathing." His thin, bony hand rested protectively on her shoulder. "Can you help her?"

"Absolutely. Let's get her in the back." Jessica stood and scanned the waiting area for a wheelchair. Spying one near the exit door, she rushed over and wheeled it back to Mrs. Cauldwell. Helping her into the chair, Jessica pushed her into the triage area. Mr. Cauldwell followed close behind.

"Val, what room's open?" Jessica called out as she moved past the nurses' station.

Valerie looked up and assessed the scene before her. She looked quickly at the triage board. "Two, Dr. Carr. I'm right behind you." She scribbled on the triage board indicating

189

treatment room two was now in use and hurried after the physician.

Jessica manipulated the wheelchair into place and assisted Mrs. Cauldwell into the bed. Valerie helped the woman change into a hospital gown and began to attach electrodes to her chest. She placed a pulse oximeter on the older woman's index finger and an oxygen mask on her face. Turning to the monitoring device behind the bed, Valerie flipped a switch, and the cardiac monitor sprang to life.

Jessica looked up at the screen and noted the numbers that began to appear. "Valerie, I'd like a met panel with cardiac enzymes; also, blood gases stat, and let's start an IV." She turned to her patient. "Tell me what's going on, Mrs. Cauldwell."

"I was fine this morning...but then all of a sudden, I... couldn't breathe. And... it hurts really bad when I... take a breath," she responded.

"What does the pain feel like? Sharp like a knife? Dull like a nagging ache? Throbbing?" Jessica reached out and placed two fingers on the inside left wrist of Mrs. Cauldwell.

"Sharp. Right here." She placed her hand on her chest.

Mr. Cauldwell interjected. "She was fine, Doctor. We just got back from Australia. We visited our grandson there. He's studying marine biology. Evie didn't have any problems there. Nothing. We've been home almost a week now, but she started feeling poorly this morning."

Jessica looked up. "Australia?"

"Yes. We were there for several weeks. We had a wonderful flight home. Nicest flight attendants we ever had. We travel a lot, but these folks were just so nice. Brought us sodas, blankets, you name it. Everything was fine, until this morning," he stated.

"I see." Jessica turned to Valerie. "I need a pulmonary angiogram and EKG stat." She wrote rapidly on the admissions chart. "I want to start her on anticoagulant meds, and call in a pulmonologist. Possible PE."

"Is she going to be all right, Doctor?" Mr. Cauldwell's worried expression intensified.

Chapter Sixteen

Jessica raised her eyes to meet his. "We are going to do everything we can to help her, Mr. Cauldwell. Your wife may have a pulmonary embolism. That's a blood clot that possibly formed in her leg. They can develop from long periods of inactivity, like a plane ride. Sometimes, they break loose and travel to the lungs. There they can get stuck. When that happens, some of the blood flow to the lungs is stopped, so a person feels a very sharp pain when breathing—"

"Is she going to die?" His wide-eyed look and whispered fears caused Jessica to reach out and touch his shoulder.

"We're going to do a few tests and give her medicines to help dissolve the clot, but I'm also going to ask the heart doctor to come and examine her. It was good that you brought her in, Mr. Cauldwell. With the right treatment and care, she should be fine.

"Right now, her blood pressure is holding, so that's a very good indicator that the clot is small. We're going to keep a good eye on her until she's ready to go home, okay? You can stay with her," Jessica reassured him.

He nodded, "Okay, Doctor. Thank you so much." He turned to look at his wife. Her eyes were closed, and she appeared to be sleeping. He looked back at Jessica. "I love her with all my heart, Doctor. Evie is my life. Please, don't let anything happen to her." His teary eyes pleaded with Jessica.

"I promise I will do everything I can, Mr. Cauldwell."

****

Later that evening, Jessica sat in the physician's section of the cafeteria, stirring her late-night dinner of tomato soup. It wasn't until the metal chair opposite her moved away from the table that she looked up.

Maggie Grant held a cup of coffee in her hand. "Mind if I join you?"

Jessica gave her a half smile. "If I said 'no,' would you still sit down?"

Maggie chuckled softly. "Yep." She sat down and took a sip from her cup. "So, what's going on? How's your brother?"

"I don't even know where to start."

"Good or bad?"

"A little of both, I guess. Caleb's still got the paralysis, but Ed's taken his case, and he's not totally convinced it's permanent, but he won't speculate as to when or if Caleb will walk again. Not that I blame him." Jessica set her spoon down.

"The good news is that Caleb's faith is more grounded now than ever. I'm so proud of him, Maggie. I think he thought everything was over for him, but after he talked with Ryan, he did a total one-eighty. He's got plans for the future and a determination to do whatever it takes to achieve his goals. Plus, the girl he loves, Bethany, she is amazing. She loves Caleb so much. She said nothing would change between them, and she still wants to marry him. And to top things off, Caleb had the opportunity to share Christ with his physician in Mexico!"

"Then why do you look so glum? It sounds like things are going very well."

Jessica picked up her spoon and started stirring her soup again. "I have some issues that I need to deal with."

"Would you like to talk about them?"

Jessica lowered her eyes and sighed deeply.

Concern enveloped Maggie's face, and she reached out for Jessica's hand. "What is it?" The uneasiness was apparent in her voice.

Jessica pursed her lips and frowned. She spoke slowly, never looking at Maggie. "I was seen in Mexico for what I thought was maybe some virus, but..."

Maggie sat quietly waiting for the rest of Jessica's explanation.

Jessica continued. "The doctor ran the normal blood tests, and the results were... unexpected."

Concern washed across Maggie's face. "What did they show?"

"My hCG was highly elevated."

Chapter Sixteen

Maggie's eyes widened. "Elevated? You're pregnant?"

Jessica looked up at Maggie through her lowered lashes, then nodded her head. "It was a total surprise to me too."

"Have you seen anyone here yet?"

"I have an appointment on Thursday."

"Okay, so why so sad? Babies are supposed to bring joy."

"I know, but under the circumstances..."

"What circumstances? God's chosen to give you a very precious gift, Jessica. A living reminder of the love shared between you and Nick. That's wonderful, and such a precious blessing!"

"I know. Ryan said the same thing. I always thought I'd have a family. I just never thought I'd have one alone."

Maggie leaned forward on the table. Her whispered voice was filled with love. "Don't forget that this baby is a gift from God."

Jessica rested her elbows on the table and held her head in her hands. "Ryan told me that I needed to trust God, and that this was all part of God's plan, and it was so easy to believe when I was in Mexico with him. Now that I'm here without him..." Her voice trailed off.

"You're not alone, Jess. I'm here. Let me help you," offered Maggie.

"Help me? How?"

"I don't know. Fixing the nursery. Throwing the baby shower. Babysitting. Stuff like that."

"Really? You'd do that?"

"Of course! That's what friends do. They help each other in times of need," Maggie began. "I'll even go with you to your appointments if you want. You know it's good to have someone with you in case you miss something the physician says or to ask the questions you forget to ask. You shouldn't be going through this alone. Please, let me help you," urged Maggie.

Despite her initial desire to stoically face the future alone, Jessica nodded to her friend. "Please," she whispered. "Please don't tell anyone. I'm not ready for that."

"I won't. I promise. What about Colin? Can I tell him? He won't say anything to anyone. I promise," asked Maggie.

Jessica smiled weakly. "Yes, of course." She swallowed a spoonful of soup. "I haven't decided what to do about work."

"What about work?"

"I don't know. I feel like my mind's not all here these days."

"Eastmont needs you Jess. It'll be fine. I'll have your back, okay?"

"You won't be with me in the operating room," protested Jessica.

"No, but He'll be there," replied Maggie confidently as she cast her eyes upward.

CHAPTER SEVENTEEN

The following Thursday, Jessica sat quietly in an examination room awaiting Dr. Rafael Santiago. She thumbed through the pages of a parenting magazine, but couldn't concentrate on anything in it. Within minutes, Rafael walked in.

"Good morning, Jessica. I was surprised to see your name on my patient list. Didn't I see you before the holidays for your annual exam?" He sat across from her on a rolling stool and pulled up her chart on a computer.

"Yes. Yes, you did."

When she didn't elaborate, he looked up from the screen. "So what brings you here today?"

She took a deep breath and exhaled slowly. "I'm pregnant."

Rafael did a poor job at concealing his surprise.

"I know," she said. "It was quite a shock to me too. It just never occurred to me that I would be pregnant, but I am. It had to have happened the last time Nick was home." She felt her cheeks warm, and she looked away from the physician.

"I understand, Jessica."

"When I was in Mexico with my brother, I was really fatigued, more so than normal. I had it checked out because if I was sick I didn't want to expose Caleb." She sighed. "I had some other symptoms, which I assumed was related to some viral infection, but they weren't."

"That's probably not the best way to find out something like this." He smiled with confidence at his colleague. "But it will all work out fine, Jessica. I'd like to get some baseline blood work, do an exam, and then we'll go from there. How does that sound?"

"It sounds like a very good plan."

****

Ninety minutes later, Jessica was back at work in the emergency room. After talking with Rafael, she felt more at ease with the pregnancy. He had given her several pieces of literature, prenatal vitamins, and most importantly, an estimated due date. Her next appointment would not be for another month, but for the first time since discovering she was pregnant, Jessica began to feel less fearful about her future.

As she stepped into the corridor from the staff lounge, she saw one pair of paramedics pushing a gurney through the ER ambulance bay doors while another pair was gathering supplies to replenish their truck. Nurses were rapidly moving through the hallway, and the intensity of the department was contagious. Jessica joined the paramedics as they wheeled their patient into treatment room four.

"What have you got?" Jessica asked as she observed the unconscious young girl on the gurney.

"Possible drug overdose, at least that's what her friends said." He turned to his partner. "On my count. One, two, three." They easily transferred the girl to the bed. "Seventeen years old. Name's Courtney Davenport. Recently broke up with her boyfriend. Her friends reported she had been drinking quite a bit before going to the bathroom. When she didn't come out, one went to check on her. Found her unconscious on the floor with an open bottle of pills. Valium. They couldn't rouse her, so they called us. Her folks are in the Bahamas, but her aunt is on the way in."

Jessica nodded as Valerie entered the room. "Val, I'm going to need a tox screen in addition to a basic met panel."

Chapter Seventeen

"You got it." As she spoke, the charge nurse attached the sensors for the cardiac monitor to the teen and adjusted the intravenous drip that had been started in the field by the paramedics. "Her friend says Courtney just found out this morning that she's pregnant."

Jessica raised an eyebrow as she looked from the nurse to her patient.

Parents gone. Boyfriend left. She was scared and felt all alone.

Jessica was jolted back to the job at hand when the cardiac monitor emitted a shrill alarm. The heart rate was slowing. The respiratory rate registered below normal, and the blood pressure was falling.

Within seconds, the room was a flurry of activity.

"Pressure's dropping!"

"Can't get a pulse!"

"Starting compressions."

"Get that epi on board!"

"Pupils sluggish."

"Open up the IV!"

The emergency room team fought valiantly to save Courtney Davenport, but her drug ravaged body responded to nothing they did.

Finally, after twenty-eight minutes, Jessica halted all resuscitative measures. She sighed deeply, then announced, "Time of death fifteen oh-five." She stared at Courtney without moving.

Did you even think about your baby?

"Dr. Carr?"

Jessica inclined her ear to the nurse. "Yes, Val?"

"You okay?"

"Yes, I'm fine. Can you let me know when the aunt gets here?"

"Of course."

As Jessica walked out of the room, Valerie began to prepare Courtney for her final goodbye before her body was transported to the hospital morgue.

Courageous Love

****

A steady influx of patients kept the ER staff busy as the afternoon sun waned and the beach lovers were now heading home from the golden sands of the southern California seashore. Jessica was finalizing the stitching of her fifth lacerated patient, a slightly inebriated surfer who had suffered a blow to the forehead from the driver of a very expensive sports car.

"You'll need to see your own physician in about 5 days to get these removed, Bobby," she instructed as she tied off the last suture. "I'll also give you an antibiotic as a preventive measure against infection. Fill it today, okay?"

"Sure thing, Doc. Thanks. Guess I should've ducked, huh?"

Jessica frowned slightly. "You shouldn't be surfing when intoxicated. That way, the next time you're carrying your board, you won't swing it into someone else's car."

"Yeah, but he didn't need to hit me. It was an accident. I didn't mean to crack the window. Besides, the dude's probably loaded. I mean, it was a Ferrari. Getting the windshield fixed, that's chump change for him."

"You broke the windshield of his *Ferrari*?"

Bobby broke into a wide grin. "Yep. I sure did. He was pretty—"

"Where is he?" A loud masculine voice echoed down the outer corridor. "Where is that nut case?" In seconds, Jessica was face to face with a huge man whose muscular build would intimidate even the most able wrestler.

"Sir, you need to wait outside," stated Jessica firmly.

"You!" He pointed a finger at Bobby and shook it vigorously. "You busted my car! You're gonna pay for that!" His face contorted in anger as he stepped toward Jessica's patient.

"I need security in here!" she yelled just as the large man pushed her roughly aside.

"Hey, man—" Bobby chuckled. "Chill out. It was just a windshield."

Chapter Seventeen

Jessica's eyes flashed angrily. "Get out of my emergency room!" She moved toward the man holding her palms out in front of herself as he recoiled his fist toward Bobby. "You need to calm down—"

The man's fist fired forward and connected with the outer edge of Bobby's right shoulder. The momentum of the blow caused his fist to continue, deflecting off Bobby's shoulder and striking Jessica squarely on her left chin. She fell against the bedside table, crashing to the floor along with an IV pole and portable cardiac monitor.

The clatter and clanging of medical equipment combined with the angry shouts of both Bobby and his attacker brought several Eastmont employees running into the room.

"You jerk! You just hit my doctor!" Bobby jumped off the bed and rammed his entire body against the big man. Together, both men slammed into the wall before Ben Shepherd and a security guard pulled them apart.

"You," ordered Ben as he glared at Bobby, "get back in that bed!" He whirled around to the security officer. "Get him out of here!" Ben dropped to the floor beside Jessica.

"Jessica! Jessica! Can you hear me?" He gently wiped the blood from Jessica's lip as her eyelids fluttered open.

"Yes, I can hear you." She tried to get up, but was too unsteady on her feet to stand on her own. "I can't believe that just happened."

"Let me help you up." He led her to an empty bed. "Sit here, Jessica. Let me make sure you're okay. Did you lose consciousness?"

Jessica shook her head and then winced. "No. No, I don't think so. Oh!" She put a hand to her chin. "This hurts."

"I imagine it does. Seems like he nailed you with a nice right hook. Your lip is starting to swell, and your chin has a small cut." Ben carefully inspected the wound on her lower chin. "A couple of small stitches, and you'll be as good as new. Claire?"

"I'm right behind you, Dr. Shepherd." She moved a bedside table to Ben's side with a suture kit ready for his use.

Jessica's eyes widened. "Stitches? You're kidding, right?"

"Well, I'd recommend it if you don't want a scar." Ben waited for her permission.

Jessica frowned as she rolled her eyes. "Okay, okay."

Claire attached a blood pressure cuff to Jessica's arm.

"This isn't really necessary," protested Jessica.

"Of course it is, Dr. Carr. You know that as well as I do." Without hesitation, Claire continued to assess the doctor's vital signs.

"Do you hurt anywhere else?" Ben leaned in and applied an antiseptic solution to Jessica's cut.

She winced again. "No, not really. A bit of a headache, I guess. I must've hit my head when I fell. Is Bobby okay?"

"He's fine. He's lucky he didn't rip his own stitches out trying to defend you." Ben completed a quick neurological assessment before addressing Jessica's chin laceration. When he tied off the last suture, he stood back and looked at her. "Hmm, I suppose admitting you for observation would be out of the question?"

Jessica raised an eyebrow. "You're not serious?"

"Well, it would be precautionary."

"How about if I just take it easy. I'll have Claire keep an eye on me," Jessica countered. "I'll still be here for quite a while."

Ben crossed his arms in front of his chest. "I'm sure I have no choice on this one."

"I knew you'd understand, Ben." She reached a hand up and gently touched her chin and swelling lip. "I don't think they pay me enough for this."

Ben chuckled as he left the room. "Put some ice on that lip. I'm going to come back and check on you in a bit."

She watched him go and gingerly felt her chin one more time before exiting the room and heading to the staff lounge.

"Dr. Carr! Are you okay?" Valerie rushed up to Jessica and inspected her swollen lip and sutured chin. "Oh my goodness! I can't believe it! You should have seen security! They wrestled that guy to the ground! LAPD came and took him away. Dr.

Chapter Seventeen

Tanner discharged your surfer guy. Oh my, that looks awful! Are you really okay?"

The door to the lounge swung open, and Maggie rushed in. "Jess? Ben told me what happened. Are you okay?"

"Yes, I'm fine."

"Are you sure? Are you really sure?" Jessica looked into Maggie's worried eyes; a silent understanding passed between them. "Yes, I really am. Completely okay."

Maggie's eyes narrowed as she peered at Jessica's chin. "Oh, that looks painful." She looked up. "Are you sure you're fine? Where did you hit?"

As she shook her head, Jessica shrugged her shoulders. "It all happened so fast. I think I fell against the bed. I'm not really sure." Her hand went to the back of her head. "Back here, I think."

"Pass out?"

"No, I never lost consciousness."

Maggie frowned; her brown eyes flashed with anger. She turned toward Valerie. "Who let that guy in here?"

Val shook her head. "I don't think anyone *let* him in, Mags. I think he just barged in looking for Dr. Carr's patient. Security got here within seconds of the call, but not before he hit the patient and Dr. Carr."

"Make sure this gets written up. Jess, you sure you're okay to stay?" asked Maggie. Worry was etched on her face.

"It's okay, Maggie. I'm okay. If I feel anything out of sorts, I promise I'll let you know," Jessica reassured her. "Besides if something is wrong, what better place to be?"

Maggie scowled, but agreed. "Okay, but you let me know if you start to feel bad."

Jessica understood clearly that it was not a request, and she nodded her head immediately. "I will."

Maggie waited until the others had returned to what they were doing prior to the fight, then whispered in Jessica's ear, "I expect you to call Rafael and tell him what happened."

Jessica sighed, but when she saw the look of seriousness in Maggie's eyes, she nodded in agreement. "I'll call him. I promise. Can I go back to work now?"

****

Later that evening, Jessica was writing a note on a chart as the ambulance bay doors opened, and once again, paramedics wheeled in a patient. She closed the chart and tossed it on the clerk's desk before moving beside the medics guiding the gurney into treatment room one.

"Forty-two year old male complaining of shortness of breath and chest pain following a traffic accident. He was driving a convertible on Highway 1 when this other car ran a stop sign. T-boned this guy's car. C-collar put on before we got him out of the car. No air bag, but he had a seat belt on. Older model car. He's tachycardic with diminished breath sounds on the left," reported the paramedic. He looked at his partner on the opposite side of the gurney. "On my count. One, two, three." They easily hoisted the man onto the ER bed. "Name's Jim Thornton. Wife's on her way in from Westwood." He handed the field chart to Jessica.

She reviewed the notes once more as Valerie entered the room followed closely by a respiratory therapist and Eric Tanner. "Let's get him on oxygen 100%." She pulled out her stethoscope and moved closer to the patient. "Mr. Thornton? I'm Dr. Carr. I'm going to listen to your chest." She bent closer to his body and extended the stethoscope.

"It hurts to breathe, Doc," gasped Thornton.

Jessica looked into his frightened eyes. "Does it hurt anywhere else?"

"The whole left side hurts."

"I'll be careful." She opened his shirt and saw several areas of bruising forming on his chest and abdomen. She gently placed the bell of the stethoscope on his chest and listened to his heart and lungs. Replacing the scope into her lab coat pocket,

Chapter Seventeen

she gently palpated his chest and neck areas, then glanced up at the cardiac monitor.

"Pneumothorax?" asked Eric.

Jessica nodded. "Val, I'm going to need a thoracostomy tray." Jessica looked at her patient. "Mr. Thornton, you're having trouble breathing because you've got some air trapped between your lung and chest wall. I need to relieve that for you, and then you'll feel a lot better. After that, we'll put a temporary tube into your chest to get rid of all the trapped air."

"Is my wife here?" His breathing came in short gasps. "I can't breathe..." His eyes rolled upward as he lost consciousness. His breathing slowed dramatically until it stopped altogether. A respiratory therapist immediately attached a manual compression bag to the oxygen facemask and artificially began to breathe for the patient. The cardiac monitor continued its quiet beeping, reassuring the team that Jim Thornton's heart was still beating.

"Oxygen's at one hundred percent. BP is holding, but he's tachycardic," reported Tanner. He looked up at the cardiac monitor and studied the various lines on the screen.

Jessica quickly donned a pair of sterile gloves and picked up a 2-inch needle, then tossed it back on the tray. "Eric, can you get me a 3-inch? He's a big guy." She prepped the left chest with an antibacterial solution and visualized her insertion site as she waited for the appropriately sized needle. As soon as Eric held it to her, she paused, then asked, "Eric, could you do this?"

His surprised eyes looked up at her. "Yes," he responded. "You okay?"

Jessica nodded. "I am, but I'd like you to do it."

Eric's lips tightened as his puzzled look disappeared. "Then I've got it."

He positioned the needle at the fifth and sixth intercostal space and looked over at her. She nodded, and he continued. Near the mid-axillary line, he pressed the needle along the top part of the rib to avoid the nerve and blood vessels along the bottom part of the bone. Within seconds, they both heard the familiar hiss of escaping air. He secured the needle and attached a flutter valve to prevent any air from reentering the pleural cavity.

"Spontaneous breathing's resumed," reported Valerie. "Heart rate's coming back down."

Eric expertly inserted a chest tube, then stepped back and turned to Valerie. "Let's get him to ICU. See if you can get Steve Lansing to take a look at him. He's one of the best pulmonologists I know, and I'd like a cardiologist to see him, so please get Markham for me."

Valerie nodded. "Will do, Dr. Tanner."

When Eric and Jessica walked into the corridor, he turned to her. "You feeling okay?"

"Yes, just thought you'd like some practice before you head off to Papua New Guinea."

"I'm not leaving any time soon." Eric stopped and turned toward Jessica. "Are you really okay? You don't look so good, and I'm not just referring to that lip."

Jessica rolled her eyes and exhaled deeply. "That noticeable?"

"Oh, yeah."

"Terrific." She looked up into his concerned eyes. "Just a little upset stomach. I'm fine, really."

He nodded, but said, "You know, you might have hit your head harder than you think. Your nausea could be a symptom of a concussion."

"Yes, or it could be that spicy burrito I had for lunch." Jessica chuckled. "So, why Papua New Guinea? I don't think you told me that, and if you did, blame your illusionary concussion."

"I could blame it on Alzheimer's," retorted Eric as he raised an eyebrow.

Jessica mouth dropped open as she looked at the resident. "I take back all the nice things I said about you," she teased.

"That shouldn't take too long." Eric winked at the doctor. "In regards to your original question, my aunt and uncle are missionaries there now. They've been there for as long as I can remember. I actually visited them last year for a week. We

Chapter Seventeen

worked with the local residents. Vaccinating kids, routine physicals, some patient education, and since it's all affiliated with a church, I also had a lot of opportunities to talk to patients about the Lord. It was so awesome! So rewarding! I knew then that that was what I wanted to do with my life. So I prayed about it, kind of laid it out before the Lord, and waited."

Eric's grin spread across his face. "I talked with my pastor and my family, and after all that, I had such peace about the whole thing. I knew then that God wanted me to go."

"What about Eastmont?"

"Honestly?"

"Yes."

"I love it here, but I believe that God wants me to be a medical missionary."

"We're really going to miss you."

Eric nodded. "I'll miss Eastmont, too, and your mentoring. You've taught me a lot in the last three years."

"You're a gifted doctor, Eric. I will expect great things from you."

"Well, I'm not leaving yet. Got to raise support and all that, which is a bit difficult with my work schedule, but I've got some ideas. After all, if God wants me to go there, He'll find a way for me to raise the money and get there, right?"

"Absolutely."

Eric paused for a moment and looked at Jessica. "I know it's not everybody's calling, but for me, well, I really believe that's God's plan for my life, and I'm going to trust Him to lead me."

"I wish the best for you, Eric. And, as I said, when the time comes, we'll miss you greatly when you leave."

"Thanks, Dr. Carr. That means a great deal to me, but I'll still be around for a while. You can't get rid of me that easily!"

"Need a doc in treatment two!"

Jessica and Eric looked toward the voice, then each other.

"I'll go, Dr. Carr. You better ice that lip some more," he said as he turned and walked briskly toward treatment room two.

Jessica shook her head as she watched him hurry down the corridor and disappear into a room.

"Hey!"

Jessica whirled around, coming face to face with Maggie.

"Did you call Rafael?"

"It's after hours."

"Really?" Maggie's displeasure was clear as she stood there with both hands on her hips.

"Really. I will call. I promise."

"Let me know when you do. I'd hate to send you home."

"Ouch. Pulling the rank card, eh?"

"If I have to."

"Okay, okay! You win!" Jessica fought to keep from smiling, but failed. "Could this day have been any crazier?" She lightly touched her lip. "Ow…"

A broad grin crossed Maggie's face. She grabbed Jessica by the arm. "Just another day at the office. C'mon, let's go get a cup of coffee while you make that call."

****

Two days later in the operating room, Jessica stood over a 15 year-old female gun shot victim. Yolanda Reyes had been hit twice, once in the abdomen and once in the chest. The first bullet had ricocheted in her chest cavity, and the damage was extensive. Two lobes of the right lung had been perforated, but miraculously the heart had been spared. Three ribs were broken, one shattered. Jessica worked furiously alongside two residents trying to stem the bleeding and locate pieces of bone that now would be considered foreign objects to the body.

"Clamp." The instrument was placed in her hand, and she applied it quickly. Her fingers worked automatically to repair torn blood vessels and feel for fragments of the bullets that had ripped through the young girl's torso.

"Dr. Carr, I can't feel anything." The first-year resident probed a cavity that was rapidly filling with blood.

Chapter Seventeen

"More suction," ordered Jessica. "Take your time. Be thorough. We don't want to leave anything in her that shouldn't be there." As she supervised the residents, she examined another area and felt for abnormalities. Blood oozed around her gloved fingers.

"Pressure's dropping."

"C'mon, c'mon. Where's the bleeder?" Jessica whispered to herself as she heard the clink of metal against metal as a bullet was dropped into a stainless steel basin. "Ah, got it!" She squinted her eyes as she clamped off and sutured the uncooperative blood vessel. "How's she doing?" Jessica asked as she continued her search for the last bullet.

"BP's low, but holding now," came the reply.

The missing bullet had entered near the umbilicus and found its way to the pelvic girdle. She gently felt around the intestines and bladder, then hesitated when she felt the touch of metal embedded in the slightly swollen muscular wall of the uterus.

"How old did you say she was?" Jessica looked up and waited for the answer she feared was coming.

"Fifteen."

Jessica frowned underneath her surgical mask. "I'm pretty sure we've got two patients here. Get an OB up here stat."

"An OB?"

"If you look closely at the uterus, you can see it's larger than would be expected," Jessica began. "Plus, it—" Her eyes widened slightly as she felt a flutter within her own abdomen.

"Dr. Carr?"

Jessica blinked the watery film away from her eyes, then looked up at the resident. "I'm sorry. I was saying that it doesn't take much for a uterus to begin contracting when stimulated. I don't want to continue until I know this baby is out of harm's way," explained Jessica. "I'm not up enough on obstetrics to know what drugs can and cannot be given at this stage of pregnancy either."

"She can't be that far along," stated the resident. "Probably doesn't even know yet."

"Maybe not, but we're here to preserve lives, therefore, we are not going to take any chances by continuing without an obstetrician here."

The resident nodded at Jessica. "Understood."

"OB's on his way, Dr. Carr."

"Thank you." Jessica turned to the nurse anesthetist. "How's she doing?"

"Vitals are stable. I backed off a bit on the sedation until OB comes, but she's still well under."

"Good. We'll wait for the OB, then we'll proceed."

Within minutes, the obstetrician had scrubbed in and took his place opposite Jessica. Under his expert instruction and watchful eye, Jessica and her team finished removing the last bullet from the uterine wall with only a few minor contractions, which ceased as soon as the sutures were in place. The developing baby was no longer in danger, and although Yolanda Reyes was transported to the ICU and expected to recover without any problems from the shooting, she was now labeled 'high-risk' and would be followed by an Eastmont obstetrician for the duration of her pregnancy.

****

Later that afternoon, Jessica sat alone in the physician's resting room. She pulled out her cell phone and punched in a number. Putting the phone to her ear, she waited for an answer.

"Hello?"

"Hey, it's Jessica! How are you?" Hearing Ryan's voice warmed her heart, reaffirming that the decision to call him was a good one.

"Jessica! It's good to hear from you. I'm fine. How are you doing?"

She leaned back into the chair. "I'm doing well. I wanted to let you know that I saw my OB. He says everything is okay.

Chapter Seventeen

I'll probably deliver some time in September. And I finally told my family. They were thrilled, and I feel so much better now that everything's out in the open."

"That's great! Still having trouble with the cough?"

"No. My lungs are used to the smog here. I guess it's just the fresh air that makes me cough!"

He chuckled lightly. "I'm glad you're better. Hey, how's Caleb doing?"

"He's started physical therapy, but as to whether or not he'll regain his ability to walk is still up in the air. He's got a great attitude though. He's going to finish his courses online, and hopefully graduate on schedule. The college has been very accommodating."

"Praise the Lord for that! So, have you started the nursery?"

"Not yet. My dad said he wants to do that project. He's been very excited about it, and it's one less thing I have to worry about."

"Ah, still working on that control issue, huh?"

She laughed softly. "Yeah, but not with great success. However, some things are falling into place. My mom has asked me if she can watch the baby when I work. Can you believe that? She said it didn't matter what my work schedule was; she would work around it. Isn't that amazing?"

"Praise God for answered prayer!"

"Yes! So tell me, how's it going there?"

"Good. I'm starting the plans for summer, and if all goes well, we'll be able to have two full camps."

"Camps?"

"Summer camps for kids. One for elementary-aged kids, and one for the older teens. Each one runs for two weeks. It's one of the highlights of our year."

"Sounds like you'll be busy."

"Yes, we've had a couple of churches that have never sent kids before saying they'll be sending some campers, plus I've got two colleges from the States sending camp counselors. It's really coming along. I'm still trying to recruit a camp doctor and possibly a missionary for the services, but I'm sure the Lord will provide them soon."

"Oh, Ryan, I'm so happy for you! I'll be praying for those positions to be filled soon. I'm here at work, but I had a little lag time, so I wanted to call you. I'm sorry I can't talk longer," she apologized.

"No problem. I totally understand. It's good to hear from you. I really appreciate the update. Tell Caleb I'm praying for him."

"I will. Take care, Ryan."

"You too, Jessica."

The call ended, and Jessica sat back in her chair.

I really miss him, Lord.

CHAPTER EIGHTEEN

"Yes, Mom. I'd love to go shopping with you. I haven't bought anything yet, although I'm starting to tell a difference in my regular clothes. Fortunately, my scrubs are pretty roomy." Jessica sat at her kitchen table drinking a cup of tea while she cradled the phone on her shoulder. It had been three weeks since she had shared her news with Caleb and her parents, and she was enjoying the freedom of being able to openly celebrate the child developing within her.

"Is Dad still designing the perfect nursery?" Jessica sipped her tea as she listened to Anne's voice happily discuss the future nursery. She set her cup down as her phone chimed softly in her ear. Pulling back, she glanced at the screen and read the caller ID.

"Hey, Mom, Caleb's calling. I'll call you later, okay? Thanks. Love you, too." She punched the icon for the incoming call. "Morning, Caleb. What's up?" She nibbled on a blueberry scone.

"What are you doing the third week of May?"

"I don't have any specific plans that I know of. Why?"

"Well…"

"Oh no," she began, "What are you up to now?"

"Bethany and I, we've decided to get married then."

"What?" Jessica sat up straight. "I thought you were going to wait until summer?"

"Yeah, we were, but now, Bethany and I are planning to get married the weekend after graduation. Nothing big or fancy, just a small ceremony with family and some friends. It's the perfect time, and of course, I want you to be there."

Jessica opened her mouth to speak, but nothing came out.

"I know it sounds soon," he continued, "but we've really thought this out. With all my medical appointments and physical therapy, and Bethany wanting to be with me, it just makes more sense. She won't need to drive back and forth from her folks to be with me. You understand, right?"

Jessica thought back to when she and Nick had decided to get married. It had been a crazy plan for them as well. She was studying to be a doctor; he was in military training, but they were in love, and nothing could keep them apart. "Yes. I do understand, Caleb, and you know I'll be there. Nothing could keep me away!"

"Jess, I have never been so happy in my life! I just can't believe God has blessed me so much! Bethany is absolutely the best girl in the world!" The joy in his voice reflected the love in his heart. "Jess, I want you to know that Bethany and I both know it won't be easy, but you of all people, know that we just don't know how many tomorrows we have. Beth and I have talked to our pastor, and we've been praying non-stop about this for a while now."

"You're really sure, Caleb? What if—" Jessica stopped herself.

"What if what? I'm not walking yet? I probably won't be. She understands. Besides, who ever said you can't wheel your bride down the aisle?" Caleb chuckled. "I can't explain it. I can only tell you it feels so right, and we both have this incredible peace about it. We've both been praying about it, and we believe this is God's will. I was totally okay with waiting, and so was Bethany, but the more we talked and shared our feelings, the more we believed we were following God's leading."

Jessica could hear the confidence in her brother's voice, and although she had her reservations, her heart was joyful. "You are going to finish school, right?"

Chapter Eighteen

"Yes, of course. It'll be the weekend after graduation. Oh, and here's another blessing. Bethany's been offered a job at this Christian school as a part-time secretary until the end of the summer, then they've told her she can move into a teaching position the next school year! Isn't God great?"

"Really? That's wonderful, Caleb! How about you?"

"I'm not totally sure yet. I have an appointment with a career counselor at the college next week. Just to see what's even available. Bethany and I still would like to go to the mission field, but we're going to wait and see where God leads us. Plus, I still have my rehab to do."

"That just seems like a lot on your platter. Be careful, Caleb," cautioned Jessica. She heard his sigh and regretted her negativism.

"Listen, Jess. I know in my heart that I love Bethany, and she loves me. We'll still be able to finish school on time, and then we'll see where God directs us. Sometimes you just gotta sit back and trust God to lead. No matter where though, we'll go there together. Jess? Are you okay? Are you crying?"

"I'm fine," she half-whispered while wiping away her tears. "And yes. Yes, I am crying." She sniffed, then continued in an encouraging tone. "My baby brother is getting married, and I couldn't be happier."

"Really?"

"Really!"

"So you'll be there, right?"

"Of course. I wouldn't miss it. When's the big day?" She inserted the date into her phone calendar as Caleb continued to talk.

****

The next five weeks flew by quickly, and on the morning of Caleb's wedding, the sky was cloudless, and the California sun was shining brightly. Awaiting her call for the preliminary pictures, Jessica stood in the church's bridal room and examined the mint green gown that fit perfectly over her slightly expanding midriff. The estimated adjustments that had been made a few weeks earlier proved to be nearly perfect for her figure.

The scoop neckline was dotted with tiny sequins, which glittered in the soft morning light streaming in through a side window. Gathered slightly above her abdomen, the silky fabric flowed over her and cascaded to the floor. Jessica stared at her reflection in the multi-paneled mirror against the far wall. Her flame-colored locks curled around her face, and the dress highlighted the flecks of green in her blue eyes. Her hands moved down the front of the dress and stopped over her expanding waist area; her eyes fixed on her mirrored image.

I can't wait to meet you, little one.

A knock on the door interrupted Jessica's thoughts. "We're ready for you."

Jessica gently lifted her dress and walked into the sanctuary. Her eyes roamed the near empty room, then rested upon Bethany standing next to Caleb's wheelchair at the front of the church. Their laughter floated through the building.

Bethany's white gown shimmered in the natural lighting that came in through the stained glass windows, and as she leaned near Caleb, her light brown curls danced near his face. He reached up to brush the tendrils away, then touched Bethany's face lovingly. She leaned over, caressed his cheek, then kissed him.

Jessica felt intrusive and averted her eyes from the tender scene. She didn't move until beckoned by the photographer.

"Ah! The groom's sister! Wonderful! Come up here, my dear."

As she walked up to the front of the church, Marty entered through a side door. He looked quite a bit older in his tuxedo than she last remembered.

As he sauntered up to the bridal couple, he noticed Jessica and flashed her a grin before turning to Caleb.

Chapter Eighteen

"I can't believe you're getting married," exclaimed Marty, then he gawked at Bethany. "Wow! You look absolutely gorgeous!"

Caleb feigned insult. "Hey, buddy, she's mine. Back off!" Marty raised both hands in front of him and stepped backward slightly. "Okay, okay." He chuckled, then became serious. "I am so happy for you both."

Bethany held firmly to Caleb's hand. "Thank you, Marty." Her smile was sweet and sincere.

"Jessica!" Caleb turned toward his sister as she moved to him. She reached out and hugged him. "You two look so perfect together."

Caleb beamed as he whispered, "Isn't she beautiful?"

"Yes she is, Caleb." She squeezed his hand affectionately.

"Hey, I forgot to tell you. I've got a surprise for you," said Caleb with a twinkle in his eye.

"A surprise?"

"Yep. But I'll tell you later," teased Caleb with a huge grin.

"Later?" Jessica pouted and put her hands on her hips. "That's not okay, Caleb. Tell me now!"

He winked at her. "I'll tell you later. I promise. We've got pictures to pose for now!"

****

Jessica stood in the foyer of the church, her nervousness well hidden behind a smiling façade. She smiled and greeted guests, shook hands and kissed cheeks of family and friends, and performed all of her sister-of-the-groom duties flawlessly.

"I was told I'd find you here."

Jessica spun around, unable to believe whose voice she heard. She froze, her mouth slightly open, momentarily lost in the dark blue eyes of Ryan Devereaux.

"You look beautiful, Jessica."

Her cheeks warmed, and she blinked several times before managing to utter, "Ryan? What are you doing here?" Her eyes fixed on his face, and she fought the urge to embrace him.

He stood before her in a charcoal gray suit, his white shirt and black tie reflecting the formality of the occasion. His eyes seemed to laugh at her reaction. "I believe I'm attending a wedding. Isn't that what you're doing?"

She shook her head as she stared at him. "I can't believe you're here! Caleb didn't say anything about you coming." She reached out and took both of his hands in hers as understanding came to her. "You must be the surprise he promised. It's so good to see you!"

"It's good to see you, too. I'm glad I got to catch you before the ceremony. How are you doing?"

"I'm doing very well. Keeping busy at work, and of course, making some future plans. How long are you here?"

"I'm planning to head home on Tuesday. I'm going to preach at my dad's church tomorrow, then spend a day with my folks."

"That's all? That's not very long."

"You sound like my mom. She'd like me to stay for a couple of weeks, but I really need to get back home. Summer time is very busy for us. Kids are already out of school, and the teen camps are only a month away. I hate to be gone too long." He glanced at his watch. "Speaking of time, shouldn't you be with the bride?"

Jessica's eyes opened wide in alarm. "Yes! Yes! I've got to go." She started to head toward the bride's room, then turned. "Save me a seat at your table?"

Ryan smiled. "I'll do that."

****

Jessica stood on her mark at the front of the church opposite Marty. Next to him, Caleb sat in his chair. All of them had their eyes glued to the back of the sanctuary. As soon as the pianist began to play the traditional bridal march, the rear

Chapter Eighteen

double doors opened, and Bethany entered on the arm of her father. The entire church rose as the bride made her way to her waiting groom.

At the front of the church, Bethany's father walked her up the two stairs so she would be on the same level as Caleb. When the pastor asked who was giving away the bride, Bethany's father responded appropriately, then prepared to put Bethany's hand in Caleb's. He turned slightly waiting for his future son-in-law to roll his wheelchair over, but instead Caleb had not moved. He stared at Bethany and smiled, then grasped both arms of the wheelchair.

A hush settled in the sanctuary as all eyes locked onto Caleb. He set his lips firmly together, took a deep breath, and pushed himself up until he was standing. Marty stepped out from behind Caleb and gave him two arm-braced crutches. Slowly, Caleb took one small step toward Bethany.

Jessica's hand went to her mouth, and her eyes filled with tears. She realized she was holding her breath. Her brother took another step, then another. Her knees felt weak, but she managed to stand and watch the miracle unfolding before her.

Caleb's steps were clumsy and arduous, but he continued toward Bethany, who was now crying. Unhindered, the bride's joyous tears fell freely as she watched her groom inch toward her. When he finally was by her side, he was breathing heavily, but a broad smile spread across his face.

"I wanted to stand beside you today, Bethany, just like I'm going to stand with you for the rest of your life," said Caleb confidently.

Bethany couldn't speak; she only nodded as tears of joy rolled down her cheeks. She gingerly slipped her arm through his as they both turned toward the pastor.

"Ladies and gentlemen," the minister began. "We are here today to join this woman and this man in holy matrimony..."

Jessica heard little of the actual ceremony. She simply stood in awe of the God who would grant her brother this moment

Courageous Love

where he could stand tall beside his bride. She knew this would be a day she would never forget.

As soon as the photographer released the wedding party, Jessica hurried into the reception area.

Where are you, Ryan?

She scanned the room quickly and saw him talking with Owen, one of Caleb's summer co-workers. She started moving toward him when her mother grabbed her arm.

Nothing was said between the two women as they embraced one another, their tears flowing once more.

Jessica pulled back and looked at Anne. "Mom, did you know?"

"No, sweetheart, neither I nor your father knew anything. Caleb only told us that the therapy was going well."

Jessica picked up a napkin from a table and wiped her tears. "I didn't know he was doing this well. I just can't believe it!"

"He only told us that he had wanted to give a very special gift to Bethany today, and he hoped we'd understand why he said nothing about it."

"Oh, Mom, Bethany is so lucky to have Caleb. He loves her so much."

Anne smiled through her glistening eyes. "Speaking of love, sweetheart, I understand I'll finally get to meet this Ryan you've spoken so much about," said Anne with a twinkle in her eye. "Which one is he?"

Jessica took a deep breath in and faced Anne directly. She spoke her words slowly and deliberately, as if chastising a child. "Mother, do not get any ideas about him and me. We are friends, that's all."

Anne smiled slightly. "Well, for just being friends, you certainly talk a lot about him."

Jessica felt the heat rise in her cheeks. She pulled her mother into a secluded corner of the room and whispered, "Mom, please. Ryan is just a friend, nothing more. Besides, it hasn't even been that long since... well, you know. It wouldn't be right."

Chapter Eighteen

Anne studied her daughter's face. She took both of Jessica's hands in her own. "Sweetheart, there is no right or wrong time for you if God is in it. However, I hope you know me well enough to know I would never meddle in your life." She hesitated a moment, then continued, "Promise me something."

Jessica sighed. "What, Mom?"

"Don't deny yourself a life of happiness with someone else if God brings him into your life, okay?"

Mom, you do know I'm going to have a baby, don't you? Do you really think a man would even remotely be interested in me at this point in my life?

Jessica forced a smile. "Of course, Mom. If God brings someone into my life, I'll think about it. I promise."

Anne's forehead wrinkled. "That's not exactly what I asked for."

Jessica kissed Anne on the cheek. "That's all you get for meddling, Mother." She smiled good-naturedly, whirled around, and walked toward Ryan and Owen, certain her mother's eyes were following her.

What am I going to do with you, Mother? Me and Ryan? That's absurd. He's a pastor. He lives in Mexico. I'm a doctor. My life is here in Los Angeles. Plus, I've got a baby to think about now.

She walked up beside the two men, who immediately turned toward her.

"Hey, wasn't that a great wedding?" asked Owen. His grin spread from ear to ear. "I wouldn't admit this to everyone, but that actually made me cry when Caleb stood up and walked. And then, those vows!"

"It was incredible," admitted Jessica. "It's not every day you get to witness a miracle."

"You're right about that. I don't think I'll ever forget this wedding," commented Ryan. "They've come through quite a lot together, and their love has done nothing but grown. I think God's going to do amazing things in their lives." He pointed toward a table. "Will this do?"

Jessica nodded. "Perfect."

Ryan pulled out a chair for her, then turned toward Owen. "Join us?"

"Thanks, but I promised Marty I'd sit with him. Good talking with you, Pastor."

Ryan nodded, then sat beside Jessica as Owen walked off. "Apparently, Caleb's therapy is going very well."

"Better than he ever let on. One day, I'll pay him back for this!" teased Jessica. "When he pulled Bethany into his lap for the recessional and wheeled out, I thought I would die! It was so Caleb." She picked up a glass and sipped the lemon water in it.

"He's going to be just fine, Jessica. They both are. Wherever God takes them, they're going to be just fine." Ryan watched the newlyweds move around the room.

"He says he's trusting God for whatever lies ahead," said Jessica.

"He's a very courageous young man."

Jessica looked up at Ryan with gratitude in her soft blue eyes. "He had a very special man help him find his way. I don't know where Caleb would be today without you, Ryan." Her voice dropped off, and she looked away.

"I like to think of it as a team effort. You, Bethany, his friends, me... all of us were part of his support team, plus Caleb was really open to the working of God's spirit. I think that made the biggest difference in his life."

Jessica nodded in agreement. "It's been kind of remarkable watching him go through this. I know he's had his moments of despair, especially at first, but now, he's got this joy that I just can't explain. Look at them." Her eyes followed Caleb and Bethany as they continued their rounds to the tables, visiting with their guests. "Don't they look so happy?"

Ryan followed her gaze. "Yes, they do. You know, I've been told that when people go through catastrophic events together, it draws them closer to one another."

Chapter Eighteen

"Really? Well, I can't think of anything more catastrophic than Caleb's accident, so I guess it must be true."

"How are your parents doing?"

"My mom had a hard time at first, but she's okay now, especially after today. I think when she saw how well Caleb was handling it, it really set her mind and heart at ease." Jessica's eyes shone with admiration. "My dad has been a rock. He's been there for Caleb from the minute we got home. He helped him adapt his apartment for the wheelchair, and even checked into getting a car for him with hand controls. Dad's been incredible! I can't wait for you to meet both of them."

"I'd like that."

Jessica looked around the room, spying her parents near the gift table. "There they are." She pointed a finger in their direction just as Anne lifted her head toward her and Ryan. "Oh dear. I think they saw us. I think they're going to come over here."

Ryan looked over to see Anne tugging on her husband's sleeve. "Is that a bad thing? I thought you wanted me to meet them."

"No. No, I didn't mean that. It's just..." Her voice trailed off as she continued watching her mother. She held tightly to the napkin in her lap and bit her lower lip.

Anne said something to the tall, gray-haired man beside her, and he bent down, his ear inclined toward his wife. A broad grin spread across his face as he looked over at his daughter. They began to walk toward Jessica and Ryan.

No! No! Go to another table. I'm not ready yet.

Jessica forced a smile on her face as her parents neared, making eye contact with her mother.

"Mother, Dad! Wasn't it a wonderful wedding?" Jessica's voice sounded strained.

"It was perfect!" gushed Anne. Her brown eyes misted over as she spoke. "Bethany was absolutely beautiful! And Caleb, well, I don't think I've seen him happier!"

Jessica glanced quickly at Ryan, then back at her parents. "Mom, Dad, I'd like you to meet Ryan Devereaux. He pastors the church in Santa Molina."

Ryan stood up and extended his hand to Paul Merrick. "It's nice to meet you, Mr. Merrick." He turned to Anne. "And you, Mrs. Merrick."

"Please," began Jessica's father. "Call me Paul, and this is Anne." He gestured to the table's empty chairs. "May we?"

Ryan nodded as he sat. "Please do."

"I wanted to thank you for all you did for Caleb after his accident," said Paul. "He was in a pretty dark place for a while, but your care and concern helped bring him out of it. You helped him realize that God still has a plan and a purpose for his life, and that gave Caleb a reason to live and fight to have the best possible life, whether in a wheelchair or not."

"I truly believe God has great plans for the two of them," said Ryan as he looked over at the head table where Caleb and Bethany were now seated. He turned back to Paul and Anne. "He's a remarkable young man."

"Jessica's told us quite a bit about you," admitted Anne. "About how you started a church in Mexico?" She leaned forward slightly.

"Well, I didn't actually start it," corrected Ryan. "I was just one in a group of several who worked there over the years. The church had already been established by a missionary pastor, but I took over when he had to return to the States for medical reasons."

Anne's voice softened as she commented, "I see God had a plan and a purpose for your life too."

Ryan smiled. "Yes, He did. It's been quite an adventure He's had me on, but I feel very blessed to be able to serve Him there."

"Jessica tells me you're starting a clinic?" asked Paul as he poured water into an empty glass.

"Yes. Right now, it operates sporadically. When doctors around the area or from the States volunteer their time, we

Chapter Eighteen

are available for immunizations, health education, physical exams, things like that. I hope to have it up and running permanently one day."

"And what would that take?"

Ryan sighed. "A full-time doctor, maybe a nurse too, but that's not easy to get. We can't offer anything even remotely close to what doctors make in the outside world, plus it would necessitate actually living in Santa Molina permanently. I can get temporary help now and then, but a full-time commitment, well, that's not as easy." He then smiled. "But, I'm trusting the Lord for that. If He wants that clinic up and running, He'll provide the staff. It's just the waiting part that's difficult.

"For instance, in situations like Caleb's. I wonder if we could have done something more for him that would have resulted in a better outcome if there had been medical personnel on site. My first aid training only goes so far."

A glimmer of sadness crossed Ryan's face, and Jessica reached out and touched his hand. "You did everything you could, Ryan. You all did."

He glanced at her, managing a small smile. "I hope so."

Paul's grey-blue eyes moved slightly to his wife, then back to Ryan and Jessica. "I agree with my daughter, Ryan. From what was shared with us, Caleb was well taken care of, both in the hospital and before, and believe me, we are very grateful."

"Yes we are," concurred Anne. "Thank you for helping *both* of our children."

Jessica felt the heat rise in her cheeks again, and she abruptly changed the conversation. "Dad, Ryan's preaching at his father's church tomorrow, and I thought I might go to hear his sermon. From what I understand, he's a great preacher."

Ryan's eyes widened slightly, and he turned toward her.

Jessica kept her eyes focused on her father, ignoring Ryan's stare. "I never got a chance to hear him when I was in Mexico, which is probably a good thing since my Spanish isn't that advanced. I'd probably have missed something in the message.

Plus, we can have lunch together before he leaves for home." She turned quickly to Ryan. "That's okay with you, isn't it?"

"Uh... sure. Of course." His dark blue eyes remained focused on her face.

"Great!" She smiled at the amused look on her mother's face. *Mom, if I could stick my tongue out at you right now, I would!*

CHAPTER NINETEEN

Jessica sat in her parked car watching others walk into the small church. White stucco accented by dark brown wooden planks gave the building a "cottage in the woods" appearance. The multi-colored pansies in the flowerbeds that flanked the open double doors on both sides danced in the early morning breeze. Jessica felt a warm welcome beckoning her.

She took a deep breath, opened the car door, and straightened her lavender and white maternity dress as she stood. She grabbed her purse and Bible, then walked toward the sanctuary.

As she entered the foyer, an elderly man in a dark brown suit approached her. Tufts of gray hair rimmed his balding head, but his eyes had a sparkle in them as he reached out to shake her hand.

"Good morning, Miss. Welcome to our church." He shook her hand firmly, then handed her a bulletin with the order of service typed neatly inside.

"Thank you." She opened the leaflet.

"There's a small paper we'd love for you to fill out and drop in the offering plate when it's passed around later," he explained.

She nodded. "I'll be happy to do that."

"We have a special treat today. Our pastor's son will be preaching this morning. He's a pastor in Mexico. We're right proud of him," boasted the man.

"I'm looking forward to it. Thank you." She walked into the main sanctuary, where the light streaming in through one beveled glass window at the front of the church caught her attention. Positioned high above a large wooden cross on the far wall, its rays illuminated the pulpit area with natural lighting.

She walked past several rows of wooden pews cushioned in brown and beige before sliding into one near the center of the church. Soft instrumental music played, and she closed her eyes as she listened to the soothing sounds of "Amazing Grace."

"You're not supposed to sleep in church, you know."

Her eyes popped open, and she found herself staring into Ryan's warm eyes.

"I'm sorry. I didn't mean to startle you," he apologized softly.

"No, no, you didn't. Well, yes, but—" She stopped abruptly, then shrugged her shoulders slightly. "I was just enjoying the music, I guess."

He chuckled slightly. "It's okay. I saw you, and I wanted to say hello before the service started."

"I'm glad you did. This is a beautiful church."

"Thanks. I have a lot of great memories here."

"Maybe you can share some of them with me during lunch?"

He grinned. "Maybe I will. I'll see you after the service."

She watched him make his way to the front of the church, greeting other members of the congregation.

He's quite an amazing man.

****

"Good morning! It is so good to see you all here today!" The man standing at the pulpit bore such a strong resemblance to Ryan that Jessica had no doubt she was looking at Ryan's father. Slightly smaller in stature than his son, he had the same deep blue eyes, the same easy smile, and the same dark hair except for some tinges of gray at the temples.

So that's what Ryan will look like in twenty years!

Chapter Nineteen

His voice was strong and sure as he continued greeting the people. "The Lord has given us a beautiful day wherein we can worship Him with joy in our hearts and peace in our souls. Please bow your heads with me as we go to Him in prayer."

When he finished praying, Jessica realized he was not only comparable to Ryan in appearance, but his voice also reflected similarities.

I wonder if Ryan's brother was as handsome as he is. Oh dear, what did he just say? I need to pay attention! I'm sorry, Lord. Help me listen and get something from You in this message.

She made a concerted effort to focus, especially now that Ryan was standing in the pulpit. He stood relaxed in a dark brown suit, accented with a matching tie against a taupe shirt. The sincerity in his smile drew her in, and she no longer had to fight to remain attentive.

"It's been a while since I've been home, and I must tell you that it's really good to be here and see you all. When my dad asked me to speak to you, I had an idea of what I wanted to share with you, but the Lord has laid something else on my heart. I hope you receive the same blessing from it as I did when I was studying for it. Please open your Bibles to Proverbs chapter three." He opened his own Bible, laying it flat on the pulpit.

Jessica set her Bible and a small purse-size notebook on her lap. Taking notes during services was something she had done since she could remember, and today was no exception. She jotted the reference down next to the date and prepared to write as Ryan shared what the Lord had laid upon his heart.

"According to the dictionary, trust is the 'firm belief in the reliability, truth, ability, or strength of someone or something.' Throughout our lives, we put our trust in different things. Some trust the financial status of the dollar; some trust specific individuals; others trust only themselves. But there is really only one thing that we can absolutely trust without fear of that trust being violated. Look with me at Proverbs 3, verses five and six. Many of you are probably very familiar with these two verses.

"'Trust in the Lord with all thine heart; and lean not unto thine own understanding. In all thy ways acknowledge Him, and He shall direct thy paths.' If you want to place your trust in Someone who will never fail you, put your trust in God, and God alone. Financial systems cannot promise they won't fail; people will let you down, and even one's own self falls short of being trustworthy. Anything you can think of that even remotely would be worthy of receiving your trust will ultimately fail you. Except God."

She listened attentively and made notes frequently as Ryan expounded on the topic of trust, and when he used Job as an example, she struggled to keep from crying.

He lost all his children! What would I do if I lost this baby?

She protectively put her hand on her abdomen.

"Although Job lost everything," stated Ryan, "he didn't sin against God. Was his heart broken? Certainly. Was he in despair? Most definitely. Did he lose faith in God? No. He trusted God and worshipped Him. That doesn't mean he didn't hurt; it meant he chose to trust God to get him through life's struggles."

At that moment, Jessica became aware of the faint movement of her child in her abdomen. She placed her hand over the spot once more and felt it again.

Dear Lord, help me to trust You completely.

She pulled a tissue from her purse, dabbed her eyes, and refocused on the message.

Ryan moved to the side of the pulpit. "Remember David? Talk about someone who trusted the Lord. He chose to trust God when he went up against Goliath. He wasn't afraid he was going to die. Instead, he relied on God to give him victory over the enemy of Israel. David had courage to face the giant. Courage to trust God, to be involved in whatever God allowed to come into his life. Saul's entire army was immobilized with fear, but not David. He chose to trust God.

"We all face giants in our lives. Giants that take courage to face. Maybe it's a chronic illness, maybe financial woes,

Chapter Nineteen

maybe the death of a child or spouse. It could be anything, and my giant may not be the same as yours. But everyone needs courage to face their own giant. The courage to do so comes only from trusting God. Especially when you have to step out alone to serve God. He's the only one who won't leave you; the only one who will *never* leave you."

He went on to talk about several other individuals in the Bible who, despite unfortunate circumstances, demonstrated great trust in God. Finally, his message became personal. He briefly shared about the death of his own wife and child, and how he learned to trust God through those losses. He quietly flipped the pages of his Bible to the book of Isaiah and then began to read. "The prophet wrote 'Behold, God is my salvation; I will trust, and not be afraid: for the Lord Jehovah is my strength and my song; he also is become my salvation.' Trusting God when I had just lost what I loved the most was the hardest thing I'd ever done, but it was the right thing to do.

"Are you searching for peace? You can find it with Christ. If you're facing uncertainty about your future, I urge you to ask yourself two questions. The first is 'What is my relationship with God?' Is there a time in your life when you remember asking the Lord Jesus to forgive your sins and save you? If you haven't ever asked Him for that forgiveness, you'll never know what it means to trust God. The good news is that you can ask Him right now, right where you're sitting. If you believe Jesus died on the cross to be the sacrifice for your sins, you can simply pray to Him where you sit. Admit you've sinned, and tell Him you're sorry. Ask Him to forgive you, and invite Him to be your Savior.

"If you're already saved, ask yourself if you've trusted God with your whole heart. Do you have confidence in God? Do you know that He can never fail? No matter how difficult things look, how bleak things become, how hopeless the situation seems, God is faithful, and He loves you with an everlasting love.

"God's Word tells me that He loves me. Not a day goes by that I don't think of Gabriela and our child. It still hurts, and I still wonder why, but I know God has a plan for me and a purpose for my life, and I choose to trust Him. Won't you trust Him today? Whatever you're facing, you can trust God. As Scripture tells us, 'Trust in the Lord with all thine heart; and lean not unto thine own understanding. In all thy ways acknowledge Him, and He shall direct thy paths.' Let's pray."

As Ryan closed in prayer, Jessica bowed her head. Her anguished soul compelled her to silently pray.

Oh, Lord, please help me trust You. I know things are coming together, but there's so much that I'm unsure of. I'm so afraid of a future alone. How am I going to raise this child? Will I be able to give this child what it needs by myself? Help me lean on You, and trust You to guide me. Help me remember I'm not alone.

****

Jessica and Ryan sat opposite each other in the small Italian bistro. She sipped her water while scanning the menu.

Ryan munched on a breadstick after he set his menu down. "I'm really glad I got to see you this weekend."

"Me too, and I'm really happy I was finally able to hear you preach." She set her menu on top of his. "How is everything in Santa Molina?"

"Pretty good."

"Have you found a doctor for the camps yet?"

Ryan shook his head. "No, but I've been in touch with the medical school in Veracruz. Hopefully, they can recommend someone for us."

"I hope so."

You could go.

Jessica looked up quickly at Ryan. "What? What did you say?"

Ryan glanced at her. "Nothing. I didn't say anything."

Chapter Nineteen

She felt an uneasiness begin to grow, and her breathing became more rapid. *You're a doctor. You could go to Santa Molina. It's only for a short time.*

"Jessica, are you okay?" Ryan studied her face.

She stared into his concerned eyes, then blurted out, "I could do it."

"Do what?"

"I could come and work as your camp doctor." She heard herself make the offer, but she found it hard to believe that she had actually said the words.

Ryan's mouth dropped open. "You?"

She struggled to comprehend from where her proposal had come. *This is Your plan? It has to be because I sure wouldn't suggest it!*

Jessica sat back in her chair and looked Ryan squarely in the face. "Yes, me," she finally said. "Why? What's so surprising about that?"

"Nothing. But you're, well, you know."

Jessica crossed her arms in front of her as she feigned irritation. "I'm what? Not qualified? No, that couldn't be it. Hmm, let's see. Too old? No, that wouldn't be it? Maybe I'm not fluent enough in Spanish. No, I don't think that would be the reason. Surely, it couldn't be because I'm pregnant, could it? No, you wouldn't discriminate against me because of that." She watched him with unblinking eyes.

He shifted uncomfortably in his chair. "That's not what I meant."

"What did you mean?"

"Jessica, you're what? Four or five months along?"

"Five."

"So, by the time camp comes around, you'll be in your seventh month. I'm guessing your OB is not going to okay you coming to Mexico to work for four weeks."

"Are you saying if he approves it, you'll accept me as the camp physician?" A slight smile appeared on Jessica's face.

Ryan sighed. "Do we have to discuss this right now?"

"Yes. Yes, we do."

"You're not going to let this rest, are you?"

Stubbornness set into her eyes. "I don't see why you're hesitating. You need a doctor. I am one."

"What about your job?"

"I'll just be starting my maternity leave a bit earlier than planned. Besides, I'm sure it won't be a problem."

Ryan looked at her with a sigh of resignation. "I'd love to have you come, Jessica. I really would, but—"

She quickly picked up the menu again and ducked behind it. "I'm glad that's settled."

Ryan sat back in his chair and pressed his lips together, stifling a response that would not have been too edifying. He shook his head and sighed deeply once more.

Jessica peeked over the top of her menu, suddenly aware that she would be greatly disappointed if Ryan refused her.

Please say 'yes.'

She lowered her eyes, but couldn't concentrate on the selections for lunch. The silence between them seemed interminable.

Glancing up at him, she saw a faint scowl on Ryan's face. She sat up in her chair and lowered the menu. "You're mad, aren't you?"

"No, I'm not mad. I just want you to be careful. I won't have any other medical person there to help you if something happens to you, and Veracruz is a long way off."

"I know, but God will be there, right?"

Ryan shook his head in frustration, unable to argue with her. "Yes, He will be, but—"

"Then I can come if Rafael gives his blessing?"

"Rafael?"

"My OB."

In resignation, Ryan sighed once more. "Fine, if your OB says you can come, I won't stop you."

Chapter Nineteen

Jessica sat quietly, not knowing what to say to break the tension between them. Finally, she softly said, "I won't go if you don't want me to. I just thought—"

"No," said Ryan. "I'm sorry, Jessica. Of course, I want you to come. I'm sure you'll do a fabulous job with the kids." He forced a smile. "But you will check with your obstetrician, right?"

Jessica nodded. "Of course I will. I promise. And if he is against it, I won't push it with him."

****

It had been difficult for Jessica to say goodbye to Ryan, and now as she sat in the nurses' station waiting for patients, her mind took her back to that moment. She had insisted on driving him to Los Angeles International airport, but when they parted, the intensity of her feelings surprised her.

She could still see him dressed in khaki slacks and a white polo shirt, wheeling a small carry-on suitcase with one hand and holding a laptop computer in the other. His hands had been full, but she knew he wouldn't have hugged her even if they had been empty. She had watched him until he disappeared into the throng of airport travelers.

"A penny for your thoughts?"

Jessica shook the blanket of memories from her mind and looked up into the curious eyes of Maggie Grant.

"I was just thinking."

"About what?"

Jessica picked up a pen and began to twirl it around in her fingers. "About Ryan."

"Ryan? My Ryan?" Maggie cocked her head slightly.

"Yes. He asked me about working there during summer camp." She suddenly felt uncomfortable.

Maggie eyed Jessica carefully as she leaned on the counter. "Summer camp? You mean as the camp physician?"

Jessica looked up slowly. "Yes."

"What? He asked you to come work there?" Maggie's voice escalated in volume. "What is he thinking? Can't he see you're not exactly—"

"No! No!" Startled by Maggie's outburst, Jessica's eyes widened, and she shook her head emphatically as she interjected, "He didn't ask! What I meant was, I volunteered."

"You what? Are you crazy?" Maggie stood up and beckoned with her finger. "C'mon. Let's take a break. We need to talk."

Reluctantly, Jessica rose and followed Maggie into the staff lounge. She looked around at the empty room.

Really? There couldn't be at least one other person in here?

"So tell me," demanded Maggie as she turned to face Jessica, both hands on her hips. "What are *you* thinking? You can't go to Mexico."

"Why not? I'm doing fine. I'll be back in plenty of time for the delivery. I don't think there's anything wrong with going."

"Really? And what does Rafael think about it?"

"I haven't asked him yet."

Maggie frowned and crossed her arms in front of her. She said nothing. She simply stared at Jessica.

Jessica shifted her feet nervously. "We were talking about his camps, and he mentioned that he still didn't have a doctor for either of them, and I sort of just blurted out that I'd do it."

She avoided looking at Maggie and walked over to pour herself a cup of coffee. "How hard could it be? I work in an ER. A camp should be a lot easier, don't you think? What's the biggest problem I could face? A broken bone? Homesickness? A bee sting?"

"Really, Jess? What about premature labor?" Maggie's irritation was obvious.

"I know it's impulsive, but…" Jessica took a swallow of the lukewarm brew, then turned around and said nonchalantly, "I just thought it would be nice to help him out. You know how hard it is to get doctors there. Besides…"

"Besides what?"

"It wasn't my idea."

Chapter Nineteen

"Really? Whose idea was it?" challenged Maggie.

Jessica looked squarely into Maggie's confrontational eyes. "It was God's idea."

"What?"

"We were getting ready to order lunch, and I felt like God wanted me to volunteer." Jessica squirmed in her seat, but held her ground. "I know it seems like a crazy idea, but I really believe it came from God." Jessica shook her head slightly. "I know it wasn't mine."

As Maggie paced the room quietly thinking, Jessica continued. "I know the risks, but I'm not due until September. I'll be back at the end of July. That's plenty of time, and frankly, if it is God's will for me to go, isn't He supposed to take care of me?"

When Maggie turned around, her worried look of concern moved Jessica to pat the sofa beside her. Maggie walked over and plopped down, and Jessica took Maggie's hands into her own. "Sometimes you just have to take a leap of faith. Isn't that what you always tell me? Besides, if God doesn't want me there, He'll close the door, right? I still have to get Rafael's okay. Maybe he won't give it. That'll shut the door, and I'll know for sure."

Maggie sighed deeply as she apologized to her friend. "I'm sorry. Forget what I said. I can be an idiot sometimes. If God opens the door for you to go to Mexico, you go. You're right. He'll take care of you."

"So you're in favor of it?"

"I didn't say that, but I'm not going to go against God." Maggie hesitated for a moment, then asked with a mischievous grin, "Are you sure there's no other reason you want to go?"

"What does that mean?"

"I mean, maybe you and Ryan—"

"No! Absolutely not! I want to help out my *friend*. That's all." Jessica felt the heat rise in her cheeks and the need to clarify her decision to go back to Mexico. "I didn't volunteer because I wanted to be with him. I volunteered because I wanted to help out with the kids at the camps."

"Are you sure there isn't another reason you want to go?"

"Absolutely not!"

"Really? You're protesting an awful lot."

Jessica's eyes narrowed, and she replied pointedly. "Maybe you're right. Maybe there is another reason. Maybe I want to get away from *you!*"

Shrugging her shoulders, Maggie replied with a teasing glint in her eyes, "I don't know. I'm inclined to believe it may be more a matter of the heart than you'd care to admit."

Jessica threw her hands up in disgust. "Oh my goodness! You sound just like my mother! Ryan and I are just friends. Nothing more."

Maggie casually retied her ponytail. "Ryan told me he enjoyed seeing you again, and that he thought you were quite an amazing person. You know, friend stuff."

Jessica felt the warmth in her cheeks again, and she was embarrassed that she was embarrassed. She twisted her wedding ring around her finger, but said nothing.

Maggie studied Jessica in the silence that followed, and as understanding for Jessica's situation became clear, she spoke. "You know, Jess, Nick would not want you to go through life alone."

Jessica's eyes closed tightly, and she took a deep breath. Wishing Maggie would leave but wanting to hear more, she kept quiet. She slowly opened her eyes, but refused to make eye contact with her friend.

Maggie softly continued. "It took me a long, long time to finally allow someone else into my life. I felt a duty to be loyal to Scott, and I was, but Scott was gone, and I was still here. I had to keep on living. I'm not going to tell you it was easy because it wasn't. I never dreamed I'd love someone again, but I was wrong. God opened my heart to love, and if I had refused to let go of Scott, I would have missed out on an amazing life

Chapter Nineteen

with Colin." As Maggie spoke, her eyes misted over. "Maybe God's opening a door for you."

Jessica shook her head. "This is crazy talk, Maggie. I'm going to have a baby in the fall. What man would want to take on that responsibility?"

"A man who has a lot of love to give."

"Look, Ryan is a nice guy. He really is, and I like him, as a friend. And he's a good friend, but Nick's only been gone for a few months. I'm not ready for another relationship."

"God's timing never seems to be the same as ours, Jessica. I had to wait a long time before I fell in love again. Maybe that's not God's plan for you." Maggie paused for a moment. "And it may not be His plan to have the two of you together, but if it is, well, be open to it. Don't push him away, okay?"

"Look, Maggie, I know you mean well, but really, Ryan and I, we're just friends. He did a lot for me and Caleb. This is just one way I can repay him for everything he's done for us."

"If you say so."

"I do," Jessica stated curtly. "Now, can we get back to work?"

Jessica walked out of the staff lounge adjusting her lab coat. Walking over to the nurses' station, she glanced up at the triage board. There were only two names written. "Still quiet?"

Valerie looked up, pen poised to sign off a doctor's orders. "Yes. It's been pretty slow. A nice change of pace. So, how's the pregnancy coming along?"

"Good. My only complaint is that sometimes this child keeps me up during the night. It likes to dance when I like to sleep."

"Oh, I remember those nights. Joy was quite active in the evening. It used to really irritate me that Will got to sleep without someone kicking him, while I had Joy pounding like crazy inside me. Pick out any names yet?"

Jessica shook her head. "No. I've been collecting suggestions, so if you have any, send them my way."

"You still don't know the gender?"

A small smile appeared on Jessica's face. "No. Rafael knows, but I told him I didn't want to know. Not now, anyway. I might change my mind later, but I rather like the idea of being surprised at delivery. After all, the pregnancy was a surprise, why not the sex of the baby too?"

Maggie walked up to the counter as if nothing had happened between her and Jessica. "Still quiet?"

Valerie nodded. "Nothing on the wire and a near empty waiting room. When does that ever happen?"

"Careful! Don't jinx it. This is nice," said Maggie as she avoided looking at Jessica.

"Well, at least I'll finally get a chance to restock the carts," Valerie picked up two bags of saline solution. "I've already sent one nurse home."

As Jessica started to move from the counter, her mouth formed a small circle and her eyes widened. Her hand automatically moved to her abdomen. "Oh my, that was a strong kick."

Valerie set the bags down and hurried over to Jessica. "Can I feel?" She held her hand above Jessica's body, waiting for permission.

"Sure. Right here."

Valerie gently placed her hand where Jessica indicated and waited. Suddenly, her hand was pushed up slightly. "Oh! I felt it!" Her eyes sparkled with excitement. "C'mere, Mags! You've got to feel this!"

Valerie reached out and grabbed Maggie's arm, pulling her over. "Right here."

Maggie resisted the pull as her uncertain eyes met Jessica's.

Jessica smiled at her friend, then reached out and took Maggie's hand in her own. She placed it on her abdomen. Within seconds, they were rewarded with another gentle kick from the growing life within Jessica's body, and this time, when Jessica looked into Maggie's eyes, all she saw was the true love of a friend, and all was forgiven between them.

****

Chapter Nineteen

"Hey, Dr. Carr!"

Jessica looked up from where she sat to see Eric Tanner approaching. The physician's dining room was nearly full, and he had to maneuver around the diners to get to Jessica's table. She popped a grape into her mouth as she gestured to the chair opposite her.

"I've been looking for you," he said as he sat down.

Her eyebrows lifted as she swallowed the sweet fruit. "Well, here I am. What did you need?"

He leaned forward on the table. "I have a proposition for you."

"A proposition?"

"Yeah." He lowered his voice. "Remember me telling you about going to Papua New Guinea?"

"Vaguely," she teased.

"Well, I heard you were planning to go to Santa Molina for a month as the camp physician, and I was wondering if I could go with you."

"Go with me?"

"Yeah. It's right up my alley, and I can get some field experience before I go to New Guinea. Plus, if anything unexpected happens, and you need a doctor, I'll be there."

Jessica eyed him suspiciously. "Really? You thought this up on your own?"

Eric shifted awkwardly in the chair. "Well, I—"

"I'm waiting." She crossed her arms in front of her.

He rubbed the back of his neck, then shrugged his shoulders. "It's not like that."

"What is it like then?"

"I really would love the experience."

"I'll consider it, but you better come clean." Jessica cocked her head and waited.

Eric sighed in resignation. "Dr. Grant thought it might be good for me, and the fact that you'd have another doctor there, well, that was just an added perk."

"Oh really?" Her skepticism was obvious.

239

A look of defeat clouded Eric's face. "I take it that's a 'no'?"
"I didn't say that."
"So you're okay with me joining you?"
"I've got the feeling I have no choice." Jessica allowed a sly smile to creep out.

Eric's eyes were hopeful. "So I can go with you?"
"Of course you can." She took a swallow of water, then added, "I think I'll work you very hard."

He grinned as he stood. "I wouldn't expect anything less, Dr. Carr." He turned to leave, then stopped and looked back at her. "Thanks."

She smiled and nodded as she watched him go.

Really, Maggie? You're sending a babysitter with me?

PART FOUR – SANTA MOLINA

*"Be strong and of a good courage, fear not,
nor be afraid of them: for the LORD thy God,
he it is that doth go with thee;
he will not fail thee, nor forsake thee."*

Deuteronomy 31:6

CHAPTER TWENTY

The flight to Las Bajadas Airport in Veracruz had taken nearly seven hours, and by the time it landed, Jessica was more than ready to disembark. She and Eric meandered through the crowds of travelers jockeying back and forth through the terminal and headed toward the baggage claim area.

"Jessica! Eric!"

Jessica stopped and turned toward the voice, knowing before ever seeing that it was Ryan who had called her. Her smile lit up her face when she made eye contact with him.

"Ryan!" She allowed him to take her carry-on bag as he directed her toward the baggage carousel.

"How was the flight, you two?"

"Long. They definitely need a non-stop one, but those comfort seats are really nice. Oh, those are mine!" Eric grabbed two large black suitcases and set them next to him while they waited for Jessica's luggage.

"Oh! That one's mine. The one with the red ribbon on the handle. And there's the other one." Jessica pointed to the suitcases.

Ryan easily lifted each bag, extending their handles. He secured the matching carry-on to one, then held his hand out. "Give me your computer case, Jessica. It'll fit right on top of this one."

"Thank you so much for meeting us. I'm afraid I packed quite a bit, and I didn't realize how difficult it would be to

maneuver all the luggage." She reached out for one of the bags.
"I can pull one."

"I've got them." He nodded toward an exit door. "We're out this way."

Ten minutes later, they were driving out of the airport and heading toward Santa Molina.

****

Eager to see where they would be working, Jessica and Eric hastened over to the clinic as soon as they had settled into their cabins. As they entered, they noticed that it had been recently cleaned and aired out, and Jessica was pleased with what she saw. She wheeled one of her large suitcases near the counter, then began to open a few cabinets.

"They're well-stocked with the basics from what I remember. You know, gauze, bandages, and calamine lotion. That kind of stuff, but let's take a quick inventory. I'd like to know exactly what we've got in case of emergency." She turned to her suitcase. "Can you set that on the counter for me?"

Eric nodded and easily lifted the case. He opened it for her, then reached for a bottle in the cabinet above him. Perusing the label on the bottle of calamine lotion, he nodded as he checked the expiration date. "Good. It's current. That's a good sign. Hopefully, everything else is also." He continued checking the various items he found.

Looking through her suitcase, Jessica started removing some of the things she had brought from home.

Otoscope, stethoscope, ophthalmoscope, glucose monitoring kit, snakebite kit, pediatric epi-pens. I hope I've got everything we'll need.

She found homes for each piece of equipment, and then rearranged some other items in an order more logical to her mind. Meanwhile, Eric had moved to the back rooms.

Chapter Twenty

"Hey, they've got some ortho stuff here. That might come in handy," called out Eric as he dug through a box with splints and slings.

Jessica walked into the room. "Really? That's great. Although, I hope nobody breaks a bone."

"Same here, but it's good to be prepared. Too bad we don't have an x-ray machine." He picked up the box. "I think I'll put these in the front room. Oh, I thought I'd get started on those files after dinner," stated Eric, "if that's okay with you."

"Of course. I hate paperwork." She smiled. "You know, I'm kind of glad you came along."

He laughed as he walked out of the clinic's back room. "I knew you'd feel that way! I'll be right back. I'm going to get my bag from the cabin."

She heard the door shut when he left, then went back to organizing the room. As she opened a second cabinet, she heard the outer door of the clinic open and close a second time.

"Eric?"

"No, it's me. How's it going?" Ryan stepped into the back room holding two glasses of iced tea. He held one out for her. "I brought this for Eric. Where is he?"

"He had to get something from his cabin. Thank you." She took the glass and sipped the tea. "Oh, this is good! And it's even unsweetened!" She rested against a counter. "You can set that over there. He'll be right back."

"You finding everything you need?"

"Yes, so far anyway. There are a few things it would be nice to have, but I think we can make it work without them. I just have to readjust my thinking from big city hospital to small country clinic. It'll be like some of my early training. I worked at a really large county hospital, but funds were always lacking, so we improvised a lot. We became very creative at times, and I'm sure I can do the same here if needed. We did rearrange a few things. I hope that's okay."

"While you're here, it's your clinic, Jessica. You do whatever you need to do," stated Ryan. "I know Maggie always

Courageous Love

spends a day of housekeeping before we open up. If there's something you need, put it on a list, and when I go into the city, I'll pick it up for you."

"Really? I wish you were in charge of the hospital's budget!" laughed Jessica. She took another sip of the tea.

"The tea is decaf. That's supposed to be better for pregnant ladies, right?" He leaned against a wall.

His thoughtfulness reminded Jessica how kind Ryan was, and for a moment her soft blue eyes were fixed upon the man who stood in front of her.

Thank You, Lord, for Ryan. He's so—

"What?" A lopsided grin appeared on his face as he cocked his head.

His questioning look caught her off guard, and Jessica realized she had been staring at him. The heat rose in her cheeks as she quickly looked down at her tea. "I'm sorry. I guess I was daydreaming. What did you say?"

"I just said I thought decaffeinated drinks were better for developing babies," he repeated.

"Oh, yes. Yes, they are. Thank you," stammered Jessica, placing the tea glass on a table. "Eric seems pretty excited to be here."

"I'm glad he's here." He lowered his eyes for a moment before confessing, "I've got to admit, with Eric here, well, my mind is a little more at ease."

Jessica smiled and playfully punched him in the shoulder. "You worry too much. You *and* Maggie."

Ryan shrugged his shoulders. "Some things are worth worrying about."

She felt the warmth return to her cheeks and quickly turned from him to look out a window. "Well, if I were you, I'd worry more about that hotshot doctor that came with me. Probably kill himself trying to keep up with the kids."

"Really? Well, I guess I'll have to keep an eye on him, but from what I've seen, it's the other doctor that's a handful. I understand she can be a bit headstrong and stubborn."

Chapter Twenty

As Jessica turned abruptly toward him with mouth indignantly open, he winked at her. "Oh, by the way, dinner's in about half an hour. Will that work for you?"

She pressed her lips together and placed both hands on her hips. Fighting back a smile, she teased, "I'm not sure I want to be in the same room with you."

He grinned at her. "See what I mean?" He chuckled as he walked toward the door. "You are eating for two, remember? I'm just here to help."

She laughed gaily. "I guess I'll meet you in the dining room then. I'll just be a few more minutes." She watched him leave, then fell against a wall, exhaling slowly as her smile broadened across her face.

If only...

Her gaze fell upon her glass of tea on the table, and for a moment she just stared at it. Turning back to the supplies, she tried to refocus on what she had been doing before Ryan had stopped by, but all she could think about was how she felt when their fingers touched as he passed her the glass of tea.

****

Thirty minutes later, she strode into the dining hall. Ryan was already there talking with Eric and Joaquin Canul, but as soon as he saw her, he excused himself and walked over to her.

"How'd you do? Everything set up?"

"There's a bit more to do, but for the most part, we're ready for business. Eric's going to start inputting the campers' information tonight, and we'll review the medical information on their forms. Hopefully, by the time they arrive on Saturday afternoon, we will know who we need to keep an eye on." She sat down at the only table with a tablecloth and place settings.

Ryan sat opposite her. "I know two or three kids are diabetic, and a few have asthma problems, otherwise I don't recall anything else. Maybe it won't take you too long to go through them. Unfortunately, most of them don't know if they have any serious medical conditions. The majority are born at home and only see a doctor if it's an emergency."

Jessica nodded her head thoughtfully. "No wonder you want to open a clinic here."

Ryan's lips formed a grim line. "We desperately need one. Hopefully, it won't be too long until we can offer more than just sporadic care."

"Eric's planning to input all the children's medical information into a database. That'll make it easier for us to keep track of the ones with meds, as well as those we've treated for minor injuries or illnesses. We can flag those files for you. After the camps, whenever you do have a physician here, that doctor will have a heads up on any previous problems if those kids return for any kind of treatment," offered Jessica.

"You can do that? That would be great!" exclaimed Ryan as Akna and her children brought out platters of food. "We've got sixty-three registered for the first camp and fifty-eight for the second."

"It should only take us a few hours to input everything." She smiled at Juan Canul, Akna and Joaquin's only son, as he set a container of hot flour tortillas in the center of the table.

"You like fajitas, *Señora*?" The tall teen's crooked smile and bright brown eyes tugged at Jessica's heart. She remembered his quiet shyness the last time she had been in Santa Molina. He had slowly approached her, only to say that he was praying for Caleb, and that he hoped all would be well with her brother.

"I do, Juan. I love just about anything your mother cooks," she replied sincerely.

With a pleased look on his dark face, he scurried back to the kitchen without saying another word.

"He's such a nice boy," commented Jessica as she dipped a crisp tortilla chip into a bowl of salsa.

"Juan? He's a great kid," added Eric as he joined them at the table. "He wants to attend Bible college after high school. He's hoping to be a missionary to the Mayan people around this area." He grabbed a hot tortilla and inhaled its aroma. "Homemade! This day just gets better and better!"

"Juan wants to be a missionary? That's a big decision for someone his age," stated Jessica. "It couldn't have anything to do with a certain doctor who's spent all day with him, could it?"

Eric shook his head. "Nope. We just started talking, that's all. He had already decided this before I even said anything about my plans."

Ryan spoke up, defending Eric. "That's true, Jessica. Juan's spent his whole life here, helping out as best he could, and at this year's revival, he came forward and said he believed God had called him to be a missionary. He accepted Christ as his Savior three or four years ago, and I've watched him grow in his faith. He'll be a great missionary to the Mayans. He speaks their language fluently, thanks to Akna. Well, one of them anyway. There are three main dialects."

"What a blessing that will be!" said Eric as he took a healthy bite of a well-buttered tortilla.

The rest of the Canul family joined Ryan and Jessica at the dinner table, and after Ryan blessed the food, the family-style fajita meal commenced. While their conversation focused mainly on Jessica's baby, Caleb's marriage, and the upcoming camps, all was centered on the Lord Jesus Christ.

****

Two days later, the *Primera Iglesia Bautista de Santa Molina,* the First Baptist Church of Santa Molina, was filled with adolescents ranging from twelve years old to seventeen from the local communities of Tres Árboles, Santa Esperanza, and Santa Molina. Jessica kept herself busy with minor abrasions and bruises, and one case of homesickness. She could often be found roaming the camp during the day, watching the children play or attending the chapel services led by Ryan or the visiting missionary.

Her Spanish was improving steadily, and she was pleased that she could understand many of the conversations around her by the middle of the first week. With her increasing understanding of the native language, the services were more enjoyable for Jessica, and she marveled at the receptiveness of the teens as the gospel was shared with them. She praised God for the numbers of young people who responded to the messages. Many made their way to the front of the church when the invitation was given at the end of each service, and her silent prayers asked God to move when counselors knelt to pray with those teens.

The role of camp doctor was more demanding than Jessica had imagined, and in spite of being in a less stressful medical environment, she was exhausted by the end of each day. Meticulous in her record keeping, she made sure every camper that had been treated during the day had an updated chart in the computer before she went to bed. After dinner, she and Eric made an effort to visit each child they had seen that day to make sure all was well before "lights out." The teens had warmed to them readily, and she found great satisfaction each night when her head hit her pillow.

Eric had endeared himself to many of the teenagers by the end of the first couple of days, and he usually accompanied them on their hikes in the surrounding jungle and hills, armed with a first aid kit and a can of bug spray. To Jessica, he seemed the perfect camp doctor, thriving in the rural atmosphere, surrounded by young people eager to learn about the Lord. As she strolled through the courtyard in the late afternoon, she often found Eric sitting with a group of teens, sharing the gospel with them or expounding on something that had been shared during chapel.

The days were filled with games, hikes, mealtimes, and chapel services, but the most memorable times for Jessica were the fireside chats. Each evening, Ryan would ignite a huge bonfire, and everyone would gather around it. He would present a short devotional from the Scriptures, encouraging

Chapter Twenty

an open dialogue with the youth to discuss what they gleaned from God's Word that day or earlier in the week. Following that, there was a time of prayer and sharing. It was during this time that some would profess their newfound salvation through Christ, while others might share how God was working in their lives.

The last night of the teen camp, Ryan rose to speak with the young people and counselors gathered around the leaping flames of the campfire. The fire illuminated the attentive faces around him, and before he spoke, his eyes swept over the assembled group. His easy mannerisms and genuine concern for them cultivated a strong relationship between the pastor and the teenagers.

"First of all, I want to thank each of you for an amazing two weeks. I could not have asked for a better group of young people to have at this camp. We've talked a lot, and we've all grown in our walk with the Lord during our time here. Tomorrow, we will go our separate ways. We will face new challenges and new situations in our lives where we each will have to decide what courses of action to take. I want to leave you with one more thing to think about as you begin to make those decisions that will ultimately impact your future. I want you to know how to determine if you're following God's will for your life."

As he spoke, he moved around the fire slowly, keeping himself in near proximity to everyone.

"Whether it's where to go to college, who to date, or what job to take, these are all examples of situations where you need to know God's will for your life. So, how do you find that out? I'm going to give you four criteria to refer to when you need to know what God's will is regarding a specific issue. David wrote, 'Thy Word is a lamp unto my feet and a light unto my path.' The Bible should always be your first reference.

"Search the Scriptures for verses to help you. If your decision is contrary to the Word of God, it is clearly not His will. He will never direct you to go against His Word. Secondly, seek advice from godly individuals. Seeking counsel from a pastor,

Sunday school teacher, or an older, wiser Christian leader can be invaluable. And believe it or not," he paused and smiled. "You could even talk to your parents."

Quiet laughter rippled through the group as Ryan continued. "This is one of the reasons God has placed these people over you. You can share your thoughts and concerns, and get sound advice from them.

"Thirdly, God has given each of you the ability to serve Him in specific ways. If your decision would take you away from serving the Lord with the gift He has given you, you must really reconsider.

"Finally, the last step is trusting the Lord to direct you. The Bible tells us to 'Trust in the Lord with all thine heart; and lean not unto thine own understanding. In all thy ways acknowledge Him, and He shall direct thy paths.' Sometimes you just need to take a step in faith. If you diligently seek the Lord for guidance, He will direct you.

"When you are on the right path, you will experience the peace that the Bible talks about; the one that passes all earthly understanding because it is given to you by God's Holy Spirit. I promise you, if you seek the Lord with all your heart in every situation in your life, not only will He answer you, He will bless you in ways that you cannot begin to imagine.

"Tonight, I challenge each one of you to surrender your life to the Lord. Allow Him to lead you. Serve Him all the days of your life, and the joys you will experience will be eternal.

"If you're sitting here tonight, and you never have asked God's Son, the Lord Jesus Christ, to forgive your sins and be your Savior, then that should be your first step in doing the will of God. He loves you more than you can imagine, and desires a relationship with you that can only happen through His Son. The counselors, other staff members, me... any one of us would be happy to show you from the Bible how you can be saved tonight and start a life knowing and doing God's will. Let's pray."

Chapter Twenty

As he prayed, several of the older boys came closer to the fire and knelt in prayer. Counselors moved beside each one, privately interceding for them and offering support and love. Jessica also bowed her head and prayed that God's Spirit would permeate each heart and reveal God's will in each life.

Later, as the group dispersed to their cabins, one older girl stayed behind. She waited until everyone had left except Ryan and Jessica, then approached the pastor.

"Julieta, did you want to talk with me?" asked Ryan as she neared.

When she nodded, Jessica turned to Ryan, "I'll go–"

Ryan shook his head slightly, then quickly turned to the teen. He gestured to a bench and said, "Let's sit here, Julieta. What's on your mind?"

Jessica sat on another bench a bit away from the two of them, but well within hearing distance.

I wonder why he wants me to stay?

Her thoughts were interrupted by the soft voice of the young girl.

"Pastor, I want to know if I am going to heaven. I was baptized when I was a baby, but tonight you said that wasn't the way." She swept her long black hair away from her face revealing large brown questioning eyes.

"Julieta, heaven is where God lives, and because He's a holy, righteous God, He can't allow anything that's not holy into His heaven. Anyone who's sinned is disqualified from going there. Baptism doesn't wash away someone's sins. Only Jesus can forgive them and take them away."

"But I haven't done bad things, Pastor. I have always obeyed my parents. I go to church. I don't understand."

"Julieta, the Bible tells us we can't get to heaven by doing good things. The book of Titus tells us that 'it's not by works of righteousness which we have done, but according to His mercy He saved us.' And then in Ephesians, Paul wrote 'For by grace are ye saved through faith; and that not of yourselves: it is the gift of God: not of works, lest any man should boast.'"

"So, I'm not good enough to go to heaven?"

"None of us are. I'm not good enough either. God's Word tells us that everyone has sinned. Here, let me show you." He opened his Bible to the book of Romans. "See right here?" He pointed to a verse. "This says that 'All have sinned and come short of the glory of God.' That means me, you... everyone. Whether we remember sinning or not, we're all guilty of being a sinner. It's something that's been passed on to us since Adam sinned in the Garden of Eden. We are all sinners according to the Bible. That's why Jesus came. You see, sin has to be punished, and God determined that the punishment was death, more specifically, eternal separation from Him. That means none of us gets to go to heaven by our own merit or good works."

"No one?" Her voice faded, and her puzzled face looked up at Ryan.

"Not unless our sin is taken care of." He continued explaining. "And that's where God's plan comes in. You see, Julieta, God loves us so much, He couldn't bear being separated from us, so He made a way for us to be able to come to His heaven. His plan was to send His Son, Jesus, to take our punishment for sin upon Himself. Jesus came to earth, and as a man, He lived a sinless life, which was something only God could do. Then, Jesus was crucified on the cross, taking the punishment for us, for all the sins of the world. After He died, He was buried, and then three days later, He rose from the grave, proving He was God, and He alone has the power to forgive sin."

He flipped to chapter six in Romans. "Look at verse twenty-three. It says 'The wages of sin is death, but the gift of God is eternal life through Jesus Christ our Lord.' Then, here..." He turned one page back. "In chapter five, verse eight, the Bible tells us 'But God commendeth His love toward us, in that, while we were yet sinners, Christ died for us." That means God showed us how much He loved us by sacrificing His only Son, Jesus, on the cross, so that we could have the opportunity to be saved from our sins."

"That's why He died?"

Chapter Twenty

"Yes. Jesus died on the cross for the sole purpose of becoming our Savior. When He rose from the dead, three days after He was crucified, He proved to the world that He was God, and only He was qualified to be the Savior. Only He could forgive sins."

Julieta thought for a moment. "I want to go to heaven when I die. How can I be saved, Pastor? What do I need to do?"

Jessica held her breath as she stared at Ryan and Julieta. Witnessing what was happening stirred her soul in a way she had never experienced before. She had never led a person to Christ, nor had she been present when someone accepted Christ as Savior. She couldn't take her eyes away from the pastor and teen, and she silently asked God to soften the young girl's heart to the gospel message of salvation. Listening more intently now, Jessica heard Ryan respond to Julieta's question.

"Julieta, do you understand that you're a sinner?"

Jessica couldn't hear Julieta's reply, but she saw the teen nod her head.

"Can you tell me what you believe about Jesus?"

Jessica strained to hear Julieta's answer.

"I know He is God's Son, who died on the cross for me. I know He didn't stay dead because He rose three days later, and now I know He is the only One who can forgive me and save me from my sins."

"Julieta, do you want Jesus to forgive you and become your Savior?"

"Yes, Pastor."

"Then you need to ask Him to do that. I can't do it for you, but I will be right here praying for you. Jesus already knows your heart, but He longs to hear you tell Him that you want Him to save you."

Julieta nodded and after a moment, bowed her head. "Dear Jesus…" She began to cry as she spoke. "I am so sorry I didn't understand before, but now I do. I know I am a sinner, and I cannot go to heaven to be with You until my sins are forgiven. I know You died on the cross for me. Would You please forgive my sins and be my Savior? I really want to go to heaven one day. Amen." She lifted her head and looked into Ryan's beaming face.

"Welcome to the family, Julieta."

Instantly, a huge smile blossomed on the girl's face. "I am saved now, right? I am going to heaven?"

"Right. You are now a child of God. And, according to the Bible, the angels in heaven are dancing around God's throne as He writes your name in His Book of Life."

"Really?"

Ryan nodded. "That's what the Bible says."

"Now what?"

"Well, the Bible says in Romans ten, verse nine 'That if thou shalt confess with thy mouth the Lord Jesus, and shalt believe in thine heart that God hath raised him from the dead, thou shalt be saved.' You should tell someone."

Her young eyes brightened, and she turned her head toward Jessica. "Can I tell *Doctora* Jessica?"

"You certainly can."

Julieta ran over to Jessica. "I'm saved, *Doctora*! I'm saved! I'm going to heaven one day!" She reached out her arms and hugged Jessica.

"I'm so happy for you, Julieta. My heart is praising God!" She smiled at Ryan over Julieta's shoulder as her own tears finally spilled down her cheeks.

The teen pulled back. "I have to tell my counselor!" She rushed back to Ryan and hugged him. "Thank you, Pastor! Thank you so much!"

Ryan and Jessica watched her run to her cabin.

"That was so wonderful!" said Jessica pulling a tissue out of her skirt pocket. She gently wiped her eyes.

"This was a pretty amazing night," agreed Ryan with a wide grin. He strolled beside Jessica, his Bible in one hand and a flashlight in the other. "What a fantastic blessing to have on the last night of camp."

"I've never done that."

Chapter Twenty

"What?"

"Helped someone get saved. It was really... really amazing. Everything you said to her was perfect. Exactly what she needed to hear. How do you know what to say?"

"That's the Holy Spirit, Jessica, not me. You just have to trust God and allow the Holy Spirit to speak through you," Ryan stated. "I will say, it is pretty awesome when I get to lead someone to Christ. It never gets old." He stopped and gazed up into the night sky. "It's hard to understand how the God who made the heavens, all those stars, loves each one of us so much that He sent His only Son to be the sacrifice for our sins because He longs to have a relationship with us."

Jessica stood silently by Ryan's side. She lifted her eyes upward and marveled at the countless number of twinkling stars. "They're beautiful."

"And He's named each one. Pretty incredible, I think."

They resumed walking toward Jessica's cabin.

"Hey, why did you want me to stay tonight? Not that I minded. I'm glad I was there."

"A couple of reasons really. One, I didn't want Julieta to be uncomfortable if we were alone, but the most important is a mandate from the Bible. It says in the first book of Thessalonians that we should 'abstain from all appearance of evil.' Some might get the wrong idea if Julieta and I were alone in the dark after everyone had retired for the evening. With you there, Julieta didn't have to fear being alone with me, plus you become the eyes and ears of the camp, so to speak. The one who can be the witness that nothing improper happened."

Jessica's eyes narrowed slightly as she frowned. "Who would think that?"

"You'd be surprised," stated Ryan. "But regardless of whether or not someone actually thinks that, God's Word tells me to be careful, so I don't counsel girls or women alone... ever. If my testimony gets tarnished, my ministry suffers for it... maybe even dies. I can't have that happen."

"No. No, you can't." Jessica hesitated as she reached for the door to her cabin. She stopped, then turned to face Ryan. "So... uh... how do you date?"

Ryan's cheeks reddened slightly as he stammered, "I...uh... I haven't since Gabriela died, but if I did, it would be out in the open. You know, no romantic dinners at the parsonage. Stuff like that."

"I'm sorry," murmured Jessica. "I shouldn't have asked that. It's really none of my business."

"It's okay, really." He shifted uncomfortably. "I'll see you in the morning?"

She tried to lighten the mood by smiling broadly. "Bright and early!" When he didn't speak, her smile lessened. "Good night, Ryan."

"Good night, Jessica." He waited until she closed the door behind her, then hurried back toward his house, never seeing the curtains of Jessica's cabin part slightly, then close together.

****

After breakfast the next day, when the long line of cars and church vans began arriving to pick up the teens, Jessica found herself continually wiping tears away as she hugged the campers goodbye. When the final group of young people drove off, Jessica felt a slight emptiness within her heart as she walked over to a bench in the courtyard.

"Well, Doc," began Ryan as he came over and sat down beside her, "how was your first camp experience?"

"It was different than I expected, but in a good way. I never thought it would be so fulfilling," she answered honestly. "I'm going to miss them."

"Maybe you'll see them again sometime. If not here, then there." He gestured upward.

Jessica smiled. "Yes, I will, won't I?"

They sat in silence for a few minutes, then Ryan turned to her.

Chapter Twenty

"I'm sorry I haven't been able to spend a lot of time with you," he said regretfully.

She shook her head. "No apology necessary. I've seen how busy you are. The kids love you! I loved the softball game! Watching you and the counselors play against them was hilarious! Everyone was so excited! What a wonderful way to end the camp, and then last night. Julieta was still beaming when she left today. I heard her tell her folks about it as she climbed into their car."

"It was pretty awesome, wasn't it? Having Julieta come forward for salvation was such a blessing! I think these camps are my most favorite time of the year."

"I can see why." She turned to him. "Thank you."

"For what?"

"Letting me come. I know how worried you've been, but I am so glad you let me come. And I'm glad Eric's here, too. I'm not sure I would have been up to all the hiking, so having him here has really been a blessing for me, too, but don't tell him!" she laughed."

Ryan smiled. "I'm glad you're both here, too. You're still feeling okay, right?"

Her smile was genuine as she replied, "I am feeling wonderful! Tired, but wonderful."

"Well, they say there's no rest for the weary, and that's us. We ought to start getting our second group of campers around three o'clock. Are you up for it?"

"Absolutely! This has been such an amazing couple of weeks for me. I can't wait to see what God does here at the next camp," admitted Jessica as they walked together back toward the main office.

****

The second camp began just as the first, and once again, after finishing with the preliminary inputting of camper information for nearly sixty elementary-aged children, Jessica remained continually busy, but it was a busyness that left her fulfilled and content at each day's end.

On the morning of the fourth day, Jessica sat out on the patio watching the younger children play around the courtyard. It had rained off and on during the past few days, so digging in the mud was a welcome adventure for the smaller boys and girls. As soon as the sun had appeared in a cloudless sky, the children scampered outside along with their counselors, who stood around chatting amongst themselves. Jessica marveled at how the children could find pleasure in simply playing in the wet ground.

Flora, a petite six-year-old girl with long, straight black hair, called out to Jessica. *"Doctora, venga a ver!"*

Jessica lowered her sunglasses to view Flora more clearly. *What does she want me to see?*

"¿Qué es, Flora?"

"Es un cangrejo con una larga cola." She squatted down and reached out her finger to touch it.

Jessica cast a puzzled look toward the girl.

A crab with a long tail?

Suddenly, Jessica's eyes widened in alarm. "No, Flora! Don't touch it! *No lo toque!*" She raced toward the little girl, but despite her efforts, she was unable to reach Flora before her tiny finger touched the pointed tail of the bark scorpion.

Flora's scream pierced the air and sent a chill through Jessica's body. Scooping up the young girl in her arms, Jessica dashed to the clinic.

"Oww!" Flora screamed as she clung to Jessica. *"¡Duele! ¡Hazlo parar!"*

"Sweetheart, I wish I could make it stop." Jessica's heart rate escalated as she slammed open the clinic door and carried Flora to a small cot. Laying the sobbing girl down, Jessica rushed over to the supply cabinet. Grabbing her medical bag, she hurried back to the scared little girl. Frantically opening the bag, she dug for the snakebite kit. From it, she pulled out the extractor and a small lancet, setting them next to her. She held

Chapter Twenty

Flora's face in her hands and looked directly into her frightened, tear-filled eyes.

"Flora, I have to make a small cut. It's going to hurt a little bit, but I need you to be as still as you can," stated Jessica. She wiped Flora's forefinger with a sterile antiseptic wipe.

"*¡Duele!*"

"I know, Flora. I'm sorry. *Lo siento.*" Jessica held Flora's hand tightly and made a small cut at the sting site. She placed the extractor over the wound hoping to create a negative pressure to withdraw any venom that had not been absorbed into the child's body.

As Jessica knelt over the girl, Akna rushed through the cabin door. "What happened, *mija*?"

"She was stung by a scorpion. I need some ice, Akna, now!" The urgency in Jessica's voice was impossible to miss.

"Of course! Do you need anything else?"

"I need anti-venom. Can you find Pastor Ryan?"

"*Sí*, I will find him!" Akna hurried out of the clinic.

Jessica's fingers trembled as she tended to Flora's wound.

Think, Jessica, think. You've got to help her. Lord, give me clarity of mind right now. Please guide me.

In moments, Akna had returned with a bowl of ice. "I called Pastor Ryan on the radio. He is on his way."

"Thank you, Akna." Jessica looked up and saw the fear etched on the older woman's face. Jessica reached up and touched Akna's hand. "If Pastor Ryan doesn't have anti-venom, we'll need to get Flora to a hospital. Will Joaquin be able to take us?"

Akna nodded rapidly. "*Sí Doctora* Jessica. He will be ready if you need him."

Jessica hurriedly wrapped some ice in a towel and placed it on Flora's swelling finger. She kept her eyes on Flora's breathing as she set the items she would need to start an intravenous line on a nearby table. She waited though, for without the anti-venom, the IV would be useless, and the ride to the hospital would be more difficult with it in the child during transport.

In less than five minutes, Ryan was by Jessica's side. "What do you need?"

"I remember seeing snake anti-venom, but do you have any for scorpions?"

"I think so. I seem to remember Maggie wanting some on site, so I ordered some from Veracruz, but that was a while ago. I don't know if it's expired or not. We don't see a lot of scorpions around here." He turned to Akna. "Office refrigerator. Grab the whole box, please." She nodded and rushed out toward the office building.

Within minutes, Akna had returned with a metal box half full of small vials. Ryan took the box and began inspecting each bottle. "Got one! Here's a few more," he announced as he set them on the table next to Jessica. "We've got five vials of bark scorpion anti-venom, and the expiration date is..." He scanned the label for the information. "It's good. Not until next year." He set the bottle on the table next to Jessica.

She turned her attention back to Flora. "Sweetie, I have to start an..." She turned to Ryan. "Please tell her I need to get some medicine into her, and I need to start an intravenous line. It will hurt a little at first, but if she's very still, I should be able to get it in quickly, and then it won't hurt a lot after that."

As soon as Ryan explained what was going to happen, Flora began to wail. *"¡Yo no lo quiero!"*

Jessica looked into Flora's wide eyes and said in halting Spanish, "I know you don't want it, Flora, but I need you to trust me. If I don't give you this medicine, you could be very, very sick. I want you to look at Pastor Ryan, okay?"

Help me, Lord. I need steady hands and a good vein.

She applied a tourniquet to Flora's lower arm and patted the little girl's hand. Several small veins popped up, but Jessica searched for a larger one higher up on the arm. Her skillful fingers softly felt for the best vein in which to stick the tiny

Chapter Twenty

butterfly needle. Finally palpating a suitable one, she wiped the skin with an antiseptic swab and looked up at Ryan.

Ryan gently turned Flora's head away from Jessica and softly spoke in Spanish to the terrified little girl. "Flora, did I ever tell you about the monkey that came to church?"

"A monkey? Really?"

"Really. It came right in through the double doors."

Jessica advanced the needle into the tiny vein and was rewarded with an immediate flashback of blood, indicating the proper placement.

"Owww!" Flora started to cry again. "¡Me duele!"

Ryan held tightly to Flora so she wouldn't move until Jessica had finished securing the IV. "I know it hurts, honey, but it's all done, Flora. You did good." He dabbed at the tears on the little girl's face.

"You did a great job, Flora," complimented Jessica. She adjusted the intravenous fluid to a steady "keep open" rate. The drops fell at regular intervals keeping the IV line patent and ready to receive the anti-venom.

"What else do you need?"

Jessica glanced up at Ryan. "I need to talk with a local doctor, preferably someone at the Veracruz ER. I want to make sure I do everything I need to do. Also, can someone notify her parents? She may still need to go to the hospital if she doesn't respond to the anti-venom, but at the very least, they should come and take her home," stated Jessica.

Ryan nodded. "Akna, will you call the parents? I'll get the physician on the line." He stepped into the outer room to make the call.

Jessica quickly read the inserts for the anti-venom, then reconstituted three vials into the appropriate amount of normal saline. She gently swirled the solutions then diluted them further according to the instructions. Slowly, she infused the anti-venom, while monitoring Flora's vital signs.

Ryan returned with his cell phone held out. "The hospital doctor is on the phone, Jess."

She took the phone and explained the situation to the Veracruz physician. As the Mexican doctor instructed her on the proper procedures for a scorpion sting to a pediatric patient, Jessica scribbled the information down. Relieved to have consulted with someone familiar with the bark scorpion, Jessica relaxed a bit as she handed the phone back to Ryan. "He said there's nothing else I need to do for the next hour. Just watch her. If she shows any signs of envenomation—"

"Any signs of what?"

"Envenomation. Effects of the venom invading the tissues. Mostly neurotoxicity is what I'm focusing on for the next forty-five minutes or so. Breathing problems, muscle twitching, frothing at the mouth. Stuff like that. If I see that, I'll need to administer another vial over thirty to sixty minutes and bring her in. He suggests she be seen tomorrow even if she's acting fine."

"She's going to be okay, isn't she, *Doctora*?" Akna's whispered voice trembled.

Jessica drew in a deep breath and then turned around to face the Mayan woman. "The doctor told me exactly what to watch for, and he said with the anti-venom, she should recover without any problems."

"Ladies, I think this would be an optimum time for us to pray." Ryan led them in a petition for Flora's well-being, and as he finished, Flora's counselor knocked on the door.

"Excuse me. I thought you'd want to know that the parents are on their way. They live in Santa Esperanza, so it will be about twenty minutes. Is she okay? Can I see her?"

Ryan motioned to her. "Come on in, Sara. I think Flora would love to see you." He stood at the doorway next to Jessica while the worried counselor sat on the bed with Flora.

"So," he whispered, "she *is* going to be okay, right?"

"Yes, I think she'll be fine. Since I was right there, we started emergency measures immediately. That's always a plus for the patient."

"I'm glad you were here."

Chapter Twenty

"Me, too."

An hour later, Flora sat nestled in her father's lap as Jessica and Ryan explained the treatment and expected outcome. Together, they cautioned the parents about the possible side effects of a scorpion sting even after treatment and recommended that a local doctor see Flora the next day or sooner if she began to act out of the normal.

As Jessica watched them leave, she whispered a small prayer. "Thank you, Lord, for being with us and watching over Flora."

"Amen," Ryan added. As they turned back toward the courtyard, they walked in silence until they reached the clinic. Ryan stopped and turned to Jessica. "I'm so glad you were here. I shudder to think what could have happened had you not been."

"I'm glad I was here, too." Her face was grim though as she continued. "You're right, Ryan."

"About what?"

"You do need a fulltime physician here."

CHAPTER TWENTY-ONE

Three days later, Breanna, a slow-moving tropical storm, crossed the Florida Keys bringing heavy rains and flooding to the string of islands. It followed its projected course and headed into the Gulf of Mexico toward the Yucatan Peninsula. Forecasters watched with a cautious eye as Breanna picked up speed and strength on the open water. With wind speeds rising, Breanna was officially upgraded to hurricane status by the National Hurricane Center in the United States. On the Saffir–Simpson wind scale, Breanna was a "1," indicating wind speeds up to 95 mph. Landfall was predicted in forty-eight hours, and the eastern coast of Mexico was on high alert.

Although Veracruz was not predicted to be in the direct path of the hurricane, it was recommended that residents in the city and surrounding communities prepare for abnormally strong winds and rainfall. As a precautionary measure, Ryan made the difficult decision of terminating the final camp six days early. Along with the staff, he made the necessary phone calls and arrangements to transport fifty-seven children safely home before the weather turned ugly.

Ryan kept a close watch on the weather reports, and when Breanna had intensified to a "2," he assembled the staff and briefed them on the situation they were facing. Twenty-three men and women sat in the dining hall and listened as Ryan shared the latest weather report.

Chapter Twenty-one

"According to the National Hurricane Center, Breanna is bearing down on the Yucatan peninsula. If you're unfamiliar with hurricanes, there will be quite a bit of heavy rain even this far north. If Breanna should veer off course and hit closer to Veracruz, we could be in for some very severe weather.

"While I have the greatest confidence that our main buildings will hold up in the storm, I can't say the same for the cabins. Therefore, I have made arrangements for the counselors to go inland until the threat from Breanna passes. The bus from our sister church in Rio Blanca will be here in about two hours to pick everyone up. They'll bring you back here after the storm is over." He paused and looked at the forlorn faces of the group.

"Don't be dismayed about our last camp ending early; the Lord gave us two amazing camp sessions this year. You have touched so many lives for Jesus, some in ways that we'll never know about until we're in heaven with God. I am so grateful for each one of you who's chosen to be here this year. You were invaluable in the work of this camp. Thank you so much for everything." His voice broke, and he took a deep breath. "Let's have a word of prayer."

Every head in the dining room bowed as Ryan spoke from his heart to his heavenly Father. "Lord God, thank You so much for bringing us all here for this year's camps. You've allowed us to share Your love with so many children, some who never heard the gospel before. We think especially of those who made decisions to accept Your Son, Jesus, as their Savior, and pray that You will help them grow in their faith. These past few weeks have been a blessing beyond measure. Thank You so much. Now Lord, You know what we are facing in the next few days. We pray for safety in travel and through the storm. Watch over each one. Please put Your hand of protection over this place and keep us up and running to possibly help others in the aftermath. We love You, Lord, and we thank You for the joy we receive in serving You. In Jesus' precious name, amen." He lifted his head, wiping his eyes. "Are there any questions?"

One of the counselors raised his hand. "So Rio Blanca won't be affected by Breanna?"

"Not likely. There's a small mountainous region between Rio Blanca and Santa Molina, so that acts as a shield for that community. You will be safe there," explained Ryan.

"What about you, Pastor?"

He smiled. "I'll be fine. I've been through a few hurricanes here. Joaquin and I usually stay in case something immediate needs to be done to the property. It's not a good idea to abandon the church unless the government issues an order to do so. I don't expect that to happen, but if it does, it's easier to evacuate a few than a lot. I would, however, appreciate your prayers." He added, "And I'll be praying for each of you."

"Can we do anything before we go?"

"If you get all packed, you can see Joaquin. He could probably use a few hands to help nail some plywood on the windows. If you have more questions, please stay and ask me, otherwise feel free to go and get ready for the bus."

As the dining hall emptied out, Jessica remained behind. She sat in her chair near the back of the room and watched Ryan as he addressed a few concerns from two more counselors. When he finished, she walked over to him.

"Do you really think it'll be that bad here?"

He shook his head. "No, unless Breanna changes course. We handle heavy rain and wind all the time, but a category two hurricane can be pretty devastating. The last one we saw here was a category three, and it did a lot of damage. No lives were lost, but we had a great deal of repair work to do."

"Are Akna and the children leaving?"

"No. She won't leave Joaquin."

Jessica hesitated, then said, "I don't want to go, and neither does Eric."

"Jessica, I—"

"Please, Ryan, don't ask us to leave. I'd go crazy not knowing how you were, and if communications were down, it could be days before I hear anything. Besides, what happens

Chapter Twenty-one

if you get hurt? Or Joaquin? Or someone else? Wouldn't it be good to have a doctor here? Even better with two." Her eyes pleaded with him.

Ryan sat down, placed his elbows on the table, and linked his fingers together. He glanced at her abdomen, then quickly looked up at her face. "I can't ask you to stay."

She reached out and touched his hand. "You're not asking us to stay; we're volunteering."

He looked at her, and for the first time, he realized he really didn't want her to go.

****

Over the next thirty-six hours, Breanna grew more massive as it moved across the Gulf of Mexico. Its wind speed intensified, and the NHC reclassified the hurricane as a category three. The trajectory of the storm put its center just south of Veracruz. As the outer bands of the hurricane neared, the sky over Santa Molina was thick with ominous gray clouds, harbingers of what was coming. Heavy rain began to pelt the canopy, and a plethora of animal calls echoed through the trees as if warning each other to be prepared for the worst.

Ryan, Eric, Joaquin, and Juan secured every building on the church grounds, while Akna, her daughters, Maria and Ana, and Jessica made sure they had easy access to food, fresh water, battery powered lights and radio, and other basic needs for at least seven days.

The skies grew darker, changing day to night in a matter of minutes. This transformation ushered in a seriousness to their preparations. Jessica walked over to where Ryan was checking the planks across the dining hall windows.

"Is there anything I can do?" she asked nervously.

"No, I think we're as ready as we can be. Most of this is just precautionary. If anything, we'll just get the edge of the storm unless it changes its course. If Veracruz takes a more direct hit, we could get a lot more rain and wind. In any case, it's easier to be proactive now than scramble to put up boards in the middle of the storm. I'm confident we'll be fine. Even if we lose power, we've got the generators, so we'll be good. If this storm doesn't lose any of its punch and alters its course toward Veracruz, then the government's priority will be getting the city up and running. Afterwards, it will send workers out into the countryside to address the needs there."

He pulled the blinds down over the planks as he talked with her. "I suspect if the city does take a direct hit, we might be on our own for a week or two."

"Really? That long?"

Ryan stopped. "Only if Veracruz is hit. Right now, that's not the predicted path, but you never know. We've got plenty of supplies here, including water. Our greatest worry will be the local rivers. With unusually heavy rains, the rivers could flood. If that happens, we'll probably end up sheltering some of the people living in Santa Molina. They know to come here for refuge."

Jessica nodded. "I suppose there hasn't been a change in the forecast?"

"Not yet. By the way, I need you to bunk with the Canul family. Your cabin is not as sturdy as their house. They've got plenty of room, and Akna is expecting you to stay with them."

"I will. Is your house okay for you to stay in?"

"It should be. It's been through a couple of hurricanes, so I would expect it to do the same this time."

"So you're going to be alone?"

He shook his head. "No. Eric will bunk with me. I'll be in here most of the time though. I can get to the office through there." He pointed to a hallway. "It's better than going back and forth from my place. And all the supplies are here, plus the television and radio reception is best here." He noticed a look of concern on her face. "Hey, don't worry so much. We're not alone, remember? God is with us, and He'll see us through."

She lowered her gaze. "I know, but—"

"We'll be okay, Jessica. I promise."

Chapter Twenty-one

She nodded and forced a smile, afraid to admit the fear that was mounting within her.

****

As predicted, Breanna slammed into the eastern Mexican coast at Alvarado, only forty miles south of Veracruz. With sustained winds close to 130 mph, the storm was expected to cause considerable damage to the coastal regions. As Breanna swung to the northwest, it lost some of its force resulting in a recategorization eight hours later to a category two hurricane with sustained winds near 110 mph. However, the devastating storm was still on the move and heading directly toward Santa Molina.

The rains and winds continued to bombard the area, and soon Santa Molina was feeling the full effects of the hurricane. Trees were being snapped like twigs, while rivers rose dangerously close to flood stage. The roar from the steady barrage of battering rain was deafening, and Jessica found herself wishing she could shut out the thunderous pounding.

Then, without any warning, everything quieted.

"Is it over?" Jessica whispered as she sat on a bench in the dining room, her arms protectively resting on her abdomen. She cast a wide-eyed glance upward as the pounding rain and howling winds seemed to magically stop. She wasn't cold, but she couldn't stop shivering.

"No," Ryan said. He moved over by her. "This is just the eye passing. We've got several more hours of this. Are you doing okay?"

"I think so. I just never imagined it would be like this," confessed Jessica. "It's so loud."

Ryan nodded. "I know, but we're safe, Jessica. I promise." He reached over and squeezed her hand. "Trust me, okay? I won't let anything happen to you." He gave her a smile. "This lull is only going to last a few more minutes. I'm going to see if Joaquin needs any help. You wait here."

She watched him leave, wishing he had stayed.

Lord, this is so frightening. I know You control the winds and the rain, but I'm not as strong as I thought I'd be. I'm sorry. Please take care of Ryan and Joaquin out there. Help this to be over soon. Keep us safe.

As she sat waiting for Ryan's return, the wind began to pick up, and she could hear the gentle pitter-patter of rain change to a more urgent rat-a-tat on the roof.

Where is he?

As the wind began to howl once more, Akna and her children came in from the kitchen with sandwiches and water.

"You need to eat, *mija*." She set a plate in front of Jessica with a chicken sandwich and fresh papaya pieces on it. Akna sat across from Jessica while the children sat at their own table to eat their lunches.

When Jessica didn't move, Akan lightly scolded her. "You need to eat for the baby. The men, they are fine, *mija*. Just checking to make sure everything is still secure."

Jessica nodded her head. "It's just that..."

"I understand. When you care about someone, it is difficult to wait when he might be in danger, but the Lord will take care of him, *mija*. His Word tells us in Proverbs 'But all who listen to me will live in peace, untroubled by fear of harm.' Trust Him. For now, you must think of your baby and eat your lunch," reminded Akna as she reached out and patted Jessica's hand.

Picking up her sandwich, Jessica took a small bite. As she chewed, it seemed as if the sky opened up once more. Rain crashed down upon the roof, and the increasing wailing of the wind made Jessica want to cover her ears and hide. Her hand shook slightly as she set her food back on the plate.

It wasn't until Ryan, Eric, and Joaquin were back in the dining hall that Jessica could finally relax. All three men were drenched, but unharmed. Akna quickly left her seat, returning with a large towel for each of them.

As Ryan dried off his arms and hair, he sat down beside Jessica. "Wow! That wind came up fast! Can you believe we

Chapter Twenty-one

got this wet just between the sanctuary and here? Everything looked good though and—"

He stopped speaking when he saw Jessica wiping her eyes. "Hey, what's wrong?" He tossed the towel on the table and turned to her. "Jessica, what's wrong?"

She shook her head and purposefully turned away from him. "I'm sorry. It's nothing, really..."

His brow furrowed as he prompted her. "Please," he said softly. "What is it?"

She pressed her lips together, thinking of an appropriate response, then finally said, "I was just worried."

"About what?"

"You."

"Me? I'm fine."

"I know that now, but when the wind and rain started, and you weren't here... I just thought..." She dabbed at her eyes again.

As understanding came, he apologized. "I'm sorry. I didn't mean to worry you. I needed to make sure everything was still in place. I'm really sorry, Jessica."

They sat together in uncomfortable silence for a few minutes until Akna set a sandwich plate in front of Ryan. She looked at him with understanding eyes, then left to go sit with Eric, Joaquin, and her children.

Finally, Jessica turned her head toward him, her eyes downcast. She slowly admitted, "I thought something had happened to you."

Ryan whispered remorsefully in his attempt to reassure her. "I'm really sorry I scared you. Nothing's going to happen to me. I'm very careful, and we always go with a partner."

She looked up at him through her thick black lashes, reached out and squeezed his hand. With a weak smile, she softly said, "I'm just glad you're okay."

They listened to the storm raging around them, and as Jessica sat quietly beside Ryan, she realized she had not released his hand nor had he pulled it away.

****

Late in the evening, the lights flickered and went out as torrential rains continued and gale force winds catapulted debris against the buildings. Some of the cabins had begun to lose their roofing, and a few trees had toppled over. The wind blew fiercely, sending rain slamming into the south side of the dining room. The roar of the storm was horrifying. Water began to seep in under the doors, and Jessica, Akna, and the girls placed hastily rolled up towels along the thresholds to try and keep the water out.

It was well after midnight when everyone went to bed, but sleep eluded Jessica. Somewhere a loose panel was banging against the side of a building. The hammering rain sounded more like millions of pebbles being thrown against the walls. The amplified sounds of the storm prevented her from sleeping, and she simply lay in her bed, her eyes wide open, her heart beating frantically.

What time I am afraid, I will trust in Thee. What time I am afraid, I will trust in Thee.

She repeated the verse in her head again and again in an attempt to alleviate her fears. Tossing and turning, she finally gave in and sat up. As she did, she felt a hard rolling motion from within. Automatically, her hand moved to her abdomen, and she bit her lower lip as she caressed her baby the only way she could.

How could God bless me with you and then put us in danger? He wouldn't do that, would He, sweet baby? It'll be okay. It has to be.

She rose and paced back and forth in her room until she could tolerate it no longer. Using her cell phone to light her way, she walked to the small kitchen. The room was dark. As she stood near the center of the room, she listened to the ferocity of the storm and shuddered.

Dear God, please make this stop!

Chapter Twenty-one

As she sat down at the kitchen table, she squeezed her eyes closed. Her lips pressed tightly together in a thin line, and her fists were clenched as she tried to pray. She silently begged God for courage to endure the deluge all around her, but the noise of the storm bombarded her thoughts, and she struggled to focus on the Lord. Her whispered voice shook as her prayer became audible.

"We will be okay, right, Lord? You will take care of us, won't You?" She hesitated for a moment, then added. "Please don't let anything happen to Ryan. Keep him safe. He's..." She stopped herself. "Please make this storm stop soon. Help me to not be so afraid. Help me to trust You. In Jesus' name, amen."

Resting her arms on the table, she laid her head down on them. The baby within her was moving back and forth, and as she allowed herself to be enveloped by the feeling, she closed her eyes and drifted off to sleep.

****

"Jessica?" The whispered voice was barely perceptible.

Someone was calling her name, but who?

"Jessica?"

This time, the voice was accompanied by a touch. She slowly opened her eyes.

"Jessica? You should be sleeping in your bed, not out here."

She felt a hand on her shoulder. Slowly raising her head, a face came into focus. "Ryan?"

"Yes. How long have you been here? It's nearly dawn." His voice was low, but filled with concern.

There was a very faint glow of light in the room, and as Jessica looked around the room and heard the pounding rain, she remembered where she was.

"Why are you out here?" he asked.

She blinked her eyes and stifled a yawn. Her hand shot up to cover her mouth. "I couldn't sleep. I thought if I came out here, maybe I could relax a little." She smiled weakly and shrugged her shoulders. "I guess I relaxed a lot."

"C'mon, let's get you back to bed." After helping her to her feet, he picked up the battery-powered lamp he had brought. He led her to the small guest room where her bed had been set up.

"Thank you. I'm sorry to be so much trouble. I just—"

"You're no trouble, but you shouldn't be wandering around at night. If you need something, just call out for me. I'm in the other room with Eric and Juan. I'll hear you," whispered Ryan. "Okay?"

Jessica nodded, then asked, "You're here?"

"Yeah. The power went out. We'll get the generators up and running in the morning when we can see better. For now, Eric and I are bunking with Juan."

"Why?"

"We think the storm's stalled a bit, so just in case, we thought it would be prudent to all be together in one place since the power's out."

An unsettling feeling arose in Jessica, but she nodded as she moved over to her bed and crawled in under the blanket as Ryan stood at the doorway.

"Get some rest. And stay in here until it's light, okay?"

"I will. Thank you." She watched him leave the room, then turned on her side and fell into a fitful sleep dreaming of a tall, handsome pastor with a boyish grin.

****

The rain and wind continued into the next day without any evidence of the storm weakening. Everyone now remained at the Canuls' home for safety's sake, riding out the storm together. Breanna had been downgraded to a tropical storm, but her fury had yet to subside in Santa Molina.

Jessica sat next to Ryan as he led the group in morning devotions. He read the entire chapter of Psalm forty-six. "Look again at the first three verses. 'God is our refuge and strength, a

Chapter Twenty-one

very present help in trouble. Therefore will not we fear, though the earth be removed, and though the mountains be carried into the midst of the sea. Though the waters thereof roar and be troubled, though the mountains shake with the swelling thereof. Selah.'

"There will be times when God is right beside us through the storm, as it's written in Psalm 23 where God is with us as we walk through the valley of the shadow of death. At other times, instead of walking through the storm with us, He simply calms it for us.

"I believe that the greatest thing God does when we are facing a storm, any kind, like this hurricane, or maybe financial problems, or even sickness, is calm our soul. We may be full of fear inside, but when we turn to God and fully trust Him, our inner spirit is at peace. It's not a circumstantial peace either; it's a peace that is eternal."

As Jessica listened to Ryan, the wind continued to blow wildly outside, but it was the turmoil in her heart that troubled her mostly this morning. She bowed her head when Ryan began to pray, but her silent prayer was vastly different than the one he offered to the Lord. She closed her eyes tightly, shutting out everything except her own heart's cry.

Dear Jesus, I know I can't stay here, but how can I leave? I can't imagine my life without him. Please help me. Show me Your will...

****

By the time breakfast was completed, it seemed as if the ferociousness of the rain had lessened. The wind was still strong, but the men were able to walk outside with minimal difficulty. Together, they checked the buildings, reinforced loose planks where needed, and removed some of the debris they came across. When they finally returned to the house, they were soaked to the skin, but rejoicing in the minimal amount of damage they had seen.

As they all sat together eating a late lunch, Ryan reported his findings. "One of the trees is down," he said. "But it missed the cabins completely. We'll have to cut it up to remove it, but at least we won't be replacing an entire rooftop, just a few of the shingles that have blown loose."

Joaquin agreed. "Yes, we have truly been blessed. There is some water on the floors of some of the cabins, but I think we will just need a good cleaning there. I am praising God for the raised bunks. It was a good idea to put the dressers and chairs on top of them, Pastor Ryan." He took a huge bite of his chicken burrito.

"I wish I could take credit for that, but it was really Juan's idea," smiled Ryan as he slapped the teen on the back.

Joaquin beamed at his son. "I am proud of you, *mijo*. You are fast becoming a man."

Juan said nothing, but a huge grin spread across his face. He glanced over at his mother through thick lashes. Akna simply smiled and nodded her head.

Jessica sipped her tea as she observed the family dynamics at the table.

Lord, the Canuls are an amazing family. Certainly not wealthy by our standards in the States, but rich beyond measure in their love for one another and their devotion to You. I hope I have that someday, too, Lord. I want my baby to grow up to love You, and to know the love of family.

****

By late afternoon, the rain was sporadic, and the winds had died down. Patches of blue dotted the sky, and it was clear that Breanna had run its course. Ryan, Eric, and Joaquin had already gone out to inspect the grounds once more, but now Jessica ventured outdoors.

She stood outside on the patio and scanned the area. Broken tree limbs were everywhere; a few roof shingles were scattered

Chapter Twenty-one

on the ground, and two planks were partially hanging from the nearest cabin. She glanced over at the clinic.

It's now or never. Let's see how you did.

She lifted her feet high as she walked, and each step made a slurping sound as her sneakers broke the suction of the mud against her shoes. When she reached the clinic, she found the door difficult to open, but putting her entire body weight against it, she managed to push it open just enough for her to slide inside, which was quite a challenge with her growing abdomen. A thin layer of mud on the floor hindered the opening of the door.

"Yuck!" Jessica frowned in disgust. "I guess I need to get some of this out the door. I need to be able to move around in here. There has to be a shovel around here somewhere."

Her nose wrinkled at the musty vegetative smell of the room, and she opened the windows as she walked through the clinic. The water line was only about a quarter of an inch high, but that was enough to be a muddy mess.

"Ugh! I'm going to be shoveling mud for days!" Jessica lamented. Finding a stiff broom, she began the arduous task of pushing the sludge out the door and away from the clinic's entrance, carefully scanning the mud-covered floor as she swept.

Hmm... I wonder if scorpions can live in the mud?

Nearly an hour later, Ryan and Eric entered the clinic. Ryan wiped his brow with his hand, leaving a thin trace of mud on his forehead. "I can't believe there hasn't been more damage. The Lord really had a shield of protection around us." He spied Jessica in the main exam room. "Jessica! What are you doing?"

She stopped abruptly, facing Ryan. "Cleaning, why?"

"No. You shouldn't be doing this. Someone else can do it." Ryan reached for the broom, but Jessica moved it out of his reach.

"Why? I am perfectly capable of sweeping a floor."

"It's not a normal sweeping of the floor. It's mud; it takes more effort to move it, and you're not the one to do it," insisted Ryan.

Jessica frowned. "Ryan, I'm not an invalid. Women have been having babies since the Garden of Eden. The world doesn't stop when they give birth. I'm not going to sit around while everyone else is working. I'm here to help, and that's what I'm going to do."

Ryan crossed his arms in front of his chest, tension in his face. "Jessica, you are not being reasonable." He shook his head. "Give me the broom." He held a hand out.

"Why?"

"Because I'm asking you for it."

"But I can do this."

"I know you can, but I'd prefer you not." He waited expectantly.

"I'm not ignorant of my situation, Ryan. I won't overdo it. When I'm tired, I'll rest. When I need help, I'll ask for it. If I were home, I'd be in the ER right now doing my job, not sitting at home counting the days until I deliver. Please let me help. That's why I'm here," she pleaded.

He looked at her hopeful face and against his better judgment, relented. "Fine, but I'm going to hold you to your word. You quit before you're exhausted, understand?"

She smiled as she saluted him. "Yes, sir."

He scowled, then relaxed his stance. "Sometimes," he began as he reached for the broom, "you are quite exasperating. Hand me the broom, and you hold the door open."

Jessica's eyes widened as she handed him the broom. "I'm what?"

Ryan just shook his head. "You heard me." He began to push the muck out the door of the clinic and whispered to himself. "And she thinks Eric is the hardheaded one?"

CHAPTER TWENTY-TWO

Dinner was ready by the time Jessica and Eric had quit their work for the day. They entered the Canuls' home, and the aroma of roasted chicken made them realize they were hungry. It was an informal meal since the dining room table was covered with supplies and items salvaged from some of the cabins.

"It smells delicious, Akna," exclaimed Jessica as she filled her plate with freshly made tortillas and *arroz con pollo*. She found a seat in the small living room and held her plate on her lap as she enjoyed the conversation around her.

Eric scooped a large helping of chicken and rice onto his plate. "This is great, Mrs. Canul. I can't wait to dig into this." He plopped down on the sofa next to Jessica and took a big bite of his tortilla. "Umm! Nothing beats a homemade tortilla!"

"Doctor Eric, a hard day's work will make any food taste good," said the Mayan woman, yet she smiled as she reentered her kitchen.

Near Jessica, Ryan sat cross-legged on the floor, his back against the wall. He balanced his plate on one leg after taking a bite of chicken, and upon request from Eric, began to explain the journey that brought him to Santa Molina. Jessica listened as he shared his story, staring at his deep blue eyes and the strands of black hair that haphazardly lay across his forehead. His voice was soothing, and she momentarily lost herself in it. Suddenly aware that she was staring, Jessica quickly averted her eyes to her own dinner plate.

What am I doing?

She hastily shoved a forkful of salsa into her mouth and immediately felt the burning sensation engulf her tongue. Her eyes filled with tears, and she grabbed for a bottle of water. In her haste, she knocked it to the floor. She bent to pick it up at the same time Ryan reached over to retrieve it. Their fingers touched, and for a brief moment, Jessica was unaware of anyone else being in the room. Her eyes looked forward and met those clear blue ones by which she had just been mesmerized. Her cheeks warmed, and she stammered, "I'm sorry... salsa... hot."

Ryan set the unopened bottle upright on the floor. "This seems to be a pattern for you." He held out his glass of milk. "Drink some of this. It'll help."

She sheepishly smiled and took a few sips. "Thank you," she mumbled. She returned the glass to Ryan, but did not allow herself to meet his gaze. She sat back on the sofa and moved her food around on her plate, oblivious to the conversation around her.

"Hey, Jess. I'd like to go over what we should take with us tomorrow. You want to get a list together tonight?" Eric's fork was poised in mid-air as he waited for her answer.

Jessica's eyes moved from Eric to Ryan, then to the others, who were looking at her. "Uh... sure. Where are we going?"

Eric grinned as he shook his head. "Where've you been? We've been talking about heading into the town tomorrow to make sure everyone is okay."

Her eyebrows lifted. "Really? I'm sorry. I guess I was daydreaming."

Ryan studied Jessica as he finished his last bite of chicken. "It has been a long day. Maybe we should all get some sleep, and we'll continue this in the morning."

"Now that sounds like a good plan. The list can wait," agreed Eric as he stood. He held his empty plate with one hand and started toward the kitchen.

Chapter Twenty-two

"Eric, now that the storm's abated, you can bunk with me," stated Ryan. "We'll have a bit more room at my place." He followed the young doctor into the other room.

Jessica watched them leave.

What's happening to me?

****

In the early morning hours, two trucks laden with food and medical supplies drove away from Ryan's church. They headed out toward Santa Molina carefully maneuvering their way along the muddy roads. Ryan and Eric rode together in one truck leading the way, while Joaquin drove the second vehicle with Akna and Jessica sitting beside him. They bounced along through deep puddles and long ruts as they made their way to the small town.

It took nearly twice as long to reach the outskirts of Santa Molina. Their first encounter with the community was encouraging. Although there was a shortage of fresh fruits and vegetables, most of the people had enough of the staples needed due to the collaborative efforts of the townspeople to pool their resources and share amongst themselves.

As they visited families, Ryan and Joaquin explained the need to boil their drinking water while Jessica and Eric managed the medical needs of the community. Akna scurried off to check on her family living farther down in the village.

It was late in the day when everyone converged at the home of Josefina and Roberto Alvarez, Akna's sister and brother-in-law. The upper floor had a window with the pane and part of its frame broken by flying debris. Additionally, a small section of roof needed to be tarped until repairs could be made to it. After surveying the damage, the three men elected to stay a bit longer and help Roberto weatherproof the house until he could get into Rio Blanca to purchase a new window and roofing materials.

Jessica and Akna decided to head for home before the sun went down, so the children would not be alone during the night. After transferring what was left of the supplies to the other truck, they began their drive. Akna took the wheel while Jessica busied herself making a list of what they should bring on the next trip into Santa Molina.

"I am so glad we were able to get out here, *Doctora* Jessica," Akna said as she steered the old truck down the road, slowly maneuvering the vehicle around a large pothole. "It is good to know my family is safe."

Jessica bounced in the passenger seat, but the seat belt, snapped below her protruding abdomen, held her firmly in place. "Me too. I'm surprised that there isn't very much damage or injury. I expected so much more."

The evening breeze began to blow through the truck, providing the women with a respite from the oppressive humidity. "Doctor Eric is a good help, don't you think? Nothing fazes him," said Akna.

"I noticed. He's going to be just fine in Papua New Guinea."

"Perhaps he will remain here with us."

Jessica glanced over at Akna. "You think so?"

The Mayan woman stared straight ahead at the road as she drove. "He is a good doctor, and we need a good doctor."

"That he is," said Jessica as she turned her head to look out the window. "I wonder what God has in store for me."

Akna smiled as she spoke. "It is not always for us to know, *mija*, but simply to trust and wait."

"I suppose so, but sometimes it would be nice to have a general idea, don't you think?"

"Maybe."

"You don't ever wonder what the future holds?"

"It is enough for me to know who holds tomorrow, *mija*. Whatever happens, I know God will do what is best for me. He is—"

"Stop! Stop the car, Akna! Did you see that?"

Chapter Twenty-two

****

Jessica climbed out of the old truck and cautiously moved to the broken guardrail. She peered over the road's edge, shielding her eyes from the glow of the setting sun. "This wasn't like this when we came through this morning. I remember because I thought about how the road was so near the drop off, and I was grateful for the railing."

"*¡Doctora! ¡Ten cuidado!* Be careful!" Akna warned as she rushed out of the truck chasing after Jessica. The gravel crunched under her feet as she neared Jessica and the road's precipice.

"There! Look!" Jessica pointed to a glint of reflected light. "Akna, that's a car! Someone's down there. I need my phone." She hurried back to the truck and retrieved the phone from her purse.

"No service," Jessica scowled as she tried to send a text message. "That's not good." She looked back toward the wreckage below.

"No, *Doctora*, you cannot go down. It is too dangerous for you. The baby! Think of the baby," pleaded Akna. "I will go down."

Jessica turned and looked into the concerned eyes of Akna. "I have to go, Akna. There could be someone down there who needs medical help right now. Look, it's not that steep, and there's plenty of foliage to hold on to. I can't just leave them there. You have to go back to Santa Molina and get Ryan and Eric. Come back as quickly as you can, okay?"

Akna hesitated and scanned the area. "I don't want to leave you here, *mija*. It will be dark soon."

"I know, Akna. That's why I need to get down there now, while I can still see the way." Jessica's eyes pleaded with the Mayan woman. "Please, Akna. I need you to go get Ryan. Bring blankets too, and water."

"But, the baby…" Akna's big brown eyes reflected the maternal fear in her heart as her gaze fell to Jessica's abdomen.

Jessica took both of Akna's hands in her own and looked into the frightened eyes of the woman she had grown to love. "God is with me, Akna. You said so yourself. He will protect me and the baby."

Reluctantly, Akna nodded as Jessica retrieved her medical bag. "Father God, protect *la doctora* and the baby," she whispered as she got into the truck. She looked once more at Jessica and called out, "Be careful, *mija!*"

Jessica nodded as she stepped cautiously onto the embankment. She hesitated for just a moment when she heard Akna drive off.

Please, Lord, give me a sure foot right now. It's just me and You.

Moving slowly with her medical bag secure in the crook of her arm, she used small plants to anchor her feet as she made the trek downward.

"Hello? Is anyone there?" she called out. "Can you hear me? *¿Estás herido?* Are you hurt? Hello?"

The way down was slick at times, but Jessica never slipped. Upon reaching the mangled vehicle, she saw that it was a small truck and trailer. The truck itself was on its side, its cab facing toward the road. The driver's door was open, and no one was inside. Shattered glass crunched under Jessica's feet when she walked around the truck. Bales of hay lay scattered below the wreckage, and Jessica saw that the trailer had been wrenched from the truck's hitch. It was off to the side, twisted, but upright.

Where are you?

Desperate for a reply, she kept calling out as she scanned the area. "*¿Dónde estás? Soy doctor. ¿Dónde estás?*"

"Please, where are you?" she whispered. Reaching out a hand to the truck to steady herself, she yanked it back quickly when she felt a sticky wetness. She glanced at the dark discoloration on her hand.

Blood! This is blood! Oh, Lord, please help me find the driver!

"Hello!" She listened carefully for any sound at all.

Chapter Twenty-two

Fumbling her way around the front of the truck to the passenger side, she peered in through the partially open door. Seeing no one, she glanced at the floor of the truck and fear welled up within her. A toy tractor rested near the accelerator pedal. Jessica winced.

A child? There was a child? Where could he be?

Crouching down as best she could, Jessica narrowed her eyes and looked beneath the truck. When she saw no body there, she murmured in relief, "Thank You, Lord," and then stood up and scanned the surrounding area once more.

"Hello!" She looked back up the embankment.

Is he up there? Could he have fallen out up there? Did I miss him?

She started to move up the hillside when a flash of color caught her eye as she turned.

What's that?

Quickly changing direction, she stumbled down toward what she thought she saw. Her eyes continued searching around her as she moved, and upon reaching an area with several small shrubs, she saw a young boy lying on his side. His blood-stained t-shirt had been torn, and now it flapped in the evening breeze.

"Can you hear me?" she asked as she lowered herself to the ground.

Please God, let him be alive.

Her fingers moved to the side of the child's neck as she palpated the carotid artery.

Thank You, Lord. It's weak, but it's there.

She started to reach for her medical bag when a strong tightening spread across her abdomen. "Oh baby, I know you don't like this, but this isn't the time to rehearse for labor." The contraction passed quickly, and Jessica continued assessing the boy. She bent near his ear. "Can you hear me? Everything's going to be all right. Hang in there, okay? I'm a doctor. *Soy doctor.*"

She pulled out her stethoscope and placed it against the boy's shirt. The dull thump-thump of his young heart was steady, and Jessica sighed in relief. She turned her attention to his lungs and listened as best she could without disturbing the position of her patient.

The sun had dropped below the horizon, and the shadows of twilight were elongating. She spoke reassuringly to the boy as she continued her examination. "You're going to be fine. Just stay with me. *Vas a estar bien.*" He had a large bump on his forehead, and his left arm was bent abnormally.

Probably a concussion and closed fracture of the left humerus.

Leaning over the boy, Jessica separated his eyelids, shining a light into the unseeing brown eyes.

Good. His pupils are reacting. What's the blood from? No obvious wounds. Only minor lacerations. Nothing that would cause this much bleeding...

She removed her light jacket and laid it upon the boy. Standing slowly, she scanned the embankment rapidly dimming from the encroaching darkness.

You're too young to have driven the truck. So where's the driver?

"Where are you?" she asked softly. She turned on the flashlight from her cell phone and looked around her. "If I had been in this wreck, I would have brought the boy here away from any potential fire, and then..." She regarded the road above her. "I would have tried to get help."

Jessica turned to light the area above her and started to retrace her steps to the road. Nightfall was now her enemy; she couldn't see the pitfalls of the uneven terrain as she climbed. Stepping on a patch of wet vegetation, she fell down roughly as her feet slid out from under her. One hand instinctively protected her abdomen; the other helped cushion her fall.

The landing still jarred her, and she sat for a few minutes willing her rapidly beating heart to calm down. Her breathing was slowing back to normal when she saw a worn boot protruding from underneath a large briar-like bush. She half-crawled to the shoe, and pushing aside the small branches, she found the driver of the truck.

Chapter Twenty-two

The dark haired man was unconscious. His breathing was shallow and irregular. She reached for his wrist; her fingers detecting a fast, thready pulse.

Something's wrong. Something's very wrong. What is it?

Jessica examined as much of the man's body as she could in the light of her cell phone, but the brush in which he was lying, combined with her pregnant state, made it difficult for her to easily access his entire body.

Jessica fought her instincts to move him, and instead tried to maneuver herself to better evaluate him. She thought for a moment, then cut off part of his shirt, rolled it up and formed a rudimentary cervical collar. Molding it around his neck, she secured it with gauze bandages and tape from her bag.

At least if I have to move you, this will help stabilize your neck.

She felt herself shaking. "Please God, I need Your help. I can't make a mistake. His life could depend on it. I can't do this alone."

What time I am afraid, I will trust in Thee.

Jessica stared at her trembling hands and repeated what she had heard in her head. "What time I am afraid, I will trust in Thee." She glanced upward. "Okay, Lord, I will trust in Thee. Please help me now." She took a deep breath and steadied her hands.

She rechecked the cervical collar. It was secure. She leaned over the man and once again put the stethoscope to his chest. She listened intently for breath sounds.

I should hear sounds on both sides, but I don't. They're only on the right. Possible collapsed lung.

She carefully moved the head of the scope inch by inch, trying to gain more information about his lungs. She straightened up and sat back on her knees taking in some deep breaths. She closed her eyes for a moment and willed her rapidly beating heart to settle down.

I can do this. This is what I'm trained for.

She moved her fingers adeptly over his upper chest, occasionally thumping the backs of her fingers, creating a dull resonance. When the pitch of the thumps changed, Jessica shook her head.

Not good.

Sliding two fingers into the palm of his hand, Jessica tried to elicit a response. "Hey, if you can hear me, please try to squeeze my fingers. *Si me puede oír, por favor trate de apretar los dedos.*" She tapped her own fingers lightly against his hand several times, then more forcefully. She felt nothing in return.

I've got to reinflate his lung. If help doesn't get here soon, he may not make it.

****

The sun had long set by the time Ryan and Eric had left Santa Molina. Joaquin had opted to spend the night with his wife's family to continue working on their house in the morning.

Once again, the ruts and washed out areas of the road made their travel slow, but they took advantage of the time to discuss God's will for their lives.

"So tell me," Ryan began. "How did you like helping out at the camps?"

"I really enjoyed it. It's a nice change from the emergency room. The kids were great, and when we were sitting around the campfire, and those kids shared what was on their hearts, well, it sure made me understand how important it is to reach everyone with the gospel. And when that one kid said he felt called to preach! That was awesome!"

Ryan swerved to avoid a dog that ran out into the road. "Praise the Lord, we only had one real emergency."

"Yeah. Jessica was great at handling that. Do you see a lot of scorpions here?"

"Not really. Not like in northern Mexico, nearer to Arizona, but we do get them now and then. That's why we stock the antivenom, but it had been so long since we've needed it, I wasn't

Chapter Twenty-two

sure we still had any. Thank the Lord, Jessica was right there. She gave Flora the anti-venom and took care of her until the parents arrived. It's been good to have you both here."

Eric nodded. "Thanks. I'm glad I got to come. It's been a huge blessing for me. Jessica's been doing great, too... considering."

"Yeah. I still worry about her, even though she's not due until the first part of September. I'm glad you came with her. It sure made me feel better. I know her OB gave her the okay to come as long as she's home by next week, but when she told me you were interested in coming, well, that was an answer to *my* prayer. I tell you, it's truly been a real blessing having both of you here."

"You two seem to get along well," commented Eric.

"I think so. She's easy to work with, most of the time, that is."

"Most of the time?" Eric lifted an eyebrow as his mouth curved upward.

"She can be a bit stubborn at times." Ryan grinned. "But she listens to reason, so it usually works out."

"Yeah, I've been on the end of that stubborn streak of hers," chuckled Eric. "More than once, too– Hey! Isn't that Joaquin's truck?" He pointed down the road.

Ryan slowed down and shielded his eyes from its headlights as the truck approached them. Alarmed, he opened the door and rushed out when he saw Akna stop and hurry out of the vehicle. "What's wrong? Where's Jessica?"

"¡Ha habido un accidente! La doctora, se quedó a ayudar."

"An accident? Is Jessica all right?"

"*Si*, she is fine. It is another car. She stayed to help, but we must help her!"

Ryan turned to Eric. Alarm filled his voice. "There's been an accident! Jessica's there!"

Akna's frantic voice cut through to Ryan's heart. "She needs you! Please hurry!"

****

"Jessica! Jessica! Where are you?" Ryan called out as he and Eric moved quickly down the embankment where the tire tracks had disappeared. Ryan fanned his flashlight out over the crushed foliage.

"Over here! Ryan! I'm down here!" came the distant reply.

"There's the truck," pointed out Eric as they hurried past the mangled wreckage.

"Jessica!"

"Here, I'm here!"

A small light penetrated the darkness.

"There she is!" Ryan pointed to the light and stumbled toward it through the brush. Eric followed directly behind him carrying his own medical kit and an old blanket. Within seconds, they had reached her.

"Jessica! Are you all right? The baby? What happened?" Ryan held her face in his hands, and his worried eyes searched it. "You're bleeding!"

"I'm okay. I fell, but I'm fine. We both are. It's him." She indicated the man. "He needs help, and down there..." she pointed. "There's a little boy."

Eric rushed down to boy while Ryan stayed with Jessica.

"He's having trouble breathing," Jessica began. "He's got air in his chest cavity. It's pressing on his heart and lungs. He needs a thoracostomy. A tube to get the air out." She turned her head to Ryan, an urgency in her eyes. Her voice was full of emotion now, and she struggled to speak. "I prayed you'd come in time. I knew you'd come. I trusted God to bring you, and He did."

"I'm here, Jessica. It's going to be all right." He reached out both hands and set them on her shoulders. Staring into her teary eyes, he stated, "It's going to be all right, Jessica. Tell me what to do to help you."

She took a deep breath and nodded her head as the doctor in her reemerged. "I need a needle. At least a 14-gauge, but larger if there's one in there. Also, some betadine, gauze, tape, and gloves."

Chapter Twenty-two

Ryan spread his jacket beside Jessica and grabbed her bag. He dumped the contents of the medical bag onto it and rummaged through them. "16-gauge! Got it!" He found the other items she had mentioned and quickly set them aside.

Jessica looked over at Ryan. "There's a good chance he has a collapsed lung. Probably one or more rib fractures. Air is escaping into the chest cavity. I have to get the air out before it interferes with his heart." She hesitated, a sliver of doubt piercing her confidence. "This isn't the most pristine of conditions for this procedure. I don't know if—"

"Do what you need to do, Jessica." Ryan reassured her firmly. "You're trained for this. Right now, you're the only one who can save his life. You've got to do this."

Jessica's eyes met his, and she nodded decisively. She hurriedly opened a bottle of the antiseptic solution and began to swab an area on the left side of the man's chest. "Ryan, can you hold the flashlight? I need it to be focused right here. Can you open those for me?" She indicated the gauze bandages he had set on his jacket. She pulled on a pair of sterile latex gloves, and with trembling hands, she removed the 16-gauge needle from its sterile packaging.

Lord, I know You're with me, so please help me now. It's hard to see with just a flashlight. Guide my hands...

She took a deep breath and felt for the body landmarks she knew were there. Feeling for the space between the fifth and sixth ribs, she held the needle just above the site of insertion.

You can do this, Jess. Easy now, just above the rib.

She willed her hands to cease their shaking once more and applied pressure to the needle. After some resistance, it penetrated through skin and muscle until a slight hissing sound could be heard.

"What's that?" Ryan whispered. The beam of light from the flashlight shook slightly.

"It's okay. That's supposed to happen. It's the trapped air escaping from the chest cavity. Hopefully, this will allow the lung to reinflate, but we've got to get him to the hospital. He needs a doctor."

"Seems to me he already has one," stated Ryan softly.

****

Four and a half hours later, both father and son were airlifted from Santa Molina to the Veracruz hospital. Ryan sat with Jessica on the tailgate of his truck as Eric and Akna drove off toward the church in the other vehicle.

"You okay?" he asked.

"Yes. I'm better now that they're on the way to the hospital."

"Are you sure you're okay? I worry about you and the baby."

"I know, but the paramedic checked me out. He said I was fine."

"I know, but I'm still concerned. You ready to head on home?"

Home?

Jessica looked over at him thoughtfully, then nodded her head. "Yes. Yes, I am."

Ryan held a hand out to Jessica as he hopped off the tailgate. She was now holding her abdomen. Her eyes were closed. "Is something wrong?" he asked.

Jessica opened her eyes and smiled. "No. Just another Braxton-Hicks contraction." As Ryan helped her to her feet, she continued, "You know, you worry a lot about me. I'm really fine."

A slight frown appeared on his face. "I know." His lowered voice sounded hurt as he looked away from her, and then he changed the subject. "You were pretty amazing out there tonight. I was very proud of you."

She contemplated his comment as he put his hands into his pants pockets. "You want to know the truth?" Jessica continued, not waiting for his reply. "I was scared. Out here is so different than working in the ER. There, I've got backup. I have equipment, and if anything goes wrong, I have every resource I need at my fingertips. But here? I have nothing. All I had was what

Chapter Twenty-two

was in my medical bag. Somehow I had to make that work, but I was afraid. Afraid for that man and his son. Afraid for me. Afraid for this baby.

"And then, I remembered what you said about trusting God, and how you told me to quote verses to help me stay focused. So, that's what I did. And I prayed. A lot. I knew you'd come. I knew God would bring you to me."

When Ryan didn't respond, she sighed and looked at the ground. She swallowed hard; a heavy ball of uncertainty sat in her stomach, and then she felt his fingers clasp hers. She cast a furtive look at their joined hands, and the unsettled feeling faded.

I knew God would bring you to me...

CHAPTER TWENTY-THREE

It was nearly noon when Jessica woke. She stretched her arms above her head and shifted her weight in the bed.

Oww! That hurts!

Opening her eyes slowly, she gingerly moved her feet over the side of her bed. Pulling herself up to a sitting position, she glanced at her watch.

Eleven thirty? Wow, I didn't even hear that crazy chicken!

She pulled a pink flowered maternity blouse from a drawer along with a khaki skirt. Slipping her feet into her leather sandals, she padded into the bathroom and glanced at her reflection in a mirror. Frowning, she picked up a brush and pulled it through her uncooperative curls.

Really? This is as good as it's going to get today?

She replaced the brush in its drawer, finished her morning duties, then walked outside into the courtyard. The sun was almost directly overhead, but large, billowy, white clouds were building.

"Hey there, sleepyhead!"

Jessica turned toward the sanctuary and saw Ryan walking toward her. His light blue shirt was tucked into a pair of faded jeans. The long sleeves were rolled up to just below his elbows. The tropical breeze had blown his hair across his forehead, giving him a carefree appearance. His eyes seemed to brighten when he saw her, and his smile warmed her heart. Jessica involuntarily held her breath as he approached.

Chapter Twenty-three

"Interested in lunch?" he asked as he sauntered up. "Akna's fixing tacos."

"Oh, that would be nice. I'm starving!" Her hand rested on her abdomen. His gaze followed her hand, and he raised an eyebrow as he met her eyes.

"Everything okay?"

"Yes. Everything's fine. I just can't wait for this baby to be born," explained Jessica. "I'm really getting excited about it. Every time I feel a kick or a contraction, I know it's going to be soon."

"Not too soon, I hope," Ryan chuckled. "I've never delivered a baby." He hesitated for a moment, then added. "You know, you're going to be a great mother, Jessica. Promise me you'll send me pictures when you think of it."

She blushed at his kind words. "I will, I promise. So, do you think it's a boy or girl?"

"Well, I'm kind of hoping for a boy."

"Why?"

Keeping his eyes focused on the dining hall, he easily guided Jessica to the door. "Because boys are cool."

Jessica took a step backward. Her forehead furrowed as she narrowed her eyes and glared at Ryan. She brought her hands to her hips. "What? Girls aren't cool?"

"Well, they're not boys," he said matter-of-factly.

"What does a boy have over a girl?"

"Tough, strong, able to leap tall buildings with a single bound. You know, boy stuff."

Jessica smirked. "You're just jealous." A hint of a smile appeared on her face.

"Of what?"

"We have more diversity in our wardrobes."

Ryan laughed. "Okay, you've got me there. Have you picked out names yet?"

She shook her head. "Not really. If it's a boy, I was thinking of naming him after Nick, but if it's a girl, well, I don't know yet. Maybe after my mom."

"Those both sound like good ideas. I guess when the time comes, you'll know what fits the baby."

Jessica felt a strong tightening move across her abdomen. She had felt them more frequently as the days had passed, and she knew that each one was merely a precursor to the real thing that would change her life completely. This time, tension mounted at her feet and moved upward through her body. As it did, her heart beat a little faster, and her old fears seemed to seep into her consciousness.

Trust in the Lord, Jessica. With all your heart, trust in the Lord.

Her abdominal muscles relaxed, and as they did, so did she. *What time I am afraid, I will trust in Thee.*

****

Jessica loved the idea of daily siestas and the guiltless feeling she had when she took her afternoon naps. Today however, she could not sleep. Unable to shake her restlessness, she opted for a short walk to the river near the far end of the camp. The sky had clouded over, but the rain had yet to fall.

She walked carefully along the path heavily padded with waterlogged vegetation. Her toes squished against the leather of her sandals as water seeped between her feet and the shoes. Off in the distance, the squawks of macaws mingled with the occasional howls of monkeys. It almost sounded like rain as she listened to the water dripping off the jungle foliage.

As she rounded a bend, she came upon the fallen trunk of a Ceiba tree. Taking advantage of the natural chair, she wiped a spot on the smooth bark and sat down. Cradling her abdomen, she closed her eyes and savored the balmy quiet of the jungle around her and the reality of the little life within her.

"Lord," she whispered. "I don't know what to do. I love what I do. Eastmont is my life. I've been there for so long, but they need a doctor here so badly. I once thought Eric was crazy

Chapter Twenty-three

for going to Papua New Guinea, and now here I am. Am I crazy for even considering this?"

How long she sat there, she didn't know, but she became acutely aware of the moment when a hardness began to spread across her abdomen, and for the first time, it was uncomfortable. She sat still, eyes closed, waiting for it to pass.

"Oh baby, that was a strong one." She spied a tiny green lizard scampering across the river's edge. It stopped, cocked its head, and displayed a bright orange flap of skin under its neck.

"Sorry. I suppose this is your territory?" She laughed softly as the lizard seemed to rock back and forth. "So, what do you do when outsiders move in?"

The lizard continued to hold its ground as Jessica admired its stand. "Such a brave little lizard. I wish I were as brave as you." She took a deep breath and stood. "Well, nice meeting you, *Señor* Lizard." She turned and headed back down the path toward the courtyard, noting the sun beginning to disappear behind the trees.

The serenity of twilight had settled over the courtyard, and Jessica looked around for any sign of life. The Canul children were nowhere to be seen, and the strange feeling of emptiness alarmed her.

"Ryan?" she called as she hurried toward his office. "Ryan?" She knocked on his door.

It opened within seconds. "Jessica? Is something wrong?"

She stood before him, her mouth open, but silent.

"Jessica?" He waited expectantly, worry beginning to etch its way across his face.

"I thought no one was here. It's so quiet."

I feel like an idiot.

Ryan visibly relaxed. "Oh. I can solve that mystery. Eric and the Canuls headed into Santa Molina to get Joaquin. They're planning to stay for supper with Akna's family, then be home later. Eric said he couldn't pass up another opportunity to have some more homemade tamales. Did you need something?"

"No. I was just wondering where everyone was." She remained at his threshold not knowing what to say.

"Just you and me for now." He watched her curiously as she simply stood there.

"Really?" She nodded self-consciously before blurting out, "What are *we* doing for dinner?"

Really, Jess? That's all you could think to say?

Amused at her discomfort, he looked at his watch as he answered, "Well, it's a bit early, but I'm sure I can drum up something." He looked up to see her gaze fixed on his face. "By the way, I wouldn't leave you here alone."

She nodded too quickly and gave him a small, lop-sided smile.

He stepped out onto the porch, closing the door behind him. "Let's go see what we can find to eat."

They walked over to the dining room, and once in the main kitchen, they managed to find all they would need to grill some burgers. Soon they were sitting down to a meal of hamburgers, fruit, and green beans.

"You're a great cook," complimented Jessica as she took a bite from her burger. "I guess I should have eaten more at lunch, but I can't seem to eat as much as before, and then I get hungry so much earlier."

"Not a problem. I probably would have forgotten to eat if you hadn't said something." Ryan wiped his mouth with a napkin. He took a bite of papaya, then followed it with a big swallow of iced tea.

"I can't believe I'll be back in Los Angeles in a few days. These past few weeks have flown by."

"They have. I'm really going to miss you. And Eric too," he hastily added. "You've really been a blessing, Jessica." He took another bite of his burger before speaking again. "I hope the hurricane hasn't dampened your outlook on camp doctoring."

"Not at all."

"So, you might consider doing it again in the future?"

She smiled at him. "I just might."

Chapter Twenty-three

****

It was nearly midnight when Ryan heard a knock at his door. He rose from the desk at which he was sitting, leaving both his Bible and laptop open. As he walked through the living room, he flipped on the overhead light, then opened the front door.

"Jessica?" His concerned eyes widened. "What's wrong?" He felt her trembling as he put a hand behind her back and ushered her into his house.

"I think... I think I'm in labor," she stammered.

"What?" Ryan directed her to sit on the sofa.

She wrung her hands in her lap. "I didn't think anything of it earlier. In fact, I thought they were Braxton-Hicks contractions, but they haven't stopped, and they're getting stronger. Uncomfortable, in fact."

"How often are they coming?" The concern was clear in his voice.

Jessica looked apologetically at him. "Every three to five minutes."

"And you're just coming to me now?" he asked unbelievingly.

She held up her hands to him. "I know," she nodded regretfully. "I know, but I really thought it was false labor. I'm not due until the first week of September. It always seems like first time mothers deliver later than their due dates, and I—"

"Really?" Ryan's frustration was not hidden. "You're not an obstetrician, and we're not exactly near a hospital. You should have come to me sooner." He stood and paced the floor.

Tears stung Jessica's eyes. "If I had even thought it was real, I would have said something earlier. I went to find Eric, but I don't know where he is."

"He's not here. He's in Santa Molina," he stated curtly.

Jessica bit her lip and closed her eyes tightly. "I thought you said— Ohh!" Her hands went to her abdomen as she bent over slightly. A tear found its way down her cheek.

"It's okay, Jessica," reassured Ryan as he dropped to one knee in front of her. "Don't cry. It'll be all right." He took her hand in his. "I'm sorry. I didn't mean to upset you." His tone was apologetic as he continued. "We'll just take you to the hospital." He stood and helped her up. "I mean, it is your first, so like you said, we should have plenty of time, right?"

Jessica leaned against the door as the contraction eased.

He grabbed his keys. "Come on." He opened the door for her, but she didn't move. "Jessica?"

She looked up at his beckoning face and said hesitantly, "Maybe we should just wait until Eric gets back. I know he can deliver me." Her strained voice was unconvincing.

"That could be a problem."

"Why?"

"Joaquin called earlier. They're staying the night. Blew a tire and can't get it fixed until the morning." He thought for a moment. "I'll drive you there. It's dark, but I know the roads. We can make you comfortable in the truck—"

"Ryan, I don't want to have my baby in the back of a truck." Jessica's nervous voice was a whisper, and her hands protectively covered her abdomen. Her anxious eyes silently implored him for another option.

"You won't. We may not have time to get you to Veracruz, but I can take you to Santa Molina. You did say that first babies take a long time, right? Wouldn't that mean we've got time to get to Santa Molina?"

"Yes, but—"

"But what?" He sat down beside her.

She looked up at him and her eyes clouded with fear. "My water broke just before I came here."

Ryan's concerned eyes searched her face for an explanation. "Okay. And that means what exactly?"

"It means the birth is closer than if it hadn't broken. Ohh...." She closed her eyes until the contraction passed, and then her voice shook as she spoke. "Ryan, I'm scared. This baby is being born six weeks early, and without the proper medical care..." She couldn't stop herself from trembling. "There may be complications."

Chapter Twenty-three

"Complications?" Ryan shook his head as he tried to focus. He ran his fingers through his hair. "Okay, I can go get Eric," he offered. "Santa Molina's only thirty minutes away. I can be back in an hour or so. Without you, I can get there quicker. We can make you comfortable before I go, and then—"

"Please don't leave me," she pleaded.

Ryan froze. His mind flashed back to several years earlier, and the voice he now heard didn't belong to Jessica.

Please don't leave me.

The memory of Gabriela was so vivid, it hurt. She had begged him to stay with her, and he had. The fear that had gripped his heart so long ago returned, and he involuntarily shivered.

"Ohhh..." Jessica grabbed her abdomen with one hand and bent forward once more. With the other hand, she reached for Ryan. "Please..."

Instantly, he was back in the present. Rushing to her side, he helped ease her back into the sofa. "I'm here, Jessica. I won't leave you. I promise." He sat with her until the contraction lessened, then showed her to the bedroom.

"Lay here. I'm going to try and call Joaquin. Maybe he can borrow a truck and bring Eric here. I'm also going to get some more blankets, okay? I'll be right back."

He hurried out of the room and punched in Joaquin's number. No answer.

"Lord, I need Your help." He prayed as he gathered supplies. "God, You know my weaknesses and my fears. Please, I am begging You, please don't make me deliver this baby by myself." He felt that old fear threaten to overwhelm him, and he forced himself to focus on the truth of Scripture.

He swallowed hard, then thought with more clarity and determination. Glancing upward, he whispered, "Lord, I know Your Word says I can do all things through Christ which strengtheneth me. Show me what I need to do to help her, and give me the courage to do it. I need You to guide me. Please, don't let this baby die; don't let Jessica die." He prayed in faith, and when he finished, he knew what he had to do.

He pulled his phone out of his pocket and dialed Joaquin's number again. It went directly to voice mail. "Joaquin, this is Pastor Ryan. Jessica is in labor, and I don't have time to get her to a hospital. Bring Eric to my house as quickly as you can... and tell everyone to pray for her and the child."

He quickly retrieved several sheets, some towels, and a washcloth before heading to the kitchen and grabbing a large basin. He returned to the bedroom to find Jessica panting and gripping the bed sheets beneath her. Her eyes were tightly shut.

"Jessica... Jessica, open your eyes and look at me. I need you to look at me," instructed Ryan.

She blinked her eyes several times, then bit her lower lip. "It hurts..." Her breathing was rapid, but as the contraction subsided, so did her respiratory rate.

"I know, but we've got a baby to deliver, and I need your help. As long as you work with me, together we can do this, okay? Adam helped Eve, and Joseph was there for Mary. Now, I'm here for you, but I need your help.

"Tell me what I need to have ready. I've got sheets, towels, clean water. What else do I need?" Ryan waited.

"Um...okay. Can you get to the clinic? There are disposable pads there, and diapers... the smallest you can find." Her breathing was rapid and shallow. "Also, grab a bottle of saline. Oh, and a nasal bulb syringe. You'll need scissors and... ohh... something... to tie... ohh... the cord with. If you can warm several towels in the microwave, you can bunch them up and maybe they'll stay.... ohhh..." She began to pant as the contraction grew stronger. "Oww... this hurts!"

Ryan held her hand until she relaxed once more. He moistened the washcloth and wiped her brow. "I'll be right back."

"Okay," she whispered, "but please hurry."

In less than ten minutes, he was back with everything she had told him to get. He quickly cleared his nightstand and set

Chapter Twenty-three

the smaller items on it. He placed sheeting and disposable pads under her, trying to make her comfortable.

"You can do this, Jessica," he said softly, rubbing the top of her hand. "I'm right here with you."

"Please stay with me..." she whispered as she clenched her teeth with the next contraction. "I'm scared..."

"You don't have to be. I'm here. I won't leave you."

He put several pillows behind her to help her sit up, and he rubbed her lower back when she asked for it. Her contractions were coming more frequently, and they were growing in intensity. He glanced at his watch, noting the duration of each contraction.

"It's... too soon," she gasped as another contraction began. "Ryan... it's too soon..." Her hands whitened as her fists clenched the bed once more.

He felt helpless, and each time Jessica cried out, he relived the agony of watching Gabriela go through her labor. The realization that he was going to have to deliver a baby unsettled him, but not nearly as much as the real possibility that he could lose Jessica, and he couldn't bear the thought of that happening.

Lord, please help this baby. We need a miracle right now. Cradle this little one in Your arms and bring it into this world without any complications.

He couldn't stop his own tears as they fell silently down his cheeks.

CHAPTER TWENTY-FOUR

Ryan observed Jessica intently as she rested after her latest contraction. She had sunk back into her pillow, breathing heavily and still clutching his hand. Beads of perspiration covered her face, and he tenderly wiped them away with the washcloth.

He sat quietly as Jessica seemed to doze off between contractions. As he watched and waited, he prayed silently for God to intervene, and somehow bless them with a delivery that would be without incident. The ringing of his cell phone interrupted his thoughts.

"Ryan? This is Eric. We're on our way, but the road is really messed up. I don't know how long it'll take us to get there. How's Jessica?"

"Doing okay, I think. Her contractions are about one and a half minutes apart, and her water broke about one and a half hours ago." Ryan looked at Jessica. Her eyes were closed, and she appeared to be sleeping, but he knew she was only resting between contractions.

"Is she pushing?"

"Not yet."

"Is the baby crowning?"

"I... I don't think so."

"Listen, I'll stay on the line with you. Just be my eyes and my hands, and we should be able to do this without any problem."

Chapter Twenty-four

Relieved somewhat by the young doctor's voice, Ryan willed himself to remain calm. "Okay. I'll put you on speaker." He set the phone on the nightstand and leaned toward Jessica. "Eric's on the line, Jessica. He's on his way, but for now we're delivering this baby long distance, okay?"

She simply nodded as Ryan brushed her damp hair from her forehead and tenderly laid another cool cloth on her brow. It wasn't long before another contraction began.

"I can't do this anymore," she cried as her body tensed.

"Yes, Jessica. You can. Think of your baby. It's time for the two of you to meet each other, but you've got to do your part," stated Ryan firmly.

"Hey, Jessica!" Eric's voice came over the speaker. "I know you can do this. You've got a little miracle inside you that's ready to come out. It'll all be over soon, but until then, you've got to do exactly as I say."

"Oh... I feel like I need to push..." She squeezed Ryan's hand.

Eric's voice crackled over the phone as he instructed Ryan on the delivery of the baby. "The baby's going to be slippery, Ryan, so use the sheet to help catch and support it when it arrives, and it's going to be very messy."

"Understood." Ryan did everything as Eric instructed, and in seventeen minutes, the room filled with the loud, lusty cry of a newborn baby. "It's a boy!"

"Is he okay, Ryan?" Apprehension resonated in Jessica's voice as she strained to see the baby.

"I think so." His voice was tender as he gently inspected the baby. "He's moving his arms and legs, and he's certainly crying enough, but he's got this white stuff all over him."

"That's normal," stated Eric. "Take the bulb syringe, depress it, then put it in each nostril to suck out any mucus. Try and hold the baby with his head downward while you do this. We're almost there!"

Ryan did exactly as he was told, then wrapped the crying baby in a warmed sheet and laid him in Jessica's arms. Ryan's eyes misted over, and with a huge sigh of relief, he offered a quick prayer of thanks to the Lord before the next phase of childbirth began.

Jessica wrapped her arms around her newborn son and held him protectively. As he replaced the sheets around her, Ryan heard her whispered plea, "Please Father, let him be fine... please."

He stood for a moment and watched the tender scene in front of him, and for a fleeting moment, he saw Gabriela and his daughter as it should have been.

The sudden slamming of the front door startled Ryan back to the reality of the moment as Eric rushed into the room.

"Don't tell me I'm too late!" His smile was broad as he snapped on a pair of sterile gloves. He moved over to the other side of the bed. "Let me check him real quick, Jess. I promise I'll give him right back."

She handed the baby to Eric, and then turned toward Ryan. "I will never forget what you've done for as long as I live. Thank you so much. I couldn't have done this without you." She reached for his hand, pulled him to her, hugged him, and cried.

"You did great, Jessica," reported Ryan softly. "I'm so very proud of you." He resisted the urge to kiss her forehead and merely said, "Congratulations, Mama."

****

Jessica sat comfortably in bed, cradling her son in her arms. As many new mothers do, she had counted his toes and fingers. His hair was so blonde, it was almost white, and his large eyes were a deep blue, almost black, in color. His grasp was firm around her finger, and in his perfectness, Jessica saw both Nick and herself.

Thank You, Lord, for my son.

Eric had deemed the baby robust and healthy with good Apgar scores. Using the baby scale from the clinic, the weight was recorded at six pounds, two ounces, but Eric had kept a close eye on the baby since, according to Jessica's information,

Chapter Twenty-four

the child was several weeks early. He assessed the cardiac and respiratory status frequently, but there had been no signs of perinatal distress.

Akna was calling the birth a miracle of God in more ways than one. She had been bustling about Jessica since arriving with Eric. She had helped her change into a clean nightgown and get resettled with the baby in a freshly made bed. Finally, she had gently held the child while Jessica made herself comfortable.

"*Mija*, he is beautiful. Praise God for this little one!" Akna kissed him on the forehead as she returned him to his mother. "He is a strong one. Look how well he nurses!" She held her hands upward. "Praise to You, O most holy One!" She smiled at Jessica once more before turning to leave the room. "I am here if you need me, *mija*."

Jessica looked at her caregiver through grateful eyes. "Thank you, Akna. What would I do without you?" As Akna closed the door behind her, Jessica settled in to nurse her son. She smoothed the blankets around him and marveled as he lay in her arms satisfying his hunger.

Fearfully and wonderfully made... You are a miracle, aren't you, my love?

Just as she had finished nursing her son, Jessica heard a soft knock at the door. "Come in," she said quietly.

Ryan stepped into the room. He had changed into a pale green, pocketed t-shirt and dark jeans. His dark, wet hair indicated he had recently showered.

His voice was a whisper. "How's he doing?"

"Wonderful!" She pulled the sheet down a little so he could see the baby more easily. The tiny eyes were closed, and every now and then a little sigh would escape the rosebud lips.

"He's beautiful, Jessica," said Ryan, pulling a chair over alongside her.

"Would you like to hold him?"

"Really? It's okay? I'd love to." He reached out and gently took him from Jessica's arms. "This is easier than the last time I held him. He's not nearly as slippery."

Jessica smiled as she watched him cradle her son. "I have a name now."

"Oh, yeah? What did you choose?"

"Nicholas, after his father, and..." She paused, then added, "Ryan."

He looked up expectantly. "Yes?"

Her eyes twinkled. "No, that's his name... Nicholas Ryan Carr."

Ryan's mouth dropped open as his eyes met hers. She smiled at him. "Nicholas Ryan Carr. After the two most important men in his life... and mine."

****

Ryan sat there speechless, his gaze moving from her to the baby. He looked up at her once again, and her smile warmed his heart.

She named him after me?

He opened his mouth to speak, but Nicholas began to stir. Ryan's attention was diverted to the child.

"It's okay, Nicholas." He stood and gently rocked the baby in his arms, holding him close to his chest. "Shh... You're safe, little guy."

Nicholas stilled, and Ryan sat back down. He looked up at Jessica. "Is there anything I can get you? Are you comfortable?"

"I'm fine, but I'm afraid I've taken over your bedroom."

"That's okay. My house has officially become a maternity ward. Akna says she and the girls are going to stay here with you for the next couple of days, and I'll be staying at their place."

Concern washed over Jessica's face. "Oh, Ryan, I'm so sorry. I didn't mean—"

Chapter Twenty-four

"I know. It's fine. What's important is for you to regain your strength and take care of Nicholas." He looked lovingly at the baby before handing him back to her. "He looks a lot like you."

"You think so?"

"I do." He reached toward Nicholas' face and pointed as he spoke. "Same cute little nose and mouth. Think his hair will stay this light?"

"I don't know. Nick's hair was blonde." Nicholas began to squirm and emit little half-cries.

"Something wrong?" asked Ryan.

Hmm... I don't think so. Maybe he needs a diaper change." She looked up at Ryan and smiled, then playfully batted her eyes at him.

"Seriously? That's the reward I get for helping deliver him?" He stood up and looked around the room. "Well, I guess I can try. I've never diapered a baby before. What do I need?"

Jessica laughed as she answered him. "A diaper. Over there. Wipes are next to the diapers, and baby powder."

He returned to the bed with the supplies and sat on its edge. Jessica scooted over to the far side of the bed, leaving room for him to lay Nicholas down beside her.

Ryan took a deep breath and looked at Jessica. "Okay, here goes."

"When you unhook the diaper, leave it over him for a second or two before you totally remove it," she advised.

"Why?" he said as he pulled the diaper off. "Whoa!" He hastily put the diaper back down on Nicholas.

Jessica giggled. "So you don't get wet."

"That was unexpected." He hesitantly started to lift the diaper. "All done, buddy?" Slowly removing it, he cleaned and powdered Nicholas before putting a new one on him. When he finally finished, Ryan sat back with a satisfied look on his face. "Mission accomplished."

Jessica supported Nicholas in her arms as she checked the diaper. "Good job!"

"Thank you. So what are your plans, Mom?"

Jessica pursed her lips and shrugged her shoulders. "I have to make some phone calls. I don't know how soon I can fly with a newborn, so maybe if it's okay with you, I could stay a little longer?"

"You're kidding, right? Of course, you can stay. Stay as long as you want. Akna will love it; she's already claiming to be his *abuela*, his Mexican grandmother."

"I can move back into one of the cabins—"

"No. You stay here until you leave. I can stay with the Canuls. It's no imposition. Besides, during the day, I'll be in and out of my office. I won't even need to be here in the house. I'll just drop in to check on you now and then, if you don't mind."

"Of course I don't mind." She dropped her head and wiped her eyes.

"Are you okay?" Ryan leaned forward, worry etched on his handsome face.

She nodded quickly.

"Jessica, what's wrong?"

"Nothing." She found it hard to speak. "It's just that you're so… you're so sweet… and you've done so much for me." She grabbed a tissue and wiped her nose. "I don't know how I'll ever repay you."

"Repay me?" His deep blue eyes filled with compassion. "You don't need to repay me." He handed her another tissue. "Hey, no tears, okay? Everything's going to be fine. You just get some rest. I'll be back a bit later."

As he left the room, Jessica's misty eyes followed him until the door closed behind him. She stared at it and whispered, "What am I going to do? I think I love you, Ryan Devereaux."

****

Later, a steady gentle rain fell, and the smell of wet vegetation filled the air. In the distance, the cries of a flock of parrots echoed through the trees. Ryan stood by the living room window

Chapter Twenty-four

looking out into the courtyard. His hands were in his pants pockets, and he didn't hear Eric come out of Jessica's room.

"Hey Pastor, how's it going?"

Ryan turned around. "Fine, Eric. Everything's fine. How's Jessica doing?"

"Good. This could almost be a textbook delivery except for the late arrival of the physician," he chuckled. "Nicholas is doing great, too. He's eating well, so that's good. I've set up an appointment with a pediatrician in Veracruz for next week. Hopefully, roads will be better by then."

Ryan hesitated, then asked. "Can I ask you something?"

"Sure."

"This baby was born... what? Six weeks early? You're sure everything's okay with him?"

Eric nodded. "Yeah. He's perfect, as far as I can tell. The biggest problem with preemies is lung development, but Nicholas doesn't have any signs of breathing problems. Maybe her dates were off."

"Maybe."

"Well, for whatever reason, they're both doing very well. I know an awful lot of prayers were being sent heavenward for her and Nicholas."

Ryan nodded as he quietly recited part of a verse from the book of James. "'The effectual fervent prayer of a righteous man availeth much.'" He smiled at the young doctor. "Listen, Eric, I really appreciate you being here. I can't explain the relief I had when you walked in the door last night."

"Hey, don't kid yourself, Pastor. You were doing a great job." Eric patted him on the back.

"Well, if you don't mind, I'll leave the medical stuff to you. It is way out of my comfort zone."

Eric plopped down on the sofa and stretched out on it. "That works for me. Hey, she's awake if you want to go in. I'm gonna catch a quick nap. Give me a holler if you need me, okay?"

Ryan nodded. He walked to the bedroom and knocked softly on the door, entering when Jessica beckoned.

"Hi there. You up for a visit?"

"Of course." Her smile was radiant. "Please sit. I'd love the company."

Ryan scooted a chair over, then reached for Nicholas. "May I?" When she nodded her consent, he lifted the boy easily and held him against his chest, inhaling the powdery fresh baby scent that accompanied the tiny infant. "I can't get over how small he is. He's as light as a feather."

Jessica studied Ryan's face as he cradled Nicholas in his arms. Finally, she confessed, "I was so worried, Ryan. Once I knew my labor was the real thing, I kept doing the math in my head. Nicholas should be a preemie. I thought—"

"Maybe your dates were off," interrupted Ryan, echoing Eric's comment. "You never know absolutely about those things, right?"

"Yes, you're right, but yesterday or the day before, I can't even remember what day it is... I should have known better. I was already having contractions, but I ignored them. I could have put Nicholas' life at risk." Her remorse was evident.

"But you didn't, Jessica. Nicholas is fine; you are fine. It all worked out. God took care of both of you," he reminded her.

"Yes, He did, didn't He? And so did you."

Ryan shifted his weight and leaned back in the chair. Nicholas slept quietly; his tiny body molded into Ryan's. "I can't get over how perfect he is." His voice was a low whisper.

"You'll get no argument from me."

"Eric says that he's doing really well. No problems at all."

Jessica lowered her eyes. "I know. It's really a miracle, Ryan." Her voice trembled. "I never dreamed..." She stopped and turned her head from him.

Ryan looked up. "You okay?"

"I'm fine, just a little tired."

"Oh, I'm sorry. I'll leave and let you rest–"

"No! Please, don't leave." She turned back toward him and put a hand out. "Not yet. Besides, Nicholas seems quite content. Please stay."

Chapter Twenty-four

****

Early the next morning, the robust cry of a hungry infant echoed throughout the house. Several short bursts of crying followed by a longer wail indicated a very unhappy baby.

Sitting in his office, Ryan turned his head from his studies and looked slightly over his left shoulder toward the main section of his house. The inner walls offered little buffering between him and the crying child.

I wonder if she's okay with him? Should I...? No, I'm sure she's fine.

The crying seemed to taper off, and soon he could hear nothing, but he was already distracted from the outline he was writing for his upcoming message. He rested his elbows on the desktop and held his head in his hands.

"Lord, what am I going to do? I never thought You'd send someone that would touch my heart the way Jessica has... not after Gabriela."

Unable to concentrate on his notes, he stood up and ambled out into the courtyard. Dark gray clouds dotted the sky, and he felt a few drops of water on his face. Hearing the door of his house open and close, he turned around to see Akna carrying a tray of dishes.

"*Buenos días*, Pastor Ryan," she stated as she neared him.

"Good morning, Akna. How is our mother and baby doing?"

"*Muy bien*. She is good. The baby, he is good too. You should go see her."

"I should? Why is that?"

"It will help your heart," she replied with a slight smile.

Ryan stared at her, his mouth slightly agape as she walked away. He watched her disappear into the dining hall, then turned slowly back toward his house.

I suppose it wouldn't hurt to stick my head in and say, 'Good morning.'

****

"There you go, Nicholas," Jessica said tenderly as her son finished nursing. The side of his head was all she could see with the thin sheets pulled up over the two of them. His contented coos warmed her heart, and she couldn't resist the impulse to gently caress his soft cheek as she fed him.

"What are we going to do, little one?" she whispered as her finger traced the side of his face. "I can't imagine leaving here. I can't imagine leaving... him." Her vision blurred for a moment, and she reached for a tissue to wipe her eyes.

A soft knock on the door interrupted her thoughts.

She glanced down at the sheet, and then replied, "Come in."

Ryan poked his head in. "Good morning! How's everyone today?"

Jessica's eyes brightened when she saw him. "We're doing very well. Did we disturb you?"

"Disturb me? Absolutely not. I was just working on my message when I heard him crying."

"So, we did interrupt you."

"Well, let's just say it was a welcome interruption." He walked over to the bed and leaned over slightly to see Nicholas. "Is he sleeping?"

She smiled. "No, not yet. He just finished breakfast. Would you like to hold him for a little while? Maybe rock him to sleep?"

"Sure," said Ryan as he dragged a chair closer to the bed. He reached down and took Nicholas from her. "Hey, little guy," he whispered as he sat down. "He's doing well?" he asked without looking up.

"Yes. He's doing very well."

As she watched Ryan cuddle Nicholas, she became more convinced that separating them would be the wrong thing to do, but she struggled with how to avoid doing that very thing.

CHAPTER TWENTY-FIVE

Sunday morning, Ryan stood behind his pulpit and looked out at his congregation. His smile brightened as his gaze fell upon each face that looked up expectantly at him. His gaze lingered for an imperceptible moment longer on Jessica, who was seated near the rear of the church. Wrapped loosely in a light blanket, Nicholas slept quietly in her arms.

"Thank you all so much for being here today. A great deal has happened in the last couple of weeks, and for many of us, there have been some very profound changes. Some of those changes are pretty exciting. Some may require some adjustments to what you've been used to, but whatever is in store for you, whether it's expected or not, your life will probably be changing, either temporarily or permanently. Some of these changes may cause you great concern. Maybe you're asking yourself, 'What does the future hold for me? My family?' Maybe you're wondering what you're going to do, how you are going to manage. Maybe you're simply afraid of the unknown.

"The answers to these questions and others are found in knowing the will of God. How you respond to these changes will be of paramount importance to you, and because of that, before you act upon these changes, you must ask yourself, 'What would God have me do?'"

He slowly panned the congregation. "God has a plan for every one of us, and it's a plan that His Word says has an expected end. It is our responsibility to seek out God's will and act upon it."

Jessica sighed to herself.

I wish I knew God's plan for my life. It would make things so much easier.

"Please open your Bibles with me to the book of John chapter seven," said Ryan as he opened his own Bible. "The key to doing God's will is to determine in your heart that you are going to follow the will of God *before* you know what it is. In this portion of Scripture, Jesus is speaking. He says in verse seventeen, 'If any man will do his will, he shall know of the doctrine, whether it be of God, or whether I speak of myself.'

"The first step in doing God's will is understanding that following God doesn't mean getting what we want, but purposing in your mind to do what God asks of you regardless of whether it's what you want or not. It involves trust. We must trust that God will only ask us to do that which is best for us, and that He will equip us with what we need to do it.

"Secondly, we need to cultivate our relationship with God. Understanding that our salvation establishes a *personal* relationship with Jesus Christ is key to understanding God's will for us. Believing in God is not enough. The Bible tells us that even the demons believe in God, but they certainly do not have a relationship with the Creator. So, how do we develop a relationship with the Lord?

"I had a Sunday school teacher who once told me that salvation was as simple as A-B-C. The 'A' meant I had to admit to God I was a sinner, and that I was sorry for my sins. Repentance is a necessary step toward forgiveness. If I don't recognize that I've sinned, I certainly can't understand why I need to be forgiven.

"The 'B' stands for believing that Jesus is God's Son, and that He took the punishment for my sin by dying on the cross, and 'C' means choosing Christ to be my Savior, by asking Him to forgive me and become my Savior and the Lord of my life. He died on the cross as man, taking the punishment for my sins,

Chapter Twenty-five

but rose from the dead three days later as God, the only one capable of forgiving me.

"That's it. A-B-C... Simple, yet life-changing, and well on the way to knowing exactly what God wants me or you to do." Ryan paused, allowing his words to sink into the hearts and minds of those in the church.

"I know many of you have heard my testimony before. I accepted Christ as my Savior as a young boy, but it wasn't until my teens that I began to develop a real personal relationship with Him. Once I spent time in private prayer and Bible study, my relationship with Jesus became deeper and richer, and I began to understand Him more, and more of what He wanted from me."

He turned and gestured toward Joaquin Canul. "Everyone here knows the Canuls. Joaquin and I are good friends. I see him almost every day. If we never spent time together, he would be no more a friend to me than someone who lives in New York City. If I never spoke to him, he would probably doubt that I cared at all for him. Our relationship has developed over time into a very deep friendship because we talk and visit with each other regularly.

"That's the way it is with God. If you don't spend time with Him, there is no way you'll develop a trusting relationship with Him. When did you last spend time in prayer to the Lord? When did you last sit down and read your Bible?" Again, he paused.

"Thirdly, you must understand the will of God as stated in Scripture. In some things, God is very specific in regards to His will. For example, the Ten Commandments give us His sovereign will, and there is no doubt as to what He wants us to do or not do in regards to those ten commands.

"It is the unspecified will of God with which most of us struggle. Things not specifically mentioned in the Bible. What job should I take? Who should I marry? Should I move to a particular place? There are no clear answers for these in the

Word of God, however, there are two things that can help you determine God's will for your life."

Ryan moved to the side of the pulpit. "God will direct you by providential circumstances and by providing an inner peace when you make a decision. These two must agree for you to know it's His will. Earnestly seek Him and His will. How? Seek out your pastor or other trusted, well-established Christian advisors. These godly people can help put you on the right path. The Bible tells us in Proverbs 'Where no counsel is, the people fall: but in the multitude of counselors there is safety.' God will not abandon you, nor will He neglect providing you with an answer."

He returned to the pulpit and looked out over his congregation. "Every time I see you, I think of how God has blessed each of you with a gift. Maybe it's the gift of hospitality. I saw quite a bit of that this past week. Maybe it's the gift of encouragement or knowledge. Whatever gift God has given you, it's your responsibility to use that gift to do God's will.

"I once knew a lady who worked as a schoolteacher. When she was asked if she would be interested in teaching a children's Sunday school class, she declined, stating that she was too tired to teach on Sunday since she taught all week long in a public school. That is definitely the misuse of God's gift. His gift should be used for His purposes before anything else."

Jessica's brow furrowed as she pondered his words.

What does that mean? Am I supposed to leave Eastmont? Can't I serve God there? Of course, I can. There's lots of Christians working at the hospital. We're not all supposed to pack up and leave like Eric's doing. So, how do I know what God wants me to do?

Ryan interrupted her thoughts as he expounded. "How do I know this? I know this because of God's sovereign will. He tells us in Exodus that we should have no other gods before Him, for He is a jealous God. This is His absolute will. We are commanded to put God's purpose ahead of the world's purpose. Is teaching in a public school wrong? Of course not.

Chapter Twenty-five

But refusing to serve God when the need is there because of working in the world *is* wrong."

She cocked her head slightly.

A need...

Nicholas stirred in her arms, and she turned all her attention to her son. He opened his eyes and stared at his mother.

What if I leave and someone else's baby needs a physician, and one isn't here? What then? What if it was Nicholas and no one was here to help him?

She slowly raised her eyes from her son and fixed them on Ryan.

"Luke tells us that 'men ought always to pray and not faint.' That means don't give up if you don't get an immediate answer. God will answer, and when He does, it may not be in agreement with our personal desires, but it will be for our best."

"As Christians, we are to be living sacrifices for God. Our calling is to serve Him. But we are to serve Him according to His will, not ours. That's our reasonable service."

He moved to the aisle in front of the pulpit. "At the age of fourteen, I never dreamed I'd be in rural Mexico, pastoring such a wonderful group of people, but God knew." His voice broke, and he stood quietly for a moment composing himself.

"I can tell you that there is no other place I'd rather be. It hasn't all been easy, but I know that God has brought me here, and I can honestly tell you 'it is well with my soul.' Isaiah the prophet wrote, 'Thou wilt keep him in perfect peace, whose mind is stayed on Thee: because he trusteth in Thee.' If it is God's will for your life that you seek, devote yourself to Him, and trust Him to lead you. Let's pray."

As Ryan led the congregation in prayer, Jessica sat thinking as she gently rocked Nicholas.

Lord, what am I supposed to do?

****

Late Tuesday afternoon, Jessica sat quietly beside Ryan as he drove them back to Santa Molina from Veracruz. The truck bounced along the road, yet Nicholas remained fast asleep, secure in a car seat fastened between the two adults.

"Seemed like a nice pediatrician," commented Ryan.

"Um-hmm," replied Jessica.

"Good report, too."

"Yes."

"Did she say when you could fly with him?"

"Yes."

Ryan glanced at her, then returned his gaze to the road. "Jessica, is something wrong? You've barely said anything since we headed back."

"What?" She looked over at him.

"Is everything okay? You're awfully quiet," repeated Ryan.

She blinked several times, then sat up a bit straighter. "I'm sorry. I guess I was just thinking."

"Anything you want to talk about?"

"No."

Ryan nodded as he drove. "Okay."

Jessica frowned and sighed deeply. "She said Nicholas could fly any time. She said it was usually not recommended that babies be on a plane for a couple of months due to the immature immune system, but if it were a necessity, it wouldn't really harm him. He just might be exposed to airborne germs."

"Well, that's kind of good, isn't it? You can go home now."

"Yes, I can."

"So what's the problem?"

She turned to look out the window. "I know my folks can't wait to see him, same for Caleb and Bethany. I probably need to go home as soon as I can, but…"

He cast a puzzled look her way. "But what?"

"Nothing. I guess I'll try and get a flight."

She reverted back to her silence, and Ryan didn't try to coax any more conversation from her. He pressed his lips together and kept his eyes on the road.

Chapter Twenty-five

When they arrived at the church, he carried Nicholas in the car seat into his house. Jessica followed close behind. When he set the seat down on the sofa, she unbuckled Nicholas and lifted him out. "Thank you for taking us into Veracruz."

"You're welcome." He hesitated for a moment. "See you later? At dinner?"

"Of course. I'll see you then."

****

Ryan walked out into the dining hall patio and looked up into the heavens. The evening's first stars were beginning to appear in the darkening sky, and a warm tropical breeze danced around him. The night sounds of the jungle began to permeate the air.

He crossed his arms in front of his chest and glanced toward his house. A faint light shone from within. He sat down on one of the patio's wooden benches, then turned his head toward the Canuls' home across the courtyard. Its inviting lights beckoned to him.

He sighed and started to rise when the front door to his house opened, and Jessica stepped out.

"Jessica? Is everything okay?"

She turned toward him and forced a smile. "Yes. Well, no, not really." She stood awkwardly, then asked, "Do you have a minute?"

"Of course. Sit down." He patted the bench next to him as he moved over.

She quickly walked over to him and spoke before she sat. "I'm sorry. I wasn't very good company on the ride back. It's just that I wasn't really expecting the pediatrician to tell me I could fly home now."

"I thought that would be a good thing."

"It is." She sat down beside him.

"Do you need some money for the ticket?"

For the first time that day, Jessica found a reason to laugh, and she did. "No. I've got enough money for the tickets. I just don't really want to go."

Ryan looked at her in surprise. "You don't want to go home?"

Jessica took a deep breath. "I do, but just not yet."

"So wait a week or so, or until you're ready. There's no rush," stated Ryan.

"But I've put you out of your home for over a week now. I can't do that indefinitely."

"Why not? I'm still able to do my work. You haven't taken over my office yet." He smiled hoping to lighten the moment.

She reached over and gave his hand a squeeze. "I feel so safe here, Ryan. Everything is working. When I go home, I don't know what I'm going to face. I'll have to juggle family with work there, and that..." She looked up and gave him a shameful look. "That scares me."

Ryan turned toward her. "Jessica, you don't have anything to be scared of. I've seen you work in the most adverse conditions, and the most unexpected. You've been amazing. You're going to find a way to be a great mom and a great doctor. You've got a fabulous support system... your mom and dad, your brother, Bethany, even the people you work with."

Jessica nodded. "You're right. It's just that..." She shook her head. "I'm so used to being in control, and for the past year or so, I feel like I've been anything but. And now, now there's no end in sight."

"Sure there's an end. It's just eighteen years down the road," chuckled Ryan, enticing her to smile.

This time it worked, and her smile was genuine as she punched him in the shoulder. "Very funny."

"Seriously, Jessica. You'll be okay. Everything that's happened, you've come through just fine. You said your mom was going to help you with Nicholas, so that's been taken care of. You certainly haven't lost any of your skills; you're the same doctor you've always been. You need to look at the future as a new chapter in your life... a new adventure, so to speak. One

Chapter Twenty-five

you get to travel with your son, and if you trust God, He'll lead you both."

When she looked up at him, her blue eyes searched his own. "So, you want me to go?" she taunted, her mouth curling slightly upward.

His eyes widened, and he spoke almost too hastily. "No! No! Of course not! I would never want—"

"Pastor! Pastor!" Ryan and Jessica both turned their heads to see Juan running toward them. Ryan stood up.

"*Juan, ¿Qué ocurre?* What's wrong?"

"*Es papá! No puede respirar. Por favor, ven rápido!*" His fearful eyes begged them to come.

Ryan grabbed Jessica's arm and pulled her off the porch. "It's Joaquin! He's having trouble breathing. You go; I'll grab your bag and be right behind you." He turned to Juan. "Stay here with Nicholas!"

****

Joaquin's eyes were closed, and his breathing was shallow and rapid when Jessica dropped to her knees beside him.

"Joaquin? Joaquin? Do you have any pain anywhere? *¿Tienes algún dolor?*" She searched his face for a clue to his condition as she reached for his wrist.

The front door opened and closed, and Jessica felt Ryan's presence before she saw him. He knelt on one knee beside her and set her medical bag down.

"How is he?"

"His heart rate is very rapid, and his breathing is shallow. Can you get an aspirin for me? If it's a heart attack, it may help."

She turned her attention back to Joaquin. Grabbing her stethoscope, she listened to his heart.

"Joaquin, can you tell me where it hurts? *¿Donde duele?*"

His hand moved over his chest. *"En todas partes, la doctora. Como una presión."* His voice was weak, but clear, and he reached for his wife.

"Everywhere? You've got pressure everywhere?" asked Jessica as she continued her exam.

Akna moved to his side, held tightly to his hand, and bowed her head. Her words, though spoken in a whisper, held great faith and power. *"Por favor, Señor Dios, no deje que mi marido murió. Ayuda Dr. Jessica hacer lo que hay que hacer. A Dios sea la gloria. Hágase tu voluntad. Amén."*

Jessica glanced at Ryan with a questioning look.

He whispered, "She's asking God to save Joaquin through your hands, but she's also asking for His will to be done, and for God to receive glory through this."

Jessica nodded as she continued her assessment. She checked his blood pressure, then helped Joaquin lay on the sofa with his feet propped up on the arm.

Jessica kept her voice low and calm as she talked with Joaquin. "We need to get you to a hospital, Joaquin. It could be your heart, but we need more tests, okay?"

"Si, *Doctora* Jessica. I trust you. I am sorry to be so much trouble." He managed a weak smile, then looked at his wife and spoke tenderly. *"No tenga miedo, mi amada esposa. Doctora Jessica cuidará de mí. Todo estará bien. Dios esta con nosotros."*

Jessica looked quickly at Ryan, who whispered to her, "He told her not to worry. You were taking good care of him, and God was with us."

CHAPTER TWENTY-SIX

The Veracruz emergency room was bustling with activity when Ryan, Jessica, and the Canuls arrived, but Joaquin was immediately taken to a treatment room when Ryan explained his situation to the triage nurse. Jessica stood, watching as Joaquin was wheeled away. Akna scurried close behind him.

"Jessica?"

She turned toward Ryan's voice as her soft blue eyes darted around the ER. She gently bounced Nicholas in her arms.

Ryan directed her to a quiet spot in a corner, and they both sat down in a pair of hard-backed chairs. "Joaquin's getting the best of care. We got him here in time. What's wrong?"

She shook her head slightly. "What if I wasn't here, Ryan? What if there wasn't anyone here to help him when this happened?"

"But you were here, Jessica, and you did what needed to be done. Now, the doctors here will do what they can for him, and we'll do what we can. We'll pray for him," stated Ryan.

Nicholas stirred, and she pulled him tighter against her chest and patted him gently until he settled back down.

"What if it's someone else next time? What if it's you?" She frowned and looked away. "You've got to have a doctor closer to you."

"I know." Ryan shifted in his chair, resting his head against the wall. He exhaled long and slow. "But that's out of my control."

Jessica glanced at him and reached out to grasp his hand. "God will send someone." Her lips formed a thin line. "He has to." Her voice wasn't convincing, but the words were still encouraging.

Ryan looked over at her. "He will, Jessica. He will send someone. All we have to do is wait."

At that moment, Akna came through the double doors from the treatment area. Her dark brown eyes were clouded, and her forehead held the furrows of worry.

"He is going to have a test. The doctor says it is a… I wrote it down." She unfolded a piece of paper and handed it to Jessica.

"An angiogram. If the test shows a lot of blockages, they will need to replace those vessels. If the blockages are small, and they determine there's not a lot of damage, they can just remove the clot. Maybe put a stent in to keep the artery open. This test is the right thing to do to know what's happening to his heart, Akna." Jessica reached over and took the Mayan woman's hand.

"I am sorry. I don't understand all of what you said," apologized Akna.

Ryan quickly translated what Jessica said, and Akna finally nodded her head in understanding.

"I am so grateful to God that you were there, *Doctora*. You saved my Joaquin. I can never repay you for that," said Akna as her voice broke and tears finally fell.

Jessica blinked away her own tears as she handed Nicholas to Ryan. She moved to Akna and put her arms around her.

"You owe me nothing, Akna. We are family, remember? Family helps each other," Jessica explained quietly. "We have to trust God that He will be with Joaquin, and that He will show the doctors exactly what they need to do. Do not give up hope, okay?"

Akna smiled through her tears. "I will not, *Doctora*. Our God, He is a good God. He sent you to us." She wiped her dampened cheeks. "May I hold the baby? He will help me be strong. I will look at him and remember how God helped you

Chapter Twenty-six

and him, and I will have the faith I need to trust Him to help my Joaquin."

"Of course." She turned toward Ryan and nodded. He placed Nicholas in Akna's arms.

Akna began to softly sing a Mexican lullaby, focusing all her attention on the child she held.

Jessica wiped a tear from her face as she struggled to control her own emotions.

How will I ever be able to say goodbye?

****

Three hours later, Joaquin Canul was resting comfortably in a bed in the coronary care unit of the hospital. The angiogram showed a small clot in one of his cardiac arteries, but the cardiologist had determined that it could be repaired by inserting a small balloon catheter into the blood vessel to compress the clot against the side of the artery. Completing this procedure in the catheterization lab, Joaquin was then taken to the CCU for continued treatment.

The hour was late, so Ryan secured two rooms at a nearby hotel; one for himself and one Jessica could share with Akna. Sitting in a nearly empty restaurant across the street from the hospital, Ryan held a sleeping Nicholas while Jessica munched her late night dinner of chicken strips and French fries.

"I doubt Akna will come to the hotel tonight," said Ryan. "I told her to call me if she decided to, so she wouldn't have to walk over alone, but I think she's going to stay with Joaquin."

"I would. If it were you," Jessica said absentmindedly as she dipped a fry into a dollop of ketchup. "I would stay."

Ryan's eyebrows rose as he pondered Jessica's comment. He reached over Nicholas to bring his coffee cup to his lips.

Jessica took her last bite of chicken and washed it down with a swallow of lemon water. "Will you call me if anything happens during the night?"

"Of course, but try and get some sleep, okay? Tomorrow could be a long day."

"I will. Oh, on behalf of my son, thanks for making that run to the market." She smiled at him. "He appreciates a dry diaper."

Ryan chuckled. "My pleasure."

After paying their bill, he walked with her to the hotel, easily carrying Nicholas in one arm and guiding her with the other. When they reached the lobby elevators, he handed the baby to Jessica.

"I'm going back to check on Akna, but after that I'll head up to my room. It's four twelve, if you need me. Otherwise, I'll see you in the morning, say around eight, or is that too early?"

"It's fine. We'll be ready." Her smile was warm and genuine. "Thank you for everything."

The elevator doors slid open and Jessica entered. She turned around to face Ryan. "You know, you're really an amazing person, Ryan Devereaux. I'm glad God brought you into my life."

The doors slid closed, and he stood there, still seeing her warm smile and beautiful blue eyes.

****

Ryan quickly walked back to the hospital to check on Joaquin and Akna. The hallway leading to the coronary care unit was foreboding, yet Ryan had a peace about Joaquin, and deep inside he believed his friend would recover without incident. As he neared the unit, the faint beepings of monitors became audible, and hospital personnel were more visible.

He peeked into the waiting room, but Akna was not there. He continued to the nurses' station, received permission to enter the unit, and went directly to Joaquin's room.

Joaquin was alone. His eyes were closed, but they opened as soon as Ryan neared the bed.

"Hello my friend," said Ryan. "How are you feeling?"

Chapter Twenty-six

A faint smile crossed Joaquin's face. "I am happy to be alive. God has been good to me."

Ryan pulled up a chair and sat down. "That He has. You're looking much better than the last time I saw you."

"I am feeling much better than the last time you saw me." He chuckled weakly. "Thank you for all you have done for me, for Akna."

"You're welcome, Joaquin." He sat back and crossed his legs. "Akna said you might be able to go home in a day or two."

"Yes, a man always rests better in his own bed," said Joaquin.

Ryan smiled. "I can't argue with that."

"I have been thanking God that *Doctora* Jessica was there." He paused for a moment. "I am hoping she will stay."

"I don't know about that, Joaquin. She has family back in California and a job. Now that she has Nicholas, she'll need to return soon to let the rest of her family meet him. I'm guessing his grandparents won't want her returning here to live," explained Ryan, a note of remorse in his voice.

"Akna and I, we will miss her."

"So will I, Joaquin. So will I."

****

Two days later, Joaquin was back home in Santa Molina. Jessica had helped him settle in and had spent time educating both he and Akna about the warning signs of heart attacks. Akna was a quick learner and carefully attended to her husband with the same skills that she oversaw her home and family. She was meticulous with his care, and Jessica knew Joaquin was in good hands.

In another four days, she was standing on the sidewalk outside the international terminal at the airport in Veracruz. Her hands were securely around Nicholas as she held him to her, leaving none free to shake Ryan's hand goodbye or wipe the tears that threatened to fall.

She watched Ryan check her bags with the curbside porter. His easy laughter floated over to her as she saw the porter smile and slap Ryan on the back. She blinked her eyes several times, trying to hold back the flood of tears that threatened to spill over. As Ryan walked back toward her, she tried to memorize the moment. The wind was blowing his dark hair; his deep blue eyes seemed to see only her; his smile was mesmerizing. She swallowed hard and forced herself to smile at him.

"Thank you, Ryan. I don't know how I would have managed without you."

"You're welcome." He reached out his hands. "Hey, let me hold this fellow one more time, okay?" He took Nicholas and brought him against his chest. He kissed the baby's head, and for a moment, said nothing, but when he did, he struggled to speak. "You take good care of your mom, okay? She's going to need your help." He handed Nicholas back to Jessica.

"I'll call you when we land," stammered Jessica. "Or when I get home."

"Call when you can."

They stood together awkwardly until Ryan finally spoke. "Have a safe flight. You've been a real blessing. I'm going to miss you and Nicholas."

"I'm going to miss you, too."

Ryan stuck his hands in his pockets. "Give my best to your family."

"I will." She turned to go, then stopped and looked back at him. "Keep in touch?"

"Of course."

"I better go."

He nodded and watched her melt into the crowd of travelers. It had been a very long time since his heart had felt such emptiness.

PART FIVE – LOS ANGELES

"Have I not commanded thee? Be strong and of a good courage; be not afraid, neither be thou dismayed: for the LORD thy God is with thee whithersoever thou goest."

Joshua 1:9

CHAPTER TWENTY-SEVEN

Jessica stood in front of the oak door, holding a sleeping Nicholas in his detachable car seat. Before she knocked, she took a moment to examine the straw wreath hanging from the top of the door. Pastel flowers of lavender, blue, and yellow were woven into it, and a tiny wooden sign with the engraved word "Welcome" hung below the wreath by a green ribbon. She rapped lightly on the doorjamb and waited, gently swinging Nicholas.

The door opened, and Jessica's Sunday school teacher, Gretchen Draper, greeted her with a smile. The older woman wore a white cardigan sweater over a beige short sleeve blouse and a dark brown skirt. She wore her graying hair in a short bob, and her grey-blue eyes twinkled with delight when she saw Jessica.

"My dear, do come in! I am so glad you could drop by!" she said as she ushered Jessica into her home.

"Thank you so much, Mrs. Draper." Jessica followed her into the living room. "I really appreciate you taking the time to see me."

"It's my pleasure, dear." She gestured to the sofa. "Please sit down."

"Thank you. You have a beautiful home."

Mrs. Draper smiled. "I thought about selling it after Robert died, but I decided there were too many wonderful memories here, so I stayed." She walked over to the sofa and peered into

Courageous Love

the car seat. "Oh, babies are so angelic when they're sleeping!" She reached a thin finger out and caressed Nicholas' cheek, then sat down in an oak rocking chair across from Jessica. "Now, how can I help you? You said you had something you wanted to speak to me about."

Jessica smiled nervously and adjusted her denim skirt. "I'm not sure where to begin," she said, looking up into the kind eyes of her teacher. "I just know that you're the one I'm supposed to talk with."

"Really? How do you know that?"

"Because when we need spiritual answers, we're supposed to seek out godly leaders, and you certainly are one to me."

Gretchen chuckled softly. "Thank you, dear. I've learned a lot in my thirty-seven years as a pastor's wife. Hopefully, I will be able to help you."

Jessica smiled. "I hope so, Mrs. Draper. I'm thinking about maybe moving to Mexico, and I want to know how I can be certain it's God's will."

"Mexico?"

"Yes. There's an opportunity there to work in a rural clinic."

"Oh? Is this the place you were just at?"

Jessica nodded. "Mrs. Draper, those people need a doctor desperately, and I could see myself as that doctor, but—"

"But what?"

Jessica folded her hands in her lap. "There's the possibility that I want to go there because of someone that I've become very fond of."

"Go on, dear."

"When I was there, there were several times when people would have died without a doctor. If I wasn't there, maybe they would have. I know that in the future there will be more situations where people will need a physician."

"So, you want to go there to practice medicine?"

"Yes, partly, I want to help establish a medical clinic. I want to help people live better, healthier lives, plus..." Her voice faded.

Chapter Twenty-seven

"Plus what, Jessica?"

"There's Ryan."

"The young man you've grown fond of?" Mrs. Draper rose and smiled knowingly. "Sounds like we could use a cup of tea." She disappeared into the kitchen.

Jessica glanced over at her son. He slept peacefully, unaware of the turmoil within his mother's heart. She traced her finger over his rosebud mouth, then tapped the tip of his nose. He stirred slightly, and she smiled as his tiny fingers clasped her own.

Mrs. Draper returned with two cups of Earl Grey tea. She set one down on the end table nearest Jessica, then sat down in the rocking chair once more, sipping her own cup. "So, tell me about this man."

Jessica took a deep breath. "Ryan's the pastor there. He's a wonderful man, and I... I think I love him."

"And that's a problem?"

"Well, yes." She sighed as she looked at her son.

"I'm not sure I understand your dilemma."

Jessica tried to explain. "I don't know how Ryan feels. We never talked about our futures, much less a future together. There was so much going on. Plus, Nick's not been gone that long, and I don't know if I should even consider someone else so soon."

"You've not given yourself permission to love again?"

Jessica smoothed her skirt self-consciously and kept her eyes cast downward.

Mrs. Draper smiled affectionately. "You know Jessica, Sometimes, when we find the courage to open our hearts, God has a wonderful way of filling them more abundantly than we could ever think or imagine."

Jessica raised her head. "What do you mean?"

"Maybe this young man *is* God's will for you. Perhaps the issue is not *where* you work for the Lord, but rather *with whom* you should be working." The older woman took another sip of tea before she set the cup back in its saucer.

"Jessica, there's no time table for love. Listen to your heart, and listen to your Lord. God is faithful to answer those who go to Him for wisdom and guidance. Continue to seek wise counsel, but not just from me. Talk to your parents, your pastor, and especially your young man in Mexico. It may be difficult to share your heart with Ryan, but before you uproot yourself from here, you must know if he feels the same way about you.

"Finally, if you *and* Ryan believe the desire to go to Mexico is God's will, take a step of faith. If He doesn't want you there, He'll close the doors, so make sure you are listening to Him. And remember, the right choice brings the peace of God to your heart. Fear and confusion is never from Him."

Jessica took a deep breath. "I seem to be hearing the same message over and over."

Mrs. Draper chuckled. "Imagine that."

Jessica felt the heat begin to rise in her cheeks. "Guess maybe I need to listen, don't I?"

The older woman smiled knowingly. "Your heavenly Father will not let you down. He loves you, and He only wants what is best for you. Ask for His direction, and you will receive it."

Nicholas began to stir in his car seat.

Mrs. Draper's eyes sparkled with delight. "Oh, Jessica! May I hold him?"

"Of course!" She quickly unfastened the restraints around Nicholas, lifted him out of the seat, and handed him to Mrs. Draper.

"Such a tiny baby! Oh, aren't you an angel, you little precious thing, you!" She held him lovingly and rocked him in her arms. Nicholas stilled, his large blue eyes focused on her face. She began to sing to him.

"Jesus loves you, this I know. For the Bible tells me so. Little ones to him belong; they are weak but He is strong..."

Jessica listened to the soothing melody, and as she watched Mrs. Draper and Nicholas, her mind went back to Mexico. She saw Nicholas resting in the arms of Akna, and she heard the

Chapter Twenty-seven

Mayan woman singing the same song, and as she remembered, her heart ached.

****

Later that afternoon, Jessica leaned over and kissed Nicholas' forehead as he lay in his crib for a nap. She turned on the overhead mobile and five little donkeys began to revolve slowly as a lullaby softly played. Each donkey wore a different colored sombrero, and as they moved, their tasseled tails swayed gently. The mobile was a gift from Ryan that had arrived two weeks after she had returned home.

She stood staring at the mobile until the ringing of her doorbell caught her attention. She readjusted Nicholas' blue and white crocheted blanket, a gift from Akna, then went downstairs.

"Mom! This is unexpected," said Jessica as she opened the door. "Come in. I just put Nicholas down for a nap."

"Hello, sweetheart!" Anne hugged Jessica. "I thought I'd drop by and visit my favorite daughter."

Jessica laughed. "Oh, I'm glad it has nothing to do with that little boy sleeping upstairs." She ushered her mother into the living room. "Would you like something to drink?"

"No. I'm fine for now. I just thought maybe you and I could chat for a bit. I know we haven't really had the opportunity to have some alone time, and I wanted some before you returned to work," explained Anne.

Jessica sat down, curled her feet up under her, and leaned against the arm of the sofa.

"It's good to have you home, Jessica. I have to say, your father and I were so worried about you. First, the hurricane, then the birth of Nicholas... well, let's just say Dad and I spent a lot of time on our knees." She rubbed Jessica's shoulder. "It's so comforting to know our heavenly Father takes good care of His children no matter where they are."

"I'm so sorry we had such terrible cell service after the storm. I would have called you sooner," apologized Jessica.

"Oh sweetheart, we know that. It couldn't be helped. Praise the Lord, you had good friends there with you."

"I did, Mom." Her voice softened. "I don't know what I would have done without them."

Anne nodded in understanding. "You know, you haven't really said much about what happened there. How were the camps?"

Jessica's face brightened. "They were wonderful. You should have seen Ryan working with those kids. When he preaches, well, it's right on target. Every service was just so… so… inspiring, and when he presented the gospel, he was so careful to make sure they really understood him. Later when we talked about it, you could tell his heart was so happy by the response of the kids. It was amazing just to sit and listen to him in the evenings when we sat around the fire. He had those kids mesmerized.

"And then you should have seen Ryan and Eric with the kids. They would jump right in and play with them. It didn't matter if it was stick ball or tag or going on a hike. And when they played softball! Oh my! The kids against the adults, it was hilarious. Ryan was right there in the middle of it all. You should have seen them! Ryan, Eric, the other counselors! It was priceless!"

"I trust you watched from the sidelines?"

"Of course, Mother!" Jessica laughed lightly. "Could you just see me running down a field? Ryan would have been so angry with me if I'd done that. In fact, he was quite protective of me."

"Apparently, he is very good at taking care of my children."

"Thank the Lord for that! I honestly don't know what I would have done without him, Mom."

"I see he's made quite an impression on you."

Jessica relaxed her head against the back of the sofa and smiled.

If you only knew, Mom.

Anne studied her daughter carefully. "He means a lot to you, doesn't he?"

Chapter Twenty-seven

"Yes, he does." She sat upright. "Mom, you should have seen him with Nicholas. He was so gentle with him. He would have made a good father."

"Would have?"

"Yes." Her voice saddened. "He was married before, but he lost both his wife and their unborn child when she went into labor. There was no doctor near enough to help."

"Oh, that's awful. I'm so sorry for him."

"Me too."

"It must've been difficult for him when he was the only one there with you to deliver Nicholas."

Jessica's eyes lowered slightly as she said, "It had to be. Sometimes I feel so guilty at having put him through what I did." She looked at her mother sorrowfully. "I know I couldn't control it, but Mom, he must have been so worried. You would have never known it though. He kept all that inside of him. He was so reassuring, so confident. I really don't know what I would have done without him."

"I am so glad he was there for you."

"Me too." She stood up. "I think I'd like a cup of tea. How about you?"

"I'd love one." Anne followed Jessica into the kitchen. "So, when do you go back to work?"

Jessica turned on the burner under her teapot. As she reached for two cups, she answered her mother. "I still have another week or so before I return. It's going to be so hard leaving Nicholas." She turned abruptly. "Not that I don't trust you, Mom. It's just going to be hard to be away from him."

"I understand completely. I think I would feel the same way," said Anne as she selected two lemon-ginger packets from Jessica's basket of teabags.

Jessica set the creamer on the counter. "I talked to Ryan last night. He said that Joaquin is doing very well. Things are pretty much back to normal there since the hurricane. You should see the people there, Mom. They all came out to help each other. It was amazing! I think they've got the sweetest spirit in that church. You know, the ladies gave me a baby shower." She became quiet. "It was so unexpected."

The teapot began to whistle, steam rising from the spout. "Jessica? The pot."

"What? Oh!" She reached for the teapot and poured the water. "Sorry."

Anne studied her daughter's face. "They must care a great deal for you."

Jessica grabbed a tissue and dabbed at the corner of her eyes. "They were so nice, Mom. On the last Sunday I was there, the ladies had a goodbye lunch for me. It was so hard to keep from crying."

They moved into the living room. This time, Anne sat across from Jessica. She drank her tea and simply listened.

"You'd love them, Mom," said Jessica as she tucked her feet under her again. "Akna is so sweet. She reminds me of you so much. She's a great cook. You should taste her enchiladas! Her kids are adorable, especially Ana. She's the youngest. She doesn't speak a lot of English. Then there's Maria. She's the spitting image of her mother; she speaks English quite well. We had several long talks. She wants to be a nurse someday. Juan is Akna's son. He's nearly a man in stature, and yet, still a boy at heart. He's the apple of his dad's eye.

"Akna's husband, Joaquin… he's the one who had the heart attack… well, he and Ryan are really good friends. They make an incredible team. Between the two of them, they keep the church and other buildings in good repair, plus the grounds. Joaquin's also a deacon in the church. Ryan's hoping one day that Joaquin will be able to attend a Bible college. Ryan says there's nothing better than a national pastor. Joaquin would be great, too. He's quite the people person."

Jessica picked up her cup and held it near her face, savoring the citrus aroma.

"I'll never forget Ryan helping me through the delivery. He was so amazing! He did everything Eric told him to do without any hesitation, and he was so encouraging. And then

Chapter Twenty-seven

after Nicholas was born, oh, Mom, Ryan was so gentle with him. It makes me cry just to think of it. To think that someone that strong could be so tender with a baby." For a moment Jessica forgot that her mother was there.

"You know, Jessica, I've been over here every day since you've come home..."

Jessica shifted on the sofa. "And...?"

Anne smiled as she set her cup on the coffee table. "And there has been a common thread in every discussion we've had. It's made me... wonder."

"Wonder? About what?"

"I was wondering," began Anne. "how you really feel about Ryan."

Jessica's overcompensated attempts to react normally fell short. "Ryan? Oh, he's a good friend. You know, he's a really good friend."

"I know. You've said that before. But something's changed."

"Changed? What do you mean?" Jessica felt uneasy and nervously focused her attention on the teacup in her hand.

Anne leaned forward in her chair. "I see a young woman who may have left her heart in Mexico."

Jessica said nothing. She sat perfectly still, staring at the cup in her hand. Finally, she lifted her guilt-ridden face toward her mother. "It hasn't even been a year since Nick died. I feel so awful."

"Awful? Why?"

Jessica didn't answer at first. She struggled with saying the words out loud. "It hasn't been that long since Nick passed. I've just had his child, but I think I'm... I think I'm in love with Ryan, and..." She looked up at her mother, tears filling her eyes. "I don't know if that's right, or if that's even what God wants for me."

Anne sat back and took a deep breath. "You do know how your father and I met?"

Jessica nodded, but Anne continued.

"At a church revival. Paul had been invited to come with a friend, and I saw him for the first time at the fellowship meal after the service. We met several times after that for coffee, and soon we became good friends. One day, he introduced me to you and Caleb." Anne closed her eyes and smiled before continuing.

She looked up at Jessica through misted eyes. "You two were such a joy to be around, and it was amazing to watch Paul with you both. When I saw him with you and your brother, I couldn't help but fall in love with him. He was such a sweet, caring father. He still is. It wasn't long before we realized that God had brought us together, and we wanted to get married. We wanted to be a family."

She rose and moved over by Jessica taking her hands in her own. "But it hadn't even been six months since your mother had passed away. We were worried what people would think, but we prayed about it. A lot. The Bible tells us in Philippians four, verses six and seven, 'Be careful for nothing; but in every thing by prayer and supplication with thanksgiving let your requests be made known unto God. And the peace of God, which passeth all understanding, shall keep your hearts and minds through Christ Jesus.'

"We truly believed it was God's will for us to marry for several reasons. First of all, if God was not part of this marriage, we knew it would not have the foundation it needed to survive, but we both loved the Lord and desired to build a home with Christ at the center. Your dad and I believed that God brought us together for a reason, and that reason was to be together, to raise a godly family, and to serve Him faithfully as long as we live." Anne took another sip of her tea.

"Secondly, we knew God was our Father, and His Word said that He wanted to give us the desires of our hearts. Our greatest desire was to be together as husband and wife, and to be parents to you and Caleb." Anne paused for a moment, then looked deeply into her daughter's eyes. "What is the desire of your heart, Jessica? Do you love Ryan?"

Chapter Twenty-seven

Jessica sat staring at her mother, nodding her head. "I think so. Mom. So what do I do now?"

"Well, if God wants you two together, He'll find a way. He always does. What you have to do is trust Him. Devote yourself to prayer; tell God exactly what's on your heart, then wait for Him to answer you. The Bible tells us that 'The Lord is good unto them that wait for Him, to the soul that seeketh Him.' So seek Him, Jessica. Read His Word. Pray. And let Him lead you."

Jessica impulsively hugged Anne and whispered, "Thank you, Mom. Thank you so much." She sat back on the sofa. "I miss Ryan so much, Mom. I don't even know how he feels. There was so much going on."

Anne reached out and squeezed Jessica's hand. "Have you made your requests known to God, sweetheart?"

"No, not really. I mean, I haven't really prayed about Ryan."

"Perhaps it's time you did." She reached for Jessica's hands and bowed her head, then waited. Praying together was something the two of them had done consistently throughout the years, and now would be no exception.

Jessica hesitated, embarrassed to pray out loud about the love she had hid in her heart for so long. Finally, she lowered her head and began to pray, opening her soul to God. She said everything she had kept to herself for many months, and then asked that He give her a true servant's heart. When her tears prevented her from continuing, Anne took over.

"Father, I come to You on behalf of my daughter. Jessica has had so much to face in this past year, but through it all, You've been with her, walking each step of the way with her, and restoring her joy through new life and new relationships. I ask that You guide her in regards to Ryan. Reveal Your will to her, and give her peace in her heart, like You gave me so many years ago when You brought Paul into my life. I thank You in advance for what You're going to do for her, for Nicholas, and for Ryan. In Jesus' name, I pray. Amen." Anne wiped away her own tears and then embraced Jessica. "I promise everything will work to the good, sweetheart, if you just trust God."

"Mom, what if God does lead me to Mexico? What about you?" Jessica's voice was filled with trepidation as she blotted the moisture from her eyes.

"Sweetheart, I will miss you and Nicholas terribly, of course, as will your dad, but we both know that the best place for you to be is where God wants you to be. And if that place is Mexico, I know God will give us the grace to accept that."

Jessica drew in a trembling breath as she tried in vain to still her tears. "Oh, Mom, thank you so much. I can't tell you how much that means to me. I love you more than I can say."

"I love you, too, sweetheart, with all my heart."

CHAPTER TWENTY-EIGHT

Her first day back at work was slow, and by mid-afternoon, Jessica was already thinking about going home early. She knew that would be impractical, but it didn't stop her from fantasizing about an afternoon outside in the fresh air with Nicholas playing happily on a blanket beside her. Sitting alone in the staff lounge, she closed her eyes and propped her feet up on a chair. In her mind's eye she saw large-leafed trees overshadowing a grassy path that led down to a sparkling brook. Cradling Nicholas in her arms, she settled down on the soft vegetation overlooking the stream. Farther down the path, a man had his back to her. Even before he turned toward her, she knew who it was from the dark hair and broad-shoulders.

"Jessica?"

Her eyes popped open. "Maggie!" Her feet dropped to the floor. "Sorry, I—"

"No problem. It's slower than ever today. I probably shouldn't complain about that, but the time certainly drags by when it's like this." Maggie sat down opposite Jessica. "So, tell me about Mexico."

"Not much to tell," teased Jessica. "Only a hurricane, birth of a baby, saved a couple of lives. You know, same old, same old."

Maggie laughed lightly. "Good to hear. For a minute there, I thought you'd gone through some pretty challenging situations."

Jessica smiled. "It was not quite what I thought it would be. The doctoring part was fairly standard, even the few emergencies that came up, but working with those kids... sharing Christ... seeing them make life-changing decisions... I don't think I could really put into words what that experience was like. Listening to Ryan share the gospel, well, that was incredible. He knows exactly what to say and how to say it.

"Now, the hurricane, well, that was definitely something I would be happy to never experience again. I've never heard it rain so hard or seen the wind blow so ferociously! If it hadn't been for Ryan, I think I would've been scared out of my wits. Maybe I was! He said he'd been through a few before. I can't even imagine that."

Maggie rose to get a cup of coffee. "Yes, and not only hurricanes, but earthquakes. You didn't have one of those, did you?"

"No. I guess I'll have something to look forward to the next time I'm down there."

Maggie slowly poured her coffee, then turned around, cup in hand. "What did you say?"

"I said I'd have something to look forward—" Jessica stopped abruptly, her cheeks reddening. "I mean *if* I go there again, I'll have something to look forward to if I go there again."

"Um-hmm." Maggie sat down again and stared at Jessica.

"What?"

"So tell me what you're not telling me."

"I don't know what you're talking about." She shied away from Maggie's probing eyes.

"You know exactly what I'm talking about."

"You'll think I'm crazy."

"I thought you were crazy when you said you wanted to go be a camp doctor in Santa Molina," stated Maggie. "Frankly, nothing you tell me now would surprise me." She grinned at her friend.

Jessica squirmed in her seat. "Why do you always make me feel like I'm on trial?"

"Really?" Maggie shook her head in mock disdain. "After all we've gone through together?"

Jessica frowned, her sigh long. "It's complicated."

Chapter Twenty-eight

"Complicated? What does that mean?"

"It means I have some... some issues I'm wrestling with."

"Issues? What kind of issues? Is something wrong with Nicholas? With you?"

"No, no, nothing like that," Jessica quickly reassured Maggie. "It's an issue of..."

Maggie leaned forward expectantly.

Jessica took a deep breath and echoed Maggie's words from their last conversation. "The heart. It's a matter of the heart."

Maggie's brown eyes opened wide. "The heart? You're not referring to a medical issue, are you?"

Jessica shrugged her shoulders with a sheepish look.

"Ryan?" Maggie waited for an answer, but when Jessica remained silent, understanding quickly came. Her hand flew up to her mouth. "Ryan? You're in love with Ryan? Does he know?"

"No. No, he doesn't, and please don't say anything to him," Jessica pleaded. "I'm not ready for him to know about this. Not yet, okay?"

"Of course! I won't say a word. So tell me, when did this happen?"

"I'm not really sure, but there's more."

"More?"

"I've been praying about God's will for my life."

A puzzled look crossed Maggie's face. "Go on."

"I've been wondering if maybe God wants me to work some other place."

Maggie's eyes widened. "You'd leave Eastmont?"

"I don't know." Jessica's apologetic eyes sought Maggie's approval. "I was thinking of... maybe... Santa Molina."

Maggie's mouth dropped open, and she sat speechless.

"Please, Maggie. I haven't said anything to anyone yet, except my parents. I'm just dabbling with the idea. Ryan hasn't asked me. He doesn't have any idea about any of this. It's just something that I can't shake." Jessica closed her eyes and dropped her head. "I can't explain it." When she felt Maggie's

349

hand cover her own, she looked up. "You must really think I'm crazy."

"No, Jessica. Not at all." Maggie's voice was filled with compassion. "If you think God is leading you there, you should pay attention to Him."

"You really think He could be? You think God would take me away from everything that I know? Eastmont? My family? My friends?" Jessica's uncertainty was obvious.

Maggie thought for a moment. "I'm not saying it wouldn't be difficult, but, yes, Jessica. If He's directing you to some place else, that some place else has got to be better for you because that's part of His plan for you. That doesn't mean I wouldn't miss you. I'd miss you so much, but I'd never ask you to stay. What did your folks say?"

"They're very supportive. I'm the one who feels like a complete heel for even thinking about taking their grandson away from them. What kind of a daughter does that? Plus, it's a foreign country. I'd be taking Nicholas away from—"

"From what, Jessica? He's too little to be aware of anything, but you. He'll do well anywhere as long as he's with you and he's loved."

Jessica stood up and began to pace the room. "I feel like I'm being presumptuous. I haven't even talked to Ryan about it. He never did anything to make me even think he might be interested, and I never brought it up, but now, it's all I can think about. And honestly, I'm really having trouble separating God's will from my own."

"Maybe they're not different," offered Maggie.

Jessica looked up, frowning. "I wish I knew. I've prayed and prayed, but I don't have any answers yet. Part of this whole thing scares me. I'm afraid God will tell me to go, and I'm afraid He'll tell me to stay. Part of me really wants to go, but the other part is afraid to leave."

"If you knew Ryan loved you, would you still be worried about going?"

Chapter Twenty-eight

Jessica brought her lips together wondering how to answer. Finally, she whispered, "I don't think so."

"Maybe it's not Mexico you're afraid of, but rather how Ryan feels?"

"Maybe..." Jessica looked up at Maggie. "Will you pray about it for me?"

"Of course, I'll definitely be praying for you."

"Thank—"

Jessica's pager went off, followed by Maggie's. They both stood up.

You were saying something about it being slow?" quipped Maggie as they walked out into the corridor.

Valerie met them midway between the lounge and nurses' station. "Two victims on the way in. Multiple gunshot wounds. Paramedics think it may be gang related," she reported. "So we may get more."

"ETA?" Jessica glanced at her watch.

"They should be here in less than ten minutes."

"Ben and Eric still here?" asked Maggie.

"Yes. Eric was just about to leave when the call came in. He said he'd stay until they arrive, in case you need him." Valerie set the IV bags on the counter, went behind the desk and grabbed a hair tie. She quickly secured her long hair into a ponytail. "Time to hit the trail running!" She grabbed the bags and hurried off into a treatment room.

Eight minutes later, the paramedics ushered in a gurney upon which lay a young dark-skinned adolescent male with a gunshot wound to his left upper shoulder. His faded blue t-shirt was covered with tiny spots of blood in addition to the large stain at the shoulder.

"I'm gonna kill him!" yelled the teen. "Just as soon as I'm outta here, I'm gonna kill him!" His right arm flailed about as he was transferred to the ER exam table. "You tell him, I'm gonna find him, and I'm gonna get him!"

"Settle down or we'll have to restrain you," ordered Jessica as she began her assessment. She pulled out a pair of scissors and began to cut away her patient's shirt. "What's your name, sir?"

"Hey! Whacha doing? That's my shirt, you're cuttin'!" He slapped her hand away, sending the scissors flying.

Jessica got down close to his face. "You need to settle down, now!" Her words were strong and forceful. "Your shirt's already peppered with holes. I need to see what I'm dealing with, or you can just bleed out right here on this table. You understand me?" Her eyes never wavered from his angry stare.

"So what if I do?" he challenged, his dark eyes narrowing.

Compassion tugged at Jessica's heart.

He's just a kid. Couldn't be more than fifteen or sixteen.

"You're not ready to meet God just yet," she said calmly as she retrieved her scissors. She set them on the counter and got another pair from a drawer.

"What? You're not a preacher, are you?"

"No. I'm a doctor." She stood poised at his bedside with the second pair of scissors in her hand. "May I?"

"This here's my clothes," he protested.

"I promise I'll get you another shirt." She waited.

"Yeah, sure, go ahead, but not the pants. You hear me?"

"Loud and clear."

As she cut the fabric, she continued questioning him. "Now, I asked you a question. What's your name?"

His narrowed eyes looked away from her as he answered. "Jerome."

"You got a last name, Jerome?"

"Nope."

She looked over at Valerie and stood up. "Put him at the bottom of the list. I've got another one to see." She stepped toward the door. "He can wait. If he dies…" She shrugged her shoulders.

The teen's eyes widened in alarm. "Okay, okay. It's Sanders. Jerome Sanders. Satisfied?"

Chapter Twenty-eight

Jessica over-exaggerated a smile. "Very. So, tell me, Jerome Sanders, you have an argument with a shotgun?"

"Something like that."

"What about this one?" She poked her gloved finger near a small hole in his left shoulder.

"Oww! Hey, what's wrong with you? That hurts!"

"Oh, does it? Sorry. Now, you were saying?" Jessica continued examining his shoulder.

Valerie stifled a giggle as she adjusted the IV dripping in through the line the paramedics had established in the field.

"I wasn't saying nothing. Just do your job."

"Oh, that's a fine attitude to have. Here I am, holding your life in the balance of my hand, and you speak to me rudely. Val, can you get me some forceps?"

"What you need those for?"

"Your body is riddled with buckshot. My job, as you so aptly point out, is to remove them from you. Then I'll tackle the bullet. You should be back out on the street by tomorrow evening."

He eyed her suspiciously. "I ain't gonna need no surgery, am I?"

"You mean the kind where we knock you out? No. I can do everything from here unless something unexpected happens."

"Something unexpected?"

"Relax. You're going to be fine. I promise."

"You can't make no promises like that."

"Why can't I?" She extracted the first piece of buckshot dropping it into a metal basin. Its tinnish clang caught Jerome's attention.

"How many of those you gotta get?"

"Oh, I don't know, twenty or thirty, I suppose." She continued removing the buckshot.

"Twenty or thirty? I should be dead!"

"Well, you probably would be if the shooter had been closer. He was probably at least fifty to seventy-five feet from you. You were very fortunate. Now this one... that's a different story." She indicated the small caliber bullet hole in his shoulder.

"I could die from that?"

"Not from where it hit you, but if it were, say, down here..." She tapped him mid-chest. "We might not be having this conversation." She dug deep for another piece of buckshot.

"Oww... can't I have something for pain?"

Jessica raised her eyes and looked skeptically at him. "Really? You can't handle this?"

He scowled at her. "You're a sadist."

Jessica laughed. "I've been called worse."

"Yeah? You probably deserved it." For the first time, he had a faint smile on his face.

"I probably did." She worked carefully, inspecting each site meticulously after she removed the shot. "How'd you get involved in something like this?"

"You mean the shooting? Aw, everybody's got a gun these days. It ain't nothing special."

"Everybody doesn't have a gun these days, Jerome. I don't have one." She plucked another piece of buckshot out of his chest.

"You ought to. A lady needs protection. You never know who you're going to run into," he advised.

"I don't need a gun."

"Yeah? Maybe not here, but how about when you're walking in the dark to your car?" His face became very serious. "You need a piece."

"I prefer to walk with God."

"I knew you were a preacher!" His eyes brightened as he teased her.

"No, I make far too much money to be a preacher," she countered. "But seriously, I feel very safe with Jesus by my side."

"Ah, you may not be a preacher, but you're one of those Christians, aren't you?"

"Yes, I am. You?"

"No. Ain't got no time for God."

"He'll wait. He's got all the time in the world. This one's going to hurt a little more. It's a bit deeper. Want me to numb it?"

Chapter Twenty-eight

"Nah. I can take it." He grit his teeth as she probed.

"You know He loves you, right?"

"No reason for Him to love me, Doc. Oww... You'd think a Christian would show a little mercy." His accusatory look made her laugh under her breath. "What's so funny?"

"Nothing. I'm sorry. You said you didn't want any numbing, remember?"

"Yeah, yeah. I remember."

"Incidentally, God created you. That gives Him a perfectly good reason to love you. In fact, He loved you so much, He sent Jesus, His Son, to die on a cross to save you from your sins, so you could spend eternity with Him."

"Forget it, Doc. There ain't no way He's gonna want me with Him for all eternity."

"You're wrong, Jerome."

"Yeah? Well, you don't know what I've done."

"True, and you don't know what I've done."

"You ever killed someone?"

Jessica stopped and looked up.

Trust God. Let His Holy Spirit speak through you.

"Unfortunately, yes, I have, but God forgave me for that."

"You're different."

"No, I'm not, Jerome. You and I are equals in God's eyes. The Bible says that 'All have sinned and come short of the glory of God.' That means me, you, everyone. No one gets a free ride. We all should pay for our sin, and that payment, according to the Bible, is death and separation from God forever." She turned to Valerie. "I'm going to need some lidocaine for this one." She indicated the bullet wound to the shoulder.

She turned back to Jerome. "But Jesus chose to pay for our sin Himself by dying on the cross. Thankfully, He rose from the dead three days later, proving He was God and had the power to forgive sins. All God requires of us now is to be truly sorry for our sins and ask His Son, Jesus, to forgive us and be our Savior."

Jerome frowned. 'That's sounds too easy, Doc. You so sure it ain't a scam?"

"Well, I don't think it's a scam, and it's what I choose to believe. And frankly, it's better than anything this world can offer. God has a plan for your life, Jerome, and it's not getting shot up on the streets. All you have to do is trust Him at His word. I promise you, if you want His forgiveness and a new purpose for your life, all you have to do is ask Him for it."

A local police officer entered the room. "Hey, Doc, can I ask him some questions?"

"Be my guest," responded Jessica as she turned Jerome slightly. She slipped her hand under his back and moved it up, then down. Pulling it out, she saw it was clean. No signs of blood.

No exit wound.

She carefully injected the anesthetic into the area around the bullet's entry point while Jerome answered the officer's questions.

Jessica waited until the officer left the room before she began her quest for the small bullet. "You ready?"

"What do you mean?"

"I have to probe to find the bullet. It may be a bit uncomfortable."

He gave her a suspicious look. "That's doctor talk for 'It's gonna hurt like crazy' ain't it?"

"We've already had this conversation, Jerome. You need to have the bullet removed."

"Yeah, I know." He winked at her. "I just thought maybe you'd show a little more—"

"Where is he? Where is that coward?" A deep voice bellowed through the ER corridor.

Jessica looked toward the door. "What's going on out there?"

Valerie shook her head, her eyes narrowing. "I don't know." She started toward the door when it flung open, knocking her backward against the end of the bed.

Waving a gun in the air, a tall, thin boy, no older than Jerome, moved into the room. His dark eyes focused on the teen in the bed. "You're a dead man!" He pointed the gun at Jerome, waving it back and forth.

Chapter Twenty-eight

"Security!" shouted Jessica. "Security!" She stepped between the assailant and her patient.

"Move it, lady, or you're gonna get hurt!" ordered the intruder. He turned his attention back to Jerome. "You killed my brother! You'll pay!" He moved slightly, then lowered the gun and pointed it toward the bed.

"Hey man, don't shoot! Don't shoot!" Jerome held his hands out in front of him with the palms facing his accuser.

"Put the gun down!" ordered Jessica, moving again between the shooter and her patient. "You need to leave this room now!"

"Get him!" Two hospital security officers rushed the gunman as the weapon discharged. Two loud explosions reverberated through the room followed by multiple screams and shouts throughout the ER department.

Jessica stood in shocked reticence as a police officer ran into the room, subdued, and then handcuffed the struggling attacker.

"I'll get you, Sanders! It ain't over! You're a dead man!"

Jessica winced as she glanced down at her hand. It was flat against her abdomen. She watched in stunned silence as a crimson stain beneath her fingers spread over her lab coat.

"Val?" Her voice faded as she fell to the floor. The last thing she heard was Valerie screaming for a doctor.

****

"Stay with me, Jessica!" Maggie worked furiously to stop the blood flow from Jessica's bullet wound. "Val, I need a line! We've got to get fluid into her now!" She turned to a respiratory therapist. "You, get the oxygen on her, then get the lab on the phone. I need 2 units of O-neg blood stat." She turned back to Valerie. "C'mon, get that line in!"

"I'm trying, but she's decompensating. Her veins are next to nothing." Valerie picked up a second needle and searched for another site to start the IV.

"Vitals?"

"BP's falling."

"Get that line in now!"
"I'm trying... Got it!"
"Get the saline going!"
"IV's running full board."
"I need—" Maggie's foot slid slightly when she moved toward Jessica's head.
"Where's this blood coming from?" Valerie asked as she moved toward the head of the bed.
The urgency in Valerie's voice prompted Maggie to follow the nurse's gaze to the side of the bed. Blood was dripping from under Jessica's left back.
The cardiac monitor alarm sounded.
"She's got no pulse, Dr. Grant!"
Maggie glanced up at the monitor, then whipped back around. "Starting compressions. C'mon, Jessica. Stay with me. Get the epi on board."
Ben Shepherd dashed into the room. "Maggie, I've got it." The doctors switched places without any interruption in compressions. "What happened?"
"Crazy guy with a gun. Started shooting before anyone could stop him." Maggie grabbed some dressings and pressed them over the abdominal wound, slowing the bleeding.
"I got it," stated Valerie as she secured the dressing in place.
Maggie grabbed another stack of dressings. "Looks like we've got another bullet." She bent down to hunt for the wound.
Dear God, help me find it, please...
"Still no pulse!"
"I need a second line in!"
Maggie frantically searched for the source of the upper body bleeding. "Here it is! She's got another entry wound under her left arm. I need some more dressings!"
"Take over, Valerie. I've got to control this bleeding," stated Ben as the pressure dressing on Jessica's abdomen was rapidly becoming bright cherry red in the center.
Valerie slid in to continue compressions as Ben moved to address the abdominal wound.

Chapter Twenty-eight

"Let's move it, people!" shouted Ben as he worked feverishly to repair the wound.

"Do we have a pulse yet?"

"Negative, Dr. Shepherd."

"Stay with me, Jessica, stay with me," pleaded Ben as he moved slightly to allow Maggie better access to the upper body wound.

"We've got to get her to the O.R., Ben. I can't stop this."

"Come on, folks. Get her stabilized. We need to move now!" ordered Ben.

"Tell them we're coming and to be ready," called out Maggie.

"We've got a pulse, Dr. Shepherd! It's faint, but we've got one!"

The ER team worked feverishly on their colleague, and within minutes, Jessica was ready for transport to the O.R. Setting the portable cardiac monitor at the foot of the bed, rehanging the IV on a bed pole, and connecting the oxygen tubing to a bedside canister happened in seconds, enabling the team to move Jessica to surgery quickly while monitoring her critical status.

"Go! Go! Go!"

In less than ninety seconds, Jessica was ushered into an operating room where Eastmont's best surgical team awaited her arrival, prepared to do everything they could to save the life of one of their own.

****

Valerie stood for a moment, watching the ER team push Jessica toward the O.R. She looked at the blood-covered floor and struggled to keep her emotions at bay. As her eyes misted over, she pressed her lips together and forced herself to tidy up the area before housekeeping arrived to do a more thorough clean-up.

As she dropped the last bloodied towel into the biohazard bin, Valerie started to shake, and her tears overflowed. She stumbled into the staff lounge, fell onto the sofa, and dropped her head into her hands. "Dear God, please help them in there," she wept. "Don't let Jessica die. Please don't..." She didn't realize anyone had approached her until she heard her name.

"Val?"

She looked up into Maggie's concerned face. "How did this happen, Mags? How could someone bring a gun into the hospital and shoot someone?" Her tear-streaked face augmented the anguish in her heart.

"I don't know, Val," said Maggie miserably. "I don't know." She sat beside her sister-in-law and took the shaken nurse into her arms. "Hold on to your faith, Val. We've got to be strong for Jessica."

"I know, Mags, but I'm so scared for her. If she doesn't make it—"

"She will. She's a fighter. She has to." Maggie pulled back and held Valerie at arm's length. She looked directly into the nurse's grief-stricken eyes. "Listen, Val, we've both got a job to do, and that job is to lift her up to the Lord. We can't forget who's really in control. It may seem like chaos, but God's still here, okay?"

Valerie nodded, pulling a tissue from her pocket and blowing her nose gently. "Do you mind if I go see Will for a few minutes. I need to tell him I'm okay, and I want to update him about Jessica."

"Sure go ahead. But don't be gone too long. I need you here, okay?"

Valerie nodded, but didn't move. She finally looked up at the physician. "Oh, Mags, I can't believe this is happening."

"I know, Val, but we'll get through it. We're not walking this valley alone, remember?"

"I know, Mags, but I'm still afraid for her."

"Me too, Val. Me too."

Maggie watched her walk away, toward the physicians' offices. She took a deep breath and leaned against the wall. Her

Chapter Twenty-eight

gaze fell upon her scrubs, which were splattered with blood... Jessica's blood.

"Dear Lord, please be with the team in there. Guide their hands and help them do exactly what they need to do. Give strength to Jessica's body. Help her get through this, please." She choked back a sob. "Please, Lord, I'm begging You..."

It took her a few minutes to compose herself, but when she did, she pulled out her cell phone. She had called Jessica's parents when she dropped off the chart in the O.R., but now she had one more phone call to make. She hesitated for only a moment, then punched in the number.

The phone rang twice before it was answered.

"Hello?"

"Ryan? This is Maggie..."

CHAPTER TWENTY-NINE

Maggie sat alone in the ICU waiting room. Her shift in the ER had ended an hour earlier, but she wouldn't leave the hospital. Jessica had been in surgery for more than seven hours, and she had arrested two more times during the operation. Waiting for updates had been excruciating, and an involuntary shiver passed through Maggie as she mentally reviewed what the surgeon had reported to her.

Injury to the spleen... massive internal bleeding... splenectomy... traumatic brachial artery injury... cardiac arrest... in recovery... prognosis is guarded...

Paul and Anne Merrick, along with Caleb, had been with Maggie to hear the surgeon's report, and when he left, they peppered Maggie with questions. She did her best to explain the procedures in laymen's terms and allay their fears, but it was challenging. Jessica was in critical condition, and the Merricks had been advised to stay close to the hospital. Maggie had stayed behind when Jessica's family was allowed into the recovery area. Now that she was alone, the fear she had kept contained threatened to engulf her. She bowed her head and tried to pray, but only tears came. Her head in her hands, she allowed herself to cry, and her body shook as she did.

She didn't realize she wasn't alone until she felt the hand on her shoulder and heard the soft British accent that was her world.

"Maggie, love. I'm here. I came as quickly as I could."

Chapter Twenty-nine

She lifted her head and came face to face with her beloved husband.

"Colin!" she whispered as she stood and fell into his arms. "Oh, Colin!" She sobbed into his shoulder, and he held her tenderly until her weeping subsided.

"Tell me what's happening." He sat down with her, and she shared everything from the moment of the gunshots until the surgeon's report.

"I called Ryan," she finally said.

"Ryan? Why?"

Maggie's fingers clasped tightly to Colin's hand. "She told me she was in love with him. I... I had to tell him, Colin. She asked me not to say anything to anyone, but after all they've been through together, I had to let him know what was going on now."

"And what did he say when you told him?"

"He's on his way here." Maggie said softly as her shoulders sagged. "I hope that was the right thing to do."

Colin put a finger under his wife's chin and lifted her face up. He looked into her sorrowful eyes. "It's all right, love. You did the right thing. If she loves him, maybe he'll be what she needs to pull through."

Maggie nodded solemnly. "The surgeon told her parents to be prepared for the worst. What if he doesn't get here in time?" She couldn't continue as a sob escaped her.

Colin pulled her to him. He stroked her hair as he prayed. "Father, we come before you on behalf of Jessica, Your child. You know her condition, Lord. We ask for Your healing touch upon her body. Please, in Your mercy, spare her life. Continue to be with those who are caring for her. Every doctor, every nurse, every technician... anyone who has contact with her, please guide them. Keep them alert to changes in her condition, and give them wisdom as they minister to her. Provide comfort for her family and friends. Your Word tells us that You are the One who gives the healing; You are the Great Physician, so we come to You now, and lift up Jessica to You for Your divine touch of healing. We will be careful to give You all the glory and honor for what is done, and we thank You for it. In Jesus' precious name, I pray. Amen."

Maggie looked up into the compassionate eyes of her husband. "It doesn't really look good for her," she confessed quietly.

Colin smiled tenderly, then pointed out, "It didn't look good for Lazarus, either."

****

The sun had just disappeared below the horizon, casting a pink and orange glow across the sky. It had been nearly twenty-four hours since Jessica had been shot. Outside the ICU, Maggie and Colin sat in the waiting room with Anne and Paul Merrick.

"The doctor said she was still critical, and he couldn't speculate on her chances for recovery," reported Paul with a heavy voice. He held tightly to his wife's hand. "He told us to be prepared... just in case."

Anne dabbed at the corners of her eyes as her cell phone vibrated. She pulled it from her purse, looked at it, then stood up. "It's Caleb. I'll be right back."

Paul watched her leave the room, then stood. "I better go with her."

Maggie nodded. "Of course." She turned to Colin. "I can't imagine what they're going through."

Colin shook his head slightly. "Me either. It's hard enough for—"

"Ryan!" Maggie jumped up and rushed to embrace her former brother-in-law as he entered the room. "You're here!" Her resolve vanished, and once again, tears were shed.

With one arm, Ryan held her gently as she wept; with the other, he shook hands with Colin.

"I'm glad you're here," Colin said as he nodded slightly toward Maggie. "It's been hard."

Chapter Twenty-nine

"I can imagine." Ryan released Maggie and sat down in a chair opposite the couple. "How is Jessica doing?" His worried eyes searched Maggie's face for a clue to Jessica's status.

Maggie wiped her tears. "She's holding her own, but she's still critical with..." Her voice broke again, and she struggled for control.

Colin squeezed his wife's hand. "Her prognosis is guarded. They've advised her family to stay close."

Ryan winced. "That's not good." He ran his fingers through his thick hair. "So what exactly did they do?"

Maggie began to explain. "She had damage to her spleen. That's one of the organs that helps the immune system. It had to be removed."

"You can live without it?" Concern washed over Ryan's face.

"Yes," reassured Maggie. "However, she'll need to be conscious of situations in which she could be exposed to illnesses. She'll need to follow-up with the proper immunizations, like the flu shot or the meningitis shot. Stuff like that."

"But otherwise, she'll be okay?"

"Well, she also had a tear in her brachial artery. That's in her arm. They repaired that, and hopefully there will be no residual nerve damage from that. She lost a lot of blood, and..." She glanced over at Colin.

Ryan saw the quick exchange, and apprehension immediately came over him. "What? What else?"

"Her body was in shock due to the trauma and blood loss, and there was a time when her circulatory system was incapable of meeting her body's demands."

"And that means...?"

Colin interjected for Maggie. "That means her heart stopped for a while."

"We started CPR right away, but—"

"But what?" Ryan's voice escalated.

Maggie shrugged her shoulders. "She needed advanced life support for quite a while. There's no real way to know the extent of any damage from that until she's awake."

Courageous Love

"Damage? You mean... brain damage?" Ryan paled as understanding came.

Maggie's head gave a barely perceptible nod. "I seriously doubt it, but we won't know for sure until she's awake and talking to us. Everything's working as it should physiologically, but right now, it's a waiting game. And the wait could be a long one. Her body's been under great stress. It takes time to heal."

Ryan closed his eyes and swallowed. He took a deep breath. "Do you think they'll let me in to see her?" he asked slowly.

Maggie managed a small smile. "You're a minister. They have full time access to the ICU. C'mon. I'll take you in." She turned toward Colin, her eyebrows raised.

"It's fine, love. I'll go get us some coffee. Ryan?"

"No. I'm fine. Thanks."

Maggie escorted Ryan into the ICU and introduced him to the staff. Together, they walked toward Jessica's room.

"I'll be outside with Colin, okay?" She waited for his acknowledgement.

"Yes." He stood for a moment just staring at Jessica's still form on the bed, then he turned his head. "Thank you, Maggie."

"For what?"

"Calling me."

She hugged him once more, then left him alone in the room.

****

Ryan slowly scanned the room. It was cold. Two stainless steel poles supported two bags of fluid, one half-filled while the other was nearly empty. Four multi-colored lines danced across the screen of an overhead monitor. The faint hiss of oxygen being delivered via a nasal cannula permeated the room.

He looked at Jessica and reached for her hand. Her skin was pale and cool to the touch. He squeezed her fingers, but received nothing in response. He spied a chair in the corner of the room, pulled it over to her bed, and sat down.

Chapter Twenty-nine

"Jessica? It's me, Ryan." His voice was low as he leaned on the bed railing and spoke. "Everyone back in Santa Molina is praying for you. You need to stay with us." He fought to control his emotions. "I've missed you. A lot. Especially every morning when I'd hear that rooster crow. I think he misses you, too."

He looked up when a nurse came in to change the IV bag. "I'm sorry," she said. "This'll take only a moment."

Ryan smiled weakly. "No problem." He continued to hold Jessica's hand, silently praying for her recovery until the nurse left.

When he was alone with her once more, he continued his conversation. "Jessica, I am so grateful to God for bringing you to Santa Molina. I really loved working with you at the camps. Watching you with the kids, well, you're really a great doctor." He paused for a moment, remembering her skill and patience with Flora Rodriguez.

He reached over and brushed a lock of her hair from her forehead. "And then there was Breanna. That was some hurricane, wasn't it? You know, most people would have gone to higher ground, but not you. The way you pitched in to help Akna and the girls during that storm. I was very proud of you.

"It was during Breanna that I first realized I had feelings for you. I think it was during lunch one day. I held your hand for the first time. It dawned on me that I... I was in love with you. I was stunned at first because I wasn't planning on ever falling in love with someone again. But I guess you don't plan love. And when God's in it, there's not much we can do to stop it.

"I never really had the opportunity to tell you; there was so much going on. Joaquin's heart attack, and of course, Nicholas, who, by the way, is waiting for you to come home. The time was never right. I'm sorry I didn't tell you before now."

He stared at her nonreactive face and reached out to trace his finger along her cheek. He felt helpless, so he did the only thing he knew to do. Bowing his head, he prayed again. "Father, please touch Jessica and restore her body to perfect health. I don't know much about how the body works, or how this surgery is going to affect her, but I know You do. And I know, it doesn't matter what the doctors say. You can raise her up. Please don't take her. Not now. Nicholas needs her, and so do I." He paused for a moment, then begged haltingly, "Please… give me the chance to tell her that I love her…"

He stood, and with the back of his hand, wiped the tears from his eyes. He swallowed hard. "Jessica, your son needs you, so you have to get well. You need to fight, Jessica. You're not a quitter. I know that for a fact. You just focus on that little boy, and remember how badly he needs his mother."

"Pastor Devereaux?"

Ryan turned around to face Paul and Anne Merrick. "Mr. and Mrs. Merrick… I… I'm sorry, I…" He stopped, unable to speak.

Anne smiled. "Thank you so much for coming." Her voice was soothing. She reached out to take his hand in hers. "Jessica spoke so often about you. You took such wonderful care of her and our grandson."

Paul held out his hand and as Ryan clasped it, he shook it with a weak smile. "I appreciate all you've done. I can't tell you." His deep voice broke with emotion.

Ryan looked back at Jessica for a moment, then returned his gaze to her parents. "It was my pleasure. She is a very special lady."

Anne looked into his anguished eyes. "She's so blessed to have you in her life. Please, stay as long as you like. We're going to run to the cafeteria and grab some coffee, but when Maggie told us you were here, we had to come see you. Would you like us to bring back something for you?"

"No, thank you. I'm fine."

Anne turned to go, then stopped. She glanced back at Ryan. "You know, she spoke so highly of you. You mean a great deal to her. I'm so glad you're here."

Paul patted Ryan on the shoulder. "Yes. Thank you for coming."

Chapter Twenty-nine

Ryan stood quietly until they left. He turned back toward Jessica. His voice was barely above a whisper as he murmured softly, "You mean a great deal to me too, Jessica." He stood for quite a while just watching her until a nurse came in.

"Excuse me, Pastor?"

He turned to face her. "Yes?"

"Do you know where the family went? They're not in the waiting room."

"Is there a problem?"

"Not really. There's just a young man who wants to come see Dr. Carr. We don't allow non-family members in without the permission from the patient or the patient's family. He's quite persistent."

"I think they went to get something to eat. I'll go speak with him if you like."

"You wouldn't mind?"

"Not at all."

****

As Ryan stepped through the ICU doors, he was met by Jerome Sanders trying to maneuver his way past Ryan and in through the now-closing doors.

"Hey, get outta my way, man!" His left arm was in a sling, so he brought his right one up to move Ryan.

Ryan put his hands out and stopped Jerome. "What's the problem?"

Jerome's eyes flashed in anger. "They won't let me in! That's the problem! Get your hands off me!" He tried to push Ryan aside, but Ryan stood his ground.

"You need to calm down. You can't go barging into the intensive care unit," stated Ryan. "And if you do, they'll just call security to drag you out."

Jerome tightened his lips angrily. "Yeah, security. A lot of good they do."

"What does that mean?"

"They didn't stop that dude from shooting the doc."

"You were there? In the ER?"

"Yeah. I was the one he was gunning for. What's it to you?"

"She's a good friend of mine."

"Yeah? So, how's she doing?" His anger began to dissipate as he waited for Ryan to answer.

"Not so good, but we're hoping for the best."

"No, man! That's not right." Jerome turned away from Ryan, raised his right fist and pounded the wall.

"Hey! Hey! Stop! Come on in here." Ryan directed Jerome into the waiting room where Colin and Maggie were quietly talking. They looked up when the two men entered the room, but said nothing as Ryan ushered Jerome toward a corner.

"What's your name?" Ryan asked as they sat down.

He eyed Ryan suspiciously before answering. "Jerome."

"Okay, Jerome. I'm Ryan."

"I saw her go down, man!" Frustration filled his response. "I told her she needed a piece, but she didn't believe me. All that God talk. Why didn't she listen?"

"What do you mean?"

"Telling me that God loved me and all that nonsense. Where'd it get her, huh? She's the one in there dying. It should've been me, not her. Why'd she do it?" His voice cracked, and he lowered his head. This time, great sorrow accompanied his rant. "Why'd she do it?"

"Why'd she do what, Jerome?" Mystified by the teen's comments, Ryan searched the boy's contorted face for a clue as what he was referring to.

"She stepped in between us. Between me and that maniac. She knew he'd hit her if he fired the gun. She knew it. Why'd she do it?" He started to shake.

Ryan sat up, shock registering on his face when he realized what had happened in the emergency room.

Jessica stepped into the line of fire? To save Jerome?

The teen continued. "She was crazy, man. You know what I mean? He told her to get out of the way, or she was gonna

Chapter Twenty-nine

get hit. But she refused to move. When he moved, she moved. She was *different*."

"Different? How?"

Jerome looked up at Ryan. "She cared, man. She didn't even know me, but she cared about me. I just wanted to tell her... I just wanted to tell her 'thank you.' She saved my life. He'd have shot me point blank, but she took it. It should've been me. Why'd she do it?"

Ryan's heart ached for the distraught young man as he quietly answered Jerome's question. "Because that's what God did for her. He sent His Son, Jesus, to take her place on the cross, so that she could live. So that she could be forgiven of her sins and be promised eternal life with God. Jesus didn't deserve to die either, but sin had to be punished, so He took the punishment for us."

Jerome's face twisted in agony. "But she was innocent, man. She wasn't involved. It was between Ricardo and me."

Ryan nodded. "Just like Jesus. His only crime was being the Son of God."

Jerome shook his head. "What is it with you Christians? Don't it make you mad that that creep shot her? If he was here, I'd kill him." The angry look on Jerome's face had returned.

"Jerome, my heart is broken that Dr. Carr is in there fighting for her life, but I know that no matter what happens, I will see her again. Maybe not here, maybe not in this lifetime, but we will have eternity together in heaven because we've both been forgiven by our Savior, Jesus. Heaven is a guarantee for us." He paused for a moment, then asked, "Is it for you?"

"What do you mean?"

"I mean, if you died today, do you know if you'd go to heaven?"

"Ain't nobody in heaven gonna want me."

"God does. He wants you so badly, He sent His Son to die for you. The Bible says 'For God so loved the world that He gave His only begotten Son, that whosoever believeth in Him should not perish, but have everlasting life.'"

Jerome eyed Ryan warily. "You're a preacher, ain't you?"

"Yes."

"I thought so. Always trying to save people, but some people just ain't worth saving."

"Jerome, none of us are worth saving. I can't explain the love of God, or why He would want to save us. All I know is that God does love us despite our worthlessness. It doesn't matter what we've done, where we've gone, what we've been. Jesus died to forgive everyone and save our souls from an eternity without Him. But God's never going to force you, Jerome. He's going to wait patiently, hoping you'll realize how much He loves you. He'll wait until you're ready to tell Him you want Him in your life."

"You sound like the doc," Jerome said quietly. "She said the same thing."

"We have a lot in common."

"Yeah? Well, tell me this then. If God loves her so much, why did He let her get shot, huh?" Despite his angry tirade, tears were in Jerome's hurting eyes.

Ryan thought for a moment, then said, "Things, good and bad, happen to Christians and non-Christians alike. We live in a sinful world, Jerome, so sinful that we're basically surrounded by it no matter where we go. But for Christians, God helps us through it, and He causes all things to work out for His good."

"So her gettin' shot is good?"

"No. I didn't say that. I said God will somehow use this situation to do something very good."

"Like what?"

"I don't really know, but it's written in the Bible that He will, and I believe it. So when it happens, I'll let you know." He forced a smile.

"Yeah, right."

"Tell me, Jerome. If that bullet would've hit you, would you have been ready to meet God?"

The teen shifted his body uncomfortably in his chair. "What's that supposed to mean?"

Chapter Twenty-nine

"It means, if you had died that day in the ER, would you have gone to heaven?" repeated Ryan.

Jerome licked his lips and shrugged his broad shoulders. "I don't know." His attempt at nonchalance was too forced; he couldn't hide the uncertainty in his voice.

"Would you like to know for sure?"

"Look, I can't promise you I'll go to church all the time, you know. My grandmother's always nagging me about that, but I ain't got time for religion."

"It's not about religion, Jerome. It's about a relationship. A relationship with Jesus. Going to church doesn't save anybody."

"Now ain't that a fine thing for a preacher to say," said Jerome with a smirk.

Ryan continued. "Probably not what you expected, but it's true. There's only one way to heaven and that's through Jesus Christ, God's Son."

Jerome crossed his arms in front of his chest. "I'm listening."

Ryan was well aware that this might be the only opportunity he'd have to share the gospel with Jerome, and he silently prayed for wisdom before he spoke again.

"Jerome, the Bible tells us that we're all sinners. Me, you, Dr. Carr... everyone. But God is a holy God. He doesn't tolerate sin, and therefore anyone who has sinned cannot go to heaven."

"Well, that pretty much keeps everyone out, don't it?" He sat back in his chair smugly.

"It would have if it wasn't for Jesus. He chose to take the punishment for our sins. He willingly let humanity crucify Him. He wasn't guilty of any crime. He never sinned a day in His human life. As God's Son, Jesus left the holiness of heaven to come down to the depraved and sinful world so that you and I, and everyone else, could have an opportunity to live with Him forever in heaven."

"That don't sound too bright to me," chided Jerome.

"Sounds like love to me," countered Ryan.

Jerome looked away.

Ryan continued, unfazed by Jerome's back. "After Jesus died, He was buried in a sealed tomb guarded by Roman sentries. Three days after that, however, Jesus rose from the dead and walked out of that tomb despite the sealed door and Roman soldiers. How? He was God. He *is* God. He alone has the power to forgive our sins, and once He does, we're holy in God's sight and promised eternal life in heaven."

"Suppose He don't want to forgive me?"

"Won't happen. Jesus became a sacrifice for all people. The Bible says, 'Whosoever shall call upon the name of the Lord shall be saved.' That means *anyone*, Jerome, including you."

"So you're telling me that all I need to do is *ask*, and God will forgive me?"

"Yes. Jesus loves you. He died for you so that He could have a personal relationship with you, but He can't have that as long as you hold on to sin in your life."

Silence blanketed the room until Jerome finally admitted, "I ain't never prayed before."

"You know how to talk. That's all you need to do. Just talk to God. He's listening."

Jerome looked around the waiting room. It was now empty. His troubled eyes returned to Ryan.

"Don't I gotta be in church or something?"

"To pray? No." Ryan studied the young man's face. "The only requirement is that you have a heart that wants to find God. It doesn't matter where you are, or who you are. In God's eyes, we're all the same. We all need Jesus." The teen's downcast face prompted Ryan to ask, "Would you like to ask Jesus to save you?"

Jerome fidgeted in his seat. He cleared his throat twice before answering. "And then I'll go to heaven? I mean, nobody wants to go to... you know."

Ryan smiled. "I know."

"And you're sure He'll forgive me?"

"100% sure. Talk to Jesus just like you're talking to me. Tell Him you're sorry for your sins and ask Him to forgive you. You do believe He can do that, right?"

Chapter Twenty-nine

"Yeah, man. I ain't stupid. I know He's God. He can do anything. I just didn't figure He'd care about me."

"Well, you were wrong about that. He loves you."

Jerome avoided looking at Ryan. "What you gonna do while I'm talking to God?"

"I'm going to bow my head, and I'm going to be praying for you, but this is between you and God. I can't do it for you."

Jerome hesitated, then finally said, "Okay. Let's do this." His voice was shaky, but he lowered his head.

Ryan bowed his own head and began to silently pray.

Jerome lifted his eyes quickly and scanned the empty room once more, then dropped his head again. "Hey God, it's me, Jerome. Look, I know I've done some pretty bad stuff, but I... I'm sorry, man. You know it's rough where I live." His voice began to crack.

"If... uh... You could forgive me, I'd really like that. I remember learning some stuff about You when I was a kid. You know, how You died on the cross. That must've really made You sad, seeing how You did it to save everyone, but they turned on You. I know what that's like. Having your friends turn on you. I guess You were pretty glad You didn't stay dead. Anyway, I don't know why You'd want to forgive me 'cause I've done some terrible things. I guess You know all about that, but, uh, I don't wanna go to... that other place, You know? This here preacher, well, he says You love me, and so did the doc, so I'm thinkin' maybe it's true. I mean why would someone..." His voice trembled with emotion, and he began to weep as he prayed. "Why would someone do that if they didn't love somebody? It's kinda hard to think You love me, but that's what this preacher says, and well, I ain't had nobody love me for a long time, 'cept my grandma and Michael, my kid brother. So thanks for that."

He sighed deeply, stammering as he finished his prayer. "And God, if You could fix the doc, I'd really appreciate it, 'cause none of this was her fault. I didn't mean for her to get hurt. She was really nice to me, God. You did real good with her. And if You make her well, I promise I'll go to church with my grandma 'cause she's always asking me to. Well God, that's all I have to say. Thanks for forgiving me, and please take care of the doc. Amen."

He looked up at Ryan, quickly wiping away the tears on his face. "So now what?"

Ryan grinned. "Now, you tell her when she wakes up."

A timid smile appeared on Jerome's face. "I will. So, I'm going to heaven now, right?"

"Guaranteed. By the way, that good thing God was going to do? He just did it."

A broader grin crossed Jerome's face. "Man, I gotta call my grandma! She ain't ever gonna believe this! I'll be right back." He stopped just before leaving the room and went back to Ryan. "Hey man, thanks." His eyes no longer were angry when he reached out and shook Ryan's hand. "I'll be back later... to tell the doc."

Ryan stood speechless as he watched Jerome leave the room. "Thank You, Lord," he whispered. He was rubbing the back of his neck when Maggie and Colin walked back into the room.

"We just saw that kid rush out of here. Everything okay?" asked Maggie as she moved nearer to Ryan. "We were praying for you... and him."

"Everything's fine. Jerome's name just got added to the Book of Life," said Ryan fighting to keep his own tears from falling.

"Praise the Lord!" grinned Colin. "Where'd he go?"

"Had to call his grandmother and tell her. Sounds like she's been planting the seed for a while. You know, that's the kid that Jessica took the bullet for."

"Really?" Maggie turned to the open door. "And he just got saved? That's amazing!"

Ryan nodded. "Yeah, pretty incredible. Apparently, Jessica witnessed to him when he was in the ER." He paused for a moment, then asked, "Any word on her?"

Chapter Twenty-nine

"No change," said Maggie. "We're going to go home, so I can shower and get into some clean clothes, but we'll be back in an hour or so. You're staying, right?"

"Yes, of course. Don't worry about me. If there's any change at all, I'll call you," said Ryan.

"Do that," said Colin as he gave Ryan a hug. "Keep the faith, brother."

"I'm trying."

CHAPTER THIRTY

Later that evening, Ryan sat alone at Jessica's bedside. He'd convinced the Merricks that they needed some rest, and he promised he'd call if anything changed. Maggie and Colin had stayed until nearly midnight, and they too refused to leave until Ryan promised to call them as well.

Now, he sat quietly, simply watching Jessica sleep. The redundant sounds of the equipment in the room faded away into his subconscious, and it was easy to ignore them. He became accustomed to the blinking lights on the monitors, and they no longer alarmed him if they changed their pattern. Occasionally, a nurse would come in to change an IV bag, assess vital signs, or ask him if there was anything he needed. Every so often, he stood and stretched, but mostly, he sat. He sat, and he prayed.

The pseudo-quietness of the ICU coupled with his recent plane trip began to take its toll, and Ryan found himself dozing off, only to be startled awake when his head began to drop. Finally, unable to keep his head up, he folded his arms on the bed rail, laid his head on top of them and drifted off to sleep.

In his dreams, he saw Jessica in Santa Molina. The wind was blowing, and she was laughing as she picked a bouquet of Mexican primrose. She twirled in the sunlight, and in the distance, he saw himself running toward her. When she saw him, she stopped and called out, but he could barely hear her. He strained to make out what she was saying.

Chapter Thirty

"Ryan?" Was she calling to him? He wasn't sure. He reached out toward her.

"Ryan?" There it was again. He did hear her! She was calling his name! It was so real...

"Ryan?" He felt her fingers brush his face.

His eyes snapped open. "Jessica?" He jumped up and leaned over closer to her face. "Jessica!"

Her dark lashes fluttered, and then her eyes stayed open.

"Praise God!" he whispered as he took her hand in his.

"Is it... really... you?" Her voice was faint and hoarse.

"Yes. I'm here, Jessica." He resisted putting her hand down, but he knew he had to call her nurse. "Don't go anywhere, okay?" He smiled at her. "I have to tell your nurse that you're awake. I'll be right back." He gently set her hand back on the bed and hurried to the nurses' station.

Meg Warner, the night charge nurse, looked up. "Pastor Devereaux, can I help you?"

"I thought someone should know that she's awake."

Meg's eyes widened. "She is? That's wonderful!" She rose immediately and headed to Jessica's room. Ryan followed her, but stood at the doorway as Meg assessed Jessica.

"Hey, Dr. Carr, how are you feeling? You really gave us a scare."

Jessica's voice was just above a whisper, but she was able to answer. "I'm really thirsty, and my shoulder hurts a little. Otherwise, I'm okay. Ryan? Is he here still?"

"Yes, he is. He's right over there by the door. I'll let him in as soon as I finish with you, okay?"

Ryan watched her for a few moments, then he stepped outside the ICU near the waiting room. He pulled out his cell phone and made the promised phone calls, then dashed back inside to await permission to return to Jessica's side.

As soon as Meg came out of the room, she smiled at Ryan. "She's asking for you."

"Thank you." He hurried to Jessica.

She had already closed her eyes, and he feared she had slipped back into the unconscious state she had been in since her surgery.

"Jessica?" Although he spoke softly, his voice seemed to resonate in the room. He picked up her hand and linked his fingers in hers. "Jessica?"

She sluggishly opened her eyes. As she focused on Ryan's face, a faint smile crossed her lips. "Hi..."

He swallowed hard, finding it difficult to speak. "Hello." His gaze fastened on her half-opened eyes, and he prayed she would stay awake. "How are you doing?"

"I don't know," she admitted. "I feel... so tired, but I don't... want you to leave me..."

"I won't. I promise. Even if I have to leave the room, I'll be right outside. I... I thought I'd lost you..." His voice broke, and he just stared into her eyes.

She smiled at him. "I'm so glad... you're here. I missed you..."

Ryan fought to keep himself composed, but his deep blue eyes misted over. "I missed you too, Jessica." He took a deep breath and exhaled slowly. "Your parents are here and your brother. They've been here ever since... since the accident."

"Nicholas?" Her troubled face looked up at him.

"He's fine," reassured Ryan. "He's with Bethany. You only need to worry about yourself right now." He held tightly to her hand, and as her fingers wrapped around his, a sweet relief filled his soul.

****

The next day, Jessica was able to lie in a semi-flat position, and she was taking fluids without difficulty. Her parents had been by in the morning, then went home to stay with Nicholas so Caleb and Bethany could come by the hospital. When her brother came into her room, he wheeled to the opposite side of her bed where there was more room for him to maneuver his

Chapter Thirty

chair. Locking the brakes when he rolled to the side of her bed, he pulled himself to a standing position to see her more clearly. Jessica burst into tears.

"Oh, Caleb! I can't believe you're here." She lifted her left arm and touched his face. "Thank you so much for taking care of Nicholas."

"No problem. It turns out, I'm a pretty awesome uncle."

"He's getting practice for the day we have our own," Bethany said. She stood near Caleb, her arm resting on the bedrail next to his. "How are you feeling, Jessica?"

"Honestly, I'm just really tired. Not sleepy, just weak, I guess. My shoulder seems to hurt more than my abdomen, but other than that, I think I'm okay."

"You look like death warmed over," stated Caleb. "Pale skin, weak muscles, man, who's your doctor? Bet you've got a scar on your belly that'll scare away zombies!"

Jessica started to laugh. "Oww..." Her hands flew to her abdomen, and she pressed down lightly to support the weakened muscles.

Caleb glanced over at Bethany, then turned to Jessica. "Sorry."

His wife simply shook her head and patted his arm. "Don't mind him. He literally believes laughter is the best medicine," said Bethany as she grinned apologetically.

"So when are they going to spring you?" asked Caleb as he sat back down in his wheelchair.

"They said I might go to the telemetry unit in a day or so. It's like a regular medical floor except everyone is still monitored remotely. Kind of like a step-down from here, but not quite the same as the standard medical floor," explained Jessica.

"Oh," said Caleb. "You mean the floor where all the call buttons are broken?" He winked at his sister. "Hey, what's this I hear about you and Pastor Ryan?"

"What?"

Jessica's startled look alarmed Bethany, who hit her husband on the arm. "Caleb!"

"What?" He looked at his wife first, then Jessica. "Mom said you and Ryan were... you know."

"She said what?" Jessica was mortified.

Has she said anything to Ryan?

"Just that you were rather fond of the pastor."

"No, no! We're just friends."

"So you're telling me you have no feelings for Ryan."

Jessica averted her eyes from her brother. "Can we please talk about something else?"

"Hey, you tell me the truth, and then I'll change the subject." Caleb folded his arms across his chest. "You know, we both share the stubbornness gene, so I can wait all day, dear sister."

Jessica pressed her lips tightly together and glared at her brother. "Look, Ryan's a good friend, but—"

"It's a simple question, Jess. Either you love him, or you don't. Which is it?" Caleb held his ground.

Bethany shrugged her shoulder and mouthed, "I'm sorry" to Jessica.

"Caleb, there is nothing simple about it. I just can't talk about it right now."

Caleb raised his eyebrows and directed his response to Bethany. "Hmm... pretty sensitive for someone who has no feelings for him."

Bethany took hold of Caleb's shoulder. "You shouldn't upset Jessica, Caleb. Maybe we ought to talk about something else."

Caleb looked up at Bethany and sighed. "Okay." He wheeled closer to Jessica and whispered loudly, "But this conversation is far from over." He turned again to his wife. "Honey, I'm kind of hungry. Let's go get something from the cafeteria, okay? That'll give Jess some time to figure herself out."

"Good idea," Bethany agreed as they neared the door.

"No need to rush back, Caleb," Jessica called out.

"Yeah, I love you, too."

He chuckled as he wheeled himself into the corridor, barely missing colliding into Ryan.

Chapter Thirty

"Hey Pastor, good reflexes!" said Caleb as he rolled past him. Bethany smiled and shrugged with a sheepish smile as she followed Caleb down the hallway.

Ryan walked into Jessica's room, pulled a chair over close to her, and sat down. "How are you feeling this afternoon?"

"I think I'm better, but I'm not sure. Maybe it's just wishful thinking," admitted Jessica.

"Caleb and Bethany look good," he said as he relaxed into the chair, crossing his legs.

"Yes. Yes, they do."

"It was good of them to come by."

"Yes, it was."

Ryan shifted in his chair, uncrossed his legs, and leaned forward. He rested his arms on his legs. "If you're tired, I can come back later."

"No. It's okay." She tried to smile. "I'm sorry. Caleb just frustrates me sometimes. I didn't mean to take it out on you."

"No apology needed. Are you sure you want company right now?" He watched her reactions as he spoke.

"Absolutely. Please don't go. I love having you here." She reached out for his hand. "Thank you for coming."

Ryan took her hand and felt its warmth had returned. "I'm glad Maggie called me. You caused quite a scare."

"Were you really worried?"

Ryan chuckled under his breath. "Who me? Listen, I save frightened ladies from raging storms, and I deliver babies in the jungle. Why would something like this scare me?" His boyish grin spread across his face. "I believe 'terrified' would be a much better word for it. When you woke up, I was so relieved."

Her eyes seemed to cloud over momentarily as she said, "I'm so sorry, Ryan. I'm so sorry I put you and everyone through this."

"Hey, don't be. I've got some great news to share with you." He handed her a tissue. "Remember the kid in the bed on the night you were shot? Jerome Sanders? Well…"

Courageous Love

****

Maggie removed a pair of latex gloves and dropped them in the biohazard bin as she walked out of treatment room two. She looked forward to the end of her shift and kept looking at her watch as she walked down the ER corridor to the nurses' station. She planned to visit Jessica in the ICU before she headed home.

"Hey, Dr. Grant, we've got another shooting victim coming in. Shepherd's tied up with the guy who went through the plate glass window, and Tanner's got a hot appy," said Claire as she added the name to the triage board.

"Sure. Where are you putting him?"

"Trauma four." Just as she finished writing on the board, the ambulance doors slid open, and paramedics wheeled in the expected patient.

"Put him in four!" called out Claire. "I'm right behind you, Dr. Grant."

Maggie followed the medics into the trauma room. "What've we got, gentlemen?"

"Fifteen-year-old black male with gun shot wound to left upper chest and right pelvic region. Name's Sanders. Jerome Sanders."

Jerome Sanders? I know that name.

"He's been in and out of consciousness since we arrived. IV started in the field. BP's low, but holding at 78 over 50, pulse 142 and thready, respirations 36 and shallow. Let's move him on my count. One, two, three!"

Maggie cringed at the amount of blood left on the gurney, and immediately began the task of saving the young man. "Claire, I need two units of O-neg blood stat. Type and cross-match for two more. Let's open up that IV and get some more fluids into him. Crank up the O-two." She turned back to her patient, then froze when her eyes fell on his face.

It's you! You're the boy Ryan led to the Lord. The one Jessica was working on when she got shot.

Chapter Thirty

"Dr. Grant? Are you okay?" Claire cocked her head and waited for a reply.

Maggie blinked rapidly a couple of times, then put her stethoscope on Jerome's chest as Claire connected him to the cardiac monitor. "Yes. Yes, I'm fine. What's his O-two sat?" She listened carefully to each lobe of his lungs.

Faint breath sounds on the left.

She held her penlight near his mouth and saw small pinkish froth on his lips.

The bullet got his lung. He's so young.

"Oxygen saturation is at ninety-one, and that's with 100% oxygen flowing," stated Claire, shaking her head.

Maggie frowned as she continued assessing Jerome's cardiac status. Even through the stethoscope, she could barely hear his heart beating. It was only by looking up at the cardiac monitor could she verify she heard anything.

He'll never survive surgery without a miracle.

"Get me—" Maggie felt a pull on her wrist. She looked down. Jerome's blood stained hand held weakly to her arm.

His dark, dull eyes stared blankly, but Maggie saw his lips moving. She bent over, her ear near his mouth.

"What? Say it again, Jerome. I didn't hear you. Tell me again."

He tried to speak, but his voice was faint. Maggie strained to shut out the noise of the ER to hear him. When he finished, Maggie assured him softly, "I will. I promise." She stood up, struggling to maintain her composure. The dark-skinned hand lost its grip and dropped to the bed.

"His pressure's dropping!"

"Moving him to the O.R.?" asked Eric Tanner as he pulled on a pair of latex gloves.

Maggie's eyes looked up through her thick black lashes. "We don't have time. Eric, I need an airway in now."

"You got it." He moved to insert the orotracheal tube for easier and more effective administration of oxygen.

Just at that moment, an alarm sounded.

No!

She looked up at the cardiac monitor. The line that indicated heart rate and rhythm was bouncing up and down erratically.

"He's in V-fib. Get the crash cart!"

"Give me one milligram of epinephrine! Start CPR!"

"Charging paddles to 250! Charged!"

"Everyone clear!" Maggie positioned the defibrillator paddles on the multi-scarred chest and depressed them.

The young man's body arched slightly, then fell back down on the bed.

"Still in V-fib!"

"C'mon, don't quit on me!"

"Charging to 350. Charged!"

Once again, Maggie called out, "Clear!" and sent an electric charge through the teen. Again, there was no cardiac response.

"What's the rhythm?"

"Still in... no, wait... he's straight-lining!"

The previously irregular line had changed to reflect an agonal rhythm. No cardiac muscle movement was evident. A straight line was all that moved across the screen. The defibrillator was of no use now.

Maggie continued the code for nearly fifteen more minutes, but when she accepted the fact that her efforts were futile, she decided to end it. There was no disagreement from the ER staff. She glanced up at the wall clock.

"Time of death... sixteen twelve."

The frenzied activity in the room vanished as soon as the patient was pronounced dead, and the clean-up began. Non-essential personnel went back to their earlier duties as an eerie calm was restored. Maggie pulled off her gloves as she surveyed the scene before her. She made no effort to move from where she stood.

"Dr. Grant? Are you okay?" Claire's concerned voice was the only sound in the room now.

Maggie remained standing, staring at the now peaceful face of Jerome Sanders.

Chapter Thirty

"I know this boy," she explained, her voice retrospective. "He's the one who was in the ER when Jessica was shot."

Claire picked up the field chart, then read the name. "Jerome Sanders." She looked up at Maggie. "I remember."

Maggie merely nodded.

"What did he say to you?"

"He said to tell his grandmother that he'd see her in heaven. And to tell Jessica... thank you. That was it." She took a deep breath as her brown eyes clouded over. "I need to inform the family. Is anyone here for him?"

"As far as I know, just the grandmother. She was in the waiting room. I'll take you to her."

Maggie followed Claire to the waiting room, then walked over to the lady that the nurse pointed out to her. Sitting quietly in the corner of the room was an elderly African-American woman. Her face appeared tired and worn, and her large arms were wrapped around a young boy, no more than nine or ten years old. The boy sniffled a couple of times and wiped his nose with the sleeve of his shirt before focusing his large brown eyes on the approaching physician.

Jerome's grandmother's head rose, and her reddened eyes watched Maggie walk over. The anguished look upon her face told Maggie that somehow, in the heart of this old woman, she already knew that her grandson was gone.

"Mrs. Sanders? I'm Dr. Grant."

"He's passed, hasn't he?"

"I'm sorry," said Maggie. "In spite of all our efforts, the injuries to Jerome were just too great to overcome. We did everything we could, but his body had suffered too much damage."

The tiny light of hope in Mrs. Sanders' eyes flickered for a moment, then faded as Maggie's words sank in.

"My brother's dead? No!" wailed the young boy. He buried his face into Mrs. Sanders' sweater. "No, Grams, he can't be dead! He didn't do nothing! They killed him for nothing! It can't be true! It just can't be!"

"Easy, Michael," she said as she patted his back. "We just need to be praisin' the Lord that Jerome found Him before it was too late."

Michael looked up at his grandmother. "Grams, he was just reaching into his jacket to give them this." He held up a crumpled piece of paper. "Weren't no gun!" He sobbed as he turned toward Maggie. "He just wanted to give them this!" He held it out and shook it in front of Maggie.

The grandmother gave a slight nod, and Maggie took the paper from Michael. She smoothed it out and stared at it. It was a gospel tract.

Maggie's tear-filled eyes met those of Mrs. Sanders. "He asked me to tell you something."

Mrs. Sanders looked up, her large, dark eyes filled with great sorrow. Her arms remained wrapped around her inconsolable grandson.

"He said to tell you that he'd see you in heaven, and that he loves you," reported Maggie. "Mrs. Sanders, I am very sorry for your loss."

The old woman managed a melancholy smile. "My loss is heaven's gain."

****

"I can't believe he's gone." Jessica shook her head solemnly. "He had his whole life ahead of him." She readjusted her blankets as she sat up against her pillow. "He was the same age as those kids in Ryan's camp."

Maggie nodded in sad agreement.

"How did it happen?" asked Ryan. He rose from his chair and walked toward a window.

"Apparently, someone thought he was reaching for a gun. Jerome was shot twice. One bullet in his left lung, and another one that probably hit his liver. He arrested, and we never got him back."

Chapter Thirty

She heard Ryan sigh deeply. "He did tell me something." Maggie paused and looked at Jessica. "He asked me to tell you 'thank you.'"

Jessica's eyebrows lifted slightly. "Thank you? For what?"

Ryan had been standing by the window, looking out into the parking lot. He spoke without turning. "For caring."

Jessica and Maggie both looked over at him.

"He couldn't understand why you cared about him, Jessica." He turned around to face her. "He couldn't understand why you stepped between him and the shooter that night." Ryan sighed deeply. "It made a big impact on him. It helped him understand what Christ did for us. To Jerome, what you did gave him a present day picture of the sacrifice Jesus made. You shared the gospel with him, and that led to his salvation."

Ryan's face reflected the heaviness in his heart, but he managed a slight smile when he said, "He saw Jesus in you."

Jessica swallowed hard, unable to speak. Silent tears coursed down her cheeks.

"I'm sorry, Jess," Maggie said as she stood up. She leaned over and gave Jessica a hug. "I need to get going, but I thought you'd want to know about Jerome." She studied Jessica's downcast face. "You'll be okay, right?"

"Of course." Jessica forced a smile. "Thanks for coming, Maggie. And will you tell everyone how much I appreciate all they did for me?"

"Absolutely." She turned toward Ryan. He had returned to looking out the window. "Hey there, brother-in-law..."

He spun around to face her. "Sorry, Maggie. Just thinking about Jerome." He held his arms out to her as she moved to him. "Thank you so much for coming to tell us about him."

She hugged him and whispered, "You take care of yourself, okay?"

"I will."

She moved back to the bed and gave Jessica's hand a squeeze. "I'll see you tomorrow, Jess."

"I'll be here."

CHAPTER THIRTY-ONE

Two days later, Jessica was moved to the telemetry unit. Her room was slightly larger now, but the machinery was less, so the room seemed huge compared to the one she had in the ICU. No longer restricted in having visitors, she was flooded with well-wishers from the hospital and her church. Get well cards and multicolored bouquets of flowers crowded her bedside table and window sill. There was no doubt that Jessica was loved by many.

Her favorite visitor, however, came in the late afternoon of her first day out of the intensive care unit. She was alone, resting with her eyes closed, but not sleeping. When she heard soft footsteps grow louder, she opened her eyes to see her mother standing beside her bed. In her arms, Anne held Nicholas.

"Oh, Mom!" Jessica reached out with her hands, careful to not hit the IV tubing that was still connected to a plump bag of normal saline. Her eyes misted over as her son was placed in her arms.

"He's missed you, sweetheart." Anne sat down next to the bed and quietly watched the tender reunion.

"Hey, there little one. It's me, Mommy." Her voice was tender and loving as she poured out little kisses on her son's chubby cheeks. His babbling delighted her, and her tears of joy fell freely. "Oh, how I've missed you, Nicholas. I love you with all my heart." She looked up at her mother. "Thank you

Chapter Thirty-one

so much, Mom." Her voice broke with emotion as she returned her gaze to the flaxen-haired baby she held.

She bent her knees and laid him against her legs. His large blue eyes fixed on her face, and when she placed her forefingers in the palms of his hands, ten little fingers wrapped around them. His grip was strong, and she was able to move his arms back and forth simply by wiggling her forefingers side to side.

"You're happy to see Mommy, aren't you, Nicholas?" As long as she talked, Nicholas lay silently staring at her. His eyes never deviated from her face, and when he blinked, his long eyelashes seemed to brush the air.

"You are adorable, Nicholas. Has anyone told you that?" He began to fuss, and soon the fussing became a dissatisfied wail. It had been so long since she had heard him cry that it broke her heart to hear it now. "What's wrong, little one?" She put him against her shoulder and patted him gently on the back. His crying stopped almost immediately, and he began to settle down, emitting little coos.

"There, there, little one. It's okay. I'm here. Everything will be fine," Jessica whispered. Her fingers gently rubbed the soft hair of his head. "Shhh... it's okay."

"Look who you've got!" Ryan walked in with a bouquet of Mexican primrose. "Anne! It's good to see you. How are you doing?"

"Much better now that Jessica's out of ICU. How are you?"

"Doing well, thank you." He turned to Jessica. "These are for you. I'll put them..." He looked around, then spied her water pitcher. "...in here!" He set the flowers inside the container before Jessica could utter one protesting word.

"Ryan! That's my water!"

He grinned and shrugged his shoulders. "I'm improvising."

Anne smiled as she stood. "I'm going to go get a cup of coffee. Can I get either of you anything?"

Ryan shook his head. "No thanks. I'm fine."

"No, Mom. I'm good. Thank you."

As she left, Ryan sat down in the vacated chair. "Well, I haven't seen you look this happy in a long time. How is he?"

Jessica beamed. "Perfect. He's absolutely perfect. I missed him so much, Ryan." She brought Nicholas off her shoulder into her arms. His eyes were closed, and he slept peacefully in his mother's embrace. "I can't stop staring at him. Every time I see him, I'm looking at a miracle."

As he watched her interact with her son, Ryan felt a longing deep within his soul, and the emptiness it caused hurt terribly.

****

The next morning, Jessica was allowed to sit up in a chair and take short walks in the hallway. She was managing very well, and her physician was optimistic regarding her discharge. He predicted she would be out by the end of the following week, and that elevated her spirits. The only cloud on her horizon was the knowledge that Ryan was leaving soon for Santa Molina. It saddened her heart whenever she thought about him going, but she felt powerless to stop him from returning to his home, not that she would if she could.

When her brother and Bethany dropped in a little before noon, Jessica was sitting up once more. Caleb rolled up to her side, leaned forward and kissed her cheek.

"Wow, these cheap rooms aren't all that bad here," he grinned. "Lots of room. Hey, are you opening a florist shop? You've got enough flowers! What's this?" He lifted up her water pitcher filled with the Mexican primrose.

"From Ryan."

"Really?"

Bethany shot a warning look at her husband. "Caleb, be nice."

"What?"

"You know what I mean."

He frowned as he turned to Jessica. "Remember before we were married when Bethany was nice to me? Well, that's

Chapter Thirty-one

certainly changed." He glanced slowly at his wife. She scowled at him as he winked at her. "But I still love her."

"I warned you, Bethany," teased Jessica.

"I know. I should've listened to you, but it's too late now," said Bethany with a small smile.

"Ouch," said Caleb. "Hey, where's your boyfriend?" Jessica's blue eyes widened as her voice rose in intensity.

"He's not my boyfriend!"

Bethany glared at her husband. "Caleb!"

"What?" He looked at his wife and shrugged his shoulders. "I just asked a question. What's the big deal? I'm just trying to get the facts straight from the horse's mouth... no offense. How hard is it to say you love somebody?" Caleb's eyebrows rose as he waited. "So, do you?"

"What if I do? It's really none of your business."

"I'm your brother. Everything you do is my business."

"Where'd you get that from?"

"You."

"Me? I never said that."

"Maybe not in so many words, but the intent was there. So, do you?" He wheeled over to the other side of her bed and pointed at the water pitcher. "I mean, he did bring you flowers. No credit for the vase though."

Jessica rolled her eyes. "Aren't visiting hours over?"

"Look, I'm just..." His voice became serious. "Mom said you were a little concerned about the timing and all. I just want to tell you that if you love him, really love him, go for it. I can't imagine living my life without Bethany, and if I hadn't listened to the people who loved me, I might have missed out on the best thing that's ever happened to me.

"If you can't imagine a life without Ryan, I wouldn't let another day go by without telling him. You ought to follow your heart. I know what you had with Nick was great, but that was then. This is now. No one's going to doubt how you felt about Nick just because you've found happiness with someone else.

"And after all you've been through together, did it ever occur to you that God let those things happen to expedite your relationship? I guess I'm nagging you about it because I figure if you say it out loud, well, it'll be real to you, and you can move forward. I love you, Jess, and I want you to be happy again… completely."

Jessica sat in silence as she listened to her brother. "You know, you're something else, Caleb. You can be so infuriating at times. I don't know why I put up with you."

"Because you love me?"

She fought to keep from smiling, but lost the battle. "Yes, I love you. But you're so annoying sometimes."

"It's genetic." He gave her a smug look. "And mutual."

Her eyes moved from Caleb to Bethany, then back to her brother. She drew in a deep breath. "What do you want from me?"

"The truth. I know it; Mom knows it. When are you going to admit it?"

She scowled at her brother. "Admit it? What makes you and Mom authorities on my love life?"

"Hey, I'm just trying to get you to see what we all have already seen."

"You can't be serious."

"I am."

In resignation, Jessica threw her hands up in the air, then shook her head as she glared at Caleb. "Fine. You want me to say it. I can say it. I love him, all right? You happy? I admit it." She practically yelled it out as she shook her head. "I'm in love with Ryan! Are you satisfied?"

Three pairs of eyes turned toward the door as soon as they heard him clear his throat.

"Maybe I ought to come back later," said Ryan as he stood in the doorway.

****

Chapter Thirty-one

Caleb was the first to speak. "Well, this is awkward." He turned to his sister. "We should probably go, Jess. I'll come by later, okay."

All Jessica could do was nod her head numbly as Caleb and Bethany left the room. She closed her eyes tightly and listened for any sound in the room.

Please be gone... please be gone... please be—"

"Jessica?"

His unruffled voice quietly broke the silence, and she sensed he had moved closer to her. She said nothing as she slowly opened her eyes. When she saw that he was looking directly at her, her cheeks grew hot, and she quickly turned her head from him.

"Jessica?" He didn't sit in the chair next to her bed, but waited for her to say something. "Should I come back later?"

Jessica pressed her lips together, keeping her head downcast. Too embarrassed to look at him, she just whispered, "I... I don't know what to say..."

"I'm sorry. I didn't mean to eavesdrop."

"I didn't mean for you to hear that."

"I figured."

Unsure of what to say next, she simply said nothing. She just stared at her hands in her lap.

"Did you mean it?"

Slowly, Jessica lifted her head and looked up at him briefly. Then, as she turned away from him, she nodded her head.

"Jessica?"

"I didn't envision you hearing it like that," she admitted softly, still averting her gaze from his.

Ryan nodded in agreement. "Probably not the most romantic way to tell someone you love them. I kind of thought my way was more sentimental. I told you that I loved you when you were unconscious and laying in a hospital bed."

Jessica slowly lifted her eyes toward him. As his words settled in her mind, understanding accompanied them. "You told me you loved me?" she whispered, turning to look at him squarely.

For what seemed like an eternity, Jessica waited for Ryan to say something. Then, when he smiled at her, she had her answer.

"Yes, I did. You probably don't remember since you were out of it." He pulled a chair over and sat down opposite her. "I guess I should tell you again. Now that you're awake and all." He reached out and took her hands in his. "I love you, Jessica. I have for a very long time. I didn't think I'd ever love another woman after Gabriela, but I was wrong. I honestly don't know what the future holds, but I..." He hesitated for only a brief moment before confidently saying, "I know without a doubt that I love you and want you to be a part of it."

She sat unblinking, her mouth slightly open. No words came as she grappled with her own disbelief at what she was hearing.

He loves me? He loves me!

Ryan released her hands, stood up, and walked around her bed toward the window. The sunlight illuminated his tall frame as he stood with his back to her. "I believe God brought you into my life for a reason. For a while, I thought it was maybe to staff the clinic, but later, I came to believe—"

"What? You came to believe what?" She spoke in hushed tones, fearful of what he might not say.

He turned and walked back to her. "I believe God brought you into my life to share it with me."

The frankness of his response shocked her, and she stared, her eyes fixed on his face.

"Jessica?"

Her trembling hand moved up to her mouth. "Oh, Ryan," she said softly. "I never thought you'd feel the same way I feel about you." Her voice was barely audible, and she fought to maintain her composure as she whispered, "I've loved you for so long."

He gave her a puzzled look. "For so long? How long? When did you—"

Chapter Thirty-one

"I don't know." She smiled sheepishly and shrugged her shoulders. "Maybe at the camp, maybe during the hurricane, maybe when you stood by Caleb through his recovery, or maybe when you first rocked Nicholas to sleep. I don't know when I first knew, but I do know that I love you with all my heart, and I have for a very long time."

He ran his fingers through his hair and exhaled deeply. When he finally sat down next to her, that familiar grin crossed his face. "I guess we have a lot to talk about before I return to Santa Molina."

****

It was late in the afternoon when Caleb finally returned to the hospital. He had spent the morning with his parents. Now, he hoped to spend an hour or so with Jessica before he left for home.

He hesitated a moment before entering her room. He took a deep breath, knocked on the door, and wheeled in. He scanned the room, then sighed in relief. She was in bed, and no one else was in the room.

"Caleb! I was afraid you weren't coming!"

For a moment, he said nothing; he just stared at her. His nervousness was obvious as he fidgeted with his chair and avoided her eyes.

"Is everything okay?" He spoke hesitantly, unsure of his welcome.

Jessica blinked and smiled. "Yes. Yes, everything's fine. Perfect, in fact! Come in!"

"Really?"

"Really."

He leaned forward in the chair. "You told him?"

"I didn't really have to. He heard it loud and clear before he stepped into the room, remember?"

Caleb nodded awkwardly. "Look, I'm sorry. I never thought—"

"It's okay, Caleb. It's really okay."

"I'm forgiven?"

Jessica's blue eyes had regained their sparkle. "Of course. You're my brother. I can't stay mad at you forever." Her genuine smile verified the truth she spoke.

Caleb moved nearer to her bed. "So, what did he say?"

"He said..." She stopped to regain control of her shaking voice, then managed to utter, "He said he loves me too" before grabbing a tissue to dab at her eyes.

A huge grin appeared on her brother's face. "Seriously?"

"Seriously."

"So what now?" He leaned forward awaiting her reply.

"Now, we wait for God."

He nodded. "Good idea. A very good idea." He reached for her hand and squeezed it. "This is a good thing, right?"

Jessica laughed lightly. "Yes, Caleb. It is a very good thing."

EPILOGUE

"Blessed is the man that trusteth in the LORD, and whose hope the LORD is."

Jeremiah 17:7

The squall passed through Santa Molina quickly, leaving behind an oppressive humidity that felt like a wet blanket had been draped over the canopy of trees trapping in the stifling moisture. Raindrops could be heard dripping off the leaves of the huge Ceiba trees, and once again, the jungle came alive with the sounds of tropical birds and monkeys.

"Remind me again why I'm here?" lamented Jessica as she wiped the sweat from her brow. She propped her feet on the coffee table while Nicholas played on the floor.

"It's traditional for the wife to live with the husband," replied Ryan as he handed her a glass of *agua fresca*. "I promise it'll get better."

"And that would be when?"

Ryan thought for a moment. "*Mañana.*"

"Tomorrow? It's always tomorrow here. Everything is tomorrow. Tomorrow this; tomorrow that. Don't you know that tomorrow never comes?" she pointed out as she sipped her drink.

"I believe I've been told that." He grinned at her, and she couldn't help but laugh.

"You know we have air conditioning back in Los Angeles."

"Where?"

"Los Angeles."

Ryan sat down by her. "You know, I think that's the first time you've referred to California without calling it 'home.'"

Jessica smiled and rested her head on his shoulder. "My home is wherever you are."

As they relaxed together, a knock was heard on their front door. Ryan rose and walked into the entryway. He opened the door to see Juan standing there.

"*Buenas tardes*, Pastor. Senor De La Cruz is here for his blood pressure check. He says *la doctora* asked him to come."

Ryan turned his head toward the living room and called out. "Jess? Mr. De La Cruz is here for a BP check."

"Tell Juan he can do it, and I'll be there in a few minutes."

When he turned back, Juan's face was beaming. "You heard her?"

"*Sí*, Pastor. I heard her!" Excitedly, he motioned to Mr. De La Cruz to follow him to the clinic.

Ryan watched Juan escort the patient toward the clinic, then turned when he heard Jessica walk up behind him. "You know, you really made Juan's day. He's on cloud nine walking over there."

"Well, since he's shown such an interest in medicine, might as well start his training now." She kissed Ryan on the cheek, then walked out the front door toward the clinic. "I can use an extra hand around here."

He watched her leave, then retreated to his study whistling '*Love Lifted Me.*'

****

Later that evening, the night sky was clear and filled with twinkling stars as a warm breeze blew softly. Jessica and Ryan sat together in a wooden swing on the porch.

Epilogue

"It's beautiful, isn't it?" She rested her head back on his arm. "That's the Big Dipper, right?"

Ryan absentmindedly played with one of the rogue curls in Jessica's hair as he gazed heavenward. "Um-hm. You know, that constellation is mentioned in the Bible. Incredible to think God's named every star, even those we can't see."

"I think it's pretty amazing how He cares about us so much when He created all this. We're so insignificant."

"'When I consider thy heavens, the work of thy fingers, the moon and the stars, which thou has ordained...' quoted Ryan quietly. "'What is man that thou art mindful of him?'"

Across the courtyard, a bush's leaves rustled, then parted as an armor-like animal lumbered toward the edge of the trees. Its long banded tail trailed behind as it made its way along the courtyard's far boundary.

"Ryan! Look! What's that?" She watched, fascinated by the odd-looking creature poking its nose into the vegetation and frantically digging.

"That's an armadillo," stated Ryan. "They're only out at night. He's probably found some ants or beetles."

"I've never seen one before! Oh, Ryan, I love this place! There's so much to see and experience!" Her eyes sparkled as she looked at him.

"Thank you for marrying me." He kissed the top of her head.

The quiet of the night was interrupted by the soft cries of a child.

"I think someone's calling you," said Jessica smiling sweetly.

"What? He cries, and you assume he wants me?"

"I assume he wants his diaper changed, and you need more practice." Her eyebrows rose as she gave him a "you know I'm right" look.

Ryan's mock frown was unable to gain sympathy from her, so he stood to walk into the house. "Really? I need more practice? I think I'm getting the hang of it." He shook his head good-naturedly as he headed for their house. "So much for being down for the night."

Courageous Love

As he walked away, his low chuckle floated through the night air, and Jessica's heart was filled with joy. She leaned her head back to gaze at the stars again, then closed her eyes and whispered a prayer. "Lord, thank You so much for my life. It's had so many challenges, but it's had so many wonderful blessings, too. Thank You for giving me the courage I needed to take this step of faith.

"Help me to be the best wife and mother I can be. Help me to serve You with my whole heart, trust You always, and love You forever, as is my reasonable service. In Jesus' precious name, I pray. Amen."

She opened her eyes when she heard the front door open and close. Ryan sat down beside her.

"Everything okay?"

"Yes. He's back asleep. I wanted to make sure he was out before I left. He's such a cute kid. By the way, changing his diaper was a piece of cake."

"That's good to know." Jessica smiled and patted Ryan's hand. "Your skills will come in handy in about seven more months."

Ryan's deep blue eyes widened with a questioning stare as he turned toward his wife. "What?"

"I said—"

"No, I heard what you said. What exactly did you mean?"

Jessica met his quizzical look with a twinkle in her own eyes. "I meant there will be lot of things to do, and it will be nice to be able to count on you to change diapers if I need help."

"Won't Nicholas be out of diapers in seven months?"

"I hope so." She remained playfully secretive. "But sometimes it takes a little longer to get out of diapers, and with another little one to take care of, well, it will be nice to know you can help."

He turned her toward him and stammered, "Another one? We're going to have a baby?"

His look of astonishment tickled her, and she couldn't help but laugh. "Yes, Ryan. We're going to have a baby!"

"You're sure?" His face maintained its shocked expression.

Epilogue

"Yes, I'm sure." His reaction delighted her, and she stifled a giggle as she sat with her head on his shoulder.

"Why didn't you tell me?"

"I am telling you."

"I mean..." A smile slowly formed on his face. "I can't believe we're going to have another baby." He leaned over and kissed her tenderly, then pulled her closer to him. He held her for a long time without saying anything as he gazed heavenward.

Finally she asked, "You want to deliver this one, too?"

Ryan's face paled, and he pulled back from her. His narrowed eyes locked with her mischievous ones. "No!" He shook his head vehemently. "For once, can we do something the conventional way?"

Jessica laughed. "Has anything we've done been conventional?"

Ryan chuckled. "No, I guess it hasn't been. In fact, it's been just the opposite, but I wouldn't trade it for anything. I love you, Jessica."

She nestled in his arms, and gazed up into the night sky. Her life would be full of tomorrows, but she knew that as long as she trusted God, the future promised to be very, very good.

A Novel

Reluctant Love

Jayne Lawson

RELUCTANT LOVE

Eastmont Series ~ Book One
by Jayne Lawson

Broken bones, third degree burns, heart attacks, respiratory distress . . . they are all in a day's work for Dr. Maggie Garrett, one of Eastmont Hospital's most gifted emergency room physicians. A career woman, she believes her life is complete, until a hallway encounter opens her heart to what is missing—love! Reluctant at first to become involved with another doctor, she finally agrees to one date and falls for Scott Devereaux. Although Maggie struggles to understand Scott's faith in Christ, their romantic courtship leads to a perfect wedding—then tragedy strikes and Maggie is left alone. Three years later, she is still trying to make sense of her personal calamity when a new man enters her life, having the same faith as Scott.

Will Maggie open her heart again? Can she let go of the past? Will she find true salvation?

HEALING LOVE

EASTMONT SERIES
BOOK TWO

JAYNE LAWSON

HEALING LOVE

Eastmont Series ~ Book Two
by Jayne Lawson

In the hectic chaos of Eastmont Hospital's emergency room, saving lives is an everyday occurrence for Valerie Garrett, a compassionate and highly respected ER charge nurse. She has everything life has to offer – a wonderful husband, a rewarding career, and a promising future — until the unthinkable happens! Now, struggling to win a battle against the same disease that took her mother's life, Valerie searches for answers in herself, her marriage, and ultimately her relationship with God.

Her husband, Dr. Will Garrett, stunned by his wife's diagnosis, fights his own personal demons as he desperately seeks to find a cure for his wife's illness. As he feels his wife slipping away, the anger he feels toward God threatens to destroy his relationship with Valerie as well as with his beloved sister, Maggie.

Will Valerie find the true healing that only God can provide? Can Will let go of his pride and allow God into his life as he faces the possibility of losing his wife?

To learn more about books written by Jayne Lawson
or to read sample excerpts, log on to
www.writingoneagleswings.com

CPSIA information can be obtained
at www.ICGtesting.com
Printed in the USA
FSOW02n1815021117
40646FS